The Grace Girls

The Grace Girls

Geraldine O'Neill

ORION

First published in Great Britain in 2005 by Orion Books
an imprint of The Orion Publishing Group
Orion House, 5 Upper St Martin's Lane, London WC2H 9EA
Published in Ireland by Poolbeg Press Ltd

1 3 5 7 9 10 8 6 4 2

A CIP catalogue record for this book is available
from the British Library

ISBN (hardback) 0 75286 010 0
ISBN (trade paperback) 0 75286 011 9

Typeset by Deltatype Ltd, Birkenhead, Merseyside
Printed and bound in Great Britain by
Clays Ltd, St Ives plc

www.orionbooks.co.uk

Acknowledgements

I would like to give a big thanks to all the staff at Orion, particularly my editor Kate Mills who is so supportive and enthusiastic about my work and is always there to lend a friendly, professional ear.

Thanks to my agent, Sugra Zaman, of Watson, Little Ltd., London for all her guidance and advice and a special thanks to Mandy Little who worked admirably with me and *The Grace Girls* in Sugra's absence.

A warm thanks to all my Scottish friends who helped with the research for *The Grace Girls*, including my nephew Nicky Mallaghan and Bob and Helen Orr, and also to my father who happily guided me through the dance-halls of the fifties.

Thanks also to my old teaching friend and fellow polio-survivor, Margaret Lafferty, for enlightening me about the 'lacquer-bug'!

I'd also like to express gratitude to my Swanwick friend, renowned Scottish writer, Margaret Thompson Davis, who gave me great encouragement in the days before I was published.

Thanks to my Offaly friend, Patricia Dunne, for accompanying me to Cavan amidst the ice and snow and for partnering me on the dance floor.

Thanks as always to Chris and Clare and to Mike for his unfailing love and support.

A final acknowledgement to all the polio survivors out there, especially those who did not escape as lightly as I did.

This book is dedicated with love to my father and mother, Teddy and Be-Be O'Neill, who always encouraged me to dance to my own music.

If a man does not keep pace with his companions,
Perhaps it is because he hears a different drummer.
Let him step to the music that he hears,
However measured or far away.

HENRY DAVID THOREAU

Chapter 1

❧❧❧

It was raining. A thick, sleety sort of rain that could easily turn into snow. The first snow this winter. It had been cold enough for it the last few days, Heather Grace thought hopefully, having always retained a childish pleasure in snow. And it wouldn't be that unusual – she often remembered walking to school in a late-November snow. But it wouldn't be walking to school in the snow now, or catching the bus into the office in Wishaw. From now on it would be walking up to the old Victorian station to catch the train into Glasgow. Right into the middle of the city.

She sat sideways on the stool in front of the kidney-shaped, walnut dressing-table, in the bedroom she shared with her younger sister, Kirsty – her brown eyes gazing out into the dark, drizzly evening, and over the shadowy, square back gardens of her neighbours. But these were not gardens where frivolous flowers grew, as most of the men grew only the earnest potatoes and carrots, turnips and cabbages they had been reared with back in Ireland.

There were a few men like her father who grew roses or hydrangea bushes under the front windows, or straight lines of wallflowers or marigolds at either of the path leading to the front door of the house. Apart from those odd floral glimpses of colour in the summer, most of the houses in the mining village remained stoically grey or stony beige.

There was a slight knuckle-tap on the bedroom door, then Sophie Grace came in carrying a plain pink mug in one hand, and a china mug decorated with freesias and the word *Mother* in gold handwriting in the other. A short while before she had changed her knitted working jumper for a soft grey fitted

I

cardigan with pearls, which showed off the trim figure that the bubbly Kirsty had inherited. Unlike her petite blonde sister, Heather had taken her mother's height, but her Irish father's stocky, more athletic build and his almost black, glossy hair.

'I have the dinner nearly ready. We'll have it the minute your father and Kirsty get in,' Sophie announced, in her local Lanarkshire accent. Unlike her Irish-spoken husband who had come over from Ballygrace in County Offaly in his twenties, Sophie was more Scottish, having been born in Motherwell to an Irish father and Scottish mother. Her allegiance at times leaned more towards her birth country and, tellingly, she had picked traditional Scottish names for her daughters, unlike her in-laws who came down very firmly on the more Irish side. 'What time did you say your film started?'

'Twenty past seven,' Heather said. 'Thanks for hurrying everything up on account of me.'

'Well,' her mother said, smiling fondly at her, 'it's not often that you go out on a Thursday night so I suppose we can make a wee bit of an effort for you.'

'I was just weighing up all this about Glasgow . . .'

'Are you having any second thoughts?' Sophie asked gently, jostling for a space on the busy dressing-table for the pink mug. She moved a small, navy glass bottle of Avon perfume and the turquoise plastic basket that held the hair-rollers and pins.

'Nope.' Heather smiled, catching her mother's eye through the mirror. She reached over to the transistor radio on her bedside cabinet, to turn down Connie Francis. 'I think . . . I'm definitely going to take it.' She put the last spiky roller in her long dark hair, and deftly stuck a small plastic pin through it to secure it. 'I'm going to hand my notice in at the office in the morning.'

Sophie patted her daughter's shoulder then sat down on the end of Kirsty's single bed.

'As your father and I told you, hen, it's your own decision. We're very proud of you getting such an important job – you've done well for yourself.'

Heather took a sip of the hot tea, enjoying the chance to talk things out with her mother on her own. 'I'm really excited about it in one way, but if I was to tell the truth . . . I suppose I'm a wee bit nervous about it as well.' Her newly plucked dark brows creased. 'It'll feel funny travelling all the way into Glasgow on the train every day,' she said in a low voice, 'but to be honest, I can't stick the thought of snooty Mrs Anderson being my boss for ever and going on the same bus to the same office for the rest of my life.'

'A lot of people do . . .' Sophie said thoughtfully, 'and you're still only nineteen.' She took a mouthful of her tea.

'I *know*.' Heather swung around on the stool to face her mother. 'But it's too good a chance to miss – a job in a *big* office in Glasgow. It's a real step up for me, and if I don't take the chance of it now, I might never get it again.'

Sophie nodded her head. 'Nothing ventured, nothing gained, as they say.'

'My Auntie Mona wasn't exactly enthusiastic when I showed her the letter last night, was she?' Heather said, rolling her eyes. 'Talk about doom and disaster.' She gave a giggle now. 'You'd think I was going to Sodom and Gomorrah the way she was goin' on, instead of Glasgow.'

Sophie smiled now. 'Och, don't pay any heed to what she says. If I listened to everything your Auntie Mona says, I'd never put my nose outside the door. She'd have me tied to the sewing machine and if I ran out of work, she'd have me down on my knees scrubbing and cleaning all day. Then when my own house was spotless she'd expect me over in the chapel to start scrubbing there as well, or maybe polishing the brass on the altar.'

'She doesn't half go on when she gets the bit between her teeth, does she?' Heather said tutting. 'And she expects *everybody* in our family to be right holy-willies just because she's the priest's housekeeper. She'd have us at early Mass every weekday before work if she had her way.'

'Och, she doesn't mean any harm. It's the way she was brought up in Galway with her uncle a priest and her auntie a nun. She feels she's got to keep up the family's standards even though she hasn't seen some of them for years.' Sophie rolled her eyes now, looking exactly like an older version of her daughter. 'She's nearly worse about housekeeping than she is about religion. I was in trouble with her again this afternoon for forgetting to bring in the washing. She'd warned me several times that there was rain forecast, and there I was, sitting down and all relaxed listening to *The Afternoon Play* on the wireless when she landed at the back door carrying the basket and the washing, telling me how she'd saved it from getting a real soaking. You should have seen her face when she realised I was sitting down doing nothing.'

'Oh!' Heather teased. 'You'll be the talk of the street!'

'If I am, it won't be the first time,' Sophie said wryly, taking a drink of her tea. 'She told me that I might at least have been doing my sewing *and* listening to the radio.'

'And you could have tied dusters around your feet and polished the linoleum while you were at it!' Heather said, giggling at the thought.

'Och, she was probably looking for that skirt she asked me to hem last night, but I've told her that I have two bridesmaids' dresses to hem before I can look at her skirt.' Sophie had a small sewing business going, and was kept very busy by the locals, repairing torn items, hemming and altering garments and running up curtains.

The front door opened, and Kirsty's cheery voice called a greeting. 'It's me-e!'

'We're upstairs!' Sophie called back.

There was the sound of footsteps thumping up the stairs and then the bedroom door was energetically thrust open. 'Sorry I'm a bit late, Mammy, I met this lassie from school that I hadn't seen for ages and we got chatting,' the younger girl explained. Her curly blonde hair and camel-coloured duffel coat glistened around the edges with droplets of rain. 'Anything new or exciting happened since this morning?' Kirsty was always looking for something exciting to happen.

Heather shrugged. 'Nothing – we're just talking about me going to work in Glasgow.'

'You lucky thing! It'll be brilliant,' Kirsty said, sinking down on the bed beside her mother. 'I wish it was me. I'd love to be in the city every day, being able to walk around the big shops in your lunch break.' Her eyes took on a dreamy look. 'I wish I was in *Oklahoma* or *South Pacific* or any of the shows that are on in the big music halls . . . then when the weather gets better we could tour around all the big cities like Edinburgh and London.' She closed her eyes. 'It would be my greatest wish . . . I'd just love it.'

'You're doing well enough for eighteen years old,' Heather reminded her. 'You're one of the youngest singers in any of the bands, *and* you're earning more money between your two jobs than I make at the office.'

'And you're certainly doing more than enough travelling, Madam,' Sophie said, stroking her youngest daughter's damp, blonde curls, which were restrained by a large clasp as her job in the local chemist's shop dictated. 'Some evenings you're hardly in the door, until you're back out it again.'

'I know, I know,' Kirsty said, her blue eyes brightening. 'We're out tomorrow night in Coatbridge playing at a dance, and then on Saturday night we're playing at a talent competition in Hamilton.'

'Well,' her mother said, her eyebrows raised in concern, 'you'd better make sure you get an early night tonight. You can't be burning the candle at both ends.'

'We'll see . . .' Kirsty said vaguely. She turned to her sister. 'Who's going out tonight?'

'The four of us,' Heather said, unpinning a roller now to check if her hair was dry yet. It was still a bit damp, so she rolled it back up again.

'And who's the four?' Kirsty persisted.

Heather made a little impatient sound. 'Oh . . . me and Gerry, and Liz and Jim.'

'Oh . . . Gerry,' Kirsty said meaningfully, then started to unbutton the toggles on her coat. 'And what are you going to see?'

Heather shrugged. 'I'm not sure . . . I think it might be some kind of a gangster film.' Her face darkened a little. 'It was Gerry's idea – so no doubt it will be a fella's kind of film.'

'Well, at least it's a night out, and it won't cost you anything if Gerry's taking you,' Kirsty pointed out.

'Sometimes *I* pay,' Heather retorted, 'and if he gets the tickets first, I often buy the ice-creams and the drinks.' She looked over at her mother. 'I must make sure that we don't stuff ourselves

5

with hot-dogs again tonight, I can feel my working skirts getting a bit too tight again.'

'Just cut out the rubbish,' Sophie said firmly, 'and you'll be fine.'

'You're daft,' Kirsty stated. 'I wouldn't be arguing with him if he wanted to pay for everything. It leaves you more money to spend on yourself. Anyway, he earns more than you – and you've been going out with him for nearly six months.'

'Maybe I don't want to let him pay for everything,' Heather said, her voice rising in indignation. Although they got on well for sisters, sometimes Kirsty really got on her nerves the way she voiced her opinions on everything so forcefully. And it was especially irritating when the opinions were about Gerry.

'Right,' Sophie said, standing up now. She could always tell when things needed diffusing between the girls. She made towards the hallway now. 'I'll go down and check that the potatoes aren't boiling too quickly and you ladies can follow me down shortly. Put that wet coat in the airing cupboard now, Kirsty, so that it's dry right through for work in the morning.'

'What's for dinner, Mam?' Kirsty asked, getting to her feet now. 'I'm absolutely starving.'

'Stew and carrots and peas.'

'Brilliant! I'll have a big plateful, because I've only had a roll and a wee Dairylea triangle since I left the house this morning.'

'You should have come home at lunchtime and I'd have made you something decent,' Sophie told her.

'I know,' Kirsty agreed, 'but the others were all staying in the shop, and anyway, it was that miserable out I couldn't be bothered walking home in case I got soaked.'

'A cheese triangle and a roll – it's no wonder you're so skinny, if that's all you're eating during the day,' Heather told her, secretly wishing she could last all day on such a small amount. Maybe her skirts would fit better if she tried to copy her sister. 'That's a really stupid way to be carrying on.' Even after a breakfast of cereal and boiled egg and toast, Heather often found herself starving by eleven o'clock in the morning, and could quite easily demolish the two rounds of sandwiches, crisps and chocolate biscuits she took to work every day for her lunch. Some days she did exactly that, and other days she made do with a bun or a hot sausage roll when the tea-trolley came around, and kept the sandwiches until one o'clock.

'Och, that's very unusual,' Kirsty said for her mother's benefit, but she pulled a face at her sister as soon as Sophie's back was turned. 'Most days I usually eat a lot more. But sometimes I could easily go all day without eating and it wouldn't bother me. If we get busy or if I'm doing my nails during my lunch break I often forget to eat – it's only when I come in the door at home and I smell the cooking that it suddenly hits me.'

'I hope you're not being silly, and making yourself ill,' Sophie called as she went down the stairs. 'Maybe you should start coming back home again for your lunch break every day where I could make sure you're havin' something decent to eat.'

Kirsty passed by Heather now, giving her a poke in the back. 'Stop getting me into trouble, you!' she said in a low, joking hiss.

'I don't need to,' Heather retorted. 'You're well able to get into trouble without *my* help.' Kirsty went out to the airing cupboard with her coat, and then returned to lean against the doorjamb. 'Are you getting fed up with Gerry?' she asked, her eyes narrowed.

'What makes you ask that?' Heather said, frowning.

'Oh, I can tell,' her younger sister said airily. 'I always know the signs. You're not bringing him back to the house as often . . . and I can see he's starting to get on your nerves already. All the little habits that you liked in the beginning are starting to irritate you . . .'

A broad smile suddenly broke out over Heather's face, and then she reached into the plastic basket. 'I'll tell you what's starting to really irritate me, Kirsty Grace—' A small pink roller came flying across the room. 'You!'

'So it's all decided then?' Fintan Grace said in his Irish lilt, beaming across the table at his elder daughter. He had come in from his work as the local school janitor and quickly washed and changed into his evening clothes.

'Aye, more or less . . .' Heather said, nodding her head. 'I'm handing my notice in tomorrow.' She moved back in her kitchen chair now, as her mother went around the table with the hot plates.

'They'll be sorry to lose you,' Fintan said, lifting up his knife and fork, 'but people have to move on.'

'I wish *I* could move on,' Kirsty said, attacking her potatoes and stew with an eager fork. 'That Sheila is driving me mad. She's got an eye on her like a hawk, and if you have a couple of minutes without a customer she finds you a cloth and tells you to wipe down the shelves or polish the glass doors.' She shook her head then lifted the fork to her mouth.

'Ah, Kirsty, don't be complaining now,' Fintan told his younger daughter in a light, teasing manner. 'You have a grand set-up there, with your half-days Wednesday and Saturday, and only a five-minute walk away from the house.'

Kirsty finished chewing her piece of stew, conscious of the table manners that had been drilled into her years ago. 'There's times it's dead boring, Daddy,' she said, rolling her eyes. 'You get fed up with moanin' old wives coming in for prescriptions who think you're only too delighted to stand there listenin' while they tell you all about their varicose veins or their husband's piles.'

Fintan shook his head, his eyes twinkling in amusement. 'You should take it as a compliment; they must think you're a real expert on all their complaints to be confiding in you.'

The conversation suddenly halted as the latch on the back gate sounded. 'Lily, I'd say,' Sophie said with a wry smile, 'and no doubt Whiskey.' Lily was the elfin, curly-blonde, ten-year-old daughter of Mona and Pat Grace – Fintan's brother – and the only girl after four boys.

'Hopefully it's not about the flamin' dog-house again,' Fintan said under his breath.

'Shhh . . .' Sophie hissed. 'Don't let her hear you.'

There was a slight tap on the kitchen door and, unrehearsed, all four chorused in unison, 'Come in!'

'It's only me and Whiskey,' a high-pitched voice sounded as the door slowly opened, and the small, grinning face appeared wrapped in a knitted red pixie-hat with what looked like two little ears at the corners. She wore a green duffle coat and red gloves that matched the hat. 'I came round to see if ye wanted any messages or if ye had any empty ginger bottles ye wanted taking to the shop?'

'It's too dark for you to be out,' Fintan told his niece. 'Does your mother know you're out of the house?' He finished the last few forkfuls of his meal now.

'Did ye not notice?' Lily said, grinning broadly and ignoring his question. She stepped into the kitchen now, still holding on to the dog lead. She pushed the door to, leaving a small space for the lead to run through but not enough room to allow the dog to squeeze inside the house. She tapped the top of her pixie. 'It's snowin'!'

'Is it?' Heather said, getting to her feet to look out of the window. 'I can't see anything.'

'Och, it's just a wee flurry,' Lily said, her eyes dancing, 'but it's definitely snowin'. You can see it on our garden at the front.'

'A wee *flurry*?' Kirsty said, imitating her young cousin. She loved teasing her, although it was always done in a good-natured way that the little girl enjoyed. 'That's a very posh word. Where did ye get that one from?'

'Out of a book,' Lily stated, her eyebrows shooting up. 'Where d'you think?'

Her gaze now shifted over to the corner where Sophie kept the empty bottles. She grinned. There were two: an Irn Bru and an American Cream Soda bottle.

'I still don't think you should be out at this time of night,' Fintan repeated. 'Who let you out?'

'Och, I just said I was taking the dog for a wee walk to the corner,' the little girl said, folding her arms now. She shook her red pixie head like a wise old woman. 'Dogs need walkin' two or three times a day – and there's not a single person in that house who would bother takin' him out, if it wasn't for me. Them lads are absolutely useless – especially our Patrick. My mammy's always tellin' him that he's nothing but a lazy bizzim.'

'Was your mother in?' Sophie cut in, not wishing to encourage the girl to be telling tales from home.

'At the chapel,' she said, her eyes sliding back to the bottles that she would get threepence each on. 'There's a funeral on in the morning – that crabbit old fella that goes into the library – and she needed to go and sort the flowers into the vases.'

'I knew damn fine she wasn't in,' Fintan said, smiling and raising his eyebrows. 'She wouldn't let you out on your own in the dark, especially on a school night. It's your bed you should be heading off to, never mind gallivanting around the streets.'

'Och, it's perfectly safe, and I'm not a bit tired,' Lily said, waving a small gloved hand dismissively. 'Anyway, I know every single person around this place and they all know me.'

'Come on,' Fintan said resignedly, pushing his plate away and standing up, 'I'll walk the pair of ye around to the shop and then back home. I could do with a packet of Woodbines.'

'Will you carry the bottles?' Lily asked, grinning with delight. She stretched her red gloves further up her wrists and pulled the sleeves of her coat down over them.

'Do you think I came up the Clyde on a banana skin?' her uncle said, his brows deepening in a mock-serious frown.

Lily went into peals of laughter as she always did when her uncle teased her.

'What about your cup of tea?' Sophie asked her husband, mildly irritated at the interruption to their meal.

'I'll have it when I come back,' he said, going to get his heavy grey wool coat from the rack beside the back door.

'Did you tell Heather about the country dancing?' Lily suddenly remembered. Since Fintan was the janitor in their school, she expected him to keep fully up to date on everything that went on.

'I never got a chance yet, bossy boots,' Fintan said, pursing his lips. 'I was just about to tell her when you arrived.'

'What about it?' Heather asked.

'Saturday afternoon at three o'clock,' Lily stated. 'Mrs McGinty said to tell you that she needs a really good dancer to help out with the practice for the Christmas show.'

'I'll have to see what I'm doing,' Heather said. 'I might have to go into Motherwell or Wishaw to do a bit of shopping.'

'Oh, but you'll have to come!' Lily gasped, her eyes like saucers. 'I told Mrs McGinty that you'd come. This practice is for a really special display for the parents at Christmas.

Everybody has to pay a shillin' each to get in – it's to buy new football strips for the school team.'

'You'd no business saying I'd come until you had checked,' Heather told her. 'I'm very busy at the weekends and I might not be able to help out.'

Undaunted, Lily looked over at Kirsty now. 'You could come too, after work, since Saturday's your half-day.' She narrowed her bright blue eyes in consideration. 'You're *nearly* as good a dancer as Heather.'

'Oh, could I?' Kirsty said, rolling her eyes. 'And what if I have other plans?'

'Out wi' your boyfriend, I suppose?' Lily said, raising her eyebrows suggestively. 'Have you got a new one yet?'

'Never mind out with my boyfriend,' Kirsty said, pretending she was getting up out of the chair, 'just get your nosy wee face out of that door before I give you a good skelp!'

'You'll have to catch me first!' Lily giggled, opening the door just wide enough to allow her to squeeze out without the dog coming flying in. 'Come on, Uncle Fintan, and don't forget the empty bottles.'

Chapter 2

T he light scattering of snow gradually turned into a grey slush as Heather and her friend Liz Mullen stood on the main street waiting for the bus into Wishaw.

'That was a big change in the weather today. I can't believe how cold it is now,' Heather said, her breath coming in white clouds into the freezing night air. She had dressed for the wintry weather in her black and white checked coat with matching black beret, scarf and gloves – plus the black umbrella she carried everywhere when rain threatened.

'It's blidey freezin'!' Liz agreed, hugging the wide collar of her blue swing coat closer to her exposed throat. Giving more attention to fashion than warmth, the collar buttoned low down on her neck, and she hadn't thought to bring a scarf. 'I only hope this film is worth coming out for. What's it about anyway?'

Heather shrugged. 'Your guess is as good as mine. Horror or gangster, no doubt.'

'Och, it's a free night out,' Liz laughed, slipping her arm through her friend's. 'And I always feel that going out on a Thursday night starts the weekend earlier. Anyway, I suppose we should be grateful that it's *us* they're spending their money on – they're two fine-looking fellas and could get any lassie they want. At least that's what Jim's always reminding me.'

Heather's face darkened. 'You should tell him to get lost! I wouldn't let any fella speak to me like that, and you shouldn't let Jim Murray speak to you like that either. There's nobody going to make me grateful to him for going out with me. I'd sooner be on my own.'

'Aw, you know what they're like,' Liz sighed in a world-weary fashion. 'Jim's always been full of big talk when there's an audience. He's different on his own, all over me. I have my work cut out trying to get him keep his hands to himself.'

'You'd better be careful with him,' Heather warned, her frown deepening. 'I told you I'd heard rumours about him with the last girl he went out with from Wishaw – there was talk that she'd disappeared down to England to have a baby.'

'Oh, I tackled him about that, and there's no truth in that whatsoever. She got a new job in Coventry and just decided to take it. And there's no fear of anything like that happenin' to *me*,' Liz said airily. 'I have the measure of Jim Murray, and there won't be anything going on until I have a ring safely on my finger.'

Feeling slightly uncomfortable with the turn the conversation was taking, she stepped out onto the road now to see if the bus was coming. 'Anyway, Gerry's absolutely mad about you, and would do anything to hang on to you,' she said, changing the subject. 'I hear all the girls in his work are daft about him, but they know they've no chance when he's going out with you.'

'I'm not sure if that's what I want either,' Heather said moodily. 'Sometimes he's a bit over-keen ... keeping tabs on every single thing I do.'

Liz stepped back into the bus shelter, relieved that she'd

succeeded in moving the conversation away from herself. 'I wasn't going to say anything ... but your Kirsty told me that she thought you were getting a bit fed up of him ...'

'She's a nosy individual,' Heather said, irritated at Kirsty butting into things as usual, 'and she should mind her own business.'

'Aw, don't finish with him, Heather,' Liz said pleadingly. 'I really like Jim ... and he's always keen if we're going out in a foursome. The longer we all go out together, the better chance I have of getting an engagement ring on my finger. Don't do anything until after Christmas – *please*.'

'I'll have to see what happens,' Heather said, not promising anything.

The girls' chat came to an abrupt halt as a medium-sized, stocky figure under a flowery umbrella came bustling towards them. 'It's my Auntie Mona,' Heather hissed. 'Don't mention anything about Glasgow.'

'Well, girls, off out for the night?' Mona stated in her Galway lilt, pushing into the bus shelter beside them and shaking the snowflakes from her umbrella. 'Cold the night, isn't it?' She turned to her niece, her brows down. 'Did you come to any decision about the job in Glasgow?'

'I've decided that I'm accepting it,' Heather said quietly, turning her attention to examine one of her gloved hands.

Mona's face was aghast. 'Don't tell me you've handed your notice in already?'

'Tomorrow,' Heather stated. 'It'll all be official then.'

Mona shook her head. 'Glasgow's not the be-all and end-all, you know. There's plenty of young girls would have been happy to work their way up in that office in Wishaw. It's one of the best in the area, and very little travel involved.' She pursed her lips. 'I'd think long and hard tonight before doin' anything drastic in the morning. You still have time to change your mind. All that travelling to Glasgow would wear a young girl out ... and you could get in with the wrong kind.' Her brow deepened. 'I've seen it happen.'

'There's all kinds of people worked in the office in Wishaw and it was fine,' Heather said, trying to sound friendly and light.

Mona shook her head. 'Take it from an older, wiser woman.

Glasgow's very different from Wishaw or Motherwell or any of the local places. And Glasgow people are very different too.'

Then, out of the drizzly, foggy night the pale yellow lights of the red bus came looming in the distance.

'Quick, Heather!' Liz said. 'Wave your umbrella and make sure he sees us or we'll miss the start of the film.'

'I'll see you, Auntie Mona,' Heather said cheerily, relieved that the bus had saved her.

'It's busy enough for a Thursday night,' Gerry said, coming back to the seat laden with ice-creams, drinks and a large bag of chocolates. He divided them out between himself and Heather.

'Thanks,' Heather said with a smile, taking the ice-cream and the bottle of Pepsi with the stripey straw from him. 'I wish you'd at least let me pay for the sweets.'

'Another time,' Gerry said, winking at her, his blue eyes suddenly looking bigger and softer. 'When you get your first wage from the new job.'

There was a little silence. 'Do you think I'm daft for giving up the office in Wishaw?'

'Not at all,' he answered, frowning now. 'It's what you want, isn't it? If you want to get on in life, you have to take a few risks, you have to make the most of your chances. I don't think you're daft at all – I admire you.'

'I wish more people did,' Heather half-muttered to herself, thinking of her aunt's doom and disaster warnings this evening. This was the bit of Gerry that she liked – the bit that had attracted her to him in the first place. He was ambitious for himself and admired ambition in others – even girls.

'We're a good team, you and me,' Gerry whispered, squeezing her hand. 'I think we could . . .' He halted, picking his words carefully. 'I think we want the same things out of life.'

There was something in the huskiness of his tone that made Heather's throat tighten, and she was suddenly aware of the lingering grip on her hand, which didn't feel as comforting to her as it used to. She took a deep breath, a kind of claustrophobia now creeping all over her. She had felt echoes of this before, but in a much more fleeting way. But now, the feeling of wanting to move away from him was more powerful and immediate. She realised she wanted to move out of the cinema seat – and out of the cinema, away from him. *What on earth was happening?* she wondered to herself. There was a time when she enjoyed every minute she spent with him. There was a time when she felt he was a really good catch.

The lights suddenly dimmed in the picture-house and the pianist struck up a rousing opening tune.

Chapter 3

'Did you get a chance to look at that suit skirt yet?' Mona Grace asked, as she came along the hallway behind the slim figure of her sister-in-law.

'It's on my list of things for the morning,' Sophie told her, ignoring Mona's resulting disappointed sigh. She had recently decided to change tactics with Fintan's bossy sister-in-law, thinking that if she took longer to do her sewing jobs then Mona might not be so keen to turn up every other week with the mountain of trousers and skirts that needing hems taking up or seams letting out.

'I wouldn't normally be rushing you,' Mona said, as they came into the living-room, where Kirsty was curled up reading in a corner of the deep, wine-coloured couch, 'only I need it for that bloomin' Kelly wedding next Saturday, and I'd feel happier if I was lookin' at it hanging up in the wardrobe all ready.' She gave a small, apologetic smile, hoping to appeal to her sister-in-law's good nature. 'You know what I'm like, I hate leavin' everything to the last minute.'

'Och, we've plenty of time,' Sophie said vaguely, lifting a pile of newspapers and books from the armchair by the fire to let Mona sit down, before seating herself in the armchair opposite.

'Hi, Auntie Mona,' Kirsty said, looking up from a sheet of

paper that held the words of a new song she was trying to memorise for the band's date the following night.

'Well, Miss!' Mona greeted her niece with a beaming smile. 'All ready for bed in your nice warm pyjamas and dressing-gown I see.'

'Och aye.' The young girl smiled, patting the back of her damp, curly hair. 'I'm all bathed and hair washed and everything. I'm gettin' all set up for the weekend early. You never know who I could meet in the dance halls on a dark night.'

'Good girl yourself!' Mona said, making a grab for her niece's bare feet – a little friendly tussle they often had. 'And if you get knocked down crossing the street, and have to be rushed away in an ambulance, at least you'll be spotlessly clean.'

'Pure as the driven snow,' Kirsty said, slapping at her aunt's hand and drawing her bare feet well in under her.

Mona laughed to herself as she sat her ample frame down into the chair. 'Purer than a lot of others around here, that's for sure,' she said. 'I hear that young Helen Kelly one is gettin' married in white after all.' She shook her head, tutting. 'How can they brass-neck it when everybody knows that she's expectin'? And her havin' to be carted out of Mass when she fainted in front of the whole village. A fortnight later the wedding invitations were out, and they're saying they set the date ages ago. They must think we're a right pack of eedjits.'

'There but for the grace of God,' Sophie said in a low voice. 'It could happen to anybody – and indeed it has. There's plenty of families have quicker weddings than they would have liked.'

There was an awkward little silence. Kirsty went back to studying the words of her song.

'I'm not sayin' it can't happen to anybody,' Mona said, her voice slightly brittle now. 'The point I'm makin' is about the *hypocrisy*. The fact that she's gettin' married in pure white, and we've all got to stand there while they're takin' photographs and everything and smile and kid on we don't know she's due in seven blidey months' time.'

There was another little silence.

'As a matter of fact,' Sophie said quietly, 'she's not actually getting married in *pure* white. I've been asked to sew a few pale pink rosebuds under the top layer of her dress and veil.'

16

Mona puffed out her cheeks. 'You're a dark blidey horse at times, Sophie Grace. Knowin' all that and sayin' nothing.'

Sophie got up and put the kettle on and a while later came back with a tray filled with mugs of tea, three thin, hot buttered crumpets and a plate of mixed biscuits.

'I saw Heather and Liz Mullen at the bus stop earlier,' Mona said, taking a tiny bite of her rolled-up crumpet. 'Off gallivantin' into Wishaw with the fellas, no doubt.'

Kirsty stared at her aunt, fascinated by how she always ate so very daintily for such a buxom woman. Kirsty often wondered if Mona ate quite so politely when there was nobody watching her or whether she wolfed things down. 'The pictures,' she confirmed, taking a much bigger bite of her own crumpet.

Mona sucked her breath in now and shook her head. 'She's decided on the big office in Glasgow, she was telling me.'

Sophie nodded, her china teacup thoughtfully clasped between both hands. 'If it's what she wants, then she might as well give it a try. Nothing ventured, nothing gained, as they say.'

'It's no joke gettin' up every morning and trekkin' up to that railway station . . . and if you miss it, you've to wait another hour for the next,' Mona pointed out. 'She only has to wait ten minutes at that time of the mornin' going into Wishaw on the bus – and if the weather's bad and the buses are stopped, she can always walk it home.' She took another little nibble at her crumpet. 'And there's every type there . . . foreign and all sorts.'

'I wish it was me,' Kirsty put in now, her blue eyes shining at the thought. 'I'd love it – going into Glasgow on the train every day. It would be dead exciting.'

'Get away with you!' Mona said, her face brightening with amusement. For all her stern, critical ways, Kirsty knew exactly how to appeal to her aunt's sense of humour.

'You're some blade to be travelling into Glasgow, so you are – they wouldn't know what hit them. How Joe Simpson puts up with you, I'll never know – it's usually the serious, brainy types like Heather that they go for in a chemist's.'

Kirsty swallowed the last of her crumpet, ignoring the inference that she wasn't as clever as her sister. 'It's because of me that all the fine young fellas come in lookin' for Brylcreem and bottles of hair oil they don't even need,' she said, winking knowingly at her aunt. 'Joe Simpson should be grateful to me for all the custom I bring in, for he would have hardly any business except for doctors' prescriptions if it was left to the miserable-faced older ones just like yourselves.'

The two older women now hooted with laughter.

Chapter 4

A small group stepped off the rattling bus at the shops in Rowanhill, and back out into the drizzly dark night. The bus engine revved up and it pulled away, leaving clouds of steamy grey exhaust fumes billowing into the nippy November air.

'Are you two going for chips?' Liz called over the bus noise, moving as quickly into the bus shelter as her high heels would allow. 'Jim says he's starving.'

The thought of the Italian shop's newspaper-wrapped chips made her mouth water, but Heather shook her head. 'I don't want any . . .' she said in a voice that sounded surprisingly convincing even to herself. She looked at the grinning, sandy-haired Jim first and then at Gerry.

'No, I'm not bothered about chips either,' Gerry said quickly, taking Heather's hand and putting it into his coat pocket.

Immediately, the claustrophobic feeling started again. 'We'll walk over to the chip shop with you, anyway,' Heather said. Then, Liz caught her eye and gestured with a nod of her head that she would prefer it if she and Jim were left to themselves.

'Well, maybe—' Heather started to say when Gerry interrupted, his hand tightening around hers.

'Tell you what,' he suggested to his friend instead, 'we'll walk on to Heather's house, and then I'll catch up with you at Liz's and we'll head home together.' The two boys lived another half-mile on from Liz's house, which was just off the main street in Rowanhill.

'Fine,' Liz said, thrusting her arm through Jim's before he had a chance to voice any objections. She wasn't too bothered about the chips, but the chance of spending any time on her own with Jim was definitely not going to be turned down – especially when there was an empty bus shelter. Especially when the last bus had gone and there would be nobody around to disturb them.

'I'm glad we've got a bit of time on our own,' Gerry said quietly as he and Heather walked down the drizzly lamp-lit street. 'You can never say too much with Liz's big ears taking in everything.'

'I don't actually think she's too interested in anything about you or me,' Heather said. She moved her hand away from him now, to allow herself to put the umbrella up. 'I think Jim takes up all her attention.'

'Here, I'll hold that for you,' Gerry said, taking the umbrella out of her hand. His arm slid around Heather's waist, pulling her closer to him. 'I've something I want to tell you.'

Heather looked up at him. 'What?' she asked.

'I got a letter from my uncle in Australia this morning,' he told her, 'and he said if I want to go over next year to work for him, that he'll vouch for me. It's easier to get in if you have a work sponsor.'

'And are you going to go?' Heather asked, surprised at the news. Gerry had mentioned his uncle in Australia several times before, but she hadn't realised that he was seriously considering a move there.

'I don't know ...' he said, pulling her to a halt under the yellow-orange light of a lamp-post. 'It all depends ...'

'On what?'

'You and me,' he said, looking her directly in the eye. 'I need to know how the land lies with us first.'

Heather took a deep breath. 'Well ... I wouldn't want to hold you back.'

There was a little silence. 'You wouldn't, Heather,' he said, with a little crack in his voice. 'Having you could never hold me back.'

'But if you want to go to Australia, things would definitely change.'

'As I've said,' he went on, 'it all depends on you and me . . . whether it would be worth my while staying in Rowanhill.'

Heather's stomach tightened and her gaze now shifted down to the wet, tarmacadam pavement. 'What do you mean?'

He moved closer to her, his head bent so close she could feel his warm breath on her face and neck. 'How serious are you about us, Heather?' His eyes searched hers, and his arm tightened around her waist.

'I don't know what to say . . .' Her voice was low and her eyes cagey. 'I haven't really thought about things like that.'

'Look,' he said, his tone brusque and determined, 'I'm not going to keep beating around the bush . . . how would you feel about us getting engaged at Christmas?'

Chapter 5

There was great laughter going on as Kirsty recounted another of her funny customers' stories from the chemist's shop, which suddenly halted when the front door sounded. A few moments later Heather came into the living-room, shaking the raindrops from her black beret and scarf. 'Hi, Auntie Mona,' she said politely, before turning to her mother and sister. 'It's absolutely bucketing down outside. Thank God I brought the umbrella.'

'Snow all gone?' Sophie asked.

'Just a bit of slush in at the kerbs, the rain's washing it all away.'

'You may get used to it,' Mona said, all joviality now gone from her face and voice, 'because you'll do plenty of running in the winter when you've to go all the way up that hill to the train station in the freezin' cold.'

'There's tea newly made in the pot,' Sophie interrupted, 'and some pancakes and crumpets in the bread bin.'

'Great,' Heather said, turning back to the hallway to hang up her damp outer clothes and to escape any further interrogation from her aunt.

Kirsty got to her feet now, pushing them into her comfortable velveteen, embroidered slippers, and tightening the loose belt on her quilted dressing-gown. 'Did you and Liz decide not to go for chips tonight?' she asked, following her older sister into the kitchen.

If Kirsty was out with her friends, the perfect ending to the night was to stand gossiping in the Italian-run chip shop waiting for their turn in the long queue. The wait enabled them to find out who had been dancing with whom in the various local dance halls, who had fixed up dates, and what romances had come to an expected or abrupt ending. Sometimes the girls found that part of the evening more exciting than the dance, for there was always the chance that some good-looking boys they fancied might just come in for chips as well, and that would prolong the entertainment of the evening.

Unfortunately, with all her commitments singing with the band, Kirsty lately found herself having to rely on Heather and her friends for the latest gossip.

'It was too wet to go for chips,' Heather informed her sister as she poured herself a hot mug of tea from the large brown pot and then added milk and half a spoon of sugar. She went over to the cooker and lit the grill with a match and slid a small pancake and a crumpet on the pan underneath. 'Anyway, I wanted a reasonably early night for work in the morning, I'm a bit keyed up about handing in my notice.'

'Did you see anybody you knew at the pictures?' Kirsty queried.

Heather shook her head as she reached up into the kitchen cabinet for a small plate. 'Nobody that I recognised – nobody from around here anyway.'

Kirsty poured herself a fresh cup of tea. 'Well, was the film any good?' she enquired now, disappointed that there weren't any snippets of news they could mull over in some depth.

'Actually,' Heather replied, her serious face breaking into a smile, 'it was great. You would have enjoyed it – it was a frightening one – *The Hound of the Baskervilles*.'

'Seen it,' Kirsty informed her, pulling a chair out at the yellow Formica-topped table. 'It was brilliant. I bet you ran all the way home from the bus stop without looking round.' The two girls laughed.

Kirsty suddenly gave a shiver. 'It's bloomin' freezing in here,' she said in a low voice, 'but I suppose it's better than listening to my Auntie Mona wittering on about what a terrible place Glasgow is.' She bent over her cup, giggling.

'She's got a right bee in her bonnet about it, hasn't she?' Heather said, tutting. She lifted her hot pancake and crumpet from the grill onto the plate and came over to the table to butter it. 'She's that obvious, too. She makes out that all the people are terrible and the whole of the city is a dreadful place, when you know fine well it's all to do with Auntie Claire who we're not supposed to mention. It's all because she met up with an older, Protestant man in an office in Glasgow, got married in the register office and went off to live in a posh part of Glasgow.'

'I love keeping Mona going about it,' Kirsty giggled again. 'I love it when she gets all aerated and indignant.'

'Well *don't!*' Heather hissed. 'It's me that gets it in the ear every time the word *Glasgow* is mentioned. Anyway I think it's terrible the way she's turned the whole family against Claire. She's a lovely person, and I always liked her. It would be like everybody trying to turn Lily against one of us in a few years' time.'

'True enough,' Kirsty said, suddenly seeing her sister's point. 'I couldn't imagine us not ever seeing Lily again . . .'

'It's terrible when you're young and people don't give you any say in things,' Heather moaned. 'I'd love to see Claire again – wouldn't you?'

'Definitely,' Kirsty agreed. She paused for a moment. 'What about Gerry?' she asked now, going onto a more interesting subject. 'Was he all dressed up as usual?'

Heather gave a little sigh, and her cheeks turned pink. 'You're not going to believe it . . .'

'What?' Kirsty gasped, her blue eyes wide with expectation. 'What's happened?'

Heather hesitated for a few moments, then looked towards the slightly ajar door and motioned her sister to close it over fully.

'Come on!' Kirsty insisted, clicking the door shut with her foot.

'I'm still in a state of shock,' Heather said. 'Gerry asked me if I wanted to get engaged at Christmas—'

'*Engaged?*' Kirsty repeated in an astonished tone. She looked down into her teacup and then back up to her sister's face. This was the last thing she had expected. The enormity of all the changes that might lie ahead – weddings, Heather moving out of the house, out of the bedroom they had shared all their lives – had suddenly struck her. 'What did you say?'

Heather shrugged then ran both hands through her thick dark hair, which was drying into soft waves around her shoulders. 'I said I'd have to think about it ... that I wasn't sure if I was ready for anything that serious yet. I said it might be better if we had a couple of nights apart from each other – have a break over the weekend just to give ourselves time to think everything over properly.' She bit her lip. 'I don't want to be out dancing with him tomorrow night with this hanging between us. Even though he says he understands ... I know he wants an answer soon.'

Kirsty took a sip of her tea, trying to digest this shocking information. 'A lot of girls think he's a good catch,' she said cagily. 'I know of a few who would love to jump into your shoes. He's good-looking with nice hair, a good worker ... a great dancer. I know he's not exactly the love of your life – but you'd be hard pushed to find somebody better around here.' She leaned her elbows on the Formica table now, and looked up earnestly at her sister. 'You might come to feel more for him later – and if you turn him down, you might regret it.'

'I know all that,' Heather said a little testily, the untouched supper in front of her now going cold. 'And I know I should be grateful ... but there's something not quite right.' She went silent. 'I know it might sound stupid – but there's times when I feel I'd rather be on my own, paying my own way, than chance making a mistake by wasting my life on the wrong person.' She paused again. 'What would you do, if it was you?'

'Well ...' Kirsty said, 'I wouldn't be too hasty.' Her eyes lit up now. 'You could always string him along for a bit longer – see what happens. It would save you money in the meantime, and your feelings could change towards him.' She dug her sister gently in the ribs. 'Alternatively . . . you might meet somebody new in Glasgow with even more money, and then you could chuck Gerry and you wouldn't have lost anything! And just think – if you get engaged now, you'll always have a nice diamond ring to remember him by.'

'Kirsty Grace!' Heather said, laughing along with her sister in spite of herself. 'I should have known better than to ask you for advice!'

Chapter 6

'Does it look OK? It doesn't make my stomach look too big, does it?' Kirsty twirled around in front of the fire in an off-the-shoulder, tight-waisted blue dress. She held out the wide skirt with the dark navy petticoat for her sister's approval.

'Gorgeous!' Heather announced with a vigorous nod of her head. 'It makes you look taller and really, really slim, and it'll look lovely on the stage, the shiny material picks up the light.'

'How's the length?' Kirsty checked, pleased that Heather said she looked a bit taller, as she was a good three inches shorter than her older sister and sometimes felt she got a bit lost with all the tall men in the band. 'Not too long?'

'Perfect,' her mother said, delighted that she'd got the hem on the dress so straight. 'It's a perfect fit on you all over.'

'*Long*?' Fintan said, scratching his head uncertainly. 'It's almost up to your knees . . . and I think it's a bit on the low side at the chest . . .' He turned to his wife.

'Could you not sew a wee triangle at the front where the bow is, and bring it up a bit higher? She's a bit on the young side to be going out dressed like that—'

'Daddy!' Kirsty hissed, rolling her eyes. 'These dresses are all the go – the Beverley Sisters and all the famous acts wear things like this. Don't forget I'm the lead singer in the band. I've got to stand out from the rest of the girls at the dance.'

'Well, you'll certainly stand out in that get-up,' Fintan said, nodding in exasperation. 'And let's hope it's for your good singing and not for all the wrong reasons.'

'I hope that oul' fella that runs the hall has the radiators working tonight,' Kirsty announced as two of the band members, resplendent in tuxedos and black bow-ties, reached their hands out to pull her into the back of the van, then went back to the bottles of beer they were drinking. Alcohol wasn't allowed in the church halls so the lads always had a few drinks in the van at the beginning of the night, and another few at the break. They didn't bother offering the young girl any, as they knew she preferred a lemonade or a cup of tea to beer – and they didn't want to have to answer to Fintan Grace if he caught the smell of drink from his daughter.

Kirsty was warmly wrapped up in her mother's fox-fur coat, with a finely knitted, blue lace scarf that her Auntie Mona had given her for her birthday back in October. A pair of sheepskin mittens completed the ensemble – Kirsty Grace was not taking any chances with the Scottish winter weather.

'Once you get up on that stage, you'll soon warm them all up,' a dark, curly headed young fellow called back from the driver's seat. Martin Kerr was the lead guitarist and the male vocalist who harmonised with Kirsty or took over a few songs halfway through the night to give her a break. He also owned the van in which they drove to their singing venues. 'When we play those new numbers we've practised, they'll all be up on the floor.'

'It's *me* I'm worried about, not the dancers,' Kirsty laughed, carefully settling herself into one of the cracked, black plastic seats, which Martin had unsuccessfully attempted to repair with peeling black duct-tape. Apart from using the van to convey the musical equipment, he often used it as a minibus taxi to earn a few extra pounds when he wasn't playing.

'I had flu for a week the last time we played in this dive,' Kirsty went on, 'and I blame that oul' fella for trying to save on the coal.' The dance hall wasn't one of their favourite venues, only being a church hall, but it always got a good turn-out in the winter when people didn't want to travel too far from home.

'There's supposed to be a big booking agent from Glasgow here tonight,' Martin called over his shoulder. 'So you never know your luck.'

'I've heard that one before,' Kirsty reminded him, feigning the world-weary attitude of an older woman. 'I won't be holding my breath. I've never seen any booking agents at the places we play in.' Then, as the van pulled away from the kerb, she turned around to the window to see if young Lily was watching out for the van. She spotted the little pixie face at her aunt's window three houses down and gave a big cheery wave. The little girl held the dog up now, and waved its paw – obviously all ready and waiting. Kirsty laughed to herself. She was very, very fond of Lily, who was much more like a younger sister than a cousin. The conversation she'd had with Heather about never seeing Lily again suddenly came back into her mind and she shivered at the thought. 'Oh, you're a right cynic, for an eighteen-year-old girl, Kirsty Grace,' Joe Hanlon, the drummer and oldest member of the group said now. For all he ran the local boxing club, Joe was known to be a mannerly, amiable type of fellow. 'Where's all the starry-eyed ambition that you used to have?' He shook his head at the two fellows opposite him. 'I can mind you only last year thinkin' that every smartly dressed stranger that came into the clubs might be a famous booking agent that might discover us.'

'Och, that was when I was daft and impressionable,' Kirsty said, waving her hand. 'A year makes a big difference. Weekends of driving from one damp, freezing dance hall to another fairly keeps your feet on the ground. Oh, there's nobody will pull the wool over my eyes now, I know what to expect. I've no illusions about it, if it gives me a bit of pocket money for clothes and getting my hair done, that's as good as it gets.'

'Famous last words,' Joe warned her. 'Famous last words.'

The hall was inarguably warmer than the previous time they had played in it, and the fellows in the band constantly teased Kirsty about how she had terrified the poor caretaker into action. She cheerfully ignored their banter as they methodically set up their instruments on the small stage, thinking to herself that the whole place could have done with a good sweep out. Then, while the boys were setting up her microphone, Kirsty went off to find the beleaguered hall caretaker to see if he could find a bit of string that might hold up one of the faded green, velvet curtains so that it would at least look as though it vaguely matched the curtain opposite. She had mentioned this along with the lack of heating to him on their previous visit, and she intended to make the point again, taking the attitude that if nothing was said, nothing would be done.

The crowd started to drift in shortly afterwards, and within half an hour, the hall was packed and the band members were all ready to begin their warm-up numbers. Kirsty had already run through her songs in her bedroom at home, making sure that her voice was ready for the harder notes as the night wore on.

They slid into a few lively Bill Haley numbers that they knew would get the crowd stirred up, and then after Martin gestured to the caretaker to dim the main lights as he was supposed to have done, they played a few slower numbers before swinging into their set programme.

As she sang, Kirsty found herself going through all the words in a perfect but mechanical fashion, having no trouble hitting the notes in any of the songs, old and new. Recently, when she was on stage, her mind kept wandering to more exotic places like the scenes from *South Pacific* and films with Mario Lanza or whatever latest musical show she had seen or heard on radio. She even found herself thinking longingly of the amateur musicals she had been involved in back in her secondary school days. That's where it had all started – her love of music and singing. With the help of an enthusiastic older music teacher who had encouraged her to go for proper singing lessons.

They stopped halfway through the night and the fellows went out into the van for their beer while Kirsty went down the rickety wooden steps from the stage into the small ante-room where a cup of tea and a small iced cake were waiting for her. She was leaning against the radiator with the fur coat draped around her shoulders and the hot cup in her hands, pondering over the latest situation with Heather and Gerry, when suddenly the door from the main hall burst open.

'Where is he?' snapped a familiarly aggressive voice, reminiscent of a movie gangster. It was a small local fellow with slicked-back red hair – well known to be a troublemaker – who had been banned from several clubs for fighting.

'You're not supposed to be in here – this is only for the band.' Kirsty stated, her brows deepening and disapproval written all over her face. They often got clowns who had drunk too much causing trouble like this.

'Fuck off and don't tell me what to do!' he said, looking back over his shoulder out into the crowd. 'Where is that big bastard?'

'Don't dare talk to me like that!' Kirsty said, moving from the radiator to the table at the centre of the small room. She slid the fur coat from her shoulders onto the back of a chair. 'You've no right to come in here cursin' and shouting your head off – and I haven't even the faintest notion of who you're talking about.'

'That blidey Martin Kerr . . . he's got it comin' to him!' His eyes were getting wilder now. 'I'm goin' to give him a right doin' over the night,' he said, his hand reaching suspiciously inside his jacket. 'When I'm finished with him, I'll make sure he'll never be able to hold a guitar again.'

'Aw, don't talk nonsense!' Kirsty said, her tone derisory now. It was amazing how drink made these eedjits so dramatic. 'He'll kill you – he's nearly twice your height and build. Don't be so stupid.' Her voice lowered; fights were part and parcel of the dance halls, and most of them came to nothing more than skirmishes. But the wild look in this fellow's eyes told her that it was best to try to diffuse the situation if at all possible – especially when his issue was with one of the band members. 'Look, if I was you,' she told him putting her cup down on the table, 'I'd just forget whatever is annoyin' you and go and enjoy your evening dancing. They'll only chuck you out and ban you, and then you'll miss all the good dances over Christmas and New Year.' She gave him an understanding little smile. 'Now, you wouldn't want that to happen, would you? Christmas is the best time of the year.'

'Fuck off, you!' was his reply. 'Nobody tells me what to do.'

Just then the door from the stage end opened and Joe Hanlon came down the steps followed by Martin.

'Kerr – ya rotten big bastard!' the little fellow said, advancing towards the men. His hand went inside his jacket again and this time it came back out wielding a toasting fork, a good nine inches long. He held the fork aloft. 'Let's see what a big man you are now!'

Joe and Martin moved backwards back up the steps, trying to size up the situation. The little fellow was known for being vindictive and unpredictable.

'I've no row wi' you,' Martin told him. 'I don't know what all this daft carry-on is about.'

'Well, I've got a fuckin' row with you!' the little guy informed him, waving the fork in the air. 'Chuckin' me off your mouldy oul' rust-bucket of a van last weekend and leavin' me to walk home two miles in the fuckin-well rain. Ma good suit was ruined!'

Martin had a vague memory of a drunken football crowd he had carried causing ructions in the back of the van and pulling into the side of the road where the worst two fellows were pushed out.

'There's no need for any of this!' Joe warned him, moving between them now. 'You can settle your arguments outside the hall when the dance is over, and without resorting to weapons.'

'Put the fork down,' Martin told him calmly, 'and we can go outside right now and sort our differences out.'

'Do it!' Joe shouted, in an authorative tone. 'Because if you use that thing, you're only goin' to get a sore face and maybe even land yersel' in jail.' Joe took up a boxing stance, his fists held out defensively, while Martin, eyes narrowed, came in close behind him. The red-headed fellow hesitated for a second, and when Kirsty saw his arm go slightly limp she came behind him and her hand shot out and grabbed the fork right out of his grip. Almost at the same time Joe moved forward and swung the fellow around, forcing his hands behind his back and his head down onto the table.

The little fellow fought back, kicking out viciously and mouthing obscenities, but when Martin put his big hand on the back of his neck he knew it was pointless.

'Now, look,' Martin told him, 'I don't know what your

problem is, but I'm going to give you one more chance to get out of here before I break your blidey neck.' He paused.

'D'you hear me?'

There was no answer. Martin's grip kept tightening until eventually the fellow gave a nod of his head.

'Aw, just get somebody to phone the polis!' Kirsty suggested in a scornful tone. 'They'll soon lock him up for the night when they see that stupid-looking fork he was carrying in his jacket.'

'Well? Have you decided which way you're going to go?' Joe Hanlon said, pushing down hard on the small fellow's arms. 'Are we going to do this the smart way and forget all about it, or are we going to have to give you a good beltin' and then let the polis take you?'

'Aye,' Martin hissed, 'apart from assault they might just do you for stealin' yer granny's toasting fork!'

The taunt caused another short but vigorous struggle accompanied by the customary string of obscenities, but both men could feel it was only token and that he had more or less given in. A few minutes later, they had him up on his feet with Joe and Martin on either side, pinning his arms behind his back. In a stiff, halting way, as if they were all moulded together, the three of them moved out of the door and into the main hall.

The little fellow made yet another token gesture of struggling as they moved across the floor, but he quietened down when the hefty Martin hissed in his ear. 'If you don't go quietly, I'll go back and get that blidey fork and stick it in your chest and eat you for ma breakfast in the morning!' Martin gave him a shove. 'You're nothin' but a belligerent wee nyaff, so ye are!'

The threat seemed to work this time and he calmed down again, allowing himself to be led out of an emergency exit door at the side of the hall.

Thankfully, Kirsty thought as the group disappeared, the other band members had gone out to the van to have a fly drink, and a lot of the young fellows at the dance had gone across to the working-men's club at the break.

All they would have needed was a crowd from the fellow's local village to decide to back him up against all the ones in the band, as a way to liven up the evening. She tutted to herself and went back into the ante-room to check her bouffant hair style was still in place, and to finish off her tea and cake.

Fellows like that were part and parcel of these places, and she had grown used to it. Most of them were just like lads she'd gone to school with – they acted the eedjit when they had too much to drink. She swallowed the last bit of her cake and then, catching sight of the offending toasting-fork, went over to examine it.

As she lifted it up, she sucked in her breath at the state of the thin, sharp prongs which looked as though they had been filed to an even sharper point. There was no doubt about it – it was a dangerous-looking thing.

She looked around the dilapidated room now, full of stacked chairs and crooked cabinets and chests of drawers, wondering if there was a safe place to hide the fork in case the little red-haired nuisance decided to come back in looking for it. She eventually decided on Martin's guitar case, and after draining her cup of lukewarm tea went back up onto the stage to put it in the case and safely out of sight.

The second part of the night disappeared without any further incidents and all in all the band were happy enough with their performance of the new songs, one of which they planned to play in the talent competition in Hamilton the following night.

'I see there weren't too many booking agents there tonight,' Joe said, winking across to the other musicians as the engine roared into life and they set off for home at the end of the night.

Kirsty was curled up in the back corner of the minibus, cocooned in her mother's fur coat again, the lacey scarf wrapped several times around her throat, taking no chances until the van heated up properly.

'Pity there wasn't,' Martin Kerr said in a droll voice, 'because there was plenty of lively talent going on there, especially in the ante-room at the break. There's many a man couldn't have held his own the way that wee Kirsty tackled that fella.'

'Well, boys, let that be a lesson to you all,' Kirsty piped up from the corner.

Chapter 7

❧❧❧

Sophie stepped out of the back door, a pink plastic baby's bath piled up with newly washed towels, her eyes scanning the morning sky for signs of the rain that was forecast. Then, deciding that it was worth getting them out into the fresh air even for half an hour, she went down the three steps and into the square drying green edged all around with a neat privet hedge.

She dropped the heavy load onto the grass that Fintan diligently kept short, and reached for the small plastic peg basket that was hooked onto one of the rusty clothes poles. Then she set about the bending and stretching that was involved in pegging out the towels. The latch on the back gate went and in came the small familiar figure of Lily.

'Are Heather and Kirsty up yet?' she asked, closing the gate behind her.

Sophie took a peg out of her mouth, delighted to see that there was no sign of the yappy Whiskey along with her niece. 'No,' she said, 'they're still in bed.'

Lily slid in past her, although the fact she was still in her slippers did not go unnoticed by her aunt. 'I'm just goin' upstairs to see them for a wee minute,' she said, before her aunt had a chance to protest.

'They're asleep! Don't bother your head going up to see them,' Sophie called, but it was too late. *'You fly little bugger!'* Sophie said to herself, and went back to pegging out her washing.

Lily stood at the girls' open door now, her hands shaped like a megaphone. 'Wakey, wakey!' she bellowed, her voice piercing the sleepy silence. 'It's nearly ten o'clock on a Saturday mornin' and youse two lazy bizzims should be up!'

Both girls moved to cover their heads with the blankets, leaving trails of dark and blonde hair visible on top of their pillows.

'Wakey! Wakey!' the shrill voice repeated.

32

'Gerrout!' Kirsty called from the bed at the far side of the room.

Lily took the response as encouragement, and took herself over to sit at the bottom of her cousin's bed. 'Are you not workin' the day?' she enquired in a chatty tone. 'You usually work the half-day on a Saturday.' Lily kept track of both her older cousins' whereabouts with great interest, and popped into Kirsty's chemist's shop at least once a day for a chat. Her other favourite place was the library, which she frequented regularly.

'Gerrout!' Kirsty repeated, her voice muffled with the covers. 'I was stock-taking late last week, so I've the whole day off. I wasn't home until late last night, so I need my sleep.'

'All right! All right!' Lily said, pulling an impish face. She skipped across the floor now to sit on Heather's bed. 'Heather ...' she whispered, 'are you awake?'

Heather moved her head under the pillow. 'Go home,' she grunted.

'But I came to see you about the country dancing,' Lily explained, totally undeterred by the unwelcoming reception she had received. 'I came to see whether you were collectin' me later, or whether I was collectin' you.'

'Neither,' Heather snapped, emerging from under the pillow. 'I've to go into Wishaw, so I probably won't be going.'

'What?' Lily gasped, her hands coming to rest on her hips. 'But you promised!' Her face was now a picture of wounded shock. 'You know fine well that Mrs McGinty's dependin' on you for this dancin' display ... and she was hopin' that Kirsty would be coming as well.'

'Away you go and stop annoying us!' Heather hissed. 'We need our sleep.'

Then, the sound of Sophie coming back into the kitchen below made Lily move towards the door. 'I'll let you sleep for a wee while longer, girls,' she said affecting a sweet, grown-up tone, 'and I'll call back later.'

'Don't bother!' both girls shouted back.

Sophie stood at the bottom of the stairs with a severe look on her face. 'You had no business goin' up them stairs without me telling you.'

Lily came down towards her, all wide-eyed and innocent. 'I

was only deliverin' a message from Mrs McGinty . . . an' I didn't hear you callin' me back.'

'You must think I'm daft,' Sophie said, her gaze sliding down to Lily's feet, 'and your mother will definitely go daft when she sees you came out of the house in those good slippers.'

Lily folded her arms and looked down at the pink slippers with the white pom-poms.

'They're not *that* good,' she argued. 'I've had them for a few weeks now.'

Hearing a noise, Sophie looked out through the open kitchen door to see the bustling figure of Mona coming in. 'You're for it now, my girl – here comes your mother.'

'I might have guessed!' Mona said as she caught sight of her daughter. 'She was warned not to set foot out of the house until she'd finished her work this morning.'

Lily stood, arms folded defensively and big blue eyes cast guiltily downwards.

'Well, Miss?' Mona said, rapping a knuckle lightly on the side of her head. 'What did I tell you?'

Lily stepped out of her mother's reach, arms still folded. 'You only said I wasn't to take the dog for a walk—'

'I said you weren't allowed out of the house until you finished cleaning the bathroom out,' Mona corrected, her finger wagging. 'Isn't that right?'

Lily shrugged. 'I was nearly finished . . .'

Mona pointed back in the direction she had just come. 'Home!' she said. 'Go home and finish off what you started.'

Lily opened her mouth to protest.

'Home!' Mona repeated. Her eyes suddenly dropped to her daughter's feet, and she sucked her breath in angrily. 'Ahhh . . . don't tell me you've come outside wearin' the good slippers . . .'

A short while later the two women were sitting in Sophie's kitchen drinking a cup of tea, and sharing a small plate of plain biscuits since it was too early for cake or chocolate biscuits.

'It's been one hell of a mornin' so far, I can tell you,' Mona stated.

'What's happened?' Sophie said, hoping that her sister-in-law wouldn't start on about the skirt for the wedding again, as she still hadn't got around to fixing it.

'The men,' Mona said, 'and the Ballygrace business rearin' its head again.' She raised her eyebrows. 'You know they're already plannin' another visit to Ireland? Pat mentioned that he wouldn't mind a wee trip over this summer.'

'Summer?' Sophie said vaguely.

'Summer, no less.' Mona confirmed. 'And here's me workin' my knuckles to the bone to pay for Christmas, and the good lad's already plannin' ahead for another trip over the water.'

'Are you sure?' Sophie said. 'I can't remember Fintan mentioning anything about the summer.'

'Sophie,' Mona said impatiently, 'would I be tellin' you if I wasn't sure? D'you think I imagined it all or made it all up?' She paused, her eyes ominiously wide. 'Take it from me, there's plans afoot for another trip on their own, and as sure as hell that will put paid to any plans I had for Butlins or a caravan holiday – just like the summer that's gone.'

'They've asked us to go with them before,' Sophie reminded her. 'Last summer they said you and me could go if we wanted, and we said we didn't fancy another wet summer in Ireland with four to a room and no inside toilets and everything. They also suggested me and you could go to Galway, Pat says it's about time you had a trip back home. You haven't been for a few years.'

'That's not the point . . .' Mona blustered.

'That was when we actually told them to go on their own without us – in fact *you* were the one that insisted,' Sophie added for good measure.

Mona took a drink of her tea and a small bite of the Rich Tea biscuit. 'I know . . . I know,' she said, clearly irritated by Sophie's easy-ozey attitude and too-good memory at the wrong times. 'But I thought they were only goin' back to help the old couple and Joe out on the farm . . . I didn't expect them to start buyin' new clothes and go out gallivantin' at night.'

Sophie laughed now. 'Gallivanting?' she said. 'I don't think there's much fear of them going gallivanting in Ballygrace! Sure, it's only a one-horse town . . .'

'Ah, but there's plenty of dances and that kind of thing in all

35

the surrounding places,' Mona informed her, her eyes now gazing out of the window. 'Don't be so easily fooled, Sophie . . . you have to keep a close eye on the men, especially when they're getting haircuts and buyin' themselves casual shirts and everything.' She narrowed her eyes thoughtfully. 'They don't get all dickeyed up in new casual shirts for shovelling dung on the farm.'

Lily made a loud slurping noise with her stripey straw in the lemonade, her eyes darting from her aunt frying at the cooker back to both girls seated opposite her at the table. 'I'm sorry for waking youse both up . . . I didn't realise you were out so late. Were you awful tired?' she asked now in on overly concerned tone. There was only three hours left now until the country dancing, and she was desperate to get one or both of the girls on board.

Kirsty swallowed the bite of bacon she was eating. 'Of course I was tired,' she said in a high voice, 'and so would you be tired if you were dancing and singing on the stage for half the night, not to mention havin' to wrestle a toastin' fork off of a wee nyaff that was ready to stab everybody in sight.'

'What?' Sophie said, dropping the spatula back into the frying pan. 'Was he jokin' or was he seriously trying to attack people?'

'Very serious,' Kirsty said. 'He was a right bad little bugger.'

'Language! Language!' Lily laughed, her eyes dancing with delight.

Sophie shot her blonde-headed daughter a warning glance.

'It's the only way to describe him,' Kirsty protested. 'He was a bad little—'

'What happened?' Heather asked, her knife and fork coming to rest on her plate.

'Och, he was after Martin Kerr over some nonsense to do with the minibus. God knows what would have happened if I hadn't grabbed the toasting fork out of his hand.' Her eyes suddenly grew large. 'I noticed that the fork was really sharp, and later on when I showed it to the lads in the band they said he had the ends of the prongs filed to a sharp point.'

'Oh, I'm not happy about that carry-on at all,' Sophie said, shaking her head. She came over to the table, frying pan in hand, to put a fried egg on top of the bacon and sausages on each girl's plate. 'It sounds far too dangerous a place for you to be singing in. Does your father know what kind of place it is?'

Kirsty shrugged, thinking now that it wasn't such a good idea to have mentioned the trouble at the club. 'Och, it's not always like that,' she back-pedalled. 'Most of the time it's absolutely fine.'

'Anyway,' Lily said, reaching a small hand across the table to Heather, 'what time d'you think you'll get back from Wishaw?'

Heather gave an exaggerated sigh. 'What time is the practice?'

'Three,' Lily said, and then held her breath.

Chapter 8

Heather got off the bus at the Household department store in Wishaw, walked briskly down to the lights and then made her way across the busy road and down to Stead and Simpson's shoe shop. She checked her watch – it was only half past one, and she wasn't meeting Liz until quarter past two. She had plenty of time to get everything done by then, so they could sit and have a good gab before getting the bus home for the dancing practice.

Kirsty had said she was coming in with her right up until the last minute, when one of the band called at the door to say they were having a final rehearsal for the competition that night. 'It'll only be an hour or two,' she said. 'I'll be back as quick as I can and then we can both run into Wishaw together. I need to get new pink shoes to match my stage outfit for tonight.'

'I can't wait until after you've finished to go shopping,' Heather had told her, rolling her eyes to the kitchen ceiling. 'Wee Lily will have a fit if I don't get back in time for the country dancing practice.'

Kirsty's face had fallen. 'Will you get me the shoes? I wouldn't ask normally ... but I really need them for tonight.'

'You wouldn't ask normally?' Heather had repeated in an

incredulous voice. 'Last week it was an underskirt and the week before it was a handbag.' She had paused, tossing her wavy dark hair over one shoulder and then giving a loud sigh. 'What kind of shoes?'

'I'll write it down,' Kirsty had said, swiftly moving over to the kitchen window ledge to rummage in a green, marble-effect vase full of pens, pencils, screwdrivers, knitting needles and odds and ends. She had found a sharp pencil, and then went into the cutlery drawer to find the small notebook that Sophie kept there for taking down people's instructions for her sewing.

'First choice is the pink patent stilettos that they had in Stead and Simpson's window last week, or pink sling-backs with a high heel from the Household. If they've sold out in pink I'll just take black to match the top.'

'Size four?' Heather had said, her brows raised in question.

'Aye,' Kirsty had said, grinning. 'And I'll give you a loan of them at Christmas if you have anything special on.'

The shoe shop was packed and Heather stifled a sigh as she had to join the end of a queue of about a dozen chairs. Eventually, a sour-faced assistant came to her. Heather gave her the description of the patent shoes, and an eternity later the woman came from the back of the shop holding up the pink stilettos in one hand and the white cardboard box in the other. 'That them?' the woman said, with a deadpan expression, taking one of the shoes out of the box and holding it up.

'Size four?' Heather checked.

'That's whit ye said, wasn't it?' the assistant snapped. 'I'm hardly goin' to get ye a size eight, am I?'

Heather forced herself to smile ingratiatingly at the rude assistant, whilst seething inside. She handed over Kirsty's money and then waited for the change and for the woman to wrap the shoe-box in brown paper and laboriously tie the package with string. After that, she made her way further down Main Street to the relatively cheap, but fashionable, ladies' shop where she and Kirsty had an account. This enabled them to buy new things as they came into the shop, and pay them off on a weekly basis. This was another job that fell to Heather, as she was in the town every day for work. And she knew that if she left it to Kirsty, there would be weeks when she wouldn't make it in to keep the account up to date.

Sometimes skirts and blouses had to be ordered in if they were very popular sizes, and Heather wanted to give herself plenty of time to make sure she had two new skirts for starting work in Glasgow. A navy and a black she had decided, as they would go with everything.

'The new pleated ones are very popular,' the young shop assistant told her. 'They're flying out of the shop as quick as we get them in.'

Heather held up a black skirt. 'Is it wash or dry-clean?' she checked.

The girl looked at the label. 'Dry-clean only ... probably the pleats might fall out if you tried to wash it.' She smiled encouragingly. 'You'd get a good few wears out of them if you buy them in a dark colour.'

'What about the pencil skirts?' Heather said, going over to another rail. 'Are they dry-clean, too?'

'No, a gentle hand-wash,' the girl read out from the label.

'I'll try one of each then,' Heather said.

'Size fourteen?' the girl said, holding a navy skirt up.

Heather's cheeks flamed at the shop assistant's assumption. 'Usually a size twelve fits ...'

'I wouldn't be too sure about that,' the girl said doubtfully, standing back to appraise her customer's figure. 'I'd try both sizes on, for the pleats look terrible when they're stretched too tight over your stomach or hips.'

Ten minutes later Heather came out of the shop with two size-fourteen skirts wrapped up, vowing to herself that she would definitely start eating less. She hurried back up the busy street towards Bairds' department store, where she was meeting her friend. The tearoom on the top floor had lovely cakes and pastries and was just around the corner from the bus-stop for Rowanhill.

'You definitely don't look as if you've put any weight on to me,' Liz said, taking a bite out of a large chocolate éclair. She swallowed it, and then scooped up a lump of cream that had fallen on the plate with her finger and popped it in her mouth. 'Look at me, I'm like a bloomin' rake no matter how much I eat.

At least you've got a bust and hips, and that's what the fellas go for.'

Heather stared down at her half-eaten lemon meringue pie. It was terrible trying to cut down, when she felt she only ate the same as Liz and Kirsty who never seemed to put an ounce on. 'The skirt waistbands told the truth,' she said ruefully. 'I could hardly get the button done on the size twelve and it was all stretched across my stomach.' Her spoon moved towards the lemon meringue pie, hovering dangerously close. Surely one more spoonful wouldn't make a big difference?

As she popped it in her mouth, Heather decided that she'd definitely start being a lot stricter from Monday.

Chapter 9

❧❧❧

'You made it back in time!' Lily said with great relief, clapping her hands. 'Your daddy's gone over to the school to put the heating on, so's it's nice and warm for us.' She'd been sitting on the edge of the couch in her aunt's living-room for the last half an hour, swinging her bright red yo-yo while she watched anxiously out of the window for her cousin's return. Sophie had given her a drink of lemonade and a Wagon Wheel biscuit and then had gone back upstairs to work. She was now in the tiny spare bedroom where her old treadle sewing machine stood resplendent amidst mountains of curtain material, trousers that needed zips putting in, and numerous items that needed taking in or letting out – and her sister-in-law's skirt.

Lily followed Heather into the kitchen now, almost afraid to let her out of her sight. 'Did ye buy anythin' nice for yerself in Wishaw?' she asked, in the manner that she imagined her nineteen-year-old cousin's friends might ask. It was Lily's greatest wish to be the same age as Heather and Kirsty and she couldn't wait to catch up.

'Just a couple of skirts for my new job,' Heather said

distractedly. She put all her packages down on the Formica table, and started to unbutton her coat.

'Did you get my shoes?' Kirsty called from upstairs, over the whirring of Sophie's sewing machine.

'Aye!' Heather called back. 'You better come down and check that they're the right ones.'

'New shoes?' Lily said, all interested. 'Are they for work or for her singin'?' When there was no information forthcoming, she pulled a chair out for herself and waited. She had to tread a fine line with her older cousins. Most of the time they were easygoing and tolerant of her inquisitive chatter, but at certain times they could take the nose off her and hunt her home if she overstepped the mark with her questions.

Kirsty came in wearing her dressing-gown after her bath, her blonde hair piled on top of her head in an elaborate style, with little imitation pink rosebuds dotted here and there amongst the pinned curls. She put her bare feet into the stilettos. 'Oh, they're absolutely fine!' she said, holding up the dressing-gown to look down at her pink shoes. She practised walking up and down the linoleum floor in them, wobbling slightly with the height of the heels as she went. 'Begod, I'll have to watch my step in these shoes tonight or they'll all think I've been at the sherry bottle!'

'Ha, ha, ha!' Lily laughed gleefully, rocking back and forward in her chair, her hands covering her mouth. This was exactly the kind of entertainment she loved with her cousins, because all she ever heard from her brothers at home was talk about football and boring old cars now that her father and Michael and Sean – her two eldest brothers – had bought one between them. The two boys were training to be mechanics, so cars were the main subject over dinner every night. Her mother was little better as she was always talking about cleaning and ironing, although it was slightly more interesting when it was to do with polishing candlesticks or dusting the altar rails in the church.

'D'you think I'll manage in these shoes all right?' Kirsty asked Heather now, her brow wrinkled in concern.

Lily looked down at the new shoes. 'If ye want my opinion, you'd better watch the way you're walkin' in them or they'll all think you're drunk! You might even fall off the stage and gie them all a great laugh.' She went into peals of laughter now again.

'Hoy, Elephant-ears!' Kirsty said, suddenly realising the little girl was taking in the whole conversation. 'There was nobody speaking to you – this is an adult conversation. Come back to us in another ten years and we'll let you join in.'

Lily turned away towards the window, looking all injured. It was hard to get it right, because sometimes the adults all laughed hysterically at things like that, and other times they gave her a right earful.

'Who did your hair?' Heather asked her sister. She came over now to examine the elaborate creation. 'It looks really lovely.'

'May Ingles,' Kirsty said. May was a neighbour who earned a bit of pin-money from doing hair in people's houses. 'She did it in the kitchen. It only took about twenty minutes.'

'Did you warn her not to put too much lacquer on?' Heather said, her tone suddenly serious.

Kirsty's eyes widened. 'Well . . . she said she had to put a good bit on otherwise it could fall down in the middle of the performance. She said all that stuff about the lacquer-bug is a load of nonsense. She said all the hairdressers got letters about it.'

All sorts of stories about the so-called 'lacquer-bug' had been flying about recently, although there wasn't a scrap of evidence that the bug actually existed.

Heather shook her head. 'They might just be saying that, because it could affect their business. Liz was telling me that two girls down in England have died from it.'

'That's probably because they hadn't washed the lacquer out of their hair for weeks,' Kirsty said, patting her coiffered hair thoughtfully. 'I only put mine up at the weekend and I give it a good wash on a Monday night to make sure I've got every bit of the lacquer out.' She glanced across at Lily, who was now over at the sink looking out of the window. Kirsty's voice dropped to a low, ominous tone, not wanting the young girl to be alarmed by the conversation. 'Did Liz say that the bug ate through their scalp and right into their brains?'

Heather nodded. 'I don't want to frighten you by going on about it,' her voice lower now than her sister's. 'Your hair is really lovely . . . but if I were you, I would change your style for the stage into a more casual one that doesn't need so much lacquer. I wouldn't take a chance about that bug thing, until there's definite proof it doesn't exist.'

'I'll wash it out first thing in the morning,' Kirsty decided, sitting down to take the pink shoes off. They were already making her feet sore and she had only worn them for a short while.

'I was just thinkin',' Lily suddenly piped up, 'you'd be better washin' that lacquer straight out of yer hair when you come in tonight. For all ye know, that bug could be eatin' right into your brain when you're asleep in bed.'

'Out!' Heather said, pointing to the back door. 'You've been warned once already about earwigging into adults' business. You can go on up to the school right now, and tell Mrs McGinty I'll be following on behind you.'

Lily flounced out of the door, biting back the comment that the two girls weren't even adults – sure, they were still only teenagers, and not a whole lot older than herself.

Chapter 10

‘**A**nd where d'you think you pair are going?' Miss McGinty shrieked to a mismatched couple – a tall thin girl, a small fat boy – who were heading in the opposite direction to all the other dancers. The rest of the group broke out into high-pitched giggles, and the dancing teacher waved furiously to the young man on the accordion to stop playing.

'Sometimes, I wonder why I bother,' the bespectacled, elderly teacher said in an exasperated tone. She turned to Heather who was standing by one of the Gay Gordons groups. 'Giving up my Saturday afternoon when I could be out having a lovely high tea in Glasgow with the rest of my ladies' group. And I'm sure the members of the school football team won't even give a thought to the country dancing once they have their strips bought and paid for.'

Heather nodded and made a sympathetic face and turned away so that Lily would not catch her eye and attempt to set her off laughing about Miss McGinty's high tea. She, too, could think of better things to do with her Saturdays than supervising a group of giddy ten-year-old Scottish dancers, but guilt at letting Lily and her father down, not to mention Miss McGinty, had brought her out. Fintan took his job as school janitor seriously, and felt it his duty to support every event that went on.

'Right, Heather,' she called now, in the same tone she had used when Heather was ten years old, 'you and I will demonstrate exactly how the Gay Gordons should be done.' She whirled around now to the grinning group, her finger pointing. 'And God help anybody I catch skitting and laughing!'

As always, Heather started off feeling rather foolish and embarrassed as Miss McGinty held her hand aloft in an over-dramatic fashion, but as soon as the music started and her feet naturally moved into the steps of the dance, she felt the same surge of enjoyment she'd always felt as a young girl.

They did several bars of the dance while the children watched, and then both women came to a slightly breathless halt. 'Back to the beginning,' Miss McGinty instructed, with an impatient wave of her arm, 'and make sure that we're all twirling round in the same direction.'

They had several more rounds of the Gay Gordons until it was ascertained that everyone knew exactly where they were going, and then they were swiftly moved on to The Red River Valley. At one particular point, when they should have been moving in pairs under a bridge made by two girls holding up their arms, Lily's group came to a mangled, giggling halt.

'What in the name of the wee man is going on across there?' Mrs McGinty called, rushing across the floor. Without a word she took Lily and Willie, the perky-faced, red-haired fellow she was dancing with, in either hand, and brought them out to the front to demonstrate exactly how the going under the bridge manoeuvre should be accomplished. Heather stood to the side of the floor, arms folded, observing her small, curly-haired cousin.

Lily stood, the focus of all attention, with head erect, and toes poised for the first bar of the music.

'Grace by name,' Mrs McGinty murmured to Heather, 'and grace by nature. When she's dancing. The rest of the time her chattering and endless flitting around would drive you to drink!'

Heather swallowed back her laughter and watched in admiration as Lily's strong little legs and feet hopped around in perfect time to the music, the knobbly knees moving as high as she could lift them. At one point the ginger-haired lad made to go off to the left instead of the right, and was swiftly jerked by the sleeve back into step, causing both the children and Mrs McGinty and Heather to titter with laughter.

'Well done, Lily and Willie!' the elderly teacher called in her prim voice, clapping her hands high in the air. 'And now, if the rest of you will make *some* attempt to follow suit, we'll run through The Red River Valley again.'

As they were nearing the end of the session, the hall door gave its usual groaning signal that someone had entered. All eyes turned towards the door to see Fintan Grace gesturing to his daughter that he wanted to have a word with her. She left her group and wearing a worried frown she hurried over to see what he wanted.

'It's Gerry,' Fintan said, pointing downstairs. 'He called at the house looking for you and your mother told him where you were.'

Gerry, Heather thought, her heart sinking. They were supposed to be having a break from each other over the weekend to think over the engagement. Usually he went along with what she said about wanting to go out or not. 'What can he want?' she asked.

'I've no idea,' Fintan said lightly, 'but he looks fairly serious.' He nodded towards the dancers. 'I'll have a wander around the hall and check they're all behaving while you're out.'

'Thanks,' Heather told her father, and then she took a deep breath and went down the stone Victorian steps to where Gerry was waiting at the janitor's office at the bottom.

As she walked towards him, Heather found herself looking him up and down – almost scrutinising him – trying to imagine

45

how she would feel about his looks – his face, his whole shape, his clothes and his dark, wavy hair – if she didn't know him.

She knew he was considered good-looking and a great catch by loads of other girls. And she knew that's why she'd gone out with him in the first place – so maybe all she had to do was look really closely at him and she would remember. She might just remember how good-looking and clever she had thought he was before she really got to know him. But the closer Heather got to him and the expensive navy woollen coat he was wearing, the more she realised she couldn't do it. However hard she tried to remind herself how good he was on the outside, she knew that he was still just the Gerry she wasn't sure about on the inside.

'I'm sorry for bringing you out of the dancing,' he said, reaching forward to take her hand in both of his, 'but I really needed to talk to you.'

The gesture was unusual and something about the way he was looking very seriously into her eyes made Heather's throat tighten. 'Is there something wrong?' she said, her voice slightly croaky.

'I need to know your decision,' he said quickly. 'I can't wait until after Christmas . . .'

Heather felt a heat rushing to her cheeks. 'Why . . . what's the matter?'

He took a folded envelope from his top pocket. 'This came through this morning.' He held the envelope out to her. 'What is it?' she said, not having the faintest clue what it was about. Then, she heard the hall door creaking at the top of the stairs and guessed that it was either her father or Miss McGinty who had come to have a look over the banister to see what was going on.

Heather still felt in awe of the older woman, even though she hadn't been her teacher for a number of years, and would feel embarrassed if she were to be seen in a heated conversation with a boyfriend. She guided Gerry by the sleeve into her father's small workroom.

'It's from my uncle in Australia,' Gerry said, sounding anxious but excited at the same time.

Heather looked up at him and then she slid the paper out of the envelope. She was silent as her eyes scanned the words, amazed at what she was reading. Amazed that Gerry had been

46

planning all this for months without saying a word to her about it.

'What do you think?' he eventually asked. 'My uncle says it's all gone through – the job's waiting for me the minute I can start.'

Heather thought for a moment, and then she shrugged. 'It's not for me to say anything,' she said in a low voice. 'I told you before – it's your decision, Gerry. If you want to go to Australia, then you should go—'

'But if we got engaged . . . or maybe even married – we could think of going together.'

Heather sucked her breath in. So this is what it was all about. 'Australia . . . I've never said I wanted to go there. We've never even talked about it.'

When he saw the look on her face Gerry went on quickly. 'Or I could go on ahead and see how the land lies—'

'No, Gerry,' Heather heard herself say in a firm, determined voice. 'I'm not ready for anything like that . . . and I don't think I'd be the right one for you anyway. I don't think I'm the right girl for you, whether it was in Rowanhill or in Australia.'

His face suddenly paled. 'When did you come to this decision?' he asked in a strangled tone.

Heather's gaze moved to the little, black-painted window. 'I'd never really thought about it before . . . but I just know that we're not right for each other.'

'You can't say that!' Gerry said, coming forward to grip both her arms tightly. 'Things were fine between us.'

'Leave me alone!' Heather said loudly, pulling away from him.

Soft footsteps sounded in the hallway. 'Are you all right, Heather?' a high-pitched little voice said.

'I'm fine, Lily,' Heather said, coming out towards her.

'Mrs McGinty sent me down to check that you were all right,' the young girl said, her eyes darting from Heather to Gerry. 'She says she needs you back upstairs for the Dashing White Sergeant.'

'You go on,' Heather said, folding her arms over her chest. 'Tell Mrs McGinty I'll be back upstairs in a minute.'

'Well, don't let me keep you back,' Gerry said. 'I'm sure

you're far too busy to waste your precious time on me! Far too busy to consider the best offer you might ever get in your life.' Then he suddenly pushed past both Heather and her young cousin, banging his way out of the small workroom and then the heavy outside school door.

'He didn't look very happy, did he?' Lily said in a hushed voice, her eyes wide. 'Did youse have an argument?'

Heather raised her eyes to the ceiling. 'Sort of,' she said, smiling faintly at her cousin.

'And have you fell out? Have you finished up?'

Heather started to walk back upstairs towards the hall and the waiting dancers. 'I suppose you could say that, Lily.'

'Never mind,' Lily said, coming over to link her arm through Heather's. 'You're startin' a new job soon – so ye might as well find yourself a new boyfriend while you're at it.'

Chapter 11

❧❦❧

'Wouldn't it be great to be playin' in a place like this every weekend?' Kirsty said, her eyes darting around the sparkly, glittery dance hall as the band headed through to the backstage rooms. They had arrived nice and early on Joe's advice to get the pick of the dressing-rooms before the other acts relegated them to a few feet at the side of the stage, as would happen to the latecomers. The fellows in the band were particularly smart tonight in their dark suits, white shirts and black dickey-bows. 'When I think of that mocket dive we played in last night, and then havin' to put up with violent wee nyaffs on top of it.'

'We all have to start somewhere, Kirsty, hen,' Martin Kerr laughed, swinging the door open, 'and if we didn't have the dives we wouldn't appreciate the decent places like this.'

'Who are you kiddin'?' Kirsty scoffed. 'That's the same thing that people say about money – that you need to have been poor to appreciate it when you have a wee bit extra.'

'It's true, hen,' Martin replied, nodding his head solemnly. 'Those that get it easy don't enjoy it as much as our kind who've had to struggle.'

She followed him in through the dressing-room door, hobbling ever so slightly in the new pink stilettos. 'Well, I don't agree with it. I think you can imagine quite easily what it's like to be skint without havin' to experience it. I'd be happy bein' rich and would love being able to buy myself nice things every day.' She wondered now if she might have been wiser to bring a spare, more comfortable pair of shoes to change into should the pink ones become absolutely unbearable. 'Oh, yes ... I could take to the high life quite easily.'

She looked around the palatial, pink-painted dressing-room with the fancy lace curtains and the framed pictures of famous singers. Then her eyes came to rest on the large, shiny, gilt mirror outlined with rows of white bulbs and the matching fancy table. Kirsty made a beeline for the mirror before one of the other acts claimed it. 'This is more like it – yes, this is definitely more like it,' she said, swinging her bulging handbag onto the table. The men looked at each other now, shaking their heads and laughing.

'Are you actually quiet when you're in bed at night, Kirsty, hen?' Joe Hanlan asked now. 'Or do you blether on all night in your sleep?'

'We're sixth in line,' Kirsty said, studying the sheet of paper that gave the running order. 'We're just before the novelty sword-dancer – whatever that is, when he's at home.'

'I saw a kiltie fella when I was in the Gents',' the drummer said thoughtfully, 'but he didnae look novelty to me, in fact he looked quite serious. He was all decked out in the kilt and sporran and everythin'.'

Kirsty looked at her reflection in the mirror, checking that all her little rosebuds were still perfectly in place and that there were no curls straying out of her beehive hairdo, then she went back to study the performance sheet. 'There's three other groups – but I've only heard of two of them. There's three women singers called Sweet Sensation that are supposed to be like the Beverley Sisters.' She pulled a face. 'And that Stella Queen wi' the screechy voice that thinks she's like Vera Lynn – and it's got to be the fourth or fifth band she's sung with. The fellas say she's terrible to work with, and she keeps fallin' out with them.' She pointed her finger around the group. 'Youse boys don't know how lucky you are havin' somebody as easy-going as me for a singer. You could land wi' a right cracker, bossing everybody around and then throwing tantrums when they don't do what she wants. You'd know all about it then.'

'Oh, don't you worry,' Martin said, 'we all know how lucky we are with you, Kirsty, hen. And we'll know even more the night if we get placed in the contest.'

Kirsty leaned forwards, her face serious now. 'D'you think there's much chance of us getting placed?' she whispered. 'Even third would be great . . .'

'A lot of it's luck with these things, hen – and your audience and judges. The judges will be swayed by the level of clappin' and whistlin'. And if they're oul' die-hard Scots, the sword-dancin' kiltie will go down well – mark my words. They always do.'

Kirsty nodded vaguely, wondering if her voice would perform at its best tonight. It was funny how she often thought of her voice as a separate thing from the rest of her – something that had a life and a will of its own. Of course, she did all the right things to help it – warming up by singing before she left the house, and trying to keep out of the smokiest parts of the halls – but that wasn't always easy. She also tried not to eat too much cheese for a few days before an important performance, as she'd noticed that it sometimes made her a bit nasally, but that wasn't easy either as she loved nothing better than a roll and cheese at lunchtime in the shop.

The dressing-room door opened. 'Don't look now, here comes the kiltie,' Martin said, under his breath.

'How's it goin', boys?' The kiltie said in a hoarse, throaty voice, as if Kirsty didn't exist. And as he walked along to a table at a smaller mirror, she noticed that he had a bit of a limp. 'The hall's startin' to fill up now. It looks like they'll get a good crowd in the night.'

'Aye,' Joe agreed, nodding his head. 'They say wi' all the

facilities that it's one of the most popular venues for this kind of thing.'

The kiltie pulled out a flowery-cushioned chair and sat down with a weary sigh. 'Thank God for a seat – the oul' leg's not so good tonight.' He gave Kirsty a friendly wink now, suddenly noticing her. 'I hope it doesn't let me down when I'm on stage. I would well and truly be on my arse then.'

The men all laughed and though Kirsty threw an amused glance at Martin, she said nothing.

The kiltie took out a packet of Capstan cigarettes, and offered them around the group, who all declined. He took one for himself and lit it with a fancy lighter. 'Och, I suppose I should give this game a bye one of these days,' he said, rubbing at his left shin. 'But whit would I do wi' myself? That's the big question. Whit would I do wi' myself in the long, winter evenings?'

His question hung in the air, then remained unanswered as the door opened and an impeccably dressed blond-haired fellow wearing a white jacket and a black bow-tie entered carrying a music folder. He gave a brief nod of acknowledgement to the others in the room, and then went and sat in an armchair in the corner where he went over his sheets of music.

'A serious type,' Bill King said, nodding in the fellow's direction.

'Nice outfit, though,' Kirsty commented, looking around the band members. 'Maybe you lot should get decked out in white jackets.'

Martin gave her a sidelong glance. 'I could just see us. They wouldn't be white for long, not wi' the oul' van.'

For the next half an hour, the dressing-room door banged opened and shut as various artists came and went, sometimes only glancing in to have a look at the competition. On one occasion, a group of women swept in with a little girl dressed as Shirley Temple and wearing a curly blonde wig in their midst.

'No . . . not in here,' a woman with an identical curly blonde wig said in a loud voice, as her eyes scanned the group.

'Definitely not in here!' the little girl echoed with a shake of her head and a distasteful curl of her lip.

'Melody should have a changing-room to herself!' the woman

stated. 'She shouldn't have to share with these people. Someone will have to complain!'

The group swept out as dramatically as they had come in, leaving a shocked silence behind them.

'If it had been Shirley Temple herself,' Kirsty said out loud, 'she couldn't have been any blidey worse – spoiled wee brat!'

'Well said, hen!' the kiltie said, clapping his hands in agreement.

A short while later Stella Queen – sporting a tall, well-lacquered black beehive – and her group arrived, all hot and flustered at being late, and after some heated debate decided to move to the changing-room at the other side.

'Thank God,' Kirsty said, 'by the looks of her crabbit face, I'd say she's caught the lacquer-bug!'

'Her and Shirley Temple should get on just fine,' Bill King retorted.

An hour later the whole tone of the place had changed, as everyone crowded around the entrance to the stage listening to each act in turn. At one point, Martin had returned from a visit to the toilet and told them in a hushed voice that there was a rumour sweeping the hall that one of the biggest booking agents in Lanarkshire was in the front row.

'I've heard that one before,' Kirsty said, throwing him a sceptical look.

When the act before them was on, The Hi-Tones stood silent, all comedy gone as each one mouthed 'good luck' to the others. Kirsty started taking deep breaths to air her lungs for the top notes, and found herself actually needing it to keep her nerves steady. Then, just as they were due to go on, there was a thud on the tiled floor in the dressing-room, and everyone turned towards the kilted dancer.

'Christ almighty!' Joe said. 'He's just taken off his leg!'

'What are you talking about?' Kirsty whispered, craning her neck to get a look. And there, lying on the floor in front of the dancer, was an artificial leg. 'I don't believe it,' she gasped. 'He's on after us . . . how's he going to get that fixed before he goes on stage?'

'It's no' our problem,' Martin said, poking Kirsty in the back. 'Get movin' – they've just announced us!'

Kirsty atomatically blessed herself, took another deep breath and walked onto the stage, head high and sore feet forgotten.

Her voice was better than ever, and as she hit her high notes easily, she knew that if the judging system was fair, they should definitely be placed somewhere amongst the winners.

As the band took a bow before leaving the stage, a dark-haired, handsome, well-dressed man in the front row caught Kirsty's eye. 'Fantastic!' he called to her, holding his thumb up and winking.

Off stage, the band all shook hands and congratulated each other on a brilliant performance. Kirsty's heart soared as each of the lads took turns in hugging her.

'This just might be our big night!' Martin Kerr whispered in her ear, in an unusually serious and slightly emotional voice. 'You were brilliant, hen!'

'If youse can just let me pass now, lads,' the kilted sword-dancer suddenly interrupted them. 'They'll be callin' for me next.'

They turned and watched, open-mouthed, as he hopped up the stairs with the aid of the banister, and stood poised at the side of the stage on one leg.

'Good lad,' the kiltie said aloud as he watched the fellow who was to accompany him on the accordion carefully place the two Claymore swords across each other in the centre of the stage. Then his name was called and off he went.

All thoughts of their own performance were forgotten as Kirsty and the group scrambled to the side of the stage to watch the unique performance.

'Would ye credit it . . .? I thought by this time in my life I'd seen it all,' Joe Hanlon said, shaking his head. 'A one-legged sword-dancer!'

Chapter 12

❧❦❧

'I wonder how she's getting on?' Sophie said, eyeing the clock anxiously. It was twenty past nine and the talent competition should be in full swing by now. She kept thinking about Kirsty, and couldn't concentrate on the intricate dress pattern she had been cutting out upstairs, so she had put it aside until she was more relaxed, and was now sitting by the fire hand-hemming her sister-in-law's skirt.

Heather nodded, lifting her head from an article she was reading about Elizabeth Taylor in *Photoplay* magazine. She'd been stuck on the same page for ages, as her mind kept flitting back to the scenes from last night and this afternoon with Gerry. 'I'm sure Kirsty and the group will do fine,' she told her mother reassuringly. 'That new song they picked really suits her, and her voice sounded great before she left the house.'

'It depends what the judges are looking for,' Fintan said warily, getting to his feet, and starting to undo the three buttons on his blue casual sweater, 'and whether the competition is rigged or not.'

'Rigged?' Sophie said, taking her glasses off and putting them down on top of Mona's skirt. 'Surely they couldn't get away with that?'

'They can,' Fintan said, pulling his sweater over his head, 'and they do. I'm going down to the club for the last hour. Pat said he'd order me a couple of pints before the bar closes.'

'I meant to ask you,' Sophie said, putting down her sewing and following him out into the hall. They went into their bedroom, which was nice and warm since Fintan had put a fire on earlier in the evening. Sophie removed the small fireguard to let more heat out while her husband was changing. 'Mona mentioned something about you all planning a trip over to Ireland in the summer.'

Fintan's brows came down. 'First I've heard of it. Are you sure? There's been no mention about it to me.'

Sophie shrugged. 'That's what she said . . . and she was none too pleased about it.'

Fintan grinned. 'That's no surprise – when is Mona ever pleased about anything Pat does?'

The doorbell sounded.

'That'll be her now,' Sophie said in a low voice, 'no doubt looking for her skirt.'

'Well, at least that's another thing out of the way,' Mona said, smiling broadly at her sister-in-law. She turned this way and that in front of the fire, checking that the hem was the same length all the way round. Sophie was great with a needle, but you could never be too careful. 'I can hang it up in the wardrobe and forget it until next Saturday morning.' She unzipped the skirt and stepped out of it, then pulled on her dark working skirt again over the black petticoat that had protected her modesty. 'Do I owe you anything for it?'

'Not at all,' Sophie said with a wave of her hand. 'It wasn't a big job.' Then, thinking that Mona might just decide to land her with a few more 'small jobs', she added, 'It shouldn't have taken me so long, but it's just that I'm snowed under with stuff at the minute. I'd say I've enough sewing to keep me going until well after Christmas.'

'Shockin', isn't it?' Mona said, tutting now. 'Christmas will be on top of us before we even know it.' She had nearly brought a few pairs of trousers of the lads over with her, but decided that it was best to get the important skirt off the lackadaisical Sophie before it got lost under the mountains of work she never seemed to get to the bottom of. 'That Lily is drivin' us mad already showing us pictures of party frocks and bikes and scooters in catalogues and going on about the toys in the Co-op window.'

'I was going to ask you what we could get her,' Sophie ventured. 'Maybe she'd prefer a toy this year . . . she might be sick of the pyjamas and *The Broons* or the *Oor Wullie* annual, although our girls haven't grown out of the annuals yet, they still look forward to them.' She paused. 'Mind you, I heard her mentioning the other day that she wanted roller skates.'

'The pyjamas will do her just fine as usual,' Mona said, with a definite nod of her head. Sophie made a pair of pyjamas every year for the little girl, picking soft winceyette with pictures of fairies or snowmen on it. 'She has enough toys and books cluttering the house up without adding roller skates for us all to be trippin' over.' She shook her head. 'Give me lads any time, they're far easier to please. They don't care what they wear and they're happy if they have a football to kick about.' She turned to her niece now. 'You're surely quiet this evenin', Miss – you'd hardly know you were in the same room. If it was the other lady, we'd soon know she was around.'

Heather went red, hating it when her aunt's full attention was focused on her. She knew that Mona didn't care for her half as much as she did for the full-of-devilment Kirsty, and any time she tried to make a joke her aunt always seemed to take it the wrong way. 'I'm fine,' Heather said. 'I'm just sitting reading and waiting for a radio play to come on.'

'No date tonight?' Mona asked. 'I'm sure I saw Liz all dressed to kill at the bus stop earlier on. She looked as if she was heading out to a dance or some such place.'

'She was down this evening, before she went out,' Heather said, nodding vaguely. Liz had called in to see what was going on, as Gerry hadn't seemed himself at all last night when he caught up with them, and he'd said that he was going to be busy for the rest of the weekend and wouldn't be going out. Thankfully, Liz had already asked Jim to go out on Saturday night with another couple from her office in Motherwell, and the arrangements had all been made, so he couldn't use the excuse that Gerry and Heather weren't going to duck out.

'So, what's happened?' Liz had asked, with big round eyes, the two friends seated on Heather's bed. 'When he left us at the chip shop to walk you home, he seemed absolutely fine. He was all over you, cuddling you into him and everythin' – and then he appeared at our gate all miserable and crabbit—'

'We're finished,' Heather had told her, 'and that's that.' There was no point in beating about the bush, because if she thought there was a chance, then Liz would try and talk her out of it.

'Finished?' Liz had been horrified. 'And you didn't bother to come round to tell me? We're supposed to be best friends – you might at least have told me a few details before everybody else knows,' she said, in a wounded tone.

Heather had sighed, knowing that every word she said could well be reported back to Jim – and then reported back to Gerry. 'Kirsty is the only one that knows so far . . . I haven't even told my mum and dad.' She bit her lip, hating even to think about it all. 'He asked me to get engaged last night,' she had said quietly.

'And what did you say?' Liz had gasped; this was all far more dramatic than she had realised. There was also a little edge of disappointment, as she had hoped to beat her friend to an engagement ring, and had been hinting to Jim about it for weeks. And even if Heather was turning Gerry down, she'd still been asked first. The situation took the shine off her own hopes.

'I said I needed time to think about it . . .'

'So, have you not given him an answer?'

'And then he turned up this afternoon,' Heather went on, 'saying that he needed an answer straightaway, because he was thinking of going to Australia in the New Year.'

'What?' Liz had said, her face crumpling in shock. '*Australia?* Gerry has never mentioned a word about Australia to Jim – not a word.' Her voice had dropped. 'What did you say then?'

Heather shrugged. 'I just told him that I wasn't ready to get engaged, and that I had no interest in going to Australia.'

There was a silence. 'My God,' Liz had said, 'I can't believe it! He must have been daft about you to ask you to get engaged and go to Australia with him.'

'I still can't believe it either,' Heather had said, tears suddenly springing into her eyes. 'I feel really guilty, as though I'd been leading him on. I had no idea what was going through his head.'

'But you must have known he was really serious about you,' Liz had pointed out.

Heather had shrugged again. 'Well, I had no notions of being serious about him, or getting engaged to him . . . I was just checking that I'd really gone off him before finishing it altogether.' She had paused, her throat feeling tight and dry. 'So maybe it was just as well the quick way it happened – it's got it over and done with before Christmas and before starting my new job. I'll have enough to think about then.'

Liz had stood up, checking her watch to make sure she didn't miss her bus. 'I suppose Jim will already know . . . I wonder what he'll have to say about it all,' she said in a flat, gloomy voice.

'Well, it shouldn't affect you two,' Heather had said quietly. 'In fact, it might help you if me and Gerry aren't always out with you.'

Liz had pursed her lips, an anxious look on her face. 'I wouldn't be so sure about that. We'll have to wait and see.'

Mona looked at Heather now, her wedding skirt clutched safely in her lap. 'Is the big romance with you and Gerry Stewart goin' off the boil, then? It's not like you to be in on a Saturday night.'

Heather attempted a smile. 'It's never really been that big a romance . . .'

'That's what they all say,' Mona stated, nodding her head knowingly in Sophie's direction. 'Then the next thing it's engagement rings and weddings. When it comes to fellas – we're all the same, us women.'

Heather felt a little pang of alarm, wondering if her aunt knew anything about the situation with Gerry. But then she decided that if Mona had known anything, she would have come straight out and said it. Subtlety was not her strongest point. 'I don't think there's any fear of anything like that,' she said, smiling again. 'Lily's fairly coming on at the country dancing,' she said now, changing the subject to one she knew would lighten her aunt's conversation.

'Is she?' Mona said, with a beaming smile. 'She certainly enjoys it anyway, she's always leapin' about up in her bedroom or down in the kitchen any time Scottish music comes on.' She rolled her eyes to the ceiling. 'She's always at something, that one. Her and that Whiskey will drive me to distraction one of these days – although I wouldn't be without her. She's the very same as your Kirsty at that age – the life and soul of every-thing.'

Obviously unlike me, Heather thought ruefully to herself, for her aunt always had a kind of edge to her voice when she spoke to her, and reserved her more light-hearted moments for Kirsty. It amazed Heather, for Kirsty was far cheekier and forward with her aunt than she would ever dare to be. Any time Heather ever tried to affect the same forwardness, Mona quickly put her in her place with a cutting word, regardless of who was there. Consequently, Heather was always on her guard.

Chapter 13

 date

Kirsty Grace floated across the stage with the deafening applause ringing in her ears when The Hi-Tones were awarded second prize in the competition, her pink skirt bobbing up and down on a sea of scarlet net underskirt and her rosebud-pinned hair still perfectly in place. All thoughts of blistered heels and rubbed toes were forgotten, as the stilettos proudly tapped their way across the painted wooden boards, leading the way for the male members of the band who trailed almost bashfully in her wake.

The band had been together for over five years before Kirsty joined them, with Martin Kerr as a fairly decent lead singer, but this was the first time they had achieved any kind of success outside of their own locality, and they found themselves somewhat bemused by it. They were also acutely aware that Kirsty Grace's voice and choice of songs for the competition – not to mention her slim, blonde good looks – had definitely helped to tip the judges' opinion in their favour.

'Well done!' the main judge had told Kirsty as he handed her the wooden plaque adorned with a silver mould of a figure holding a microphone. He had then bent his shiny, bald head towards her, his subtly expensive aftershave lingering between them.

'You have a great voice on you there, hen – and I'd say a great future in singing.'

'Thanks very much!' Kirsty had said, beaming with delight, then, suddenly realising that she shouldn't be conducting a personal conversation on stage, she had blushed and moved to let him shake hands with the others, almost tripping in the pink shoes as she went. The spoilt, quarrelsome Shirley Temple – who turned out to have a far better voice than the real one – had walked away with the first prize, and Kirsty and the band had cheered with great gusto when the one-legged Highland dancer walked with great dignity across the stage wearing his artificial leg to receive third prize.

Back in the dressing-room, the lads all toasted their win with a complimentary pint of beer from the bar, and Kirsty decided to risk her father's wrath by accepting a Babycham, which she was assured by the men would have little or no effect on her.

'When you show him that plaque your father will be that delighted he'll be offering you a drink himself!' Joe Hanlon said, his face red with all the excitement and the beer.

'I'll tell him you said that,' Kirsty joked, taking a sip of the sweet, fizzy drink. It was so nice and harmless-tasting that she took a bigger gulp straight afterwards.

Then, there was a knock on the changing-room door, and the bald, fragrant-smelling man who had presented the awards came in and made straight over to the band. 'There's someone outside who would like a wee word with you, Miss,' he said, indicating the door to Kirsty. 'It'll only take a few minutes.'

There was a sudden silence. 'D' you mean all of us?' Kirsty said, looking around the others.

'I'm quite sure he said just *you*,' the man said smiling, his gaze never straying from Kirsty. It was obvious from the way he was standing, with his back to the group, that they were not wanted or needed.

'Who is it . . . and what does he want?' Kirsty said, her brows deepening now. She turned again towards the others, an anxious look on her face. This didn't seem right, that people wanted to talk to the youngest, least experienced member of the band.

'It's a personal friend of mine,' the judge said, 'with some very good contacts in the music business.'

'Go on out and see, hen,' Martin Kerr said in a low voice, touching her elbow, and Kirsty noticed that he had a strange, resigned look on his face. 'If you need us for anything, we're all just in here.'

The judge led Kirsty through the crowd towards the dazzlingly lit bar. As they walked along, people kept stopping them to congratulate Kirsty on her great performance and her fine voice. She smiled and thanked them all, and silently wondered if her feet would last the rest of the night in the shoes, as they were really starting to pinch at the toes. Then she found herself being guided into a seat at a table to the side of the bar, and there sat the handsome, smartly dressed man who had been sitting in the front row.

'Larry Delaney,' the man said in a refined Irish accent, holding his hand out towards her. He looked up at the judge. 'And this hugely talented young lady is . . .'

'Kirsty Grace from The Hi-Tones,' Kirsty answered, knowing that the judge probably only knew the band's name and not the individual members. She realised the dark-haired man was still holding his hand out, and quickly offered her hand to him.

'Kirsty Grace,' Larry said with a smile, showing a row of perfectly even, white teeth. 'It works better than the band's name.'

Kirsty smiled back at him, feeling more relaxed now she knew he was Irish. All the Irish people she knew both in her family and in the village were always warm and friendly.

The judge looked at Larry now. 'Same again?' he said, motioning to the bar.

'That'll be fine,' Larry replied, 'and whatever Kirsty here is having.'

'A Babycham, please,' Kirsty suddenly heard herself saying, as though she had been ordering the drink all her life. She had left half of her drink in the changing-room, and she decided that another one would do no harm. As the boys in the band had said, it was a special night and deserved to be celebrated with more than just a glass of lemonade.

'How long have you been singing, Kirsty?' Larry asked, taking a fancy packet of cigarettes from his pocket. He offered Kirsty one, which she declined, before taking one himself.

Kirsty shrugged. 'I suppose I've been with the band for nearly a year.'

'And have you enjoyed it?' His eyes looked deep into hers now, and he was listening intently as though what she had to say was of the utmost importance.

Kirsty shrugged again, feeling a bit unsure of herself. She knew these questions were leading somewhere, but she wasn't exactly sure where. 'Aye,' she said, 'they're all nice fellas, and they're a good laugh.' She paused. 'They look after me well . . . and make sure I get home safe and everything.'

'Very important,' Larry agreed, his head nodding in approval. He paused to light his cigarette. 'Have you ever thought of branching out on your own?'

'How d'you mean?' Kirsty said.

'I'm going to be very direct with you,' Larry said, politely blowing the cigarette smoke away from her, 'because I can tell you're a mature, intelligent girl. I mean you could do an awful lot better for yourself *without* the band. You're far more talented than they are. They're only an average club band, if that.' He paused. 'Have you ever thought about going it alone?'

Kirsty took a deep breath, suddenly realising what this was all about. A picture of Martin's resigned-looking face came into her mind, and she immediately felt guilty. Before she had the chance to reply, the judge appeared back at the table with three drinks – the Babycham and two large whiskeys and water – balanced on a fancy silver tray.

'I think you and I are of a like mind on this one, Frank,' Larry said to the judge, 'aren't we? We both agree that Kirsty could have a very big future in singing, if we were to sell her as a soloist.'

Kirsty listened, bemused by the conversation that was taking place around her. Could they really be talking about *her*? And using words like 'very big future' and 'selling', which obviously meant there could be big money involved.

'No doubts about it,' Frank said, winking at Kirsty. 'Maybe a wee change of image . . . a more sophisticated, glamorous one.' He lifted the small blue-labelled Babycham bottle and proceeded to pour the golden bubbly drink into the elegant glass with the picture of the little dicky-bowed deer on the side. He stopped for a moment, allowing the bubbles to subside, and then he filled the glass to the top and handed it to her.

'What age are you, dear?' Larry suddenly asked.

'Eighteen and a bit,' Kirsty said, then immediately felt silly for adding the 'bit', as only immature schoolgirls did that.

'Old enough,' Larry said half to himself and half to Frank.

Old enough, he thought, to make her own decisions and not have to have her parents too involved.

Kirsty went to lift the glass to take a sip of the lovely liquid, when Larry lifted his whiskey glass and moved it towards hers and then Frank's. 'Cheers!' he said, turning back to meet Kirsty's blue eyes. 'And may you have a very long and very successful career in the music business.'

Chapter 14

There was a weary, depressed kind of atmosphere in the minibus going home that night and, instead of dozing as usual, Kirsty was staring out through the steamed-up, grimy windows, pondering over the happenings of the night. She felt strangely alert and excited, and couldn't decide whether it was due to the proposition that had been put to her, or whether it was the effect of the couple of Babychams. Either way, it felt good to have something different to think about, even if it all came to nothing, rather than the same old routine.

Thank God it was men she was working with. She found them so much more reasonable than the girls and women she both worked with and was friends with. Girls were far more bitchy and jealous, Kirsty thought. Instead of being all catty and accusing, the lads in the band, even Martin, had just been quiet and had steered well away from asking her any awkward questions about Larry Delaney and the judge.

Kirsty drew the collar of her mother's fur coat around her neck, feeling the warm softness against her skin and inhaling the familiar Coty L'Aimant scent from the collar. Maybe, she mused, she might be able to afford her *own* fur coat if she was to have that exciting, successful future in singing that the two men had been going on about. Maybe she might be able to afford a lot of things. It was funny how she saw the fellows in the band as 'lads' but Larry and Frank as 'men' – or maybe, more rightly, *gentlemen*. However she referred to them, they had definitely treated her as a lady as opposed to a girl.

She went over the conversation in her mind: how her image could be moulded into something along the lines of Marilyn Monroe or the English equivalent, Diana Dors. She almost laughed at the thought. Imagine anyone thinking that she could look all sexy and sophisticated like that, with her blonde hair loose and hanging over one eye.

'And even better,' Larry had said, raising his dark eyebrows, 'is the fact that you're younger ... and genuinely more innocent.'

Frank had looked at Larry then, and raised his eyebrows too. 'Just a wee bit of moulding here and a wee bit of moulding there would make quite a difference.'

Kirsty bent her head to look out of the van window now, up into the dark, starry sky. Even if it all came to nothing, it was certainly worth giving a bit of thought to.

Some time after midnight, as she waved goodnight back to the boys on the minibus, Kirsty wondered who would be the best person to ask advice about her singing. She felt very torn between her ambitions and loyalty to The Hi-Tones. She could think of no one who would really understand. Heather would listen and give an honest opinion, but she didn't know what she was talking about when it came to the world of singing and clubs.

Her mother and father would give their opinions, but it would be coloured by old-fashioned views about the places she would be going to and the people she would be meeting. And if she asked her Auntie Mona, it would be all about whether she was singing in chapel halls or clubs that were frequented by Catholics.

The boys in the band were the only ones she could have relied on, but given the fact that she would be dumping them to move on to better things, they were hardly going to be full of advice.

When it came down to it, she would have to make the decision herself.

The van pulled away from the opposite side of the street, leaving a trail of exhaust dust in the cold, damp air. Kirsty turned to walk the few yards to her own gate, when she suddenly noticed a shadowy movement in the back garden.

'Is that you, Daddy?' she called, thinking that it was Fintan come to meet her as he occasionally did.

But there was no reply.

'Uncle Pat?' she called, catching sight of a man's coated figure crossing over the back fence into the next-door neighbour's garden. Then, a cloud moved from in front of the moon, and she saw the figure of a man quite clearly jumping a fence into the next-door neighbour but one's garden.

She wondered now if it could be her Uncle Pat. Sometimes when he had a drink, Pat did daft things that he would never do sober. It would be just like him to take a short-cut through a fussy neighbour's garden, delighted that they wouldn't be able to see him trampling on their carefully cut grass.

Whoever it was, it wasn't anyone who wanted to make themselves known to Kirsty.

It was only later, when she was lying in bed, recounting the whole evening in her mind, that it dawned on her that the stocky dark-haired figure looked a bit like Gerry Stewart. She looked across at her sleeping sister, and wondered if she should wake her to tell her about it. Then, she thought better of it.

In all honesty, she couldn't be really sure who the fellow was, and if she was wrong, it would cause a lot of trouble.

She turned her face into her pillow and decided that it might be best to say nothing.

Chapter 15

Heather rubbed a gloved finger on the steamed-up train window and thought how she would have to be much smarter at pushing on the train this evening if she wanted a seat. The whole procedure of boarding the train reminded her of fighting to get on the school bus when she was twelve or thirteen. She hadn't imagined that adults would behave in the same manner, desperate to get a seat for the half-hour journey into Glasgow.

In fairness, the air of desperation earlier was probably because it was not only a cold, wintry morning, but because it was also raining. People were trying to put their umbrellas down, shake the rain off them and board the train at the same time. Also, Heather hadn't realised that certain passengers, who had already boarded the train at an earlier station, kept seats for their friends. As she passed the empty seats marked for someone else with a coat or a handbag thrown over them – or a briefcase when it was a man – it dawned on her that there was a knack to getting on this train, finding an available seat and grabbing it before anyone else.

By the time she had pushed her way up and down the crowded, smoky carriages, she realised that she might as well stay put at one of the doorways where there was a bit of room, or she would be forced to stand in the aisles where there was always the risk of falling in an ungainly heap over another passenger. She'd travelled lots of times by train when she was going into the city shopping with her mum and Kirsty or Liz, but that had been on a later train – she'd never had to negotiate anything like this bustling commuter one.

Eventually, the train came to a shuddering halt at the Central Station. Heather moved smarter this time, and was one of the first off the train and weaving her way towards the ticket clerk with her weekly ticket held up for inspection. Then, as she came to leave the main station building, she stopped for a few seconds to check if she needed to put up her umbrella. She decided that her hat would fend off the worst of the light rain, and moved into a quick walking pace uphill towards her new office in Bothwell Street.

By the time she had arrived at the granite-stone row of offices, the rain had eased, she had warmed up considerably, and found she had actually enjoyed the walk. She was slightly out of breath as she joined a crowd of people who were entering the big lift.

'All in?' the elderly, uniformed, lift attendant checked. He dragged across the first set of white wrought-iron gates, and when they were securely in place, he dragged across the second set, and then the lift took off.

Heather felt a mixture of excitement and anxiety as the lift moved up floor by floor, as she listened carefully to the lift attendant call out the list of offices on each one. She knew perfectly well from her interview that her office was on the fourth floor, but she listened intently and didn't move out of the lift until he called out Seafreight amongst the other offices on that particular floor.

There was no comparison between the small, three-roomed office in Wishaw and the city shipping office that took up a whole floor, and even had its own kitchen and separate – very elegant, Heather thought – Gents and Ladies toilets. The walls were painted cream and were hung with large, elaborately framed pictures of very serious sea-going vessels with large, windswept sails. There was liquid soap in a glass dispenser, and piles of freshly washed blue and white towels folded in an old sea-chest.

'I think we'll start you on the filing and the post this morning,' Mr Walton, the office manager, said with a kindly smile, walking her in the direction of the smallest office where two smart middle-aged women were hanging up their coats, scarves and hats. 'And then maybe after lunch, we'll check out your shorthand and typing skills.' He'd paused then, indicating to one of the women. 'Talking of lunch, Miss Ferguson – Muriel – will sort you out with luncheon vouchers for the week, and I'm sure some of the other girls will be only too happy to suggest places that you can use them.'

'Thanks, Mr Walton,' Heather said, trying not to show how delighted she was about the luncheon vouchers. They had been one of the attractions of the job. Apart from saving her the bother of making sandwiches or having to pay for her own lunch, it gave her a reason to try all the exciting city places that had the LV sign on the door.

Mr Walton now introduced Heather to Muriel and Anna, and then they went back out to the main office. 'You can put your coat and things on there,' he said, pointing to a long wooden rack, 'and there's an umbrella stand by the door.' He gave a little sigh. 'At this time of the year it's well used.'

Heather deposited her damp umbrella in the stand and then hung up her belted tweed coat and matching hat, then Mr

67

Walton took her over to a group of large grey filing cabinets in the centre of the largest office, and explained how the numerical system worked for the shipping documents. He indicated a table piled high with documents. 'They're all numbered according to the files in the cabinet,' he said, showing her the stamp on the corner of the top sheets. He gave an apologetic smile. 'I'm afraid we've got a wee bit behind since Janice left.'

'I'll manage,' Heather quickly reassured him. 'I've done plenty of filing in my old office.'

'Oh, I have every confidence in you,' the older man said, then he motioned to a thin-built man in his late thirties to come over and be introduced to her, and two girls around her own age called Sarah and Marie. Various other members of staff were brought over to the filing cabinet to meet Heather, and others wandered over of their own volition.

Two fellows who looked to be slightly older than Heather came over together, one dark-haired, on the small side although well-built, and the other almost six feet tall, going bald with slightly bulging eyes. She had noticed them chatting at one of the desks and caught them looking over at her on several occasions. When she saw them coming across to her, she could feel her cheeks starting to burn.

'Danny Fleming,' the smaller of the two said, greeting her with an outstretched hand and a big cheery smile. He indicated to his colleague now. 'And this is Maurice Smith.' Both shook hands with her, trying not to make it too obvious that they were over for a closer look at her.

'Heather Grace,' she replied, hoping she didn't look as embarrassed as she felt. Then she added rather needlessly, 'I've just started here this morning ...'

'Is that an Irish name?' Maurice asked. He thumbed to the fellow beside him. 'Danny's family are all Irish.' He gave a little smirky kind of smile. 'That's something you both have in common already.'

'Aye ...' Heather said, her face going even redder. There was a little pause, and she suddenly felt she should say something. 'My father's from County Offaly.'

'Mine's from Mayo, a wee place in the middle of nowhere,' Danny said in a pronounced Glasgow accent that gave no hint of his Irish roots. 'Never heard of Offaly – whereabouts is it? Are ye sure that's the name of an Irish *county*?'

Then, before she had a chance to reply, Mr Walton came rushing out of his office clapping his hands for attention. 'Just to remind you all that the window-cleaners are outside on their cradle-things this morning, so don't get a sudden shock if a face appears at the window beside you.'

'Well, ye don't have to be completely mad to work here,' Danny Fleming quipped, winking at Heather, 'but sometimes it helps if ye are.' He glanced over his shoulder. 'And it helps if ye can look busy even when you're not, especially if oul' Walton is around.' He dropped his voice. 'He's a dangerous man to work for. Ye never know how ye'll find him – he's all great laughs one minute and then very next he could caw the head off ye for nothin'. Isn't that right, Maurice, son?'

Maurice nodded his head solemnly in Heather's direction, then his eyes widened making them bulge even more. 'A right moon-man at times – so be warned.'

She nodded her head now, alarmed to hear this about the man she had thought was really nice. 'Thanks for telling me,' she said quietly. 'I'll bear it in mind.'

After about an hour, Muriel Ferguson came over to Heather and said she had a few minutes to spare to show her the postal system. Another hour flew by as Heather became acquainted with the weighing scales for envelopes and parcels in the office, then she checked the postal rates on a table and franked each piece of mail accordingly.

At eleven o'clock, the office suddenly slowed down and people started looking for handbags and heading for the door.

'Break-time,' Muriel Ferguson said, indicating towards the big round, mahogany clock with the Roman numerals that had once adorned the sea-going office in a famous Clydeside ship. 'There's a small canteen on the floor below that everybody goes to.'

Heather reached for her bag. 'Great,' she said, 'I could just do with a cup of tea.' They walked down the stairs together and as they entered the canteen, Heather was hit by the comforting smell of warm sausage rolls and bridies. She looked over at the glass oven that kept the food warm, and her mouth watered at the sight of the pies and hot bacon rolls.

She had promised herself that she would start to cut down a bit, so that she would fit into nice dresses for Christmas, but the look and smell of the lovely food made her shaky willpower waver even further.

'They have a great selection,' Heather said to the older woman as they joined the queue. 'I can't decide what to have.' Her gaze came to rest on a tray of buttered treacle scones and lovely cherry scones with jam.

'Some of them come into work without having any breakfast,' Muriel whispered in a disapproving manner, 'and then they wolf into all this heavy stuff as if it was lunchtime. You'd think they'd never seen a bite in their lives.' She sniffed, lifting a plain white cup and saucer from the tray in front of the urns. 'I have a good breakfast before I leave the house in the morning, so a cup of tea does me just fine at this time.' She passed her cup across to the lady serving. 'I would hate to have all that stodgy stuff lying on my stomach at this hour of the day – and I'm sure it must affect their work. How can your brain be sharp if your body's sluggish from all that stodge?'

Heather's heart sank as she realised that it would look terrible now if she went for any of the tantalising things that Muriel had described so disparagingly. She even felt embarrassed at the thought of buying one of the lighter items like a scone or a doughnut. She reached for a cup and saucer, pondering over her predicament, when she felt a hand on her shoulder.

'Where did ye say that place was in Ireland that yer family came from?' It was the small, dark-haired fellow who had come across with his friend earlier in the office. He lifted up a large paper plate, his eyes scanning the array of snacks.

'Offaly,' Heather said, turning around to face him. 'It's one of the smallest counties . . .'

'Imagine it being a county in Ireland,' he said, shaking his head, 'and I've never heard tell of it.'

He reached into the glass oven and lifted out a hot bridie and put it on his plate, then stretched across the counter for a jam doughnut, holding onto his spotty blue tie in case it draped across any of the buttered scones or sugary doughnuts on display. 'Do you go to Ireland much?' Danny asked now.

Heather shook her head, hardly able to concentrate for looking at all the lovely things she desperately fancied. 'We used to go for a month every summer when we were at primary school, and we went over for a few Christmases, but now that me and my sister are both working, we don't go as often.' She passed her cup across to the lady behind the counter who filled it up with tea.

'We don't either,' Danny said. 'Once ye start work ye don't have the same time off. But I try to get over for a week every year.' He grinned now. 'We have some brilliant times over there goin' to hurling matches and everythin', and the pubs stay open half the night.' He now passed a large blue mug across for his tea.

Heather turned back to face the front of the queue and realised that Muriel Ferguson and her cup of tea had vanished. She gave a quick glance around the canteen and then saw Muriel disappearing out of the door with another older lady.

'Would you mind passing me a plate?' she said to Danny. 'I think I might have something to eat after all.' Then she reached her hand into the glass oven for the lovely, golden sausage roll she had been eyeing since joining the queue.

'They're brilliant, by the way,' Danny informed her, taking a bite of his bridie and sending little flakey crumbs down over his shirt and tie. 'They get all the stuff delivered fresh every mornin' from Crawford's the baker's.'

'It looks lovely,' Heather said, picking up a small slice of millionaire shortbread. *Tomorrow*, she promised herself. *Definitely tomorrow, I'll start cutting down.*

The rest of the morning flew as piles of parcels and envelopes arrived to be weighed and franked, and when they eventually dribbled down to ones and twos, Heather took a break and went back to the filing cabinets. This time, as people moved up and down the office, and often stopped to pass a few words, she felt less self-conscious. As it grew nearer one o'clock, however, she started to feel a little anxious about where she might go at lunchtime. Then, Sarah, one of the girls she'd met earlier in the morning, came across to her.

'Muriel asked me to give you your Luncheon Vouchers,' she said, handing her an envelope. 'There's a few of us going to The Trees restaurant down at the station, if you want to come.'

'Oh, that would be great,' Heather said, giving a relieved smile. 'I wasn't too sure where to go . . . I only know Glasgow for shopping.'

'Oh, we know it well for shopping, too.' Sarah laughed, her long, straight mousy-brown swinging as she did. 'Where d'you come from?' she asked now.

'Rowanhill,' Heather explained. 'It's out near Wishaw . . .'

Sarah's brows came down. 'Never heard of it – but then I don't know too many places outside Glasgow.' She paused. 'Sometimes a few of us go into the shops on a Friday evening after we've got our wages. We go for something to eat in the café at the station. If you fancy it, you can come any time.'

'That's a great idea,' Heather said, delighted to be included. 'I could just get a later train home.'

As she sat back in the train on her return journey that evening – squashed between a heavy-built woman and a young boy – Heather felt grateful and pleased with herself for actually having a seat. She had bought a magazine from the paper shop in the station to read as she travelled home, but she decided now that there wasn't enough room to hold it comfortably. She looked out of the window at the other commuters running to catch their various trains, then, as the train pulled out of the station, she ran over the day's events in her mind, and felt she had made a very respectable start.

The afternoon had passed quickly after a nice lunch in The Trees. The three girls had all picked fish and chips with a small dish of trifle to finish, then they had sat chatting over a cup of tea, swapping information about themselves. Then realising the time, they'd all hurried through the bustling streets and back to the office. Mr Walton had brought Heather into his office and got her to take a letter down in shorthand, and then he'd asked her to type it up. When she'd brought the finished document to him, he said he was perfectly satisfied with the standard of her work, and that he'd chat to the other women about giving her some more of that work for the following day.

All in all, she thought, her first day at Seafreight had gone well.

She was relieved that when the train reached Cambuslang Station, the heavy woman and the boy got off, and Heather moved in towards the window, glad to have a bit more space. She was just reaching into her handbag for her magazine, when she looked up to see a figure in a dark winter coat coming to move into the empty seat beside her.

'Hello,' a familiar voice said, 'I thought it was you.' He sat down beside her, an evening newspaper in one hand and a few carrier bags of different sizes in the other.

'Gerry ...' Heather said, her voice suddenly sticking in her throat. She swallowed hard, feeling all flustered and embarrassed. 'I didn't see you getting on the train ...'

'Oh, but I saw you,' he said, his face quite serious. 'I saw you queuing at the barrier in the station. I was a bit behind you.' He organised the carrier bags into a tidy group on the floor under the table.

'Aren't you usually working at this time?' she asked. 'You don't usually go into Glasgow during the week ...' She suddenly wondered if he'd remembered about this being her first day in her new office, and whether he'd worked out that she'd be getting on this particular train. There were only two that went to Rowanhill around the time that the shops and offices closed, so it wouldn't be hard to work it out. But then, she thought, he could meet her in Rowanhill any time, he didn't need to come into Glasgow just to sit beside her on a train. What would be the point in that?

'Day off,' he said, folding the newspaper over and fitting it into one of the bags. 'I had a few things I needed, so I decided to take a trip into the bigger shops while it was quiet at the beginning of the week.'

There was an awkward silence, during which Heather pondered over how she should react to suddenly being flung beside her ex-boyfriend for the next twenty minutes. She turned to look out of the window, signalling to him that the conversation was ended. She definitely didn't want to come across as being too friendly with him and giving him the wrong impression. She moved her handbag nearer to her on the table, then glanced down at Gerry's shopping, and could see the names of the Gents' Outfitters shops on the bags.

He had obviously been treating himself to some new clothes. She wondered now if they were for going to Australia after Christmas.

'How are your plans for Australia going?' she suddenly heard herself ask in a reasonably friendly tone.

There was a pause, then a little smile came to his lips. 'I'm still considering it,' he told her. 'But I've had another option come up at work. When I told the boss I was thinking of going, he came back to me a few days later and offered me a good promotion.' He indicated the bags. 'I thought I could do with a new suit and a few good shirts and things, whatever I decide to do . . .' He turned sideways in his seat now, facing her properly. 'I was thinking about you this afternoon . . .'

Heather felt her stomach tighten. *How on earth had he managed to catch the same train as her? And why did he have to have found one of the few available seats beside her?*

'How did your first day go in the new job?' he asked casually.

'Fine,' Heather said, nodding her head but looking straight ahead. He had obviously remembered about her starting in the new office, and wanted to let her know. 'Aye, it went really well . . . the people in the office are all nice. I think I'm going to enjoy it.'

Gerry nodded, his face thoughtful. 'I think maybe you were right,' he suddenly said in a low voice, 'about us having a break . . . maybe it's not a bad thing. We both have things to be getting on with, your new job and my own situation.'

There was silence for a moment while Heather wondered if he had purposely used the words *having a break* as opposed to *us breaking up*. Whichever way he had meant it, she decided it would be safer not to make any comment. She reached into her bag and brought out her magazine now, hoping he would get the hint and maybe read his paper.

'Are you going out at the weekend?' he said after a while.

Heather shrugged, still looking at the magazine. 'I haven't

given a thought to the weekend yet,' she said casually. 'It seems like a long way off.'

'I'm fairly booked up already,' he told her, a note of smugness in his voice. He shifted the bags into a straight line again with his feet.

'Good for you,' she said lightly. She turned over a page in her magazine and concentrated on a knitting pattern for a lovely jumper in a lace design. She often knitted and, having finished her last top a few weeks ago, had been pondering over what she would knit next. The one in the magazine was exactly the kind of jumper she needed to go with her tartan suit when it was too cold to wear a blouse under. She kept looking at the pattern, trying to work out which colour of wool she would buy – anything to keep her mind off her unwanted companion.

'How's Kirsty doing?' Gerry enquired now. He turned to the side again, trying to engage her in a deeper, more serious conversation. 'Liz was telling me and Jim that she's got a new manager.'

'She's fine, it all seems to be going well,' Heather said, giving a little sigh that she hoped would indicate her irritation at being forced into talking to him. He took the hint. He turned back in his seat and after a few minutes he leaned down and got his newspaper out of the carrier bag.

Heather looked at her watch and willed away the minutes until the train arrived in Rowanhill.

Chapter 16

K irsty stared into the crammed, white-painted, wooden wardrobe she shared with her sister, trying to decide what to wear. This was something she'd never had to plan for before – a meal out in a posh hotel, especially with an older, sophisticated man like Larry Delaney.

When he had called in to see her at the chemist's shop that afternoon – all dressed up in an expensive grey and black herring-bone coat and soft grey wool scarf – and casually suggested that they go out for the evening to discuss her singing future under his management, Kirsty had eagerly agreed, presuming they were going to a café or a quiet pub lounge somewhere. Then he had said that they could talk over dinner at a nice hotel in Lanark and that he'd pick her up at the house in his car at seven o'clock. It had all happened so quickly that she had just agreed, not really taking in what she had agreed to, then after he'd left Kirsty had felt a little knot forming in her stomach.

Kirsty had never actually been out for a meal with *any* man, as her escorts up until now had always been boys her own age, who would have been more terrified to walk into a restaurant or a hotel than she would have been.

She had rushed out of the chemist's shop as soon as the lights were off and ran all the way home to make sure she had plenty of time to get ready for this special night out. With her coat still on, she'd rushed upstairs to the airing cupboard to check that the tank was filled with enough hot water for a bath, then rushed back downstairs to tell her mother she wouldn't be having any dinner.

'You're going to a *hotel* for your dinner?' her mother had said in a high, surprised voice.

'Where?'

'I think he said Lanark,' Kirsty said, hanging up her duffle coat. 'And I haven't a clue what to wear or what I'll talk about when I'm out . . .'

'You'll be fine,' her mother had said, coming over to put her arms around her. 'Just wear something nice and tidy, that makes you look as if you know what you're talking about.'

Kirsty rifled through the hangers, vaguely muttering to herself as she did so, and every so often lifting out a dress or a suit and throwing it on top of the growing pile on Heather's bed. She hoped to have picked an outfit and have everything back in the wardrobe before her fussier, tidier sister came in and started complaining about the state of the room.

The wardrobe was split into two distinct halves, with the girls sharing the hanging rail and each having a shelved section at either side of the mirrored wardrobe. Normally, Kirsty kept strictly to her own section because Heather was extremely fussy about the order things were hung in. She liked skirts and dresses all together, blouses on hangers and jumpers carefully folded on the shelf, and she hated Kirsty touching her stuff. But tonight Kirsty was desperate for just the right outfit, and she was counting on her sister to understand.

'The bath's ready, hen!' her mother called from along the hallway. 'I've turned the taps off so's it doesn't run over ...' There was a pause. 'Are you sure you don't want a wee plate of home-made soup before you go out?'

'No thanks,' Kirsty called back in a high voice, irritated with the interruption. She picked out a reddish-blue tartan suit of Heather's, which had been covered in a polythene dry-cleaner's bag, and then she swung the wardrobe door closed to see what it looked like held up to her in the long mirror. It had a lovely, single-breasted jacket caught in at the waist with a half-belt and a tight-fitted skirt. She knew that Heather had bought it in Glasgow last Christmas, and had only worn it a few times because it just fitted her and no more. She was always hoping to lose a few pounds so that it would look and feel better on her. Kirsty looked at it now, her eyes narrowed in thought, turning her head to one side and then the other. It was definitely the best so far, and she knew that it would easily fit her with room to spare, and if she wore it with her tight red sweater, with a nice broad belt, it would look lovely when she took the jacket off.

'I've a big favour to ask,' Kirsty said, meeting Heather at the top of the stairs wearing a dressing-gown and with a towel wrapped around her damp hair. 'I've got a really important meeting tonight with that manager, Larry Delaney ...' She bit her lip. 'He's taking me out for a meal, and I need to look my very, *very* best ...' She paused. 'I haven't anything suitable amongst my own clothes ... You know I wouldn't normally ask, but it's *really*, really important.'

Heather gave a loud sigh and unpinned the green beret she was wearing from her dark hair. Kirsty was forever doing this, and the number of times she had returned things with buttons missing and hems coming down had resulted in her older sister putting a ban on them borrowing clothes from each other.

Heather moved from the top step to the hallway outside their bedroom door. 'Which outfit exactly are we talking about?' she asked, on her tiptoes now, holding the beret and trying to see past her sister in through the open bedroom door.

'I promise I'll pay to get it dry-cleaned again as soon as you feel it needs it,' Kirsty rushed on, almost barring the way into the room where the suit lay spread out on the bed alongside the red sweater and a fancy garnet brooch she'd borrowed from her mother. 'So . . . is it OK if I take a loan of one of your suits?'

Heather's eyes narrowed. 'It's not the good tartan suit you're talking about?'

A pained expression came on Kirsty's face. 'I wouldn't normally ask . . . but it's a *really* special occasion, and I need to make a good impression.'

Heather shook her head. '"You know fine well I've only worn that about twice . . . I was keeping it up for Christmas.'

Kirsty's shoulders sagged and she looked almost wounded. 'I've *nothing* of my own that would look as nice,' she said in a low, uncertain voice, 'or anythin' that looks kind of professional. If I'd had time, I'd have run into Glasgow or Motherwell and bought myself somethin' new, but he only asked me this afternoon . . .'

She looked at Heather now, and Heather looked back at her.

'Aw – go on!' Heather finally said. 'Take it – but you'd better—'

'I will, I will!' Kirsty said, hugging her. 'I'll really look after it, and I promise I'll get it dry-cleaned at the weekend.'

Sophie and Heather stood at the side of the curtain as Kirsty and Larry went down the little path still flanked with the straggly remnants of the autumn wallflowers, Kirsty walking with great dignity in a pair of reasonably comfortable black stilettos. They watched as Larry moved forward to open the passenger door on the shiny Wolseley to let Kirsty in first.

'Good manners,' Sophie murmured, nodding her head in approval, 'that's the sign of a real gentleman.'

'My daddy always lets you in the car first,' Heather said. They both watched now as the car pulled away. *Not that our car's as fancy as that*, Heather thought to herself.

'That's exactly what I mean,' Sophie said, smiling. She started drawing the curtains now to keep in the heat. 'And that's one of the first things I liked about your father. He might be rough and ready in certain ways, but in other ways he's always been a real gentleman ... always had that wee touch of romance.'

When Heather turned to look at her mother, there was a dewy, far-away look in Sophie's eyes that made her feel a little uncomfortable, along with the thought of her father being described as *romantic*.

'Kirsty looked well in the suit,' her mother said now. 'It made her look older and more confident.'

'I wish it fitted me as well as it fits her,' Heather said ruefully, smoothing down her dark pleated working skirt. 'I need to cut out all the biscuits and things in the office at the break times.'

'I think you look as though you've lost a few pounds already,' Sophie said, going over to check if the fire needed more coal. Fintan had left a heaped bucketful before going up to put the heating on in the school hall for the boys' guild that met there every Thursday night.

'D'you really think so?' Heather said, smiling now. 'I've noticed that my skirts aren't just as tight, right enough.' She sat down on the edge of the couch, picking up the *Daily Record* to check what was on the radio that night.

'All that running up and down to the station and the walk up that hill to your office will be helping to keep you trim,' Sophie told her, as she picked a few big lumps of coal from the bucket with the tongs, and threw them into the heart of the fire.

'Aye,' Heather said, feeling the little gap in the waistband of her skirt that wasn't there when she bought it a few weeks ago. 'If I cut out all the sweet things, it might make a good difference by Christmas.'

Sophie sat down in the armchair by the fire, a thoughtful look on her face. 'What did you think of that manager fella?'

Heather shrugged, flicking through the paper now. 'He seemed nice enough ... what did you think?'

'Aye,' her mother said, nodding, 'he seemed a nice man. Well dressed and well spoken.'

'That's what you'd expect from a manager or an agent, or

whatever he's called,' Heather commented. 'They've got to look the part for people to take them seriously.'

'Aye,' her mother said again. 'But he's a handsome-looking man, and I'd say he knows it only too well.' She looked up at the clock, checking when Fintan would be back in for his cup of tea. 'Kirsty was takin' their night out very seriously anyway, she was like a scalded cat running up and down the stairs and checking she looked all right.' She halted. 'I hope she doesn't take it all too seriously, for he's the type of man that would have plenty of women running around after him.'

'Mammy!' Heather said, rolling her eyes in mock horror. 'Kirsty's not going to be in the slightest bit interested in the likes of him, apart from her singing.' She started to giggle now, amazed at the daft ideas her mother came up with. 'He's ancient! He must be about thirty at least . . . Kirsty wouldn't look twice at him. If she heard what you were saying, she'd die laughing.'

Sophie smiled now and shook her head. 'Don't be too sure.'

'Get away – he's far too old for her,' Heather said, still laughing at the thought.

'Famous last words,' Sophie said quietly. 'Famous last words.'

Chapter 17

'**A** Babycham, if I remember correctly?' Larry said in his rich Dublin accent, smiling warmly at Kirsty.

'Lovely,' Kirsty replied, smiling back, delighted that he'd remembered.

They had arrived half an hour before the restaurant booking, as Larry said it would give them plenty of time in case the roads started to get icy, but the drive up to Lanark had turned out to be lovely and the roads had been perfectly dry and clear. They had veered off the main road just outside the town and climbed a narrow winding road past lovely big old houses up to the Clydeside area.

Then they had driven on a little further and suddenly when

they turned a corner, the old Victorian sandstone hotel was just in front of them. Larry had parked at the side of the hotel, and then moved quickly again to open the passenger door for Kirsty.

When she got out of the car and looked around her at the beautiful gardens still miraculously in colour in winter, and the other fancy cars that were parked, Kirsty had felt a pang of nervousness.

The thought of having to walk into the imposing building had suddenly made her remember her father's uncomfortable attitude when they had days out on the train to Edinburgh and Glasgow, and their mother suggested going into places like this for afternoon tea or a cup of coffee and a cake.

'They're not for the likes of us,' Fintan would venture as they stood outside the hotels, debating whether or not to go in. The thought of having to give orders from complicated menus to waiters in tailed coats and bow-ties filled him with dread, and there was always the matter of negotiating the tiny china cups with his large hands, which were much more suited to shovelling in coal or fiddling with the Victorian plumbing in the school. They would walk on for another while past homely tea-rooms or big bustling restaurants frequented by people more like themselves, but eventually they would turn a corner to be confronted by another formidable establishment and that would start Sophie off again.

'But I would really like to go in,' she would argue in a low voice, 'and our money is as good as anybody else's. We're all dressed up for the day, and it lets us see how the other half live.'

'I'm not in the slightest bit interested in how they live,' Fintan would sigh.

Sophie would then pause. 'I want the girls to feel confident – to know they can walk into places like this when they're older and be every bit as good as the next one. After all, it's only once a year ... it's not as if we're out together as a family every weekend. It's only a bit of a treat ...'

And their father would give in, as the girls knew he would. The easy-going Sophie made few demands on him, and it would have been churlish of him not to agree. And then all four of them would walk into the nice hotel or restaurant, where the three females would enjoy the smart surroundings and the small fancy cakes – and after a stiff Irish whiskey, Fintan would eventually relax and endure it.

Bolstered by her mother's words now of being *as good as the next one*, Kirsty had straightened her back and lifted her chin and smiled at Larry Delaney as if she was used to walking into posh places every night of the week.

She watched him now from her high-backed green leather Chesterfield chair as he crossed the floor in the surprisingly busy small bar, and wondered if there was ever a time, back in Dublin years ago, when he would have been nervous in a place like this. She watched as he caught the barman's attention through the crowd with a mere nod of his head, and then had a light, friendly conversation with him as he ordered the drinks, and decided that Larry Delaney must have been born confident.

Kirsty thought it might have been quiet tonight since it was only a Monday, and was amazed to see so many people being able to afford to go out for a meal on a working night.

She took the opportunity to have a good look around the elaborately decorated, dimly lit lounge while she was on her own, starting with the glass-topped table in front of her, which was underlaid with the same green leather as the chair. She leaned forward to discreetly examine the chunky crystal ashtray that matched the crystal candle-holder, which had a round well in the middle holding a small thick candle. She lifted the candle-holder a few inches off the table and was surprised at how heavy it was.

While Larry was at the bar, Kirsty took advantage of his absence at the table to remove her suit jacket and make sure that her red sweater was smoothed down and sitting just perfectly. Then she discreetly checked in her compact mirror that her lipstick and hair were fine and the garnet and gold brooch was still properly pinned on. Satisfied that she looked decent, she then sat with a straight back in the leather chair and surveyed the other people around her.

Most of them were much older than her, and probably a bit older than Larry too, and they all looked very much at home. Kirsty wondered if they lived in some of the big houses they had passed on the way up here – the sandstone ones that looked like smaller versions of the hotel. Then, she became aware of a striking, dark-haired woman gazing across the room at her and she suddenly went back to feeling all self-conscious again. She started to fiddle with the clasp on her brooch, just to give herself something to do. When she lifted her eyes later, the woman was engaged in conversation with a man and two other women, her hands waving expressively, and her dark hair swinging around as she laughed out loud.

Larry came back to their glass-topped table with the drinks and while he was pouring Kirsty's drink into her glass, a young – obviously new – waiter rushed over with a dish of nuts, apologising for not having been there to take their drinks order. His red-faced awkwardness reminded Kirsty of some of the boys in her class at school, and she started to feel a little more relaxed.

'This is a lovely place,' she said, taking a sip of her sweet, bubbly drink.

'Good,' Larry said, 'I'm delighted you like it . . . I hoped that you would. It's one of my favourite places around here.'

There was a little silence, during which Kirsty took another drink of Babycham and wondered who Larry usually brought along to his 'favourite places'.

Then, he unexpectedly leaned forward and patted her hand and Kirsty felt a funny little tingle run through her. 'We need to get down to the serious business now—' He halted, looking up as a figure suddenly appeared by the side of their table.

'Hello there, Larry,' a low, refined Scottish voice cut in. 'I thought it was you . . .' It was the glamorous, dark-haired woman who had been staring at Kirsty earlier. Close up, Kirsty could see that she was older than she had appeared at a distance, probably even older than Larry, but very good-looking and beautifully dressed in a simple black shift dress with long black gloves and pearls.

'Fiona . . .' Larry said, a smile crossing his handsome face. It wasn't a broad smile – more a careful, quizzical smile. He stood up now to embrace her and kiss her on the cheek. 'What are you doing in this neck of the woods? This is a wee bit out of your usual area, isn't it?'

'It's not that far from Hamilton,' she said. 'I'm out on what you could call *business* . . .' She smiled up at him, giving her head a little shake, which sent a long dark wave covering one eye. 'Although – as you well know, Larry – it's very easy to mix business with pleasure.'

Larry nodded, then he seemed to hesitate for a moment. 'How are Helen and David? Have you seen them recently?'

Fiona's eyes narrowed. 'I see them regularly, and they're both well,' she said quietly. She tilted her head, as though studying his reaction. 'Helen made a wise decision . . . very practical and one that works well for all concerned.'

Larry nodded again, but this time he said nothing.

Fiona turned now to Kirsty, raised her eyebrows expectantly and waited for some explanation as to who she was.

Kirsty gave the woman a smile, and then, as she found herself being scrutinised, her stomach tightened and her smile disappeared. Then she felt her neck and face start to burn with the deep red flush that always let her down when she was nervous – and the more she worried about it, the worse it got.

'We're out on a professional nature, too,' Larry told the woman with a casual smile that showed his even white teeth. He put a hand on Kirsty's shoulder, the way her father sometimes did when he was introducing her. 'This young lady is Kirsty Grace . . . a brilliant new singing talent that I've had the great good fortune to discover.'

'Imagine!' Fiona said, smiling broadly, but Kirsty was quick to notice that the smile didn't reach her eyes. 'Imagine *actually* discovering a new talent . . . I look forward to hearing her some time.' She gave a tinkly little laugh, as though she had just heard something funny. 'You're so very clever at all this, Larry, aren't you? Discovering new talent.'

'I have no doubts that you will hear her,' Larry said, with a little edge to his voice, and his hand still lingering on Kirsty's shoulder. 'Now, would you like to join us for a drink?'

'No, no . . . not at all,' Fiona said, glancing back in the direction of the table where she'd been sitting. She pushed her black hair back over her shoulder. 'I have to go . . . we have a table booked in the restaurant and I think it's nearly time.'

Larry nodded. 'We're heading in there ourselves.'

Fiona's eyebrows shot up again in surprise, but she said nothing. She gave another little smile. 'I'm sure I'll see you later,' and then with a flick of her glossy black hair, she set off back to her table, her high heels silent in the deep pile of the carpet.

'Who was that?' The words were out of Kirsty's mouth before she could stop herself.

'Fiona McCluskey,' Larry said in an even voice.

'And is she in the music business, too?'

'No,' Larry said, 'she's involved in a number of businesses, but music isn't one of them.' He took a sip of his whiskey. 'Now, back to our discussion . . .'

The meal went smoothly, much to Kirsty's relief, and it was helped by the one glass of cold white wine that Larry had poured for her – the first wine she had ever tasted. 'I wouldn't want your mother and father to think I was leading you into bad habits,' he'd said earlier, laughing as he ordered a half-bottle between them. 'And if we're going to be working closely together, it's best if I don't start off on the wrong foot with them.'

Kirsty almost said that she would have preferred another Babycham or a small sherry with her meal, but something had held her back. She wasn't sure why she had said nothing when he ordered the wine, but later when she looked back on the evening, she realised it was when she noticed Fiona's group with *two* bottles of wine on their table that she decided wine was obviously a social nicety she needed to learn about. And even though Larry seemed kind and understanding, Kirsty thought it best not to enlighten him that the only wine she knew anything about was tonic wine.

She could feel herself burning with embarrassment again, as she recalled having half a tumbler of the strong red wine one Christmas at an elderly neighbour's house, which she'd downed in two gulps, and had felt her head spinning for the rest of the afternoon. In Rowanhill and the surrounding villages, Buckfast and Sanatogen wines were regarded by decent people as lethal, and only bought by the lowest of the low, heavy drinkers, or old ladies who indulged in a tiny glass now and again, supposedly for their health. Sadly, some of the poor old souls got so used to it that they were often seen discreetly buying bottles of the stuff on a daily basis.

When the waiter had carefully poured their wine from a cold bottle wrapped in a white damask linen napkin, they had clinked their wine glasses together, and then Larry had started talking, outlining all the great plans he had for her.

He talked first about her having a course of singing lessons with a renowned teacher from Motherwell, just to 'sharpen up her voice' on the high notes.

'I used to go for singing lessons when I was younger,' Kirsty told him, slightly defensively.

'Good,' Larry said, smiling. 'It will be no bother to you learning breathing techniques and scales again.' Then he talked about her changing her whole repertoire of songs, which he felt would attract a more sophisticated audience.

'It might take a month or two before you're ready to go on stage again, but when you do, you'll be a very different type of performer. You'll be in a different class. We have to get it right from the very beginning – voice, songs, clothes, hairstyle . . . everything.'

'But that's going to cost a fortune.'

When Kirsty had looked alarmed at all his plans, he had taken her hand between his and squeezed it reassuringly. 'Don't worry about a thing – it'll all be taken care of.' He had leaned forward and looked into her eyes. 'I understand that you're only a young girl, and you can't be earning a huge amount in that chemist's shop . . .'

'It's not a bad job,' Kirsty said sounding defensive again, annoyed at being described as *only a young girl*. 'There's nothing wrong with it, it's handy for home and a chemist's is a nice clean place to work.' She sat upright now, straightening out the rib of her sweater for something to concentrate on, without having to look at Larry. 'It's as well paid as anything around here . . . and I've made a bit extra from singing with the band.'

Larry nodded, and held his hands up apologetically. 'I'm not saying anything about your job, Kirsty,' he said in a low voice. 'I'm sure it's a fine job . . . for a girl who doesn't have your *outstanding talent*.'

Kirsty registered his two last words, and she suddenly felt her heart soar. 'Do you really think so?' she whispered. 'Do you really think I've got a good singing talent?'

Larry laughed out loud now, and Kirsty felt all self-conscious again. She hoped that Fiona wouldn't look across and think he was laughing at something silly she'd said.

'Would I be out here with you tonight, if I didn't think you had talent?' he said quietly, his face suddenly becoming more serious. 'Why else would I be sitting here with you? I'm a very busy man, and I haven't time to waste on things that aren't important to me.'

Kirsty dropped her gaze now and started fiddling with her napkin. Now she *did* feel silly.

'Well,' she said, giving a little shrug, 'I don't like to act big-headed or anything ... and there's a big difference between thinking you're not a bad singer in a local band and somebody like you sayin' that I have ... a *real* talent.'

'You have a real talent, make no mistake about it,' Larry confirmed. 'So we won't waste any more time debating it.' He tapped his fingers on the lace tablecloth. 'I was trying to say you're not to worry about the singing lessons and the clothes being out of your reach ... we can come to an arrangement.'

'How?' Kirsty asked, her brow furrowing. 'What kind of arrangement?'

'Well, I can always put the money up front,' he explained, 'and then we can deduct it from your wages when you start earning decent money from your singing. It's fairly standard in this business ... it's the professional way to do things.'

There was a little silence. 'I have savings in a post office account ...' Kirsty volunteered. 'I don't really like the idea of owing anybody money.'

'We'll see,' Larry said. His eyes were dancing with amusement, but he kept his face straight just in case she took further offence. For someone who was used to dealing with all sorts of people, he suddenly realised he'd never actually met anyone like Kirsty Grace before – and certainly had never worked with anyone like her. One minute she seemed quite confident and mature beyond her years, and the very next minute she was a touchy, prickly teenager. He reckoned he was just going to have to play their working relationship very much by ear.

But one thing was sure: Kirsty Grace had a voice like no other singer on his books. He would just have to be patient and understanding with her, and hopefully she would become wiser in the ways of the business world.

Larry talked and talked throughout the meal, and Kirsty's confidence soared as she listened to him praising her singing, and then at one point she suddenly realised she was relaxed and enjoying herself in this posh restaurant.

The array of gleaming silver cutlery that had caused her heart to sink had gradually began to make sense as she followed Larry's example with each course, starting with the obvious soup spoon. And she had heaved a small, silent sigh of relief when the strangely shaped object – which turned out to be a fish knife – had been removed by the friendly waitress and replaced with a more recognisable wooden steak knife.

And then – feeling reckless since she hadn't made a fool of herself – she decided to be brave and pick an Italian-sounding dessert because she liked the description of the *coffee-flavoured liqueur* in the centre. When the dessert arrived, she was disappointed to discover that it was darker and the liqueur was much more bitter than she had expected. But funnily enough, the more she ate of it, the more she got used to it. Like the man sitting beside her.

At first she wasn't sure what to make of him. But the more time she spent in his company – the more she got used to him.

Chapter 18

❧❧❧

DECEMBER 1955

This was not half-hearted, melting-before-it-dropped snow. This was *real* Scottish snow – crisp, hard snowflakes that would lie on the ground to be joined by millions of others, mingling together to make a hard white carpet. A carpet that would be enjoyed for days to come in the lead-up to Christmas – and Lily Grace was determined to get out and about in this real white stuff as much as possible.

'Can I have a shillin', Mammy?' Lily asked, hopping from one foot to another in an unconscious Highland step. She was all decked out for the wintry weather in a green woollen suit, with trousers and hooded jacket lined in a creamy fleecy material and fur-lined, leather, zipped ankle boots. Pat often teased her that she looked like a little leprechaun in the outfit.

'A *shilling*?' Mona repeated in a high voice, as she drained the excess milk from a slow-cooked rice pudding that would be eaten in two seconds flat by the boys that evening. There were two dishes, the large one she had just drained for the family, and a smaller one which was for Father Finlay to have this afternoon. The priest preferred his main meal in the middle of the day, and was happy with a cold plate of something in the evening, even in the winter.

'Ye see, I want to buy my daddy a wee present for Christmas,' Lily explained, coming to a standstill, one hand on her right hip and the other occasionally waving in the air for emphasis. Now and again she threw a glance at the slightly mottled, but fancily framed, mirror above her mother's head to see how she looked as she was speaking. Anything that resembled the mannerisms of Kirsty or Heather's age-group was the general aim. 'Ye see, I'm sixpence short for this lovely pen I saw . . .' Her voice dropped now. 'And I owe the paper shop sixpence for a comic.'

Mona plonked the rice on the draining board and whirled around. 'Did I just hear right?' she gasped, her eyes almost bulging. She rubbed her damp hands on the floral apron tied around her thickish waist, and then she tucked an irritating strand of hair behind her ear. 'Did I hear you sayin' that you owe the paper shop money?'

Lily's little hands were quickly stilled by her mother's tone, and moved to join together behind her back. 'It's just this once,' she said, biting her lip. 'You see, there was a bit of a mix-up . . . but it wasn't my fault.'

'Don't tell me!' Mona said, raising her eyes skywards. 'Don't tell me, you've muddled them all up changing comics again? Not just before Christmas when they're up to their eyes selling books and annuals and everything?'

'It wasn't me – honest!' Lily protested. 'It was that Sammy again. I tell him to write it in the book last week, but he must have forgot.' The hands were out waving expressively again, just in case the words weren't getting the point across to her mother. 'You see, I telt him that I wanted to change from *The Dandy* and *The Beano* to *The School Friend* and *The Girl*.' She took a deep breath to continue. 'I felt since I was ten now, it was about time I was gettin' more girls' stuff ...'

The outside door sounded now, and Lily offered a silent prayer that it was her father, who might just get her out of this situation, and not one of her brothers, who just might make it worse.

'Wait until you hear this,' Mona said as Pat came in, taking his bus driver's hat off. He got the half-day off every second Saturday. 'This lady's only been getting stuff on tick up at the paper shop again.'

Lily's eyes opened wide in indignation, and her mouth moved into a circle of denial. 'It wasn't my fault – it was that Sammy,' she said, her voice now high and bordering on hysterical. 'It was all a big mistake!'

'No – it's *you* that's the big mistake,' Mona countered.

'Now, now,' Pat interjected, 'don't be sayin' things like that to the child—'

'Can you not just do what you're told for once?' Mona went on. 'The last time this carry-on happened, you said it would never happen again.'

Lily joined her little hands as though in prayer. 'I promise I never asked for tick. I went up to collect my comics as usual, and he handed me two instead of one.' She turned to Pat now, her eyes filling with tears, and her lip trembling. 'Ye see, two of the comics come out on a Tuesday, and two come out on a Thursday – and I wanted to change to a different one on each day ... if ye get what I mean.' Her father's face was more patient than her mother's but it was blank, showing that he didn't get what she meant at all. 'But that stupid Sammy didn't write it down ... and he was too late to cancel them for this week, so that's how I ended up owin' them sixpence.'

In actual fact, it was sevenpence ha'penny that Lily owed the shop, due to the fact that one of the new comics was fourpence ha'penny as opposed to threepence for the rest. But she had worked it all out that if she got the sixpence at least, she could always make the other threeha'pence up with an empty ginger bottle.

A fairly straightforward transaction – if the adults didn't complicate things as usual.

'Isn't that some carry-on?' Mona said to her husband. 'A right ha-hoo over blidey ould comics. We've never owed a penny in our lives, apart from at the Co-op, and if she had her ways, we'd be owin' money right, left and blidey centre.' She pursed her lips and gave a long, weary sigh. 'We'll be ashamed to show our faces in the shop after this.' She looked at Lily with a severely pained expression. 'We'll be the blidey talk of the place wi' you and your blidey comics.'

Pat hung his bus driver's jacket and hat on the back of the kitchen door. 'How much?' he said, his hand now jingling coins in his thick working-trouser pocket.

'I'll leave you to it, if you want to bale her out,' Mona stated, with a dismissive wave of her hand. 'But she'll learn nothin' about managin' money if she gets it handed to her every time she spends money she doesn't have.' Her finger was now wagging in her daughter's direction. 'And I hope she's going to tell it all when she's next at confession.' Mona flounced out to check how the fire was doing in the living-room, hoping that her husband and daughter would feel that she was so upset she had abandoned the two dishes of rice pudding on the sink drainer. In actual fact, she had left them there to cool, but it made a handy dramatic exit, and kept up her status as a beleaguered wife and mother.

'About a shilling altogether . . .' Lily whispered, relieved that her mother had left the kitchen, and hoping that her father wouldn't find out that he had just paid the last instalment on his own Christmas present.

The business was duly sorted out at the paper shop thanks to the shilling that Pat had come up with and threepence that her brother Declan gave her on the way up the road. Lily had slid all her way to the shop, making good use of the icy pavements, paid her debts, and slid onwards to the library, which closed early on a Saturday, to show the librarian her scrupulously washed hands and then pick up her books for the weekend. The librarian was a nice type, but she had been told off by the County Librarian for letting careless children into her little private toilet to wash their grubby hands before handling the books. Lily Grace had taken the lesson to heart after the one occasion when she had been sent all the way back home in the rain to wash her hands.

She had deposited the two *Famous Fives*, a *Just William* and the newly released *Secret Seven* she'd been waiting weeks for, back at the house. Then she slid over to the school for the very last Saturday-afternoon Scottish country dancing rehearsal before the fundraising concert.

Mrs McGinty had been surprisingly good-tempered, and on two occasions had brought Lily and her wee partner Willie out to the middle of the hall to demonstrate the more intricate moves. 'Just like your cousins,' she had told Lily in front of the whole class. 'The Graces are gifted with light feet in the family.'

She hadn't seemed too annoyed about the fact that Heather hadn't turned up for this important last rehearsal, she tutted and just gave Lily a note for Heather, saying not to forget the actual dance display the following Saturday afternoon, which was the week before Christmas.

'And make sure you all have your proper dancing shoes and socks,' Mrs McGinty reminded the group, 'and a tartan sash to go over your school skirt and blouse. If your mothers haven't managed to make the sash themselves, then tell them they've to go straight to Lily's Auntie Sophie, and make sure she knows it's for next Saturday.'

Lily's hand had shot up. 'My Auntie Sophie says she's done a few extra sashes,' she said importantly, 'so if anybody needs one, they can just go straight to the house with a shilling and buy one.'

After the dancing, Lily had spent another wee while playing snowballs out in the schoolyard with Willie and some of the other boys and girls, and then they had all slid up to the Co-op to press their noses against the window and stare longingly at the colourful Christmas display of toys and books.

'I want that and that and that off Santie!' Lily said, pointing to a baby doll, a chalkboard and easel and *The School Friend* annual.

'And I want that and that and that off Santie!' Willie echoed, pointing to a red-painted wooden sledge that stood in the corner of the window, a football annual and a big jar of Quality Street.

The three other children followed suit, chanting their preferences and then they all had another game of snowballs and sliding.

Later, when Lily got back home and complained of having sore arms and shaky legs and generally not feeling well, Mona told her that less running about and less sliding would help both her legs and the soles of her new zip-up boots.

Chapter 19

'This is the first Saturday night I've had off for ages,' Kirsty stated, as she jostled for a place at the bathroom mirror beside her sister. She turned the tap on very carefully, to let a drop or two of water fall onto her Max Factor cake mascara, then she rubbed the brush onto the damp block to work up a good paste. 'I can't believe it! I feel all excited at the thought of a night out at the dancin' in Motherwell Town Hall. You'd think I was a schoolgirl let loose for the night.'

Both girls were all dressed up for going out – Kirsty in a fine red wool sweater, with a fashionable, tight black pencil skirt and a shiny black belt nipping in her waist. She had black suede ankle boots with a black fur trim to wear with her black swing coat for travelling, and planned to carry high black stilettos in a bag to change into when she arrived at the dance. Her blonde hair was loose down over her shoulders, with the waves kept in place by a light setting lotion as opposed to gallons of sticky lacquer for the swept-up creations.

She had taken Larry Delaney's advice about getting rid of the beehive for singing on the stage; he said men found loose hair far more appealing and it would set her apart from the other female singers who all seemed to go for the more formal, pinned-up style. Kirsty found she preferred it down now for going out, and at the back of her mind was relieved not to be running the risk of the dreaded lacquer-bug. Anyway, this wavy style was much easier to comb out at night.

Heather's outfit was slightly more subdued than her sister's, with a dark-blue circular skirt and a blue boat-necked fitted top, her waist also emphasised with a broad black patent belt.

'I'm still not sure if I should go ...' Heather said now, a worried frown on her face.

'Don't be daft,' Kirsty told her indignantly. 'Surely you're not goin' to let that Gerry put you off? He's bound to have got the message by now.' She halted, unable to avoid another little playful dig. 'Mind you, I still think your timin' was bad – I'd have definitely waited until *after* Christmas to finish with him, until I'd got an engagement ring or at least a decent present out of him!'

'It's all right you making jokes,' Heather told her in an injured tone. 'You don't now how it feels having somebody watching every move you make.' She combed out her long dark hair, carefully put in an off-centre parting, and then caught one of the sides up in a large pink and blue jewelled clasp. 'It wasn't you that had him acting all strange last weekend – everywhere I went he was there, with his eyes boring into mine.' She paused, shaking her head. 'I'd no idea he was like that ... and I'd no idea that he had such serious notions about me.'

'Look – forget him!' Kirsty advised her older sister in a no-nonsense tone. She still hadn't told Heather about the night a few weeks back when she thought she saw him lurking around in the back garden. She probably wouldn't bother mentioning it now, as the more time passed, the less sure she was that she had actually seen anything. It had probably just been a neighbour or something innocent like that. 'If he keeps annoyin' you, get my daddy to have a wee word in his ear. Or if that doesn't work, get my daddy to give him a good oul' box in the ear!'

'I'd feel a bit stupid dragging my father into it,' Heather sighed, searching in her make-up bag for her pink lipstick. 'I'll just have to see what happens when I meet him again.'

Kirsty jostled Heather's elbow. 'Anyway, I'll be there tonight, and if he so much as looks at you, he'll have *me* to deal with. I won't be long in givin' a good right hook.' Her arm shot out now to demonstrate. 'Or failin' that I'll take off my stiletto and batter him over the head!'

Heather laughed, in spite of her concerns. 'I wouldn't put it past you!'

'Here,' Kirsty suddenly remembered, 'talking about stilettos – I've giving up on those pink ones. I should have got them in a bigger size.' She motioned to Heather's feet. 'Why don't you try them? They might fit you, we're both about the same size, and pink would go nice with that wine dress you have.'

'Thanks,' Heather said smiling gratefully, 'that's really good of you.' Although truthfully, she felt the shoes were a bit too bright for her. Kirsty was braver with colours than she was. 'I'll try them on later and see how they look.'

Kirsty stood on her tiptoes to apply the black mascara on both top and bottom lashes. Then she stopped midway, suddenly giving a guilty giggle. 'Thank God for the oul' age pensioners!' she said. 'I wouldn't be goin' out here tonight if it wasn't for them. Imagine cancelling a Golden Wedding just because there's a bit of snow!'

Although she had more or less decided to leave The Hi-Tones she still had a number of bookings with them over Christmas and the New Year that she had said she would honour. They had been more than understanding about her leaving, but Kirsty still felt guilty and didn't want to leave them in the lurch at their busiest time. Besides, if she waited until after Christmas, it would give them that bit longer to get a new female vocalist.

'Have you seen outside recently?' Heather asked her, thumbing towards the window. 'It's more than just a *bit* of snow. I was just beginning to think that maybe we're mad going out in it ourselves.'

'As long as the buses are still running, we'll be fine,' Kirsty said, opening her eyes really wide to let the black mascara dry. 'Is Liz going tonight?'

Heather gave a long sigh. 'Don't mention Liz ... she's been going on to me non-stop about how I should get back with Gerry. She says Jim Murray isn't botherin' with her half as much now because they're on their own. She said Jim liked havin' Gerry to walk home with at the end of the night, because it's a good ten-minute walk from her house to his in the dark.'

'What a bloomin' big Jessie he is!' Kirsty said scornfully. 'Going to finish with Liz just because he's scared of walking home in the dark! That definitely doesn't say much for what he thinks of her.' Her eyes suddenly felt irritated and she blinked to clear them. There was a moment's silence. 'Oh, damn it! I've just smudged all my mascara!' She turned to grab a piece of toilet roll to blot it off before it was too late. 'Blidey hell! It's that oul' Izal toilet paper again!' she moaned. 'How can I rub my eyes with that?' She tutted loudly. 'I'll have to go into the bedroom for some paper hankies. I thought my mammy was supposed to be buying that new soft Andrex paper from now on? Honestly! There's times when you'd think we were still livin' in the Dark Ages in this house.'

Chapter 20

⊗⟪⟫⊗

The bus ground to a halt opposite the Town Hall in Motherwell. The snow had eased, and the council workers had diligently kept the main roads clear apart from small grey drifts at the side.

'So did Jim definitely say he'd meet you in at the dance?' Kirsty quizzed, as all three girls stood waiting for the bus to pull away and let them cross over safely.

'He said *something* like that,' Liz said, 'but I don't want to look *that* desperate that I'm going to turn up here on my own.' She gave a small laugh, looking from one sister to the other. 'Well, I am actually desperate – but it's just that I don't want him to know it.'

Kirsty rolled her eyes at Heather, amazed that any girl would contemplate running after a fellow in such an obvious way. But Liz had made it plain to her friends from the start that she was out to capture Jim Murray by hook or by crook.

'Well, if he's not here, never mind,' Kirsty said dismissively. 'There's always plenty more fish in the sea.'

Then all three linked arms and ran across the road and into the welcoming warmth of the dance hall.

It was around the fourth or fifth dance that Heather realised with a jolt that Gerry was standing at the side of the floor, staring straight across at her. He was with Jim and another lad, but he was standing slightly separate from them, so he could watch the dancers. The fellow Heather was dancing with whirled her around enthusiastically to 'Rock Around the Clock' and when she came back to face the same direction, there he was again – still staring. The minute the dance finished and she made to go back to join the other girls, he was at her side.

'Can I have a word with you?' he said in a low, urgent voice. '*Please.*' He was dressed immaculately as usual, in a dark striped suit with what looked like a brand-new white shirt and a red and navy striped tie. His dark hair was newly cut and well-groomed with just the right amount of oil and, as always, his shoes would be gleaming. Gerry always made an effort with his appearance, but there was something about him tonight that said he had put in that little bit of extra effort.

From the glances the other girls beside them were giving him, Heather knew that Gerry wouldn't have had to ask any of them twice to dance – they were only waiting and hoping. Why was it that she didn't feel like that about him any more? Dancing with him, feeling his arms around her, was the last thing she wanted to do now.

She took a deep breath and deliberately shifted her gaze to the floor. 'I've nothing to say to you, Gerry,' she said in a low, firm voice. She swept her dark hair back over one shoulder, desperate to be away from him. 'Nothing's changed since we last spoke. I really don't want to fall out with you ... but I think you should let this go.'

'I realise now that I rushed you ... I should have waited – given you more time. The Australia thing was only a notion ... I'm not even sure if I want to go myself.'

'It wouldn't have made any difference,' she said, looking directly at him. She shook her head sorrowfully. 'I don't feel the same way, I'm still young and I'm not ready to get engaged or settle down with anybody yet.'

'You made a good pretence of being ready,' he told her, his voice rising now. 'Asking my advice about your new job and telling me about your plans for the future. That kind of talk would make any fellow think you were serious.'

'Well, you're wrong,' Heather said, suddenly conscious that the other dancers could tell they were arguing, and realising by the tone of his voice that he had probably had a few more drinks than he usually had. 'And it's not my fault if you took it all too seriously . . . it didn't really mean *anything* serious to me.'

She saw his face stiffen at her words and the hurt and pain in his eyes, and a pang of guilt and regret washed over her. Guilt for having caused this situation by leading him on – and regret for not ending it sooner.

Then she felt a hand gripping hers.

'Come on!' Kirsty said, moving between them. 'I thought we were having a night out with the girls?'

'We were talking, if you don't mind, Kirsty,' Gerry said. He was polite but there was an edge to his voice. He had always got on well with Kirsty and Heather's other friends, but now this situation seemed to be changing everything.

Kirsty looked at Heather, her eyebrows raised in a question.

'I'm coming,' Heather told her, then she waved across to the table where Liz and some of their other friends were sitting, just to make the point to him. She turned back to her old boyfriend now. 'I'm sorry the way things have turned out – but these things happen. It doesn't mean we can't be friends . . .'

Gerry looked at her, his eyes narrowed and thoughtful, and then he silently nodded his head and turned away.

'You're daft, Heather – you shouldn't have got into any conversation with him,' Kirsty told her as they walked across the floor. 'You have to be cruel to be kind.' When they sat back down, she turned to Liz. 'I've just been telling Heather that she needs to totally ignore Gerry. Don't you think she should just walk in the other direction when she sees him?'

'Listen to Marjorie Proops here!' Liz said, laughing and thumbing in Kirsty's direction. Liz was much more light-hearted now that Jim had put in an appearance, and she didn't want to jeopardise her own situation by being seen to snub his friend. 'None of us would ever have a fellow if we took her advice. How many weeks is it since you've had a date, Kirsty?'

'I've been asked out on loads of dates over the last few weeks,' Kirsty retorted, with an exaggerated grin and a roll of her eyes, 'and I'm happy to say I've turned them all down. Unlike some people, I'm very fussy who I go out with. I'll wait until I find somebody that's really decent.'

'Famous last words!' Liz said, batting her eyelashes. 'There's plenty of ould maids that thought like that, and they all ended up on the shelf.'

'Well, it'll be a while before I'm interested in another fellow,' Heather said ruefully. 'The way Gerry has been carrying on has put me off boys completely.' She gave a lopsided smile. 'I'll fill my weekends from now on doing country dancing with Mrs McGinty and The Legion of Mary. And I've always got my knitting.' She took a sip of her lemonade, a thoughtful look on her face. 'That might not be too bad an idea – I could do with a few new jumpers for work.'

All the other girls laughed now. 'I can just see you sittin' in every Saturday night knitting away,' Liz teased, making gestures as though she were knitting herself.

'Och, it's just your bad luck with this particular fella,' Kirsty told her sister. 'How were you to know how it would turn out? Gerry Stewart looks nice and he seemed a nice enough fella, but he's obviously a bit odd in the head the way he's carryin' on.' She lifted her glass now and gave a little sigh. 'I'm beginnin' to think that a lot of them in here tonight are odd. It wasn't worth the effort of getting dressed up and coming out in the snow.'

'Speak for yourself,' Liz stated. 'There's some of us are quite happy with the choice.'

A few minutes later the band struck up another rock-and-roll number and within seconds a group of fellows appeared at the table looking for partners. The first two in Teddy-boy suits made a beeline for the Grace sisters. Kirsty's eyes lit up with amused surprise when she recognised the fellow she was dancing with as a boy from her class in school. When she got onto the dance floor, she stepped back for a minute to get a good look at his grey drainpipe trousers and matching long, draped jacket with the black velvet collar. She shook her head and laughed when her gaze dropped to the white socks and black, thick-soled suede shoes.

'I didn't recognise you in all that fancy get-up, Terry McGinn. When did you turn into a Teddy boy?' she demanded, taking no trouble to disguise her amusement. He had always been a rather quiet, studious boy at school, and seeing him in the outrageous outfit was more than a surprise.

'A few weeks ago,' he said, grinning back proudly, although there was a slight tinge of embarrassment around his cheeks. He then reached into his inside pocket for a small comb, which he quickly ran through his heavily Brylcreemed quiff.

'Whit d'ye think?' he asked, holding the jacket open. 'Does it look good or whit? Does it suit me?'

Kirsty clapped her hands together now and laughed heartily. 'It depends on what ye think looks good! Put it this way – if I didn't know you, I'd say you looked as good if not better than any of the other Teddy boys.'

'Coming from a good-lookin' lassie – that'll do me!' Terry told her, with a delighted grin. As they jived to the music, Kirsty found herself enjoying herself in spite of her earlier reservations. 'What does your father think of your new fashion?' she asked, as Terry whirled her around. His father was a rather sombre, staid insurance man, who visited the Graces' house every year when their subscription was up for renewal. He was definitely not the sort who would be associated with Teddy boys and their ilk.

'My father doesnae know!' he replied. 'I keep the suit at ma pal's house, and I change into it there before comin' out. He'd skin me alive if he saw it – and so would the oul' dear!'

Kirsty laughed even harder at this information, and couldn't wait to get off the dance floor to impart it to Heather and the other girls.

'Any chance of me and Frankie seein' you and Heather home the night?' Terry asked as soon as the dance ended.

'None whatsoever,' Kirsty smilingly informed him, with a little friendly tap on the cheek.

'We could just go for chips if you like,' he suggested, walking across the dance floor with her now in the direction of her table. 'It's a freezin' night and you'd be glad of them to warm you up.'

Kirsty shook her head, her blonde waves bouncing around her

shoulders. 'We're with a crowd of our friends. Anyway, we're not the kind of lassies that you Teddy boys would want to be seen with. We're too tame and old-fashioned for you!'

'Aw, c'mon now, Kirsty,' Terry said, his hands spread out and his face looking all injured. 'There's nobody could ever call *you* tame ... and anyway, I'm hardly a *real*, rowdy kind of Teddy boy.' He leaned forward and whispered. 'It's only the suit and the hair that makes me look like this.'

'Come back in a year or two when you've a car and plenty of money, and I'll think about it,' Kirsty said airily, and then with a toss of her flowing hair added, 'and thanks for the dance.'

Kirsty's tale about the Teddy-boy suit being kept at the pal's house and Heather's recounting of the dance she had with his friend, Frankie – who had two left feet – kept the table entertained in between dances. Then, Heather had felt greatly relieved when Liz dug her in the ribs during one of the slow waltzes to point out Gerry dancing with a beautiful, small, auburn-haired girl.

'Tell me the honest truth – does it not make you feel dead jealous when you see him with another girl?' her friend asked. 'Even when you go off them, you like to know they still fancy *you* the most. That's how I feel about any of my old boyfriends.'

'I'm delighted to see him dancing with somebody else,' Heather said honestly, 'and I'd be even more delighted if he started going out with somebody else. I've no feelings for him whatsoever.' She paused. 'She's a nice-looking girl ... I hope Gerry Stewart decides he's better off with somebody like her than me.'

'She's had all the fellas after her this evening,' Liz whispered, craning her neck to get a better look at Gerry's partner. 'Thank God I never saw Jim anywhere near her.' Earlier on in the evening all the girls had been admiring her gorgeous black lace, low-necked dress, which they all said must have cost a fortune, and could only fit someone with a twenty-inch waist.

Heather stole a quick glance at them, and was surprised to see that Gerry looked quite relaxed, and was dancing easily with the stunning-looking girl, his head bent down towards her, listening attentively to whatever she was saying. And even though she tried not to look, Heather couldn't help but notice that several dances later, he was still with the girl. Then, some time later, she watched as he went off to sit at a table with her.

'It looks as though you finally have Gerry off your hands,' Kirsty commented at the break, when they were all in the Ladies', touching up their lipstick and checking their hair. 'Either that, or he's trying his best to make you jealous.'

'Well, it hasn't worked,' Heather told her. 'I've no interest in anything he does.'

Whether he had left or whether he was in some dark corner of the dance hall, Gerry was nowhere to be seen towards the end of the night. Liz had been delighted when Jim took her up for several dances in a row, and then suggested that they leave early. After explaining to the girls, she went off with a great bright-eyed flourish, grabbing her bag and rushing off to get her coat and things from the cloakroom.

'Pa-thetic!' Kirsty had pronounced as Liz swept out on Jim's arm. 'If I ever get like that over a fella,' she told Heather, 'shoot me!'

The rest of the evening passed quickly, with the girls missing only the odd dance when their feet needed a rest.

'It wasn't a bad night, after all,' Heather said, as they queued to collect their hats and coats in the draughty corridor.

'You looked as if you were enjoying yourself when you were up dancing,' Kirsty said, dropping her voice in case any of the other girls queuing could hear her, 'especially when you were jivin' with the Teddy boy.'

Heather laughed as she handed her coat ticket over to the small, dumpy lady behind the counter. 'I did enjoy myself, and I definitely felt a lot more relaxed after Gerry left,' she admitted. 'Did you feel you had a good night?'

'Aye, I suppose I did,' Kirsty said, but there was a slight note of reservation in her voice. She smiled benignly at the cloakroom attendant as she took her coat and hat from her. 'I got several offers, but the boys all seem really young and immature at times. There's absolutely *nobody* I'd have let see me home.'

A picture of the handsome Larry Delaney suddenly flashed into her mind, and it dawned on Kirsty that she had enjoyed herself far more in the older man's company the other night. There were parts of the time she had spent with him that had taken a wee while to get used to, but once she had, she discovered that it was just a different way of doing things. As she looked around at all the other girls bustling around the cloakroom now, she decided that anything she had done with Larry was a lot more interesting than what she was doing with all these people her own age.

'Quick,' Heather said, looking at her watch, 'we'll just make the eleven o'clock bus if we hurry.'

The girls pulled on their coats and hats, then scarves and gloves. Then the Grace sisters set off, arm in arm, into the cold, white night.

Chapter 21

ophie, wide awake and lying silently beside her husband, was just planning how she would slide out of bed without waking him, to have the fried breakfast cooked and eaten well before ten o'clock Mass. She moved when she heard the gate bang open and the footsteps half-running, half-sliding up the path, and was pulling on her dressing-gown when she heard the doorbell ringing and the clatter of the letter box all at the same time.

'It's Lily!' spluttered Patrick Grace, Mona and Pat's gangly, fifteen-year-old son. He was the one that Mona sent on all the messages, being the most trustworthy and the one most intimidated by her. 'She's not well – she can hardly talk, she's all hot and she complainin' about her arms and legs. My mammy says can you come straight over and see what ye think?'

'Fintan!' Sophie called up the stairs. 'Fintan!' Then, when she heard a mumbled response she called again. 'There's something wrong with Lily . . . I'm going across now.'

'She was all hot and couldn't breathe last night,' Patrick explained as they went along, his voice coming out in little white puffs into the snowy winter air. 'My mammy gave her aspirins and some Lucozade and she fell asleep. But when they woke this mornin' she was just lyin' there hardly able to talk and she couldnae move her legs very well . . .'

'Have they phoned for the doctor?' Sophie asked as they ran up Mona's front path. She pulled her dressing-gown tighter over her chest, suddenly conscious of the silent but searing cold.

'He's still there, and he's sent our Declan up to the priest to phone for an ambulance. He said she'll need to go straight to the Strathclyde.' The Strathclyde Hospital in Motherwell was the nearest General Hospital, and served Rowanhill and all the surrounding local villages.

'Oh, dear Jesus!' Sophie muttered to herself, feeling the clouds of worry and illness envelop her like a damp, cold blanket as she entered the house. She heard a whimpering sound coming from the kitchen, and she stopped for a moment to look in through the open door, and there, curled up in his basket and looking out at her very dolefully, was Lily's constant companion, Whiskey. Sophie made a vague comforting tutting noise at the dog, and then followed Patrick straight upstairs to where the family were all standing outside Lily's little room.

Mona came forward to grasp her sister-in-law's hands, and Sophie could feel the desperation in the tight, trembling grip. 'It's her arms and legs . . . Please God, it's not polio!' she whispered, her breath coming in little gulps. 'Please God – don't let it be that . . .'

'No, no . . .' said Sophie, her arms coming around Mona. 'Sure, that's all over . . . there haven't been any cases of polio this long time.'

Mona shook her head violently. 'The doctor said there's been another outbreak . . . they must have been keepin' it quiet . . . a baby and a wee boy in Motherwell just yesterday.'

'What else did the doctor say?' Sophie asked, dreading the reply, but feeling it was the right thing to say. Then, a bitter draught wrapped itself around her bare legs and her slippered feet as Fintan and the girls entered the house.

'He just doesn't know . . .' Mona whispered. 'He says it's not for him to diagnose . . . that the hospital will do all the tests.' She moved towards her daughter's bedroom door, bringing Sophie along with her, still desperately grasping her hands.

'Maybe it's just the flu . . .' Sophie suggested, but as they entered the room to see the doctor kneeling by the prone little body, she knew instantly that whatever it was, it wasn't just the flu.

For two cold, snowy days and nights everyone held their breath, waiting on news of Lily Grace. It was as if the light and life had left the Grace family houses and all the ones surrounding them. Nobody could believe that such a vivacious, impish little creature as Lily could suddenly be struck down in such a way.

And struck down she surely was. Within hours the local hospital realised they were not dealing with a straightforward case of pneumonia, and murmurs amongst the doctors that Hairmyres Hospital outside Hamilton would be better equipped to diagnose the child led the whispers of polio to reach out into the hospital corridors.

One of the senior doctors who had been on duty overnight was called from his bed. His face – grim from being woken out of a much-needed, deep sleep – became grimmer when he checked over the now hot and coughing Lily. An ambulance was hurriedly arranged, and the little girl was wheeled out on a trolley with breathing equipment and various tubes attached to her.

Pat and Mona went along with her in the ambulance, and the boys followed closely behind in their father's Ford Anglia. Initially, they all milled around in the unfamiliar hospital corridor as a group of doctors and nurses shut themselves away with Lily. After a while, Pat and Mona were led into a small waiting room whilst the boys were ushered out of the building to take refuge in the Anglia in the car park, as they all waited for news.

Eventually it came.

Lily Grace, it was now confirmed, had contracted the dreaded poliomyelitis germ. It was now a matter of waiting to see the extent of the damage the germ had done.

Chapter 22

❧❧❧

Heather Grace shielded her eyes against the dazzling lights of a car coming towards them on the dark country road. So far the journey had been easy, since it was as pleasant a night as you could get in December and the roads were fine and dry. A much better night than most since Lily had been brought into the hospital over a fortnight ago.

'What did you say you've brought for Lily, Mammy?' Heather checked from the back seat of her father's car where she was sitting with her sister. 'Was it Ludo or Snakes and Ladders?'

'Both,' Sophie said from the front seat, holding up a rectangular box wrapped in brown paper and tied up with white string. 'The board has one game on one side and one on the other – so Sammy in the paper shop informed me when I bought it.'

'I've got her the new *Malory Towers* book she wanted for Christmas,' Kirsty put in, 'so the wee devil's gettin' it earlier. She'll be delighted wi' that.'

'And I've got her a teenage dressing-doll set and loads of packets of those cherub and angel scraps she likes,' Heather said, and then she halted. 'I nearly bought her a box of Milk Tray, then I remembered that she's still not able to swallow very well . . . God love her,' Heather added her voice cracking a little. 'I still can't believe it's happened . . . I can't believe that wee lively soul is paralysed. I can still picture her hopping about, lifting her legs up to her chin in the country dancing.'

'She won't be doing any dancing for a long time,' Kirsty said quietly. 'She could be lucky if she's able to walk again.'

'She's coming on,' Sophie reminded the girls, 'and that's the most important thing to remember.'

'Aye,' Fintan chipped in, 'she's over the worst, thanks be to God and his Blessed Mother. It didn't kill her, so we've a lot to be grateful for.'

A silence descended on the car as they approached the entrance to Hairmyres Hospital, and then Fintan negotiated his way in through the gates and up to a parking space beside Lily's ward. They got out of the car and walked towards the building.

'Who else is visiting tonight?' Heather whispered as they walked along the brightly lit, low-ceilinged corridor to Lily's ward.

'Mona and Pat as usual,' Sophie whispered back, 'and probably some of the boys. There's usually a good few of them in every afternoon and night now they're on school holidays. Father Finlay has been coming in regularly and so have a lot of the kids from school.'

'I think the whole of Rowanhill has been in to visit her,' Kirsty said smiling. 'She's one of the most popular wee girls in the place and in the school.'

The ward was busy as usual, with small groups around each of the twenty beds. Lily was halfway down on the left-hand side, the top of her bedside cabinet full of flowers and cards.

'There's Pat and Mona,' Sophie said, giving them a small discreet wave of her gloved hand, 'and Patrick and Declan are there, too.'

As soon as he saw them, Pat moved the boys to collect spare chairs from the surrounding beds to accommodate the extra visitors. After the initial bustle of taking off coats and gloves and assorted outdoor garments, they all moved towards the white-painted bed with the high safety-sides, where Lily was propped up on pillows and grinning delightedly to see them, her bright eyes flitting from one to the other. She had on a fancy new pink nightdress with white gathered lace and ribbons at the neck. Her long, curly blonde hair had been brushed and tied back in her customary ponytail.

Heather caught her breath at the sight of her cousin, thinking how tiny she looked amongst the stiff white sheets and the pale blue, basket-weave blanket – but like the others, she smiled and hid the little pangs of sorrow.

'Well, how's the wee blether-box the day?' Fintan said, leaning over the bed to give his niece a careful hug.

'Fine, Uncle Fintan,' Lily said in a strange, thin little voice. 'The doctor says I'm an awful lot better.'

'An' you're lookin' it, too, darlin',' he said in a voice hoarse with emotion. 'That oul' school hasn't been the same without ye,

Lily. Your teacher told me that on the last day before the holidays. She said all the other children were sayin' how the country dancing display wasn't as good this year.' He halted then gave her a wink. 'And Willie fairly missed you, they'd to get him a new partner from the class below, and he said she wasn't a patch on you. The way they're talkin' I think the whole school have missed you.'

Lily blushed slightly at the mention of Willie, as her brothers often teased her about him being her boyfriend. Thankfully, nobody reacted to her classmate's name.

'Have they really all said they missed me?' she said, looking very pleased at the thought.

'Missed ye?' Fintan repeated incredulously. 'They've me driven up the wall asking about you. And the teacher said you could tell the difference without you there. Sure, the class were as quiet as mice – it wasn't the same at all.' Lily gave a little giggle now, and he was delighted to see her response.

'Are you going to move over and let the rest of us in?' Sophie joked now, elbowing Fintan out of the way. 'How are you, hen?' she said, giving Lily a cuddle. 'You're looking a whole lot better today.'

Heather and Kirsty moved in after their mother, hugging Lily and showing her the presents they had brought her, and reading all the get well cards and letters that had been sent in by the children and adults in Rowanhill.

'You're a fly wee thing,' Kirsty teased. 'Picking the right time to be in the hospital. Gettin' all these presents now and then you'll have piles more next week for Christmas.'

'They might be lettin' me out for Christmas!' Lily said, her voice sounding a little stronger. She looked at Mona with big wide eyes. 'Aren't they, Mammy?'

Pat turned away, pretending he was looking at something across the other side of the ward. Mona knew instantly that he was leaving the delicate business to her. 'Now, they didn't say for definite, Lily,' she said, her face pained, and her heart even more pained. 'They said we'd have to see. You have another few days yet.' The thought of Christmas this year was like something way, way off in the future to Mona. She had become so used to taking things a day at a time – and often an hour at a time.

'But my arms and legs are movin' again!' Lily said. 'Look!'

Everybody's gaze moved now to the bottom of the blue-covered bed. A very slight – but very definite – movement could be seen under the covers.

'Well done!' Sophie said, starting them all off in a carefully muted clapping session, so as not to disturb the other patients and their visitors too much.

'And my arms ...' Lily said, her blue eyes dancing with excitement, but her voice now beginning to show signs of strain. 'I can lift them up a wee bit as well.' She suddenly started to cough – a choking, breathless kind of cough – and those at the top of the bed moved aside to let her mother in.

'Take it easy now,' Mona said, coming to stand beside her. She leaned over to dab the side of Lily's mouth with a folded tissue. 'Just take easy breaths like the nurse showed you ...'

'She wasn't just an ordinary nurse, Mammy,' Lily rasped, 'she was a *phys-i-o-ther-apist* – so she was.' She leaned back in her pillows, taking deep breaths as she had been instructed.

A few minutes later Lily was back to feeling reasonably comfortable, and everyone relaxed around her bed again, chatting and showing her the presents they'd bought.

Heather took the cardboard, teenage dressing-doll with the imitation hair out of the box, and held outfits up to Lily to allow her to pick what the doll should wear. She and Kirsty took turns dressing the doll, making a great, exaggerated show of hiding it from the boys when it only had its underwear on. Each time they did it, everyone tittered with laughter. When Mona called a halt to the laughing for fear of disturbing other patients, and of getting Lily too excited, the Enid Blyton book was produced.

'There's an older girl called Margaret,' Lily whispered to Kirsty and Heather, 'who's allowed out of her bed, and she comes up and sits beside me and reads to me because I can't hold the book myself. Sometimes she just holds the book out for me and I read it.' She stopped. 'I'll probably ask her to read me the book you brought me tomorrow.'

'Where is she?' Heather asked in a low, conspiratorial voice, which she knew would engage Lily's attention further. 'Now don't try to point or move yourself . . . just describe where she is so that we know what she looks like.'

'Nosy got hung!' Kirsty said to her older sister in the childish banter they used when they were young. 'She'll know we're talking about her if everybody looks around.'

'Look to the right,' Lily said, giggling, swivelling her blue eyes dramatically in the direction, 'and down three beds. She's wearin' a green dressing-gown and she has her hair in two pig-tails.'

'Clocked her!' Kirsty said. 'She's sittin' up in bed reading all her get well cards to her visitors. She looks a right wee bookworm – and you forgot to mention she was wearin' glasses. You forgot to say she was a specky-four eyes!'

Lily giggled some more. 'Oh, you're terrible!' she said, her brows coming down in mock disapproval. 'Margaret's not a *real* specky, for your information – she only wears them for readin'.'

'Well, she looks a right wee specky from where I'm sittin'!' Kirsty teased.

Lily started laughing in a heartier manner now and after a few moments the coughing came back with a vengeance.

'Come on now, my wee darlin',' Pat said, going over to comfort her. 'Will I give you a drink of Lucozade?'

Lily nodded now, trying unsuccessfully to control the spasms. Tears started to trickle down her cheek with the effort, but after a while the coughing subsided again, and she was able to take a drink from a plastic feeding-cup, supported by her father. All the other visitors watched them anxiously, whilst making half-hearted attempts at light conversation to keep the atmosphere as normal as possible.

Mona caught Sophie's eye and shook her head, tears glistening in the corner of her eyes. Whatever problems life had thrust in their direction before was nothing compared to the devastation that this illness had wreaked on the whole Grace family. This vicious, silent germ had crept into the most vulnerable part of their lives, the very centre of the family's heart.

Lily.

This precious little daughter – the apple of their eyes – who had come after the four boys, when they had almost given up hope of ever having a girl.

When she'd settled down again, Pat leaned across the bed, his arms around his little daughter, and whispered soothingly into her ear. 'You'll be fine soon, Lily – you'll be all fine for Christmas. And Santie's going to bring you the biggest surprise you've ever had in your life.'

The little face lit up again, and she looked directly into her father's eyes. '*You'll* get me home in time for Christmas, Daddy,' she whispered, 'won't you?'

Chapter 23

❦

Two nights later, just as Sophie and Heather were clearing up after the evening meal, Pat Grace came to the kitchen door. 'Is the big fella in?' he enquired in his rich Irish accent. 'Or is he up at the school?' Pat was much more serious these days since Lily's illness. His usual jocular manner with males and flirtatious manner with the women had all died down.

'Oh, he's inside having a second cup of tea by the fire and listening to the news,' Sophie said, stepping back to let her brother-in-law through. 'If you go on in to him, I'll bring you a cup in a few minutes. What's the news of Lily today?'

'Still sore and stiff . . . but movin' a little bit more every day, thanks be to God.'

'Who's going in to the hospital tonight?' Heather asked.

'Just myself and Mona,' Pat replied. 'The boys were in this afternoon, so they can stay at home and the older ones can have a quiet visit tonight.'

'Kirsty's out rehearsing,' Heather said, 'but Mammy and Daddy and me were thinking of going in to see her for half an hour.' She hesitated. 'That's if you don't feel it's too much for her.'

Pat nodded and smiled, although the smile didn't quite reach his weary eyes. 'She'll be delighted to see you,' he said softly.

'When you and Kirsty are around, the rest of us could go home as far as she's concerned.'

Heather's eyes suddenly filled up, and her throat felt tight. 'She'll be home soon . . .' Her head moved downwards and her dark hair came over her sad face like a curtain.

Pat nodded again. 'How's the job going in Glasgow?' he asked now. His tone was as friendly as usual, but his manner was distracted and his eyes flickered towards the hallway.

'Och, it's fine, Uncle Pat,' Heather said in a falsely bright voice, shaking her hair out of her watery eyes. 'The work is great and the people are nice and friendly.' She didn't bother to elaborate as she could see Pat had more on his mind.

'Good girl,' Pat said, turning out into the hallway. He tapped on the living-room door before walking in.

Fintan got to his feet immediately and switched the wireless off. He indicated to the seat at the opposite side of the fire. 'Well,' he greeted his brother, 'any news this evenin'?'

'Ah, nothing much,' Pat said, sitting down. 'She's coming along slowly . . . feckin' oul' polio.' He paused, then let out a long, low sigh. 'I don't suppose you got in touch with Claire, did you?'

Fintan sat back into his chair, his face lightly flushing at the mention of their estranged sister. He rubbed his hand over the light stubble on his chin. 'Well,' he said in a low voice, 'I asked Sophie to phone her up on Sunday . . .'

The job Fintan had delegated to his wife had been an awkward one for two reasons. The first was practical – the complications involved in using the public phone box, sorting out the correct coins to pay for it and then the business of finding the code for Glasgow and dialling it. The second part was even more difficult – having to speak to the younger sister who had turned her back on her Catholic family.

Or, as Claire put it, the sister the whole family had shunned for marrying out of her class and her religion.

Whatever the rights and wrongs of the arguments, Fintan had been pathetically grateful to his wife for agreeing to make the difficult call.

'And how was she?' Pat asked, looking decidedly awkward

himself now. This was just the sort of conversation he dreaded, and usually avoided at all costs.

Fintan pursed his lips. 'By all accounts she started cryin' the minute she heard Sophie's voice . . .' He paused. 'She wanted to know what was wrong . . . that there must be something wrong for anybody to phone her.'

Pat nodded, his gaze now on the floor, and his forefinger pressing on the point at the bridge of his nose. This was all very painful to hear, because Claire and he had been the closest out of the family before the rift had occurred – before Mona had made her feelings plain to everyone. 'I suppose she would say that . . .'

'Sophie felt she might as well tell her straightaway,' Fintan went on, 'she said there was no point in tryin' to make small talk on the phone all the way to Glasgow.'

Pat lifted his eyes to meet his brother's. 'How did she react to the news about Lily?'

Fintan's head was nodding now. 'Well . . . I suppose you could say that she took it fairly bad . . . with her being Lily's godmother and everythin'.' He sucked his breath in. 'It's understandable, seeing her regularly since she was born, and then not having seen her for the last two years.'

'So what did Claire say?'

'Well, the main thing is that she's just heart-broken about Lily having polio,' Fintan said, trying desperately to remember all the details his wife had given him. 'She was nice enough to Sophie, and she said she was more than grateful to her for phoning . . . but she felt it was awful bad that we had to wait for this kind of news to get in touch.'

Pat sighed loudly and shrugged. 'What can I do? Mona won't hear Claire's name mentioned.' His voice rose now. 'The feckin' Christmas and birthday cards are ripped up the minute they come in the door. She wouldn't even let Lily have an oul' doll Claire sent.' He held his hands out, palms up. 'And I have no say in it – none at all. When women get started on each other they're the very worst. They're more vicious and devious than any man.'

Fintan sat silently, his gaze focused on the flames in the fire.

Pat ran his hands through his wavy dark hair, now starting to fleck with grey. 'An' I have to live with her, don't forget. Mona can be awkward at the best of times, but when it comes to religion there's no movin' her. For myself, I couldn't care less. Claire could be married to a feckin' Hindustani for all I care. She's still the same girl to me.'

'And me an' all,' Fintan said in a low voice. 'I hate all this carry-on ... but we can't just blame Mona for it. There's Tommy's wife, Janey, over in Wishaw who's every bit as bad.'

'Well, Mona's the one that won't bode any discussion on it in our house, and it's me that's affected by it there ...' Pat said bitterly. 'I thought it was only over the wedding, with it being in the register office. I thought that once we'd made the point about not attending the marriage service it would all settle down, and that we'd at least visit Claire in Glasgow now and again – and have her visit us.' His shoulders slumped. 'If I'd realised the extent that things would go to, I'd have put my foot down at the very beginning.'

'We all would have,' Fintan stated. 'But it's the way things are around here between Catholics and Protestants – the way things were back in Ireland. And it's got to be harder for Mona being the Priest's housekeeper – it puts her in a more awkward spot than most. Father Finlay isn't the type to be givin' comfort to any family who let the side down. You're lucky he's still letting Patrick and Declan serve on the altar, for he stopped the O'Brien lads when their sister got married in the register office.'

'I don't know what's going to happen,' Pat said. 'Another Christmas comin' up and Lily nearly at death's door, and the family are split down the middle.'

Fintan pursed his lips together thoughtfully. 'Maybe some good will come of this terrible situation ... maybe when Lily's feeling more like her old self we might have a wee bit of celebration and we could all meet up.'

A tap came on the living-room door and Sophie came in carrying a tray with a mug of tea and some biscuits and set them down on the small coffee table for Pat.

'We're just talkin' about all this nonsense about Claire,' Pat blurted out. 'Fintan was sayin' that you phoned her?'

'I did,' Sophie said, pushing a wing of hair back behind her ear. 'And I felt sorry for the girl. I felt sorry having to tell her that news about Lily ... but then I felt sorry for her over the wedding, too. I told the other women as much.'

'Well,' Pat said, lifting the mug up from the table and then nursing it between his big hands, 'that was decent of you – gettin' in touch with her – but it should have been her own flesh and blood that put the hand of friendship out to her.' He took a sip of the hot tea.

'Life's too short to have all this animosity between families. I'm determined to do something about all this after Christmas. When I feel Lily is on the mend a bit then I'm going to tackle Mona.'

'Go easy on her,' Sophie said softly. 'She's been through a lot these last few weeks, and whatever she might say, she's not as tough on the inside as she makes out.'

Chapter 24

Kirsty finished the last note of Patti Page's 'Let Me Go, Lover', to a round of applause by the four band members and Larry – who was on his feet and clapping. 'Brilliant!' he said to her as she dismounted the steps at the side of the stage, her heels echoing in the empty ballroom. He took both her hands in his and then kissed her on the forehead. 'Absolutely brilliant! You can tell the singing lessons are paying for themselves already.' He led her over to a table at the side of the hotel function room, the heels on her black stilettos keeping time with his expensive leather-soled Italian shoes. Even on a midweek night where there were only rehearsals going on, Larry didn't let his standards drop and he always stood out compared to the other men in the clubs or hotels. This evening, the fellows in the band he had hired were all in white open-necked shirts and plain black trousers, while Larry wore a red golfing sweater with the crest of some exclusive Dublin club over a red and white striped shirt and dark checked trousers.

'How about "Unchained Melody"?' Kirsty checked, anxious for reassurance and further praise. With The Hi-Tones she was lucky if she got the odd thumbs-up from the boys, and if she had an off-night, they didn't seem to notice or were too nice to say anything. 'Did I hit all the right notes?' She took a gulp of the deliciously cold lemonade he had waiting for her.

'Definitely,' he said, smiling warmly at her. 'You never missed a note.' He paused, his mind ticking over. 'If it wasn't for the commitments you have with the lads in the band, I could easily have got you bookings all over Christmas. It would have been a great time to launch your solo career.' He took a packet of cigarettes from his pocket and a fancy silver lighter.

Kirsty's face fell. 'I couldn't have let them down . . .' She still felt bad about leaving The Hi-Tones and knew they were finding it hard to replace her with either a male or female lead singer. But they hadn't let it affect their working with her up until she left, and were still as friendly and teasing towards her as they'd always been.

Larry patted her hand. 'Relax,' he told her, lighting up a cigarette. 'We've plenty of Christmases ahead of us.'

'I hope so,' she said, smiling now.

'I was just thinking—' Larry broke off as the musicians called over to say they were leaving. He went across the dance floor to have a word with them, and to check how they felt about the rehearsal.

'Champion,' the pianist said, smiling and nodding vigorously, while the others echoed their agreement. 'She's got a great voice for a young girl – I'd say she has a great future ahead of her.'

Larry came back to the table, his forehead furrowed, pondering a thought that had just occurred to him. 'When is your last booking with the band?' he asked lightly.

Kirsty put her blonde head to the side, working it out. 'I think it's the twenty-ninth of December,' she said.

He inhaled deeply on his cigarette. 'You're not working New Year's Eve then?' he checked, his piercing blue eyes narrowing against the smoke.

'The boys like to have the New Year off,' Kirsty told him. 'Anyway, most of the pubs and clubs close about ten o'clock to let everybody get home for Hogmanay.'

'What about yourself?' he enquired. 'Have you any plans?'

Kirsty shrugged. 'We'll probably just be at home or at friends or relatives.' She pulled a face. 'There's no buses running from early on and the taxis cost a bomb – double or even triple.' She halted, then a defiant little gleam came into her eye. 'Not that somebody like you would know, with a fancy car to drive about in, any hour of the day or night.'

Larry's eyes danced with amusement now, but he stopped himself from laughing out loud as he knew it would only infuriate her. He had already come to realise that Kirsty Grace – while young and naive in many ways – was no pushover. She couldn't possibly be a pushover and survive amongst a group of men who were playing in some of the roughest clubs in the West of Scotland. She was definitely a survivor. And yet, despite her occasional brittleness and sharp tongue, there was a delicate, feminine contradiction about her that brought out the protective instincts in men.

'If you've nothing more exciting on, how do you feel about singing at a New Year dance?' Larry said casually.

Kirsty looked startled. 'I thought you said it would be well into January or February before I'd be ready to go on stage . . .'

'I know, but I've had a cancellation . . . a singer I'd booked has had to go into hospital for an appendix operation, and I'd say she won't be fit to go on stage for a while.' He took another deep drag on his cigarette, and then stubbed it out in the ashtray. 'In my opinion you're more than capable of filling her shoes – you're a far better singer. It's just that she's been around a few years and knows how to put a song across with confidence.' He paused, watching her reaction. 'What do you think?'

'God!' Kirsty said, putting her hands in a praying gesture over her mouth. 'I don't know if I feel ready yet . . .' Standing up on the stage alone tonight had felt strange, even though there had only been a handful of people in the room, but the thought of standing up when the room was packed and expecting a great night with it being New Year's Eve was terrifying.

'You've surprised *me*, Kirsty,' he said in a low, sincere voice. 'I didn't think you'd be ready for a while yet, but you've really mastered those new songs, the pitch, the timing – everything.' He halted, looking straight into her eyes. 'Although you're a young girl – with these new songs – you come across with the authority of an older woman.'

'How d'you mean?' she asked, draining her glass of lemonade.

She wasn't too sure if she liked the 'older woman' bit. 'D'you mean I'm sort of *old-fashioned*?'

'No, Kirsty,' he said patiently. 'What I mean is that you sang "Unchained Melody" and "Let Me Go, Lover" like it had really happened to you – as if you knew all about passionate, intense, grown-up love affairs.'

Kirsty started to giggle now, and a slight blush came to her cheeks. 'I don't know exactly how to take that . . . but I've seen enough about it all in the films and read about it in books.'

Again, Larry stopped himself from smiling at her naivety, realising that she might back off and lose confidence if she thought he was laughing at her. 'Well,' he said, touching her cheek with his forefinger, 'you're a very good little actress as well as being a wonderful singer.'

Feeling flushed with all this unexpected praise, she suddenly felt confident enough to ask, 'Where is the dance? Is it local or further away?'

Larry gave a slow smile. 'It's not too far away, and it's somewhere you know.'

She smiled back at him, easier now she knew it was somewhere familiar. 'Come on!' she said, jokily prodding the table. 'Which club is it in?'

'Ah,' he said, 'I never said it was a club. The idea of you going solo was to get you away from the clubs – to move into a higher league.'

The smile slid from her face, to be replaced by irritation. 'Is it a dance hall then?' she snapped, beginning to feel he was teasing her.

'Calm down, Miss Prickly Briar,' he told her. 'It's a hotel. A very nice hotel with very nice people.'

'Which hotel?'

'The Clyde Valley Hotel – the one we had a meal in a few weeks ago. You liked it there, didn't you?'

Kirsty's throat narrowed in fear. How could he even imagine that she was ready for a place like that? 'I couldn't sing there . . . it's really posh,' she stuttered, hardly able to get the words out. 'They would be expecting a real professional . . . somebody like themselves. It would be all older people from the posh houses in Lanark . . . there would be nobody like me there.'

'Nonsense!' he stated, shaking his head vehemently. 'You *are* a professional – you're a first-class singer.' He ran his hand through his thick dark hair and gave a long, low sigh. 'I can't believe you could have such a low opinion of yourself, after all I've just said to you about your wonderful singing.' He paused, and then his tone dropped to a lower, kinder one. 'Have more faith in yourself. You're as good as any of the people who will be there and better. They're only interested in having a bit of a dance and a nice place to bring in the New Year.'

Kirsty's head drooped. 'That's all right for you to say,' she muttered. 'You don't come from an ordinary council house . . . I bet you live in a big fancy house like all those people.'

'You don't know a thing about my background,' he said quietly. 'And what kind of houses either of us have come from has absolutely *nothing* to do with it. The people at the dance won't care where you come from – they'll only be interested in your singing voice and having a dance and a bit of *craic* for the night.'

Then Kirsty lifted her chin and a defiant look came into her eyes. 'Not that I'm ashamed of where I come from or my family. Our house is spotlessly clean and we've nice furniture and everything. It's just that I know the types of people there will be all uppity and full of themselves – and I hate the way people like that make me feel. I've one or two that come into the chemist's and they talk to you as if you're beneath them.'

'Kirsty . . . Kirsty,' Larry said in a low whisper, taking her hand into both of his. 'You'll be grand, I promise you – you'll be absolutely grand. You're the best little singer I have on my books.'

There was a truce-like silence for a few moments, during which she became acutely conscious that he was still holding her hand. She wondered whether she should ease her hand out of his, then she wondered if he was even aware that he was still holding it. He smiled at her now, gave her hand a reassuring squeeze and then gently let it go.

'What,' she asked now, in a resigned, wavery voice, 'would I have to wear for this "do"? I don't know if I've anything suitable. I couldn't ask my mother to start making me an outfit at this late stage, she's up to her eyes in sewing for Christmas.'

She stopped. 'You see, I was going to wait until the January sales to go into Glasgow – to the big shops and buy a few really fancy dresses for the stage.'

'Let me sort that out,' Larry said to her. 'I'm sure I can put my hand on some very nice dresses in your size that would be suitable.' Then, seeing the surprised look on her face, he smiled. 'Contacts, Kirsty – in this business it's all about contacts.' He looked at his watch and, realising the time, he finished his brandy in one gulp and pushed his chair back.

Kirsty stood up too. 'I'm beginning to wonder if it would have been easier staying with The Hi-Tones,' she said ruefully.

'Nothing ventured, Kirsty,' Larry Delaney said, smiling and wagging his finger. 'Take my word for it – you were meant for much bigger things than The Hi-Tones.'

Chapter 25

☙✥❧

The hospital was the usual hive of activity for the evening visiting. 'It's a crisp enough night,' Mona said, running her hand along a white radiator as they walked along the corridor to Lily's ward, 'but it's nice coming into the heat. They keep the hospital lovely and warm – although in the summer they say that it can be far too warm, that they keep it on all night for the older patients.'

No one responded to her observations, just vaguely nodding and keeping to their own thoughts as they walked along.

Once again, Mona realised, she had caught herself saying something just for the sake of it. Daft, meaningless talk just seemed to pour out of her these days – talk about normal, everyday things when nobody walking along the corridor found the situation normal at all, talk that drowned all the unspoken words of dread and worry about her precious daughter.

Mona and Sophie walked down the ward first, followed by Heather and the two men. Each one went to the head of the bed and kissed Lily and had a few words of encouragement for her, then sat down in a chair or went to another bed to locate a spare one.

'More presents!' Lily said gleefully, as Pat put a large brown paper bag on her bedside table, then bent to give her a kiss on the forehead.

'From oul' Mrs Kelly at the bottom of the street,' he told her. 'D'you want me to open it for you?'

'Aye,' Lily said, making an effort to nod her head. She took a breath, holding it in to expand her lungs as the physiotherapist had told her to do. 'I'm dyin' to see what's in it.' Then, as Pat opened the paper bag and withdrew the colourful contents, she gave an excited gasp. 'A selection box!' Then her brows came down. 'What kind of sweeties are in it, Daddy?' She quizzed. 'Is there a game on the back of the box?'

Pat smiled and made a show of rolling his eyes to the ceiling in exasperation, and then as he moved closer to the bed he started to rhyme out the contents of the Christmas-decorated cardboard box. 'Chocolate Buttons, a bar of chocolate, a chocolate Santie Clause—'

Lily cut him off midflow, having made her decision. 'I'll have the bar of chocolate and we can all have a square,' she told her father.

'Are you sure you're allowed chocolate at this hour of the night, darlin'?' Mona checked anxiously.

'Aye, aye,' Lily replied, her eyes watching Pat's every move as he opened the box and extracted the chosen bar of chocolate, which he then proceeded to break into individual squares as his daughter had instructed. 'Our Patrick and Declan will be ragin' they're not here to get a bit of the chocolate!' she giggled now, then went into a small spasm of coughing, making everyone look at each other anxiously.

After she finished coughing, Pat gave her a drink then he lifted the chocolate again from the bedside cabinet. Lily had the first square and Pat was handing the rest of the chocolate around when he became aware of two well-dressed figures making their way towards the bed. He turned to look, and his face suddenly drained of colour.

Mona looked curiously at him first, as he stood planted on the spot, then she turned around to view the visitors. There was a sudden heavy silence, then everyone around the bed turned to see what had caused the reaction.

'Claire . . .' Pat finally said, moving forward to greet his sister and the older, prosperous Protestant husband that had caused all the trouble by daring to fall in love with her and then marry her.

'Hello . . .' Claire said in a low, hesitant voice. She was smaller and slimmer than her brothers, but there was a definite likeness. She had also rounded off the thick brogue they had all arrived in Scotland with, but the soft warmth of her local Irish accent was still evident.

She and her husband Andy paused just a few feet from the bottom of Lily's bed, both dressed to the last in obviously expensive clothes, and drawing curious glances from the other visitors. They had to be somebody of note with the man's thick black overcoat, pin-stripe suit and pristine shirt and tie. Something about the well-cut grey hair, the clothes and the way he carried himself, plus his wife's rig-out, made them whisper that he must be somebody really important. He was definitely not just an insurance man or a bank-clerk type in a suit.

Claire's hair was shorter than the last time anyone had seen her, and looked blacker and sleeker in a Cleopatra-style bob. She was wearing a dark brown cashmere coat with a creamy-coloured, luxurious fur on the collar and cuffs and she had a crocodile-leather handbag slipped over her wrist.

Sophie, who decided to stay put in her chair for the moment, glanced anxiously over at Mona and saw her whole body suddenly stiffen up, as though she had received an electric jolt.

Mona, stony-faced and injured looking, turned her back on the others now to face Lily and Heather, as though the visitors were but a brief interruption who would go away as quickly as they had come.

Fintan, red-faced and awkward, moved out of his chair to join his brother and sister, while Heather slid up to the top of the bed beside Lily, because she didn't know what else to do. She didn't know how she should greet this aunt who she had been close to only a few years ago and who now looked like a beautiful, dark-haired stranger. A stranger whom her Auntie Mona had been obsessed with for the last two years, and whose presence might just make Mona blow up at any minute.

From the safety of the corner at Lily's bed, Heather decided that she would wait and see how the real grown-ups handled this delicate situation. She was especially watching Mona, who looked like she was going to have something in the line of a heart attack or a stroke, as she listened to Claire's refined voice explaining that this was the first chance they'd had to come out to see Lily.

After speaking quietly to her brothers for a few minutes, Claire moved towards Sophie on the opposite side of the bed from Mona. 'How are you, Sophie?' she asked, then without waiting for a reply, she looked across at her other sister-in-law. 'Mona?'

Mona sat rigid, staring silently ahead as if she hadn't heard her.

'I hope you don't mind us just landing out here ...' Claire went on, moving towards Lily, 'but I wanted to come out to see my little god-daughter as soon as I heard.' She squeezed Heather's hand as she passed, and then turned now to the bright little face propped up on the pillows. 'How are you, pet?' she said, her manicured hands coming to stroke Lily's hair and cheek.

'I'm fine!' Lily announced, giving her aunt a beaming smile. 'I haven't seen you for ages ... Where have you been?'

Mona's shoulders rose and her back straightened in her wine wool coat as though gearing up for anything that came her way. And she was more than ready to meet it, even if it came from Pat – her treacherous husband – who had been the first to move towards the uninvited and most definitely unwanted visitors. She looked around the group at the bed now, and wondered who amongst them had taken it upon themselves to let this pair know about Lily being in hospital.

'I live in Glasgow now,' Claire said softly, smiling at the child and trying to ignore the tears that were prickling at the back of her eyes. 'It's a good bit away from here ...'

Lily's face was now more serious. 'How did you not come back to see us?' she demanded. 'It's about two or three years.'

'Well, I'm back now, darling,' Claire said, carefully skirting around the question. She rubbed a finger to the side of both eyes. 'And I came to see you just as soon as I could.' Claire turned and gestured towards her husband who was standing chatting with Fintan and Pat. 'You know your Uncle Andy, don't you, girls?' She looked first at Lily and then at Heather. Both girls looked blankly back at her, vaguely uncomfortable and unable to remember if they had ever met this tall, silver-haired man before.

'Andy ...' Claire beckoned, and he came towards the bed, smiling warmly at anyone who caught his eye. 'This is little Lily and,' she put her arm through her older niece's, 'this is Heather. You've heard me often talk about Heather and Kirsty, her younger sister.'

'Of course I have,' Andy said, beaming at them. 'You've talked about them so often I feel as if I know them well myself.'

He put his hand out to Heather and she shook it, suddenly feeling that this was really a very nice, polite man, and not the monster that Mona and some of the other family members had constantly castigated.

'Hello,' Heather said, averting her eyes from the stern-faced Auntie Mona. 'I'm pleased to meet you ...' After that, she couldn't think of anything else to say to him.

'And young Lily,' he said, coming to lean casually, but carefully, on the metal side of her bed. 'I hope you're feeling much better, young lady.'

Lily nodded her head. 'I'm fine,' she told him, delighted at all the attention. 'I wasn't very well for a while, but I'm getting better. They might be lettin' me out for Christmas.'

She turned to her mother now. 'Have you asked the doctor yet, Mammy?'

Mona's face went a deep red. She was caught in the spotlight now with all eyes on her.

'They're giving you till the end of the week,' she replied in a small, terse voice, 'to see how you are then.' She looked back to the nurses' station at the end of the ward as though seeking some kind of telepathic confirmation about the situation.

Heather glanced across at her mother and for a few seconds their eyes met, and she knew Sophie was finding it as painful and awkward as herself.

'Every day,' Lily announced, to her new audience, 'I'm getting better and better – I can move my legs and arms more now. Look,' she said, moving her arms very slowly from beneath the covers. 'I can nearly lift them up in the air.' After a few seconds, her arms dropped back onto the bed and the effort it had taken was plain on her little creased face.

'She's a great girl, hardly ever complains,' Sophie spoke out now, feeling that she should contribute something towards the conversation, and wanting to let Claire and her husband know that she had no axe to grind with them. She never had – she'd always liked Claire, and the girls had adored her. But it was hard to be heard when Mona and the other women shouted down anyone who went against the Church. In the end, being the peace-loving soul that she was, she'd given in, deciding that this was something the Grace family should sort out between themselves.

And thankfully Pat and Fintan had finally moved to do something about it. And now, like the men, she was aware she would have to answer to Mona for her involvement. She would be blamed for getting in touch with Claire, but she was well used to handling her sister-in-law's wrath and would deal with it somehow when it descended upon her.

Since she knew she was already in deep trouble for not ignoring Claire now, Sophie decided 'in for a penny in for a pound'. 'You're looking very well, Claire – living in Glasgow must be suiting you.'

'Oh, it's grand,' Claire replied, a warm, grateful smile spreading on her pretty face. She moved to sit beside Sophie on the chair that Heather had vacated. 'I've surprised myself, I've really settled in well in Giffnock. The neighbours are all nice and friendly—'

Mona's chair made a scraping noise as she suddenly stood up. 'I'm goin' out for a breath of fresh air,' she announced to no one in particular, her lip curling and her eyes raised to the ceiling. 'The air in here has got too warm for my liking.' Then she made her exit, without looking directly at anyone.

Claire turned to her husband now, as though Mona's little scene hadn't just happened. 'Have you the card and little present for Lily?'

'Indeed I have!' Andy said in his refined Glasgow accent. He reached into his inside pocket and withdrew a stiff white envelope and a small gift-wrapped box that obviously came from a jeweller's shop. For a moment, he hesitated, realising that the little girl couldn't manoeuvre herself into a position to take them from him, and then he laid them both down on a smooth part of the bed.

'Thanks, Auntie Claire and Uncle Andy!' Lily said, her gaze flitting from one to the other then falling on her cousin. 'Will you open it for me, Heather?' she said, twisting around in the bed to get a good angle from which to watch the present being opened.

The card with Disney characters was passed around for everybody to look at, then Heather carefully took off the ribbon and the pretty outer wrapping and opened the velvet box and held it out for Lily to get a good look at.

'A locket!' Lily gasped. Then she noticed the little ticket in the box. 'A *real* gold locket!' She looked at her father with wide, shining eyes. 'It says it's eighteen carat gold on it, Daddy – it must have cost a fortune!' She suddenly gave a giggle. 'And it's not even Christmas yet!'

Everybody laughed now and Heather heaved a sigh of grateful relief that Mona hadn't been there to witness the fuss that was being made of Claire and the expensive gift.

'All my pals at school will be dead jealous,' Lily rattled on, as Claire fastened the locket around her thin little neck. 'They'll all be wishin' they caught that polio as well, when they see all the stuff everybody's gave me!'

There was an awkward pause, which Lily didn't even notice in her excitement, where Pat found a huge lump coming into his throat. 'I'm just goin' out to see your mammy, darlin',' he told her hoarsely, moisture glistening at the side of his eyes. 'We'll be back in a few minutes.'

For another ten minutes or so, Heather and her mother and father and Claire and her husband sat chatting and laughing with Lily, and then Claire looked at the delicate watch on her slim wrist.

'I think,' she said to Andy, 'that it's time we headed off, and let the family have some time on their own with Lily.'

'Whatever you like now,' Andy said, giving a quick smile and casting a glance towards the bottom of the ward. There was still no sign of Mona or Pat returning.

Claire stood up and started fastening the buttons on her fur-collared coat. 'I'll make sure we don't take so long to come and see you next time, pet,' she told Lily. 'And we might come out to Rowanhill to see you when you get out of hospital.'

'You and Andy are welcome at our house any time, Claire,' Fintan said, standing up to see them off.

'And always remember you and yours are welcome at our house,' Andy said, his face and tone suddenly serious. He pressed a small white business card into Fintan's hand. 'That has the house and my work's phone number on it. Phone any time you or the girls want to come out to visit us or stay the night.'

The atmosphere in the car on the way home was as frosty as the clear night turned out to be – the three women in the back seat and the two men in the front.

'The blidey cheek of them!' Mona muttered several times in a row, obviously expecting some kind of a response, but no one in the car was forthcoming. Eventually, she could stand the silence no longer and went full steam ahead venting her anger.

'Turning up at the hospital like Lord and Lady Muck ... looking down on the rest of us from a great height. That Claire was always the same, but you'd think she could have found an uppity type amongst her own kind. There's plenty of teachers and well-educated fellas around that would have suited her – but oh, no! Why she had to put the nail in the coffin by marryin' that grey-headed oul' Protestant yoke that's old enough to be her father, I'll never know.' She halted to take a breath. 'She's made a holy show of the whole Grace family ... I'm squirmin' every time I'm at a meeting of the Catholic Mothers or the Parish Council in case anybody asks me how she is. And then she has the cheek to turn up at the hospital as large as life with that oul' Church of Scotland relic along with her.'

'Give it a rest, Mona,' Fintan said from the front seat, 'you've had your say now.'

Heather was squashed between her hefty aunt and her mother in the back seat, with her hand pressed firmly against her mouth. Never had she seen Mona in such an agitated, angry mood – and she dreaded where it was going to finish. There were often disagreements and atmospheres between her mother and aunt, but they had never been as vicious as this one-sided tirade.

Mona made a loud indignant-sounding grunt and then turned sideways in her seat towards Sophie, although she could only see her silhouette outlined in the dark of the car. 'And ye needn't sit there in silence. I know fine well that none of you agree with me. You're obviously all prepared to be walked over – to let yer own standards and the Catholic Church's standards down as well. Where would we all be if them that defected were welcomed back with open arms? She knew the rules and she deliberately broke them – so now she can pay the price that we would all have to pay.'

'Maybe some of us don't feel as strong as you do, Mona,' Pat said sharply. 'Maybe some of us couldn't give a damn what other people do.'

Heather's stomach churned at the thought of this turning into a full-scale row between husband and wife, and was grateful when the men started a conversation of their own about football.

Mona sucked in her breath, then started off again in a lower tone directed at the females. 'Men and lads not speakin' out I can half understand,' she said in a derisory manner, 'but us *women* need to stick together. An' it's not that I'm pickin' on Claire Grace here – there's plenty of others up to the same carry-on these days. Tommy's wife, Janey, was sayin' that only the other day, about a niece in her own family that's gettin' married outside the Catholic Church, and all the rows it's caused.' She tutted loudly now. 'The Church depends on us mothers to hold the family's standards together. And there's no good in being all mealy-mouthed and weak when one of them decides to step outside the fold. We need to stand firm or we'll have them all doing it.'

Sophie finally spoke up now, unable to take much more. 'I don't think any of us could be described as mealy-mouthed,' she said, leaning forward and looking towards her sister-in-law. 'And there's plenty of stories in the Bible where you're told you should hold out the hand of friendship to people of all creeds and colour. Look at the Good Samaritan and Mary Magdalene.'

'Well, you're surely gettin' all religious, Sophie Grace, quotin' the blidey Bible!' Mona said incredulously. 'And the Good

Samaritan and Mary Magdalene ...' She paused for breath. 'Father Finlay says it's not for us to be reading and translatin' the Bible – that's what the priests are there to do, to explain all that in the Gospel on a Sunday. Readin' the Bible – sure that's what the oul' Protestants do, wi' their Bible-reading classes and the like.' She gave a sarcastic little laugh. 'It's a bad day when ye can't be proud of your own religion and heritage. When ye think of all the poor souls that starved to death durin' the famine in Ireland for their faith, and there's folks nowadays wouldn't have the guts to even admit they were Catholics if it was any way awkward for them.'

There was a silence, as everyone looked out of the car windows into the white frosty night and hoped Mona had exhausted her grievances and would let the subject drop.

'Lily looked better tonight,' Heather said, as the car slowed down and turned into the main street in Rowanhill. 'She's moving better and she's not coughing as much as she was before. D'you think there's a chance she will get out of hospital for Christmas?'

'I spoke to the ward sister tonight,' Mona said, her voice flat and weary. 'She said there's a possibility that we might be able to bring her home on Christmas Eve for the night – to be in her own house for Santie coming. They're not promisin' anything as they said they'll need to see how her breathing is between now and then.'

'I'll say a wee novena that she does get out,' Sophie said.

'Thanks,' Mona said quietly, with an audible catch in her voice. 'After what she's gone through, the wee soul could do with all our prayers.'

Chapter 26

❧❦❧

In the last few days leading up to Christmas, there was more than the usual activity going on in the Grace households. Lily, it had been confirmed, was now deemed well enough to have both Christmas Eve and Christmas night at home. This was on the strict understanding that with any signs of breathing difficulties or the slightest deterioration in her condition, she would have to be returned to hospital immediately.

On the Thursday afternoon, Sophie was ensconced in her little sewing-room with a stack of dresses, skirts and trousers that all needed to be hemmed or taken in or let out for the Christmas festivities. On a small table behind her was another pile of curtains and other functional items that would have to wait until the holidays were over.

A rap came on the back door and she heard Fintan's footsteps as he went to answer it. Hearing Pat and Mona's voices, Sophie stopped the machine, glad of an excuse to have a break, and came down to hear the latest news on Lily. As she walked along the hallway, she was relieved to hear Mona laughing and chatting, as she had dreaded a cold war between them all over Christmas.

'Wait until you hear this,' Mona said, as Sophie came into the kitchen, 'the big fella here is heading into Wishaw to get us a television set!' She was still in her dark working jacket and full white apron, obviously having just come from the Chapel house.

'A television?' Sophie repeated in a shocked tone, looking from Mona to Pat. 'When did you decide this?'

'Yesterday,' Pat announced.

'A television – imagine!'

'I'm on the early shift this week,' Pat explained, 'and I've been takin' a run around all the electrical shops after work. I've got a good deal wi' one in Wishaw, and they said I could collect it this afternoon.' He nodded at his brother. 'I was just wonderin' if you wanted to take a run in with me to pick it up.'

'Grand, I've nothin' much else to do this afternoon,' Fintan told his brother. 'I've already been up to the school to check the pipes and the boiler are OK.' He nodded his head. 'It'll be interesting to see how they rig the television up, and see how the aerial works and all that kind of thing.' He glanced out of the window to see if it was likely to rain. It didn't look too bad; the sky was grey but it looked as though it would hold. 'I'll just get my overcoat.' He went out to the hall to the coat-rack.

'The television is for Lily, really,' Mona said now, her face serious. 'We wouldn't bother for ourselves. It was her that made us make up our minds.' She bit her lip, for a moment looking as if she might burst into tears. 'We'd planned on gettin' her a new two-wheeler bike. I had it ordered up at the Co-op and everything . . . but she's not going to be able for that for a long while. So there's no point in havin' it rusting out in the shed, and us havin' to look at it every time we go to get coal.'

Pat cut in now. 'She's not going to be fit to do much this Christmas except lie on the couch, so the lads suggested that we all chip in and get a TV for her. Seemingly, they have kids' programmes and everything on it, and then in the dark evenings the whole family would get a bit of pleasure out of it.'

'It's a great idea,' Sophie said, going over to the sink to top up the lukewarm kettle. 'We're always saying that we'll see into getting one ourselves, but as usual we've never got organised.'

'Oh, the radiogram will do us just fine for a while,' Fintan said, 'and anyway, we won't need one now that the rich neighbours will have one. We can go round and look at theirs.'

Everyone laughed, knowing that Fintan was only half-joking. There were very few people in Rowanhill with televisions, and anybody that did usually got a crowd in to look at it over the weekend or if there was a big football match on.

'Just as long as you bring a few shillings for the box,' Pat said. 'We said we'd try one of those slot tellies that you put your money in.'

'Is that right?' Sophie asked. She was hugely interested in getting a television herself and had nearly succeeded on several occasions, aided and abetted by the girls. Fintan was the fly in the ointment. 'And how exactly does it work?'

'They have the money box attached at the back of the television, so that it can't be seen . . . to give you a bit of privacy in case there's anybody around that you wouldn't like to know your business,' Pat explained. 'Then, seemingly, you put a shilling in the box and you can watch it for two hours. The idea with the box is to always keep a few bob handy so that you're ahead of yourselves.'

'Well, we'll have to see about where we'll keep the money,' Mona mused, 'for it won't last long in a dish where those lads are around. That Patrick and Declan are forever borrowin' money out of the two shillings I keep for the electric box, and they never pay it back.'

'Well, they've said they'll all take turns at putting their shillings in,' Pat said, in a no-nonsense tone. 'And if they don't keep it up, we'll get a payment book and they can all chip in every Friday for it.'

Mona waved her hand dismissively. 'We'll cross that bridge when we come to it. We'll get the telly and Lily home for Christmas, and we'll worry about paying for it in the New Year.'

The two brothers headed away on their business into Wishaw, and Mona took her coat off and settled down at the kitchen table for a cup of tea. Sophie moved about in her slow way, pouring water into the teapot then searching around in the cupboard for a packet of Cadbury's chocolate fingers that she'd hidden from Kirsty the other day. Every time visitors came there wasn't a single decent chocolate biscuit in the house. They were eaten in jig-time, leaving the plain digestives or custard-creams. Heather wasn't so bad at the minute, with her trying to cut down on sweet things, but when Kirsty was in the mood, she could eat a packet on her own.

Sophie tutted to herself, half-listening to her sister-in-law while she opened all the cupboards that she might have hidden the biscuits in.

'I meant to ask you,' Mona said, 'did your goose arrive this mornin'?' All the Grace families received a decapitated goose as a Christmas present from Pat and Fintan's brother, Joe, who was still home in Ireland on the small family farm.

Sophie nodded, still opening cupboard doors. 'Fintan brought it in. I'm glad he was here for it's a ton weight.'

'Thank God now that they came in plenty of time,' Mona went on. 'Ours came in the post van around eleven o'clock. By the time we got it in and soaking in cold water, the van had gone out of the street and I'd missed seein' whether he'd stopped at your house.' She looked around the kitchen now. 'Where have you put it?'

'Out in the shed,' Sophie told her, 'in cold water. I spent a good hour plucking it this morning, and then I gave up and left it to Fintan to finish off. It's the most horrible job, that and gutting it. The smell of it would put you off.' She laughed. 'The girls run a mile when they see it with the feathers on and the blood all around the neck. If they look at it too much, it'll put them off and then they won't have it for their Christmas dinner. That's why it's out in the shed until it's ready for the oven.'

'Oh, I don't mind it a bit,' Mona laughed. 'I get the lads to take turns on the feathers and then I give it a good clean out in salty water. It always reminds me of back home in Galway when we were children. My granny kept geese and ducks and everything.'

'I ordered a large-sized chicken at the butcher's just in case the goose didn't arrive,' Sophie said, now on her tiptoes looking in the cupboard she kept the baking trays in, 'so I asked Fintan to take a walk up to the shop and let the butcher know that I'll leave the chicken until the New Year.'

'We're lucky getting the geese,' Mona stated. 'Chicken is what most of them have around here for their Christmas dinner. A goose in a luxury.'

'You're right,' Sophie agreed. 'We should all be grateful, even if it is hard work.'

'It's a mild enough day for December,' Mona said, nodding towards the window. 'Thank God, I would hate it to be awful cold for Lily comin' home. We'll have to be fierce careful about keeping the house warm enough for her. We've brought her bed into our bedroom because it has the biggest fireplace and so we can keep a close eye on her.'

'Oh, she'll be fine,' Sophie said, her head half in the cupboard that held the pots and pans. 'She's come on great every time I've seen her, and she's moving her arms and legs and breathing a lot better.' She suddenly spotted the blue wrapping and emerged triumphantly with the chocolate fingers.

Tears suddenly shot into Mona's eyes. 'It's taking an awful long time ... When I think of her just weeks ago, running around and dancing all the time, and then I look at her now, still hardly able to move.' A tear trickled down her face. 'God knows if she'll ever be able to walk again ... or whether she'll be left crippled. That little McKay fellow up the road – he's left in a wheelchair.' Her head dropped into her hands. 'Oh, God, Sophie,' she moaned, 'I lie awake every night thinkin' of her, and Pat's often awake too. What did we ever do to deserve this?'

Sophie came over to sit by her and put her arms around her sister-in-law. 'You did *nothing*!' she whispered. 'It's a germ that could have attacked anybody ... it has attacked loads of people, grown-ups and children.' She rocked very slightly, trying to comfort Mona.

'It's the hardest thing we've ever had to endure,' Mona said, her voice thin and cracking. 'And it had to be the smallest and the weakest.' She gripped Sophie's hands with all her might.

'Lily will be fine,' Sophie said, tears now tripping down her own cheeks. 'Lily will be fine.'

Mona finished her cup of tea, and then leaned across to pick one more biscuit. 'You'd better take them out of my sight,' she said to Sophie, 'or I'll end up eating the whole packet.' She shook her head. 'It's no wonder you're as thin as a rake, you only pick at the odd one.'

'Chocolate doesn't bother me,' Sophie replied. 'I can take it or leave it most of the time. It's only at the bad time of the month that I take a notion for it.'

'Don't talk about that,' Mona said, rolling her eyes. 'Mine are all over the place. They're here early one month then gone for two. I don't know where I'm up to, and I'm terrified to let Pat near me. Before I could work out the safe time of the month, but now I haven't a clue.' She gave a little laugh now. 'I'm tryin' to outsit Pat every night, so that he's asleep when I go up. I tell him I'm ironing or listening to the radio but some nights he stays up late himself, and it means that I'm not gettin' to bed before twelve.'

'What about going up earlier, and trying to get a good night's sleep?'

'Tried it,' Mona said, lifting her eyes to the ceiling, 'but he only follows me up ten minutes later.'

'Has he not guessed that there's something wrong?' Sophie asked, surprised and slightly embarrassed that Mona was speaking so personally. Sex was not a common subject for discussion amongst the circle of women they moved in.

'Oh, I'm sure he has,' Mona sighed, 'but he'll just have to keep guessing. I don't want to start explaining all of *that* to him, and knowing Pat, he might blame everything on it and say it's me gettin' older . . . that I'm on the change of life.' She took a small bite of her chocolate finger. 'I've just said I'm not in the mood for you-know-what, with all the worry about Lily and Christmas and everythin'.'

'Are the lads all finishing work tomorrow for Christmas?' Sophie enquired now.

Mona nodded, then she swallowed the remainder of the biscuit. 'Michael and Sean have the half-day, and Declan and Patrick are off school and college already. What about Heather and Kirsty?'

Sophie had to think for a moment. 'Heather's finishing early tomorrow,' she said, 'and then the crowd in the office are all going out to a pub for a Christmas meal. They said it would be easier havin' it in the afternoon for the ones that have a distance to travel home.'

'That's sensible,' Mona said, 'because you can't trust those trains, especially late at night.' Her brow deepened. 'And you never know who could be lurking about on them when they're half-empty. A good-looking young girl on her own in a carriage – anythin' could happen to her.'

'Don't say that, you'll only get me worried,' Sophie said, clearing up the cups and plates. She turned the hot tap on to fill the basin and then squirted some Fairy Liquid in and swished it around with her hand. Mona was an expert at putting her finger on the sore point, she thought ruefully. And when things did go wrong, she wasn't slow to point out that she'd noted all the drawbacks in advance. She kept her back to her sister-in-law, rattling about with the cups and saucers in the comfortingly hot water.

'Well, she was hell-bent on going to work in Glasgow, and

that's what these big cities are all about,' Mona said with a sigh. 'Oh, Heather Grace is just like her Uncle Pat: once she makes up her mind, there's no movin' her.' A smile suddenly spread across her face. 'And how's poor Kirsty? She must be exhausted – on her feet all day in that chemist's and then out two and three nights in the week for rehearsals.'

'Oh, she's none too pleased at the minute,' Sophie said, grateful that they'd moved on to the safer subject of Mona's favourite niece. She often wondered if Mona made the difference between the girls deliberately, or if it was something she wasn't aware of. 'She's working right through until the half-day on Christmas Eve.'

'Is she?' Mona said, her eyes wide with surprise. She clucked her tongue in disapproval. 'I suppose oul' Simpson is hopin' to sell a few more soap an' bath-cube sets at the last minute.'

Sophie shrugged, lifting the delft out of the basin and placing them on the draining-rack. 'I suppose it's for prescriptions as well, with them being closed the Monday and Tuesday. I think having Christmas on the Sunday this year has confused things as well because they have to get an extra day off for the bank holiday.'

'True,' Mona said, her round face thoughtful. 'That's a nice Irish fella Kirsty's workin' with at the singin' ... good-lookin' and well-dressed too. Is it Dublin he's from? What's his name again?'

'Larry Delaney, and he is from Dublin. He's been very good to her,' Sophie said, warming to the conversation. She left the dishes to dry on their own and came back to sit down at the table. 'He called round last night and dropped off half a dozen beautiful dresses for her to pick from for that big New Year's ball. You should see them, all sequins and pearls and one has a fancy shawl to go with it. He even brought long gloves to match each dress.'

'And are they upstairs?' Mona asked, lifting her eyes to the ceiling, interested. 'I'd love to get a look at them.'

Sophie frowned and adjusted her glasses on the bridge of her nose. She really only needed them for reading and sewing, and most of the time she forgot to take them off. 'God knows what state the room will be in ... they're always rushing at the last minute and I haven't had time to make their beds yet or anything.' She felt cornered now; the last person she wanted to have nosing around the bedrooms was the fussy Mona who made a virtue of being up early every Monday to clean her windows after making all her beds and hanging her washing out. 'I usually tidy the room for them first thing in the morning, but I've that much sewing to do I never got the chance to make my own bed, never mind theirs.'

Sophie suddenly got to her feet now, thinking that if she got a few steps ahead of her sister-in-law, she might manage to close all the other doors and not have her peering in at the towels that Fintan had probably dropped on the bathroom floor after washing this morning.

Mona got to her feet, waving her hand dismissively. 'Don't be so silly, Sophie, sure there's nobody lookin' at the beds or the state of the house.' She shook her head incredulously, smiling benignly, as if she were the most easy-going housewife in the world. 'All I'm interested in is seeing these fancy stage rig-outs, no' lookin' around for dust.' She followed Sophie out into the hall, keeping as close behind her as she could. 'And where did you say that he got the dresses from?' she asked as they mounted the stairs.

'I'm not sure,' Sophie replied, trying to get a step or two ahead of the heftier Mona. 'I think he has a finger in a lot of pies, and he must know somebody that hires them out or something like that.'

'Well, I'll tell you something,' Mona said, cracking out in laughter, 'with looks like that, he can stick his finger in my pie any day!'

'Mona Grace!' Sophie said, coming to a standstill a few steps from the top. She was laughing along with it, but fairly shocked at the same time. 'That's not what you were sayin' earlier when you were talking about poor Pat.'

'Poor Pat, me arse!' Mona said, her chin jutting out. 'He's been well looked after in that department all these years, and there's five children to prove it.'

Sophie continued up to the landing, casually reaching out her left arm to close the sewing-room door and then swinging her right arm to close the door to her and Fintan's room.

'As I said before,' Mona said airily, 'this isn't a house inspection. My own isn't too tidy at the minute with Christmas presents and paper shoved into wardrobes and drawers.'

Yes, Sophie thought ruefully, *but mine are scattered all over the floor and on top of the dressing-tables.*

'Beautiful! Absolutely beautiful!' Mona said, her voice full of awe. She fingered the little beads on the bottom of one of the dresses. 'They must have cost an absolute fortune.'

'The material alone to make them,' Sophie informed her, 'would cost more than two or three frocks in the Household or Bairds.' Both department stores in Wishaw were patronised by the females in the surrounding district for outfits for special occasions.

'Oh, she'll look stunning in them,' Mona said wistfully. 'With the lovely little figure Kirsty has on her, she can wear anything – absolutely anything.' She held up a strapless taffeta dress, the red bodice sewn with tiny black seed pearls, with a plain black skirt flaring out underneath. 'Oh, my God!' she breathed. 'What would you give to get into something like that again?'

Sophie lifted a midnight-blue, off-the-shoulder dress from the hastily tidied bed where they were all spread out, ignoring Mona's comment, because she knew perfectly well her own weight and shape had hardly altered since she was Kirsty and Heather's age. Mona just liked putting everybody in the same boat as herself and the couple of extra stone she was carrying. She looked closely at the blue dress, wondering if it was a bit too plain for the stage, and the dark colour a bit too sombre.

'I think your Heather's lost a bit of weight,' Mona commented, her brow in a disapproving furrow. There were no compliments forthcoming, as there had been for Kirsty's slim figure. 'I suppose it's all that running up and down to the station, and then the walk she has to the office. I'm not sure if it suits her ... she looks a wee bit drawn to me. She's not run down or anything, is she?'

'She's fine,' Sophie said, almost snappily. 'She's just been cutting out the sweeties and biscuits to wear some of her nice fitted things for Christmas.'

'This is a lovely dress,' Mona said, changing the subject. She lifted up a boned black lace dress with a plunging neckline and the tiniest of straps. 'But I don't think Kirsty has quite enough on top to fill it! She'd need to shove a couple of socks into her brassiere.'

'I think I'd need to shove a couple of socks into mine to make it fit!' Sophie laughed. 'This one's lovely, too,' she added, holding up a short-sleeved green satin empire-line dress with a small bow in the middle. 'I think that colour would suit Kirsty.'

'Mmm,' Mona mused, pursing her lips together. 'I think the red and black one is my favourite. I think it's more festive-ish. It would go lovely with the long black gloves.'

Suddenly the doorbell went, and Sophie threw the dress down on top of the bed. 'Just leave them there,' she told Mona. 'I'll hang them all up later.' Then she rushed downstairs.

Mona picked up the lace dress and examined the label. It was one she didn't recognise, but then she hardly thought the dress had come from Marks and Spencer, even though she bought her own best clothes from there. She laid it in her lap and then turned to have a proper look around the untidy bedroom, tutting to herself as she did so. Her own lads were tidier than this, she thought – and the windows all needed a right good clean. Even downstairs in the living-room and sitting-room, the windows weren't gleaming the way they should. It wasn't that Sophie didn't clean the windows, it was a case of not putting enough effort into it. They all needed buffing up with a bit of elbow grease and damp newspaper. Mona looked at the wardrobe mirror now, thinking that a rub over that wouldn't go amiss either. It could all be fixed with just a bit more time and care spent on it.

But she knew that wasn't likely to happen, because perfect housekeeping wasn't a priority in this particular household – and young girls needed training and goading into keeping standards up.

There was no doubt about it – the blame lay at one door, and one door only: Sophie's.

'Mona!' Sophie called back up to her now. 'It's your Patrick looking for you. He says a van has just pulled up with the new television!'

'The television! Jesus, Mary and Joseph!' Mona exclaimed, dropping the dress she was examining onto the bed. She came tearing down the stairs, breathless by the time she reached the bottom. 'That blidey Pat, I'll flamin' well kill him!' she panted. 'Leavin' me to deal with this and him gone into Wishaw to collect it! What am I going to say to the man? What am I supposed to know about televisions and aerials?'

An hour or so later, when Sophie was downstairs getting the evening meal ready, Fintan came in.

'That was a bit of a fiasco,' he said, taking his coat off and laying it across the back of one of the chairs. 'They told us at the shop that the television had already been sent out in a van. So, there was no need for us to go into Wishaw at all, and it was absolutely jam-packed.' He shook his head in despair. 'Nothin' but women and weans out doing last-minute Christmas shopping.'

'I bet Pat was raging,' Sophie said. 'Did he go mad at the man behind the counter?'

'No,' Fintan said. 'I was surprised myself. He just said he must have made a mistake. Maybe with Lily comin' home tomorrow and everything, he just got mixed up.'

'So what did you do?' Sophie said, frowning, and putting down the knife that she was cutting potatoes with. 'You were away a long time for just one shop.'

'We went for a pint,' Fintan admitted. 'I think Pat wanted to have a chat.'

'What about?' Sophie asked.

'Oh ... everything and nothing. Lily, mainly. He's awful worried about her, and then he went on about Mona.' He looked over at Sophie, his eyebrows raised. 'I think she's giving him a hard time in every way.'

Sophie nodded her head slowly. 'Once Lily's out of hospital it'll all blow over.'

Chapter 27

The restaurant was lovely, and just on one of the roads up from the Central Station. It was quite modern, with a fancy bar with coloured lights and lovely glass vases filled with real red carnations all over the place. They had a beautiful big imitation Christmas tree in the corner, Heather noted, lavishly decorated with different coloured tinsel and glass baubles. Just the perfect kind of tree, she thought, and no fear of pine needles dropping everywhere. The red velvet curtains and the thick white lace at the window gave a cosy feeling, and with the small lit candles on the tables it felt as though it was night-time as opposed to half past two on a Friday afternoon.

The staff of Seafreight had taken over two of the biggest tables in the restaurant, all done out in white linen tablecloths and festive paper napkins. Sprigs of holly and ivy, and smaller vases of red carnations, had been placed at intervals on the table beside candles. Heather looked along the table she was sitting at, discreetly glancing from under lowered eyelids at each of the eleven other people beside her – all wearing gold cardboard party hats just like herself. Everyone was dressed in their best – the women in dresses or pretty blouses and skirts, and the men all in well-starched shirts and fancier ties than they wore to work.

She had only been in the office a few weeks, and yet as she looked at all the friendly faces, she felt she'd been there for ever. And the new things she'd learned in that time were unbelievable. She was now taking letters in shorthand for all the more prominent men in the company, and had no problems going to check any words she wasn't sure of. She'd been given a practically brand-new typewriter and a fancy, high-backed swivel chair and, contrary to what the lads in the office thought, she found Mr Walton a lovely, understanding man to work for.

'That's only because you're a girl,' Danny Fleming had told her with a sceptical note in his voice. 'He's always nice to the girls, but he can be a real tyrant with the men. He gave Maurice a right going-over this morning for making a mistake on a bill of lading. Maurice was that annoyed he said if it hadn't been the Christmas holidays he'd have felt like telling oul' Walton where to stick his job.'

Heather never knew which way to take Danny because he was always joking and messing around. She decided she would take each member of the staff as she found them. Consequently she kept well out of Muriel Ferguson's way and one or two others. Muriel, she discovered, was constantly moaning about every-thing, and after being stuck with her at the break once or twice, Heather made sure she walked down to the canteen with some of the younger staff. And when she found she was really weakening with her food, she asked Danny or one of the girls to bring her up a cup of tea so she didn't have to put herself through the agonies of avoiding the cake stands.

She looked down at herself now, delighted with the ten pounds she'd lost since starting work. When she'd looked in the big mirror in the Ladies this morning, she had been very pleased with her piled-up hair that Kirsty had helped her with before work, and the pink ruffled blouse and black pencil skirt she was wearing. Both were both sitting perfectly on her – no gaping at the buttons or stretching too tightly over her hips – just sitting perfectly and making her look taller and slimmer with the pink shoes that Kirsty had given her. Eating less had definitely paid off, and she was going to make up for all the nice things she'd missed recently by enjoying everything that was put in front of her today.

She lifted the small, fancily decorated menu card in front of her and read down the list. There were three starters, three main courses and half a dozen choices of dessert.

'What are youse all havin'?' Danny asked the group around him. He listened intently, head cocked to the side, as they all rhymed off their order. Most of them were going for the soup to start and the chicken with all the usual Christmas trimmings.

Danny was still not sure what to pick. 'I don't know whether to have the chicken or the steak.' He paused. 'Och, I suppose I'll be eatin' plenty of chicken over Christmas . . . so maybe I'll just have the steak.'

Heather wondered whether to give everyone a laugh about the

goose that they got sent over from her Uncle Joe in Ireland every year. She and Kirsty joked about it with their friends, as several of the others had relatives in Ireland with farms as well, who sent poultry over.

This year's goose had arrived as usual, carefully wrapped in reams of strong brown paper and tied with rough, thick string, the kind of hairy string that hurt your hand if you had to carry a parcel by it for any length of time. And no matter how carefully Uncle Joe wrapped the goose, the wrapping didn't last long. Every year without fail, the poor goose arrived bloody and battered with the string hanging off and the brown paper tattered and congealed with blood and the unfortunate goose's innards. The sight and smell of the sad decapitated bird was quite awful. Thinking and talking about it always made Heather want to heave.

Some Christmases the bird got held up in the post – stuck in some unimaginable place like the dark and dank hold of a ship, amongst thousands of other more ordinary Christmas parcels, or maybe just stuck under a pile of post in the overflowing parcel department of the local depot.

On those annoying occasions, the goose would stink to high heaven, and would leave Sophie and Fintan hovering around wondering whether it was actually safe to eat. One year it didn't arrive until almost New Year and the normally placid postman had complained bitterly about having to deliver such a disgusting, rank package.

'Ye should just have dumped the feckin' thing,' Fintan had told him, mortified at the situation.

'Against rules and regulations, pal,' the postman had said, still bristling. 'You could land in court – tamperin' with Her Majesty's Mail is a serious business. Even if it is a stinking rotten bird.'

'That's the last,' Fintan had said to Sophie. 'I'm going to have to tell Joe not to send any more. We can't have that happening again.'

But as usual, he had never got around to it. And, thankfully, the last few years the goose had arrived in the few days leading up to Christmas in reasonable condition.

Listening to her workmates chatting away about the menu

now, Heather decided against relating the goose story, thinking that it just might put them off their lovely meal. The waiter arrived bearing a big tray of drinks that Mr Walton had ordered for his staff as part of the Christmas treat. There would be a glass of wine with the meal, and then another drink to finish off while they all chatted in the bar afterwards. A few of the lads had rushed off ahead of everyone else and, by the looks of their beaming faces, had downed a few drinks before the rest arrived.

A sherry schooner was put down in front of all the girls at Heather's end of the table. She looked at it now, surprised at the size of the glass. It was far bigger than the little sherry glasses her mother had at home, and it was plain glass, unlike Sophie's, which had *A present from Portobello* written on them and a picture of Portobello beach.

She took a careful sip from the glass and was pleasantly surprised at the sweet taste. She had been going to order her usual lemonade shandy, but changed her mind when the girls all said that since Mr Walton was paying, they should have a *proper* drink. She was looking forward to trying the wine later, so she could go back home and compare it with the time Kirsty had it up in the hotel and Lanark.

After they'd had their soup and main course, everyone pronounced it was all lovely, then sat back sipping the remains of their wine and chatting about their plans for Christmas and New Year. 'How d'you fancy comin' to the Pavillion with us, Heather?' Sara asked. 'A crowd of us are goin' to see Lex McLean the day before Hogmanay.'

Heather smiled broadly, delighted to be included. It made her feel she had really settled in. 'I'd love to come,' she said. 'but I'll have to check about how the trains or buses are running for getting back and everything.'

'You could always stay the night at our house,' Sarah offered, flicking back her brown hair. 'I've got a double bed to myself.'

'Thanks,' Heather said, smiling again, but not quite knowing how to feel. She and Kirsty had always had single beds, and she didn't know how she would react to sleeping next to someone else. 'I'll find out what's arranged at home and let you know.'

Danny drained the last of his wine, making a loud, satisfied noise. 'If Heather doesn't want to stay,' he put in, 'then ye can put my name down to stop overnight, but I canny promise that I'll keep to my own side of the bed!'

'Do I look that desperate?' Sarah said, grinning and giving him a push so that he fell against Maurice, who gave him an even heftier push back.

Then the desserts arrived, and the younger group at the bottom of the table looked at their own then had a good look at everyone else's.

'Och, I wish I'd gone for the trifle,' Danny moaned a touch dramatically, craning his neck to see what the people at the other end of the table had. 'The Christmas puddin' is that tiny you need a microscope to see it!'

He dug Sarah in the ribs and then caught the attention of the other girls. 'Watch this,' he said, winking and with a slight slur in his voice. 'I think I'll put the wind up oul' Frosty Ferguson.'

'Oh, don't dare!' Heather said, half-laughing and half-afraid.

Danny put his elbows on the table and leaned forward. 'Hey, Muriel!' he hissed in her direction. 'Any chance of swappin' my Christmas puddin' for your trifle?'

Muriel Ferguson looked startled. 'What?' she asked incredulously.

'Swappin',' he said, gesturing to his dish of pudding and cream. 'I know you're not as greedy as me, and I thought you might prefer a wee bit of Christmas puddin' instead of that big dish of trifle. I know you're a healthy eater, and all that sweet stuff isn't good for you or yer figure!'

Muriel shook her head disapprovingly, deciding the offer wasn't worthy of a reply. 'It's worse you're getting instead of better,' she told him curtly, and turned to speak to the person next to her as if Danny had just disappeared out of sight.

The girls were all helpless with laugher, and Heather was trying to look as if one of them had just told a joke.

'You've a blidey nerve, Danny Fleming, so you have,' Maurice told him. 'And don't think Muriel will forget it – you'll be paying for it this time next year.'

'Aw, stuff her,' Danny said, brave with the wine and beer. 'I'll not be losin' sleep over it anyway.' He leaned across the table to touch Heather's hand. 'How'd you like me an' Maurice to walk you down to the station later on?'

Heather drew her hand away, but laughed good-naturedly at him so he wouldn't take offence. 'It's only a two-minute walk,' she told him.

'Not if we go slow,' he replied. 'We could go that slow that we could make it last all night.'

'Would you listen to that, patter-merchant!' Sarah scoffed, shaking her head. 'Who d'you think you are, Danny Fleming? James Dean or Frank Sinatra?'

'I can be whoever Heather likes,' Danny said, sighing loudly and leaning back with his hands clasped behind his head. Then, in an unexpectedly good voice, he started to croon, 'I'm Dreaming of a White Christmas', causing uproars of laughter at the table.

Later, as she walked to the Central Station, linking arms with the small, stocky Danny on one side and the lanky Maurice on the other, and Sarah and Marie linking the boys on the outside, Heather couldn't believe how much she had enjoyed herself with the crowd.

She reached the station red-faced and glowing – her dark hair now flowing freely – with Danny singing what he thought was a slowed-up romantic version of 'Jingle Bells'. All the girls were giggling and laughing, the five of them still linking arms as they walked through the station concourse heading for the Edinburgh train that passed through Rowanhill.

The seven o'clock train hadn't arrived yet, so the gate to the platform wasn't open and groups of last-minute Christmas shoppers and other office-party people were milling around the platform entrance.

'We'll stay wi' you till your train comes,' Danny told Heather. 'I wouldn't like to leave you on yer own. You don't know what could happen to a good-lookin' girl like yoursel'.'

She shook her head. 'I'll be fine – honestly. There's no need to keep you all back. There's a good few people waiting here, and I'll probably know some of them.'

Maurice laughed. 'We're better off standing here than back drinking in the pub.' He gestured to his smaller friend. 'If he has much more, I'm going to have to throw him over my shoulder and carry him home!'

As they all stood chatting and laughing, Danny turned to Heather. 'Whit's yer sister like?' he asked, his Glasgow accent more pronounced with a drink in him. 'Is she as good-lookin' as you?' He inclined his head slightly, looking at her from under his brows in the moody manner affected by James Dean and Marlon Brando.

'Better,' Heather said airily, throwing the other girls a glance that she hoped indicated that she needed rescuing, but it went right over their heads.

'Is she dark-haired the same as you?' he said, reaching a hand out to touch the bottom of her hair.

'No,' Heather said, moving out of his reach. 'She's blonde actually. A bit smaller and thinner than me and blonde.' She stood up on her tiptoes now to see if the train was coming in the distance.

'A blonde, did you say? She sounds a bit of all right to me,' Maurice chimed in. 'When do we get to see her?'

Heather started laughing. 'Never – Kirsty's far too busy to be bothered with boys at the minute. She's putting her singing career first.' Kirsty had never said those exact words, but it was obvious where her priorities lay at the moment. She was either up in their bedroom doing strange singing exercises to strengthen her voice or out rehearsing and meeting people with that Larry Delaney.

Eventually, the train appeared in the distance – a small black dot with a flickering light – and then very slowly it snaked its way into the station.

'Right, that's me,' Heather said, joining the moving queue towards the gates that were now being opened. She gave a little wave. 'Have a happy Christmas, everybody – even if the weather forecast says it's not to be a white Christmas!'

'You'll let me know about the show at the Pavillion?' Sarah checked. 'You've got the number of the phone box across the street from us?'

Heather nodded, glancing back at the queue.

'When anybody answers,' Sarah reminded her, 'just say it's for Sarah Fox and they'll run across to the house and get me.'

'Hey, Heather,' Maurice Smith said, suddenly rushing up beside her. Heather turned around to see the lanky, balding Maurice holding a small plastic twig of mistletoe above his head and bending down towards her for a kiss. 'Away you go!' she giggled, but she wasn't quick enough to retreat, and he landed a smacker on her cheek.

'My turn now!' the smaller Danny called, elbowing Maurice out of the way.

'Oh, no!' Heather said, backing off. Then, seeing the hurt look in his eyes, she immediately felt sorry for him. She pressed a finger to the middle of her cheek. 'There,' she told him with an exaggerated sigh.

'You've made my Christmas,' Danny whispered, then planted his warm lips on the spot she had indicated.

It was only when she was getting off the train at Rowanhill that Heather realised that Liz and Jim had been on it too. She concealed her surprise at them being together shopping in Glasgow, and especially being on their own, because Jim had always been loud in his protests about getting involved in female activities like that.

'How on earth did I miss you at the station?' Heather asked them, as they walked down from the station to the village together. It was a pleasant walk as the night was surprisingly mild, more like early October than the latter part of December.

'We were up at the very front of the queue,' Liz explained, with a pained expression, 'because we just missed the six o'clock train and had to hang about for another hour. We were making sure we got on this one OK.'

'Did you have to hang about in the station all that time?' Heather asked.

'No,' Jim said, grinning. 'We went to a pub just down the road and I had a couple of pints while we were waiting.'

Liz dug him in the ribs with her elbow. 'After Christmas you'll have to cut out all the drinkin'.'

'New Year,' he countered, a frown on his face now. 'I'll definitely be having a few drinks over the New Year. You canny *not* drink at the New Year.'

Liz gave a great exaggerated sigh and shook her head at

Heather. 'What is he like?' she said, casting an adoring smile in Jim's direction.

'I'm not the worst,' Jim said airily, moving the heavy carrier bags from one hand to the other. 'Are you OK carrying those other bags?' he checked with her now.

Liz nodded. 'Aye, I'm fine – they're not that heavy.' She turned to Heather. 'I bet you never thought you'd see the day when Jimmy would be actin' the gentleman?'

'Gentleman Jim,' he said, making a little bowing gesture. 'That's what they call me.'

It suddenly struck Heather as they walked along chatting that there was a big change in the way Liz and Jim were getting on. Usually he was all cocky and full of himself, and the one making all the decisions about where they were going and what they were doing. But now Liz seemed more confident and in control, while he seemed far more eager to please. Heather wondered what had brought about the big change.

She motioned towards all the shopping bags they were carrying. 'What on earth have you two been buying? You look as if you've bought half of Glasgow.'

'We went into the Barrows,' Liz told her, with a delighted grin. The Barrows was a huge weekend indoor market in Glasgow that sold absolutely everything a lot cheaper than the shops. 'They've great bargains now wi' it bein' Christmas Eve tomorrow,' she went on. 'They're sellin' loads of things off cheap. You should go in tomorrow yerself.'

'I have all my Christmas present bought weeks ago, and anyway I can't,' Heather explained. 'Lily's comin' home and we're all going to be at the house waiting for her, a sort of welcome-home party.' Her face suddenly became serious. 'I wouldn't miss that for the world, not after all the wee soul has been through.'

'Aye, right enough,' Liz said, looking more serious herself now. 'I got her a small Christmas present from the Barrows, so I'll maybe drop down with it tomorrow. I wanted to have a word with Kirsty anyway.' She glanced up at Jim, as though checking something, and he gave a slight nod.

Heather bit back the words 'What about?', realising that it would appear really nosy. It's just that it was strange that Liz would want to speak to Kirsty when she was Liz's best friend. Kirsty and Liz got on fine, but it had always been Heather and Liz, and they knew most things about each other.

They slowed up as they came towards Liz's house on the main street. 'How's the job goin' in Glasgow? D'you like it as much as the office in Wishaw?' she asked.

'Great,' Heather said. 'They're all nice and friendly, I had a lovely Christmas meal out with them all this afternoon. When you come to the house tomorrow we can catch up on each other's news. My mother will make you one of her famous Advocaat and lemonades.'

'Brilliant,' Liz said, beaming. 'I love them, and I only ever have them at Christmas at your house.'

'Have ye seen Gerry around lately?' Jim asked, trying his best to be casual, but you could tell by his awkward stance that he had been waiting for an opportunity to ask.

'No,' Heather said quietly, 'but then I wouldn't expect to see him. It's not as if we're still going out or anything.' She paused, pushing her dark hair behind her ear. 'I suppose he's busy making plans to go to Australia after Christmas.'

'No,' Jim said quickly, 'he's not going now. He's postponed it till the summer. He decided to take the promotion at work here instead and see how it goes. If it all works out and he decides to stay, he's talkin' about buying a car and everything.'

'You might regret that you finished with him,' Liz put in. 'Especially when you see him driving about in a fancy car. And there are loads of girls after him. I've even had girls I work with askin' all about him.'

'I think you'd still have a chance, if you've changed your mind,' Jim said. 'I don't think he's as keen on any of the other girls he's been going out with.'

Heather suddenly felt uncomfortable. 'That's all over and done with,' she said, looking at her watch. 'I need to go, there's a radio programme I want to catch at nine o'clock.'

'See you tomorrow then,' Liz said cheerily. 'And we'll swap our own Christmas presents then too.'

'Fine.' When Heather turned to give them a wave, she was surprised to see Jim going into the house with Liz. Normally he was in a big rush to get to the pub or the local Miners' Club on a Friday night. She walked on home, mulling over the situation, and still wondering what had brought about such a change in Jim Murray.

'I kept you a bit of fish,' Sophie said, looking up from her Christmas edition of *Woman's Own*, 'and there's some chips cut that will only take ten minutes to cook if you're hungry.' She had just finished clearing and washing up after herself, Fintan and Kirsty's customary Friday-evening meal of fish, chips and peas.

'No thanks, I'll just have a cup of tea,' Heather called from the hallway where she was hanging up her coat and things. 'I ate loads at the Christmas meal and I'm still full.' She came back into the kitchen, where her mother was now pouring them both a cup of tea from a freshly made pot. 'It won't go to waste, I'm sure my daddy will eat it for his supper later. He loves fish between bread and butter.' She sat at the kitchen table beside her mother. 'Has Kirsty gone out singing already?'

Her mother nodded. 'She's out with the band. She's only tonight and another night next week and then she's finished with them.'

'She's done brilliantly getting taken on with that Larry Delaney,' Heather said. 'Although I think she's going to find it very different from all the laughs she's had with the band. This is far more professional and serious.'

'If she doesn't like it,' Sophie mused, 'then she can always leave.'

'She's got to at least try it out though,' Heather said, 'hasn't she? I was in a similar position with the job, and I'm really glad I took it now. Can you imagine my last office taking us out for a fancy Christmas "do" or anything like that?'

'Was it a nice meal?' Sophie asked.

'Fabulous,' Heather breathed, picturing the Christmas tree and the lovely table in her mind all over again. 'It was the nicest place I've ever been in, and the dinner was beautiful.'

Sophie put her elbows on the table now, intrigued. 'What did you all have?'

Heather went over the evening in great depth. 'We had

sherry and wine as well,' she suddenly remembered. 'Mr Walton paid for all the drinks out of his own pocket.'

Sophie looked warily towards the hallway. 'Be careful about sayin' anything about drink to your father,' she warned in a low voice. 'He mentioned to me just the other night that he was sure Kirsty had had a few drinks after she'd been out rehearsing.' She gave a little sigh. 'He wasn't a bit happy about it. He said anything can happen to young girls if somebody gives them drink . . . they can be taken advantage of.'

Heather's brows came down. 'It's Christmas, for God's sake,' she said, shaking her head in disbelief. Her father could come over all awkward about nothing at times. 'I could count the number of drinks I've had in my life on one hand, and I've never seen Kirsty drinking anything with alcohol in it apart from a lemonade shandy.'

'Well,' Sophie shrugged, 'your father worries . . . two young girls goin' out into the world. And even though you're my own, I have to say that you're not two bad-looking girls either.' She looked down at her *Woman's Own*, thinking of some of the articles she had just read. 'Times are changing, and it's not just drink. Look at that young Helen Kelly, barely eighteen and having to get married.'

'Well, there's no fear of that happening to me or Kirsty,' Heather said briskly. 'I want to see a bit of the world before I get tied down, and I'd say Kirsty has bigger ambitions than pushin' a pram around in the next few years.'

'Well, I wasn't suggesting that,' Sophie said, putting her hand out to cover her daughter's. She gave it a little squeeze. 'Oh, by the way,' she suddenly remembered, 'you and Kirsty got a Christmas present each in the post.'

'Who from?' Heather asked, trying to shrug off the feeling of irritation with her parents. Really, she and Kirsty had given them very little to be worried about over the years, and instead of being grateful for that, her mother and father seemed to grow even more protective – especially her father. You'd think he'd ease off a little especially since it was Christmas.

Sophie went to the ribbed-glass kitchen cabinet and brought out a small box wrapped in gold paper. 'It's from your Auntie Claire,' she said quietly, handing it to her. 'She sent us a lovely

Christmas card and a present each for you and Kirsty.'

'That was really good of her,' Heather said, feeling her earlier annoyance draining away, like air seeping slowly from a balloon. 'She hasn't sent anything since she got married, has she?' There weren't that many adults in the family who gave them presents now the girls were older, and those who still did were greatly appreciated. Sophie shrugged. 'She made it quite plain when nobody would go to the wedding that it would be up to us to make the first move.'

There was a little pause. 'Well,' Heather sighed, 'I can see her point. She must have felt really rejected. It must be horrible to be cut off from your family. I couldn't imagine it.'

'Well, it's never going to happen to you, is it?' Sophie smiled. She looked thoughtful then. 'Claire has sent Lily things every year since it happened, because she felt she was too young to understand, and because she's her godchild, but I don't think Mona told Lily who they were from. And there were one or two things that I don't think she even gave her. Pat mentioned something about a doll that Mona threw in the bin.'

'Auntie Mona can be very hard,' Heather said, giving a loud sigh. 'She was terrible to Claire at the hospital; it was really, really embarrassing having to sit through it.'

'She doesn't mean to be,' Sophie said, feeling sorry for her bristly sister-in-law. 'And this Christmas we need to give her a wee bit of leeway, because she's been under a terrible strain.'

'She's always under a strain,' Heather said in a low voice. 'She gets too wound up and has to have an opinion on everything.' She turned the box around in her hands, guessing it was some kind of jewellery because it was the same size and shape as the box that Lily's gold locket was in. She looked up at her mother, smiling now. 'Should I keep it until Christmas Day?'

'It's up to yourself,' Sophie told her, relieved that the tension was disappearing between them. She shook her head, laughing. 'Kirsty opened hers – but then Kirsty's never had any patience when it comes to waiting for presents. She was delighted with it – they're really lovely.' She hesitated. 'The only thing is, she's wearing hers tonight, so you might see it on her if she doesn't know you're waiting.'

'I'll open it now then,' Heather suddenly decided. Carefully, she unwrapped the gold paper and then opened the velvet box to reveal a charm bracelet. 'It's gorgeous!' she breathed, lifting it out of the box. It was the sort of thing she had dreamed of having when she was older and with money to spare. The chain had fairly heavy gold links with a heart-shaped lock on it, and she had four charms already dangling from it – a pair of ballet shoes, a lucky dice, a shamrock and a small cross.

'I felt terrible when Kirsty opened hers,' Sophie confessed, 'because we never even thought to send a Christmas card to them. We didn't have their new address until the other night, and I never gave it a thought.'

'Maybe we could take a run out over the Christmas week,' Heather suggested. 'We could take a nice box of chocolates or something like that. What d'you think? The weather's good for travelling, it's been clear every day this week.'

'We'll see what your father says,' Sophie said cautiously, 'and what the weather forecast is sayin' – it mightn't stay this mild for much longer. Last year we had sudden snow in January and it lasted for weeks.'

Heather held the bracelet up, examining it more closely. 'D'you know, Mammy,' she said in surprise, holding the trinket out for her mother to examine, 'she has even gone to the trouble of having an "H" engraved on the heart.'

'Has she?' Sophie asked, taking it from her. 'Kirsty never noticed that, we must tell her when she comes in tonight, then you'll both know how to tell them apart.' She looked thoughtful for a moment. 'That's just typical of Claire Grace – she always took care over the wee details. Even when she was young, she was always a thoughtful girl.'

Heather's face darkened. 'But isn't it terrible that the whole family has turned against her just because she got married to a Protestant?' She let the charm bracelet trickle back into the box, link by link.

'It's not as simple as that, Heather,' Sophie sighed, hating this sort of discussion with either of the girls, especially around Christmas. 'Religion causes major problems in families, and we're actually not as bad as some.' She paused, trying to find the right words. 'The Graces have always been staunch Irish Catholics, and to have one of their own turn her back on their religion is awful hard for them to take. Especially when it's one of the girls.'

'I still don't think it's fair,' Heather persisted. 'Andy seemed a nice polite man, and he obviously thinks the world of Auntie Claire.'

'That's all true,' Sophie agreed. 'But Claire knew what would happen if she married him – she went into it with her eyes wide open.'

Chapter 28

'Is there *definitely* no snow?' Lily asked, as she was being taken in a wheelchair out to the waiting ambulance. 'I thought we might at least get some snow for Christmas,' she said in disgust. She was all bundled up in trousers and jumper and a woolly pixie-hat, and wrapped in two warm blankets. There would be no risks taken during this short first visit home.

'It's too mild for snow, hen,' the young nurse accompanying her said kindly, as they came to a standstill beside the open door of the waiting ambulance. 'And we don't get snow *every* Christmas. As least we won't be slipping and sliding getting you in and out of the ambulance.'

'Aye, I suppose so . . .' Lily said, but there was an ungracious note in her voice, because she really didn't 'suppose so' at all. Christmas wasn't the same without snow, *everybody* knew that.

'All ready, Miss Grace?' the kindly ambulance driver asked. She giggled at being called *Miss Grace* and nodded, and then he and the nurse came either side of the wheelchair and very gently lifted Lily out.

They carried her up the three fold-down metal steps, their feet clanging as they went, and into the ambulance, where she was then seated on a long, soft bench. It reminded Lily of the kneelers in the church. Something soft on top of something hard.

Then she looked around her at the other two people in the

ambulance – a man about the same age as her daddy and a girl with pale red, straight hair about the same age as Kirsty or maybe even Heather. The girl had a white plaster on her arm and a white sling supporting it.

Lily smiled across at them, thinking how much she was looking forward to being home.

'Are you all right, hen?' the man asked kindly.

'Aye,' she answered, her curls bobbing up and down. 'I'm fine now, thanks.' She wondered what the man was doing in an ambulance; he didn't look as if he had anything wrong with him at all. She scrutinised him a bit more – her eyes narrowed a little – but came to the same conclusion. He didn't look as if he had a single thing wrong with him. Maybe he was just getting a lift home in the ambulance, she decided.

'And are ye lookin' forward to Santie comin'?' the man asked now.

Lily nodded her head vigorously.

The nurse wrapped the blankets tightly around Lily's top half, keeping her weak arms well supported. Then a moment or two later, the ambulance shuddered into life, and set off towards the hospital gates. 'She's a great lassie, this one,' the young nurse said, putting a hand up to check that her navy hat with the badge was still clipped in place. 'I don't know what they're going to do in that ward without her. She kept the whole place going – she was even singing for them all last night.'

'Well, ye see,' Lily said, her blue eyes more expressive now she couldn't use her hands in the same way, 'it was only *easy* Christmas carols, and we learn the *exact* same ones in school every year.'

'And are you a good singer?' the red-headed girl asked, joining in.

There was a little pause while the younger girl thought. 'Well, I wouldn't like to say it *maself* . . .' she said modestly, batting her eyelids. 'It's different if other people say – but if I said I was a good singer, then that would be *really* showin' off.' She paused. 'My big cousin Kirsty is a real singer on the stage, right enough – an' sometimes people say I take after her.'

The man suddenly started laughing, and shaking his head. 'You're a right wee blether, aren't you?' he said. 'I'd say they'll all be glad to get you home for Christmas.'

'I hope so,' she said. 'I've been in it for weeks an' I was just gettin' a bit fed up.'

'And why were you in the hospital, hen?' he enquired.

The nurse lifted her head sharply to look at him, but it was too late.

'That oul' polio thing,' Lily said, very matter-of-fact, looking across at the girl now. She wondered if her arm was broken or just hurt. She decided it must be broken or she wouldn't have the stookie plaster on it.

The man's jaw dropped and he looked mortified at having asked such a tactless question. Polio was not a subject people touched on lightly. 'Och, I'm really sorry, hen,' he said, all flustered, looking from Lily to the nurse. 'I'd never have asked . . . I thought it was just a bad dose of flu. There's a lot of it goin' about.'

'It's all right,' Lily said, wishing she could see out of the blacked-out ambulance window to check where they were. 'The doctor said I'll soon be back to my old self.'

They were all waiting for her. Most of the family was watching for the ambulance from the window in the house, while the two younger lads, Patrick and Declan, were hanging about with a crowd of youngsters by the gate.

Sophie and Fintan and the girls had decided to wait until she'd had a wee while with her own family, but were also watching for the ambulance from their own window.

'You wouldn't believe the crowd that came into the chemist this morning,' Kirsty said, taking a bite out of her roll and cheese. 'All the men – lookin' for last-minute Christmas presents for their wives.' She gave a derisory giggle. 'Half the women in Rowanhill don't know that I ended up picking their Christmas presents for them. They'll all be walking around smelling of the same perfume, for there's not much choice in Simpson's. It's either 4711, Cusson's Lilac Blossoms or Evening in Paris.'

'They're all lovely perfumes,' Heather said. 'I wouldn't mind any of them myself.' She couldn't resist a joke at her father's expense. 'And it's far better than getting a new teapot.'

The three women went into titters of laughter.

'That's nice,' Fintan said, 'laughing at your poor oul' father.' He was laughing himself now, although slightly self-consciously. 'Your mother said she needed a new teapot, so I bought her a nice fancy one – what was wrong with that?'

'If a man bought me a teapot,' Kirsty squealed, 'I'd batter him over the head with it!' Then the two girls fell against each other giggling, while Sophie and Fintan looked on in bemusement.

'There's the ambulance comin' down the street!' Kirsty suddenly said, and the laughter came to an abrupt halt as they all moved towards the front door.

As they waited for the ambulance to pull up, Heather pointed to the H-shaped aerial on her Uncle Pat's roof. 'I didn't noticed that when I came in last night,' she commented. 'But I suppose it was a bit too dark.'

'There's more of them goin' up every few weeks,' Fintan said. 'I think the television's eventually going to take over from the wireless.'

'Mona was complaining that it's not a great picture,' Sophie said. 'There's times it's like faint snow moving across the screen.'

'Well, at least you can listen to it as well,' Kirsty pointed out. She dug her father in the ribs. 'I can't wait until we get one.'

'Well, try and find some patience,' Fintan told her, putting his arm jokily around her neck, 'because you'll be waitin' a while before a telly comes into this house.'

When the ambulance doors opened, a cheer went up from the group gathered round Pat Grace's gate, then everyone fell silent as first the wheelchair was brought out, and then the ambulance driver and the nurse came out carrying Lily, still wrapped in the blankets. She had her eyes screwed up against the piercing brightness of the winter sunlight.

'Move away now, and let her through,' Pat Grace instructed as he went forward to meet the little party from the hospital, Mona only feet behind him. When he saw the small white-faced bundle in the blankets, a big lump formed in his throat. He had been looking forward to her coming home all morning, for some ridiculous reason imagining her running about like her old lively little self. But seeing her now brought the severity of her illness into sharp focus. Seeing the brightest little light in his life being lifted into the wheelchair, just as he used to lift her as a small baby into a pushchair.

'I feel far happier now I've seen her in her own house, and I think she's lookin' quite well, considering,' Kirsty announced after the four of them had been over to see Lily. They were all sitting around the fire, with the radio on in the background, Sophie hand-stitching a hem on her own skirt and Fintan reading a novel by one of his favourite Irish authors, while the two girls were flicking through the Christmas editions of their weekly magazines. 'She's moving her arms and legs much better, and she's well able to sit up now, with a couple of cushions behind her.'

'Thanks be to God and his Blessed Mother,' Sophie said, making the sign of the cross on her chest.

'Did you hear Pat saying about the look on her face when she saw the television?' Fintan put in. He laid his book, spine up, on the arm of his chair. 'He said for once in Lily's wee life she was speechless! Then she started going on about *Andy Pandy* and *The Woodentops*, and all these programmes she been hearing about.'

'That was a great idea,' Heather said. 'It means that she'll never be on her own downstairs in the evening while the television is on.'

'And Mona has warned all the boys that Lily's to choose whatever she wants to watch or listen to on the radio over Christmas,' Fintan laughed. 'It looks like she'll be ruling the roost, the very same as always.'

'Thank God,' said Sophie. 'We'll know she's back to normal when she's bossing the boys and Pat about.'

'And the priest!' Fintan said. 'Did you hear Mona sayin' that he's coming out to the house tomorrow before eleven o'clock Mass to give Lily communion?'

'No, I missed that,' Sophie replied, her eyebrows raised in surprise. 'I must have been chatting at the time.'

'Talkin' about the priest – are any of you going to Midnight Mass?' Kirsty suddenly put in.

'Your father and I thought we'd go in the morning,' Sophie said, looking across at Fintan. 'We've been on the go since early this morning, so we thought we'd head off to bed around ten or eleven tonight.' She yawned now, shielding her mouth with the back of her hand. 'But there's nothing to stop you two from going on your own.'

'Are you going?' Heather checked with her sister. 'I'll go if you're going.' Midnight Mass was usually very nice and sociable. If it wasn't raining, a group of them often met up outside the church afterwards and went back to one of the houses for a cup of tea and toast or maybe a bit of Christmas cake.

Kirsty shrugged. 'OK then, we might as well get it over with, and have a long lie in the morning. Anyway, you always get a good laugh wi' the drunks that come in after the pub.' She went into peals of laughter at the thought. 'D'you remember Michael Murphy last year? He hadn't a leg to put below him, and then he missed the kneeler at Communion and banged his knee onto the floor!'

Heather started tittering at the memory. 'And what about the year the choir got all mixed up and half of them were singing the wrong hymn?'

'Enough now, ladies!' Fintan warned, his face suddenly serious. 'That's no way to be talkin' about the Church on Christmas Eve – it's no way to be talking about the Church at any time.' His eyes flicked from one to the other. 'I'm very surprised at ye both now.' The girls looked across at each other now, realising they'd gone too far. Their father was usually so easy-going that sometimes they forgot that religion was a touchy subject.

He nodded towards Heather. 'You were happy enough going to the Legion of Mary for years.' He looked over at his younger daughter now. 'And up until a couple of years ago, Kirsty, you used to paint the statues for the crib every Christmas.' He stopped for breath, and to calm himself down a little. 'I don't mind the odd little joke . . . but after all the problems we've had wi' poor Lily and everythin' – it's to our religion we should be turning and not making a mockery out of it.'

'Och, you know we were only kiddin', Daddy,' Kirsty said in a low, placating voice.

'You know we're not serious when we're goin' on about anything to do with the Church, isn't that right, Heather?'

'Of course,' Heather confirmed. 'We were only carrying on.'

'Well, you might try to find something more suitable to be skittin' about,' Fintan said, but there was definitely a lighter note in his voice now.

They all halted now as the doorbell went.

'Oh, that might be Liz,' Heather said, getting up from the sofa. She turned back to Kirsty.

'She said she wanted a wee word with you when she was here.'

'What about?' Kirsty asked, surprised. Liz was Heather's friend and although they often went out in a crowd together, she normally wouldn't have anything very private or personal to say to Kirsty.

Heather shrugged. 'I haven't the foggiest what she wants, she never said.' She looked at her mother. 'If it's all right, I'll take her into the kitchen for a cup of tea and see if she wants anything to eat.'

'There's a fancy tin of biscuits in the bottom cupboard that I bought for Christmas, and if you like I'll come in later and make you both a Snowball,' Sophie offered.

'That's awful nice of you!' Kirsty said, her face a picture. 'I made a cup of tea for everybody earlier, and nobody mentioned Fox's biscuits to me!'

'You're not a visitor,' Fintan said, winking over at her, 'and you just have to wait until one comes, like the rest of us.'

Kirsty laughed, relieved that her father had let the argument go.

Chapter 29

Heather and Liz went into the kitchen, where they first of all exchanged Christmas presents and then Liz showed her the Mickey Mouse jigsaw puzzle that she'd bought for Lily. She'd left the end of the Christmas paper wrapping open, so that she could just slide the jigsaw out to show Heather. 'Jim said the best thing to get her was something that other people could help her with – you know with her arms not being as strong as before. He said that it would keep her from bein' too bored either in bed or lying on the couch all day.'

'That was really sensible of him,' Heather said, nodding her head in agreement. 'She loves things like that, and it'll definitely pass the time. I was sitting with her this afternoon, while she was reading one of those pop-up picture books, and she had to have it propped up on a cushion, while she had a cushion under the arm she was trying to turn the pages with.'

'That polio is a blidey curse,' Liz said, wrapping the jigsaw back up again and sticking the ends down with the small roll of sticky tape she'd brought in her handbag. In certain things, Liz was very organised. 'And Lily was lucky, because she looks as though it's going to wear out of her system. We had a cousin from England that had it about five years ago, and he was in one of those iron-lung things for ages.' Her voice dropped. 'But he's never been right since. He's in a wheelchair and he can't walk or anything.'

'Well, the doctors are keeping a close eye on Lily,' Heather reassured her friend, 'and they said that all the right signs are there for a good recovery.' She bent down to the bottom cupboard and took out the gold biscuit tin.

'Well, I'm delighted for her,' Liz said now. She tied the red string she'd brought around the wrapped jigsaw puzzle now that her friend had inspected it and deemed it suitable. 'I'll leave that on the windowsill,' she said now, 'and I'll drop it in at Mona's on my way home.'

'So what's brought about the big change in Jim?' Heather asked as she struggled with the strong tape that ran all the way around the seal on the biscuit tin.

'What big change?' Liz said, a defensive look creeping into her grey-blue eyes. She took off her black-and-white checked wool jacket and hung it on the back of the kitchen chair, then she sat down with her thin legs crossed.

'Well,' Heather said, going into the drawer for a knife, 'for a start, you're always complaining that he never seems keen on going into your house, and yet he went in quite happily yesterday.' She found a small bone-handled knife. 'And secondly, he was far nicer to you than he usually is.' She glanced at her friend's tight face. 'And don't go getting all annoyed with me for saying it, because it's you that tells me all these things.'

A blush came to Liz's face, and she gave a small embarrassed laugh. 'OK,' she said, nodding, 'maybe there is a wee bit of a change in him . . .'

'Well?' Heather said, waiting. She tucked her wavy dark hair behind her ears, and then attacked the sticky tape around the biscuit tin with the knife.

'Can you keep a secret?' Liz said, looking anxiously at the door that led out to the hall. 'We don't want anybody to know until tomorrow.'

Heather put the knife and the biscuit tin down on the table, and turned to give her friend her whole attention. 'What?' she asked, not having the foggiest idea as to what her friend was talking about. 'What's going on?'

'You're not going to believe it,' Liz said in a softer voice now. 'Jim's asked me to get engaged.'

Heather's mouth opened and shut in shock. 'Oh my God!' she said, not knowing quite what to say. This was the last thing she'd expected, because the last few times she'd spoken to Liz, she'd been convinced that Jim would finish with her and start spending more time in pubs and at the dancing with Gerry.

'Well,' Liz said, with an injured look on her face, 'you might say *Congratulations* or something like that . . .' Her head and shoulders drooped now, the way they always did when she was upset.

Heather immediately felt guilty. 'Of course I'm pleased,' she said, leaning across to put her arms around her friend. 'If it's what you want, then I'm delighted for you.'

Liz lifted her head and looked Heather straight in the eye. 'It's what I've always wanted – I've loved Jim since we were at school together.' She paused. 'You know I've always loved him.'

'Well, if he's asked you to get engaged,' Heather said brightly, 'then he must love you a lot as well – so it's absolutely brilliant news.'

'What's brilliant news?' Kirsty said, coming in the door. Her blonde curls bounced as she looked from one to the other. 'Come on, come on!' she demanded. 'What have I missed?'

Heather shot a glance across at her friend, not wanting to say anything she might be blamed for later. If Liz wanted to tell Kirsty all about it, then that was up to her.

'Oh, I'm awfully sorry – I've obviously butted in on some highly confidential information,' Kirsty said, rolling her eyes, and closing the kitchen door tightly behind her. She sat down at the table beside them now and waited. She knew eventually that something would be said one way or the other.

'You won't breathe a word?' Liz said at last, two pink dots appearing on her cheeks.

'You promise, Kirsty?'

'Of course I promise,' Kirsty said indignantly. 'Who am I goin' to tell anything to?'

'Plenty of people,' Liz said, looking at Heather knowingly. 'You work in the local chemist's for a start, and it's the kind of place everybody yaps about everybody else in.'

'Everything that goes on in the chemist's is professional and confidential,' Kirsty said indignantly, prodding her finger on the table for emphasis. 'It's just like the doctor's. I would be sacked on the spot for talking about customers – we're not allowed to discuss the prescriptions they come to get filled or anything like that.'

'Well, that's good to hear,' Liz said, sounding just slightly impressed, 'because that's exactly how it should be. Who wants the whole village knowing if you've got piles or verrucas?'

'Anyway,' Kirsty went on, ignoring the jibes, her eyebrows were meeting in the middle with curiosity, 'what's this big secret?'

Liz took a deep breath. 'Jim bought me a ring in Glasgow yesterday – an engagement ring.'

'What!' Kirsty exclaimed, her eyes growing bigger. 'I don't believe it. That's some bolt out of the blue.' She looked across at Heather. 'Did you get a big shock when you heard too?'

'Well, I suppose I was a wee bit shocked . . . but I'm delighted for them both,' Heather said diplomatically, getting up again to finish opening the biscuits, and pour out the tea.

'There's plenty of people get engaged out of the blue.' Liz suddenly felt slighted for the second time that night. The pink dots of awkwardness grew larger on her cheeks. 'And it's not as if we've only been going out a short time. It's been years on and off.'

'Aye, and sometimes more off than on!' Kirsty joked, then seeing Liz's agitation growing she smiled broadly and hurriedly added, 'Well, congratulations. I'm delighted for you both. Are you havin' a party or anything?'

'My mammy and daddy thought we might invite people in for a wee drink around the New Year to celebrate.'

'You should have a big party in the church hall and make a right do out of it,' Kirsty suggested. 'You've big enough families on either sides, and you could give all your friends like us a good night out. Couldn't she, Heather?'

'Well, it's up to them what they want to do,' Heather said, lifting down three mugs.

'We thought there was no point in wastin' money on the engagement,' Liz said, her voice sounding slightly strained now. She paused, growing redder and hotter by the minute. 'The thing is – we don't really want to wait. There's nothin' to hold us back ... so we were actually thinking of gettin' married early on in the year.'

There was a little silence, during which Heather poured the three cups of tea and made sure she avoided catching Kirsty's eye. She knew her sister would be thinking the exact same thing as herself. Then, for a split second, Heather wondered if she was really understanding the conversation that was taking place. Maybe she was putting the worst interpretation on it. She decided it was best to say nothing for the moment, and let Liz explain it all without interruptions. She turned back to occupy herself again with the opening of the biscuit tin, and reached for the knife.

'That's what I wanted to speak to you about,' Liz went on. 'I wanted to ask you if you and the boys would play for us at the wedding?' She drummed her nails gently on the kitchen table, a habit she had when she was anxious. 'I know you're splitting up from them, but you're still doin' odd nights, aren't you? I'd like them because they're local.'

'Well, sort of. It all depends on what Larry's got booked up for me. Have you got a date in mind?' Kirsty said, all businesslike, as if all of this wasn't the biggest surprise that had descended out of the blue. Being businesslike, the way she always was when people approached her about playing at private functions, was the only way she could handle this particular conversation. Otherwise, she was afraid she might start to laugh or say something stupid.

'How early would you have a Saturday free in February,' Liz ventured in a small voice, 'or even late January?'

Heather stifled a sigh of satisfaction at finally opening the biscuit tin, not wishing her friend to mistake the sigh as some comment on her news. Then she took the layer of grease-proof paper out of the box and stared down at the contents. There was a lovely, luxurious mixture of dark, milk and white chocolate-coated biscuits in every shape and size. Before she could stop herself she had lifted a small hexagon-shaped dark chocolate biscuit and popped it whole into her mouth.

As soon as she bit into the chocolate delicacy, she felt a slight pang of guilt at breaking out before Christmas Day as she'd promised herself. But as she placed the open tin on the table in front of her sister and her friend, she decided that the sweet biscuit was in some way medicinal – necessary to get her through this awkward situation. Whether it served the purpose of keeping her tongue quiet and unable to ask all the questions that most people would ask – whether it was the soothing chocolaty sweetness that made the awful situation more palatable she didn't really know. All she knew was that the biscuit made her feel slightly more calm and relaxed, and that was very necessary for the moment. She went to the pantry to get the milk for the tea.

'Pity you hadn't come around yesterday before I saw Larry,' Kirsty said, 'because he has a list of all the dates we have booked over the next few weekends. He said he would bring me some music over Christmas, so I'll check with him then or I might even give him a ring on the phone.' She paused. 'Have you any idea where you're havin' the wedding?'

'Jim's going to have a word with the priest about the chapel hall,' she said quietly, 'and if that's booked up he's goin' to try the Miners' Club.'

Kirsty nodded and smiled. 'Och, well,' she said, 'it sounds as if you're all organised.' What else was there to say? She pulled the biscuit tin towards her to examine the choice.

Heather put a cup of tea in front of Liz and then she put another at her sister's elbow. 'Help yourself to biscuits,' she offered, going back to the worktop to get her own cup.

Kirsty pointed to her mouth, into which she had just stuffed a white chocolate circle. 'Thanks very much, but I've already helped myself!' she said, laughing through the crumbs.

'What's your engagement ring like?' Heather asked, trying to sound all excited – excited in the way she would have done in any other circumstances. Excited in the way she would have been if her friend wasn't having a shotgun wedding.

Sophie had come in and made them all their glass of Advocaat and lemonade and cut them all a slice of Christmas cake, and a while later Heather got another surprise as she saw her friend off at the door.

'I wanted to ask you if you'd like to be my bridesmaid,' Liz said in a low voice, fearful of Sophie or Fintan overhearing. 'Since I've only got two brothers, and you're my oldest friend . . .'

'I'd love to,' Heather said, giving her a hug. 'And I'm delighted and honoured that you've asked me.' She reached back into the coat-hooks in the hall and lifted Kirsty's working duffel coat. 'I'll walk down the road to Mona's with you,' she said, pulling it on.

'There's only one thing about the wedding you might not like,' Liz said quietly as they walked along, their breath coming out in small white clouds in the cool, still December air.

Heather's throat tightened as she waited to hear confirmation of her friend's pregnancy.

'Jim's asked Gerry to be the best man . . . and I know you won't feel very happy about it.' There was a little pause. 'They've been friends for years, and it wouldn't be fair to make him choose somebody else. You see, Jim's got a funny feeling that Gerry might still go off to Australia, and if that happens he might never see him again.' She rushed on, obviously anxious. 'You know Jim thinks the world of him.'

'It's your wedding day,' Heather said softly, hiding her true feelings about the situation very well, 'and I'll agree to whatever makes you happy.'

'Oh, you're a brilliant pal!' Liz said, her voice sounding all emotional. 'And some time soon we'll get a chance to have a decent chat about everything ... Are you goin' to Midnight Mass tonight?'

'Aye, Kirsty and I are going,' Heather confirmed, thinking that Liz might invite her back to the house for a heart-to-heart after Mass.

'Well, I might see you there,' Liz said. 'Then me and Jim and my mammy and daddy and the boys are invited over to my Auntie Mary's for a glass of that terrible dandelion wine she makes every year. It's just a family thing like.'

It wasn't going to be tonight, Heather thought. Liz wasn't going to say anything tonight about expecting.

Chapter 30

❦

Heather was in the kitchen in a little world of her own, ironing a blouse for Midnight Mass. Her thoughts kept flitting around, and she was half-thinking about her friend's dilemma and half-listening to the seven-thirty news when the doorbell rang. When it went for the second time, she realised that nobody else was going to answer it and went rushing down the hallway to get it. She remembered then that her parents had gone to Mona and Pat's for a television programme and Kirsty had said she was going to have a bath.

'Is Kirsty there?' a rich, well-spoken Irish voice asked. 'I was just passing and I thought I'd drop off this music I'd promised to give her.' He put his hand out. 'I'm Larry Delaney, by the way . . .'

'I'm Heather . . . Kirsty's sister,' Heather said, looking up at him. He had his heavy winter coat loose over a wine-coloured polo-necked sweater, a navy tartan scarf draped casually around his neck. It was the sort of style that Gerry had aspired to, but Heather instinctively knew that this older man's clothes came from a more expensive tailor than Gerry's.

Larry smiled in an open, friendly way at her, and she suddenly she felt all flustered and lost for words. She put her hand out to meet his, and was surprised by the warmth and strength of his handshake. 'Come in,' she said, opening the door wide, 'and I'll run upstairs and tell her you're here.'

Kirsty was sitting on the bed in her dressing-gown with a towel wrapped around her damp hair, the wardrobe door flung open wide as she decided what she would wear to church. She wanted to look her best for tonight, as going up the aisle to communion at Midnight Mass – where everyone was dressed in their winter best – was like running some kind of fashion gauntlet. It was the very same at Easter when anyone who could afford the latest spring fashions and fancy hats took the chance to show them off.

'That Larry Delaney is downstairs in the hall,' Heather said in a breathless voice. 'You'd better come down to see him.'

'Oh, that's brilliant,' Kirsty said, smiling. 'I can check out those dates for Liz's wedding while he's there.' She stood up now, taking the towel off her head, and shaking out her thick, curly hair. She reached for a brush on the dressing-table to tame it down a little.

'Surely, you're not coming down in your dressing-gown, are you?' Heather asked, frowning in disapproval.

'I'm decent, amn't I?' Kirsty stated, dragging the brush through her hair and wincing as it caught on the odd damp tangle. She pulled the tie-belted towelling gown tighter around the waist and checked that it wasn't in any way low or revealing at the chest. 'It'll take me ages gettin' dressed, and you'll have to sit chatting to him until I'm ready. Anyway, he only wants to drop somethin' off, so there's no point in me wasting time getting all dickied up just to speak to him for a couple of minutes.'

'Are you not embarrassed at the thought of him seeing you like that?' Heather said, knowing she would die rather than be seen by a lad in her dressing-gown. It just didn't seem right.

'Not a bit,' Kirsty replied airily. 'Doesn't my daddy see me like this every night of the week?' They moved towards the bedroom door. 'I'm sure he's got sisters of his own,' Kirsty said as they went out into the hall, 'and at his age, he's not likely to see anything he's never seen before!'

'You're unbelievable!' Heather hissed, starting down the stairs.

Kirsty began to giggle as she followed behind, and then quickly stopped herself when she looked over the banister and saw the top of Larry Delaney's dark head.

For the first time ever, Kirsty saw her new manager look slightly disconcerted when he realised he'd come at a bad time. 'Oh . . . I'm sorry for disturbing you now, Kirsty,' he blustered, his Dublin accent more pronounced than normal. He held up a large brown envelope. 'I was passing by Rowanhill and I thought I'd drop off the music for 'This Ole House' and 'Only You' that I'd promised you. You said you'd like to look over the words during the Christmas holidays.'

'Oh, that's really decent of you,' Kirsty said, beaming at him and thinking how he was always as good as his word. When Larry said he would do something, you could always guarantee that he would. She motioned towards the living-room door. 'You can't stand out here in the freezin' cold – come on into the living-room where it's warmer.'

'No, no,' Larry said, holding his hand up. 'I only called for the minute, and I don't want to be disturbing your family on Christmas Eve.'

'There's only me and Heather in,' she said, touching him on the elbow, 'come on in and have a wee drink at least. My mother would go mad if I let you go without something.' She moved down the hallway towards the door into the living-room.

'No, honestly,' he protested, reaching into his coat pocket. 'I haven't time, I need to get back to Motherwell . . .' He held out a small rectangular-shaped box wrapped in very classy unusual paper. 'I wanted to give you this . . . I thought it would give you that little bit more confidence for New Year's Eve.'

'What is it?' she said, not quite sure whether it was something practical to do with her singing or a proper Christmas present. When she took it from him she noticed the House of Fraser logo on the wrapping.

He smiled. 'It's just a little gift . . . and you're not allowed to open it until after twelve o'clock.'

'Oh, I feel terrible,' Kirsty said in a low voice, 'I never thought . . .'

'It was just a last-minute thought when I was in Glasgow this afternoon,' he told her gently, 'and as I said, it'll just help to give you that little boost when you're all dressed up.' He paused. 'You're happy with the dress you picked?'

'Definitely,' Kirsty said, her head bobbing enthusiastically. 'It's gorgeous.'

'Grand,' he said, turning towards the door. 'Are you doing anything on St Steven's Day night?' When he saw the confused look on her face he corrected himself. 'Boxing Day . . . I still think of it in Dublin terms.'

'Och, I should have known that, my daddy often calls it that, too.' She paused for a moment. There was a dance on in one of the chapel halls in Newarthill, but she still wasn't sure who was going. Liz had told Heather that Gerry was going so she wasn't too keen on it. 'I've nothing big planned,' she told him, shrugging her shoulders.

'There's a band playing at the Trocadero in Hamilton with a lead female singer, and they're supposed to be really top stuff. I wondered, if you were free, if you fancied going just to see what their programme is – see if we can pick up any ideas.'

'That's great,' Kirsty said. 'It sounds like a good night out . . . better than anythin' else I've got planned so far.'

'Are you sure?' he checked, opening the outside door again. 'I don't want you to think that I'm taking over your social life – a young girl like you might prefer something that's a bit more of a laugh with lads and girls your own age . . .' For a moment Larry Delaney actually sounded a little bit uncertain.

'No,' Kirsty said, with a definite note in her voice. 'I think it's a great idea, and it's a far nicer place than the other ones I'd be going to.'

'OK,' he said, smiling warmly now. 'I'll pick you up around

half past six on Monday night.'

'Oh, Larry,' Kirsty suddenly remembered, 'I want to check a few dates with you around the end of January.'

Chapter 31

❧❦❧

'I'm still in a state of shock,' Heather said in a low voice, as both sisters lay awake in the early hours of Christmas morning, the usual excitement over the big day keeping them awake as well as all the shocking news about their friend. 'I can't believe that Liz would go to that length just to keep a boyfriend. I'm sure she wouldn't be that stupid.' She paused. 'You don't think that we're jumping to conclusions, do you? She didn't actually say why she's in such a rush about everything.'

'Are you kiddin'?' Kirsty scoffed, not having the same emotional attachment that her sister did. She leaned up on her elbow now, facing Heather's bed. 'She's definitely expectin',' she hissed. 'No doubts about it. It was written all over her face.'

'It's just that her and me had a conversation about the girl Kelly who got married a few weeks back, and she sounded as though it was the last thing she'd let happen to her.'

'Famous last words,' Kirsty said, like a woman of the world. 'Well, she's certainly changed her tune. I'm not a bit surprised, she's been all over Jim Murray since day one. All she's ever wanted is a ring on her finger. It was just a matter of time until it happened.' She paused. 'Are you going to mention it to my mammy?'

'Not yet.' Heather sighed. 'I mean, we don't really have any definite proof, do we? And it doesn't exactly look good on me, when she's my best friend, does it? She might think I've been getting up to things I shouldn't have, too. And I don't fancy mentioning things like that in case she tells my daddy. He was a bit on the touchy side about us laughing about chapel tonight, wasn't he?'

'Och, you know what he can be like at times.' Kirsty said dismissively.

'Well, I just don't want to have everybody going on about Liz to me.'

'Don't be so daft,' Kirsty said, in her forthright way. 'You're not Liz Mullen's keeper, are you? What she gets up to is her own responsibility and nobody else's.' She moved her elbow closer to the edge of the bed and lowered her voice. 'Did you know she was gettin' up to no good wi' Jim?'

'No, indeed I did not!' Heather said indignantly. Trust Kirsty to come out with something like that. 'That's why I couldn't believe my ears when she was sitting down in the kitchen tonight. I nearly died!' She gave a weary sigh. 'As far as I know, they've never had any time on their own together for them to get up to anything. They're always at the pub or the dancing, and usually in a group, so where could they go to get up to anything?'

'How about behind a wall or in the chapel grounds like plenty of other couples?' Kirsty suggested, then suddenly went into a fit of giggles at the thought. She started to laugh so hard that she had to turn her face into the pillow for fear of waking her parents. 'If my daddy heard me sayin' that about the chapel he'd skin me alive!' she tittered.

'I'm going to sleep,' Heather said rather huffily. 'I'm glad you're finding it all so hilarious, Kirsty Grace, because it happens to be my best friend you're laughing at, and I'm afraid I don't find anything at all funny about it. Liz is far too young to be getting married and havin' a baby.' Her voice dropped. 'And I'm absolutely shocked at her getting up to all those things with Jim. It's disgusting, so it is . . . and it's against all the Church's teachings.'

Kirsty laughed even harder now. 'You're soundin' just like my Auntie Mona!'

Heather reached down to the floor for the little black and white teddy bear that lay on her pillow during the day. 'Shut up, you!' she hissed, throwing it across the room at her sister.

After a few minutes' silence, Kirsty started again. 'Are you still awake, Heather?'

'No,' Heather whispered back, as they used to do as children in the same beds in the same room. 'I'm fast asleep.'

'So am I,' Kirsty giggled. 'No, seriously, what did you think of Gerry Stewart bein' at Mass with the new girlfriend? He looked dead proud as he was parading her up the aisle at communion time.'

'I'm absolutely delighted,' Heather said honestly. 'I feel a lot better knowing that he has somebody else to take up all his attention, although I must admit that I felt a bit awkward when he marched over to introduce her to us.' She paused. 'He obviously wanted to show her off, with her being so good-looking and very fashionably dressed.'

'I think there's something a bit weird about it all,' Kirsty mused. 'I'm not a bit convinced.'

'Convinced about what?' Heather said, losing track of the conversation. She was actually beginning to feel tired, and in a minute she would stop answering Kirsty, and eventually her irritating sister would give up and they would both go to sleep.

'The way he kept watchin' you . . . as if he was doing it all to see what your reaction would be.' Kirsty paused, trying to work it out. 'As if he's only doing it to make you jealous.'

'What?' Heather said, suddenly more alert. 'Surely you're not saying that Gerry Stewart would go to all the trouble of taking another girl out for *weeks* just to make me jealous?' She gave a little snort of disbelief. 'I think you're havering, Kirsty Grace. Are you sure my mammy didn't put too much Advocaat in your Snowball?'

'There's no fear of that,' Kirsty said, 'although I sneaked a wee drop more in when she was out of the kitchen.'

'Oh, you're the absolute limit,' Heather laughed. She halted, suddenly remembering. 'Hey, imagine that Larry fellow buying you that expensive perfume from Fraser's!'

'I know,' Kirsty whispered. 'I nearly died when I opened it and saw it was Chanel No. 5. I think I've only ever seen it advertised in magazines, I don't remember ever seeing it in any of the shops in Motherwell or Wishaw or anythin'. And we definitely don't sell it in the chemist's.'

'It must have cost him a bomb,' Heather mused. 'And he must have plenty of money. I saw his car from the bedroom window and it's a really fancy one as well.' She paused. 'And he's definitely got high hopes for your singing, Kirsty, to spend all that time on you.'

'He's a good manager,' Kirsty said, 'and although he's a real businessman, the more you get to know him, the more ordinary and down-to-earth he seems. At first, I used to be a bit nervous when I was with him, but now I feel quite relaxed. It's funny how people can be totally different when you get to know them.' She turned over onto her back, staring up at the faint circles of lights on the ceiling that shone in from the street lamppost, musing over her changed opinion of Larry Delaney.

Ten minutes later, the bedroom was in both darkness and silence as the girls lay awake with their own private thoughts.

Heather was once again thinking over the situation with Liz, trying to work out how her best and closest friend could have been having a proper *sexual* romance with Jim Murray without her even knowing. They had shared everything from when they were young girls, and she'd thought there wasn't one thing about Liz and Jim's romance that she hadn't known about up until this evening's shock.

She had presumed the romance between Liz and Jim would go the same way hers and Gerry's had gone. That one of them would outgrow the other and that it would all fizzle out. Maybe even a more dramatic ending, because Heather knew that Liz was mad about Jim and, as she'd said tonight, she always had been.

This was obviously what the whole thing was all about – Liz had demonstrated to Jim just how much she loved him by letting him do all those unbelievable, *personal* things to her, because her friend couldn't possibly have enjoyed it. The things that Heather always shied away from – didn't want to think about. The things that almost frightened her, like when Gerry kissed her too roughly and pressed his hard body too close to hers. The personal things that she would put off worrying about until she got married.

The news had made Heather feel all funny, as if she hadn't really known Liz at all. In a way – which she knew was childish and stupid – she felt rejected. It was as if Jim Murray had suddenly stepped into her shoes as Liz's closest friend and confidante, and was now the person who knew everything about her life. The thought of that made Heather feel very silly and, worst of all, sort of lonely.

Who was she to go out with now? Of course she always had Kirsty, and as they got older, she enjoyed her younger sister's company more and more. She wasn't quite so irritating these days, and at times could be quite entertaining and sensible. And Heather still had other friends from school and her old office. But it wasn't the same – she still needed a *best* friend, somebody she could moan to about Kirsty and the rest of the family. Somebody she could let off steam with who wouldn't remind her about it in the morning. Somebody who would share the ups and downs of working life and love life with her. Somebody who had been Liz.

Heather turned her face into the pillow and tried to sleep.

Kirsty had drifted into a sleep more quickly than her sister and within a short while found herself entangled in the strangest dream. She awoke some time later with a start – hot and sweating – and then sat bolt upright when she remembered what she had been dreaming about: Larry Delaney. *Oh, my God . . .* she thought, horrified as the recalled pictures ran through her mind. She dreamt she had been in bed with him . . . and not only in bed with him. She dreamt she had been lying *naked* in his arms!

She sat in the dark for some time, head in her hands, trying to work out why on earth she had been dreaming about her manager in that way. Not for even one minute before had she thought about him in anything other but a business sense. So why on earth had she had this weird, sexy dream about him? A sexy dream in which she had felt very relaxed and comfortable lying next to Larry Delaney with no clothes on. Even though the bedroom was winter-cold, little beads of perspiration started to form on her hot forehead.

Kirsty had never come close to anything in real life that resembled the situation she'd just been dreaming about. She'd often thought and *wondered* about sex, but decided it wouldn't be an issue until the time came around when she met someone she really, really fancied. And so far that had never happened.

She'd gone out with boys from school and then later fellows

she'd met at the dancing, but it had always been more of a laugh than anything and usually ended up with her being bored by the boys' immature chat and she found she preferred the company of her girlfriends.

As she thought about it now, it gradually dawned on her that the nights she and Larry Delaney had spent together rehearsing her songs, with Larry encouraging her and suggesting this and that change, had been some of the most enjoyable nights she'd spent with any man.

Yes, it had been hard work and at times she felt it was all beyond her – that she didn't have the ambition and confidence in herself that Larry Delaney had in her. But the more she rehearsed and pushed herself, the better she felt. She discovered that whilst she had been afraid initially, she now looked forward to trying out new things, and stretching her talents to the limit. When she was with him, she felt that anything was possible.

She lay back in bed, pondering the whole thing, wondering if the dream was some kind of indication that deep down she liked or even fancied the older, more worldly wise Larry Delaney. A man who must be nearly fifteen years older than her. A man who she didn't know an awful lot about.

Kirsty felt a little shiver and, suddenly conscious of the chilly winter darkness, she snuggled back down under the warm covers. And when she closed her eyes, she slowly drifted back into the heavy and dreamy world where she once again imagined herself wrapped in the strong warmth of Larry Delaney's arms.

Chapter 32

The morning had started around ten o'clock when the girls got up to collect their childish Christmas stockings – which Sophie still filled with small trinkets she collected over the preceding weeks – and to open their modest piles of presents from each other and their parents. There were no presents from aunties and uncles – apart from Claire's bracelets –

as that had stopped when they left school. Given the number of children in the Grace families, cost was a big factor, and the adults had decided some years back that the younger children were the priority as those now working could look after themselves. As always, on their way downstairs they called Sophie and Fintan to come down and open their presents along with them, and then they switched on the three-bar electric fire to warm the chilly living-room until Fintan had lit the coal fire.

Sitting side by side on the sofa, the girls rummaged through their stockings first, finding bars of Avon soap and tins of talcum powder, a diary each, sets of pens for work and other small odds and ends. Then they started on the bigger presents.

'Oh, brilliant!' Kirsty stated as she held up the pink towelling Marks and Spencer dressing-gown with white embroidery on the collar that she had hinted to her mother about several weeks ago. She watched, smiling, as Heather opened the same size and shape of parcel to reveal an identical blue dressing-gown. The girls weren't surprised at receiving several identical gifts, because as long as they could remember, they had always been treated the same.

Heather held up a rectangular-shaped present. 'Guess which annual?' she said, grinning at her sister.

Kirsty screwed her eyes up, thinking. 'Let me see ... let me see. It must be the ... *Oor Wullie* this year!' she suddenly calculated. The Scottish cartoon book came out every second year, with *The Broons* book on the alternative year. They had received a copy of either one of the annuals every year since they could read the words that went with the pictures, and it was the one Christmas gift which Fintan always took upon himself to organise.

Heather ripped the paper off the present to reveal the *Giles* annual, and they all laughed heartily as Kirsty opened hers which was in fact the *Oor Wullie*.

By the time all the wrapping had come off, between them the girls had presents of romantic novels, gloves, scarves, make-up sets, plus numerous bath-cubes and fancy soap sets from friends like Liz.

Sophie was delighted with the joint gift of a lovely navy and white wool Chanel-style suit from the girls, which Heather had spotted at a bargain price in a shop in Glasgow and they had both paid half for. She went into the kitchen to put on the kettle and the grill for toast for the girls, and was delighted with the lovely smell coming from the oven. She opened it to check on the goose, which had been cooking slowly overnight. After poking and prodding it for a bit with a sharp knife to check how far on the cooking process was, she covered the bird up again and turned the temperature up a bit higher to let it brown while she was at church.

Then Sophie suddenly decided to quickly take off her winceyette pyjamas and pull on the navy suit while she was there. A few minutes later she came back to show her daughters it was a perfect fit on her slim figure, and after hugging them both, declared that she would wear it to eleven o'clock Mass that morning.

Fintan was slightly less effusive but still thankful for the shirt and tie the girls had bought him, along with a miniature of Irish whiskey, which they had given him every Christmas since they were little girls. He would – as he always did – have the whiskey in his mug of tea when he came back from Mass, since both he and Sophie were fasting for communion. The women all sat chatting and examining each others' presents while Fintan raked out the ashes in the grate and started up a fresh fire from the hot cinders, some small pieces of dry wood and screwed-up newspaper.

While their parents went upstairs to get ready for church, the girls went into the cold kitchen to make tea and toast and chat about their plans for the next few days, referring every now and again in whispered tones to the shocking situation that Liz was in. Later, when their mother and father had gone off to Mass and they were on their own, curled up in the chairs at either side of the now-roaring fire, they were able to talk freely.

'I was delighted when Liz asked me to be a bridesmaid,' Heather told her sister, 'but I nearly died when she said that Gerry was going to be the best man. It's not as if I can refuse, it would look terrible, and she might think that I'm just trying to get out of being bridesmaid because she's expecting.' She gave a weary sigh. 'If you were me, how would you feel about having to spend the whole day sitting and even dancing with your ex-boyfriend?'

Kirsty took a bite of her toast and crunched it while she was thinking. 'Blidey annoyed,' she finally stated. 'But with no choice. You've got to do it.' She paused. 'You'll probably get invited along with a partner, so why don't you ask another fella to go with you? It means you've got a ready excuse to go over and sit with him and dance and that kind of thing.'

Heather looked sceptical. 'Who would I ask? And anyway, if I did ask somebody to come with me to the wedding, they would only think I fancied them.' She took a sip of her tea. 'I haven't the foggiest who I could ask . . . and the invitation will likely be just for me. Liz said it's a small wedding, so they won't be looking for single people to bring partners.'

'Well, don't forget *I* might be there if the band's free to play at the wedding,' Kirsty reminded her gleefully, 'so I'll keep a close eye on him.' She paused. 'Maybe Gerry will bring his new girlfriend and then you won't need to worry at all. He'll be too busy looking after her, because she won't know anybody.'

'That's true,' Heather said, her dark head nodding, but she didn't sound wholly convinced. 'It's just that when I met Jim coming off the train with Liz on Friday, he was going on about how he thought Gerry would still be keen if I changed my mind—'

'Och, don't heed that Jim Murray,' Kirsty said scornfully. 'He just wants to see everybody else tied down now, just because he's landed himself in hot water with Liz.' Just as she said that, Kirsty suddenly remembered her dream, and felt all funny thinking about it again. Surely, she didn't really fancy a much older man? How could she?

She wondered now if she should mention it to Heather – just casually ask her what she thought of him, and get the opinion of somebody her own age. But she stopped herself. Heather had only met him briefly once, and didn't know him well enough to offer any kind of opinion. She would only go on Larry's looks and his snappy kind of business manner – the things that Kirsty herself had first noticed about him. Heather wouldn't know anything about Larry's good sense of humour, his intelligence and the lovely cologne that he wore – so maybe it was best to say nothing.

The girls sat opposite another while reading their annuals and dipping into a box of Quality Street, then Heather looked at the clock. 'We'd better get dressed so that we're ready for my mammy and daddy coming back from Mass. They said we'd all go over to Mona's to give Lily her present and see what else she got.'

'There's no big rush,' Kirsty said lazily, her eyes fixed on the cartoon book. She reached across for another chocolate, and then unwrapped the crinkly purple cellophane and popped the caramel and nut sweet in her mouth.

Apart from feeling a tiny bit squeamish with all the chocolate, she was nice and comfortable now by the lovely crackling fire and couldn't be bothered moving even if it was to see Lily. Another ten minutes wouldn't make any difference. 'They'll probably have a cup of tea and something to eat before they go and my mammy will want to check on the goose and everything. You know what she's like.'

'Come on, lazybones!' Heather said, suddenly grabbing the book out of her hand. 'I'll race you up the stairs.'

Chapter 33

Lily Grace was definitely not in a festive mood – in fact, she was decidedly grumpy considering it was Christmas Day. 'That telly's a load of rubbish,' she complained, her perky little nose and eyes peeping out from under the quilt that covered her on the settee. Whiskey was curled up at the opposite end of the sofa, his head resting on her feet. 'I thought children's programmes were on the whole day, but it's only for a wee while. It's a rotten swiz so it is.' The latter comment was one she'd picked up from the new *Billy Bunter* book that her brother Sean had bought her, and moaning gave Lily the chance to try it out.

'Never mind complainin',' Mona told her briskly, knowing that commiserating with Lily only made her worse. She tucked the pink satin quilt tidily around her daughter, and then planted a kiss on her forehead. 'You've loads of other things you got from Santie to keep you occupied, you've got your books and your jigsaws and everything. And there's plenty of children in this street would be delighted to have a television in their house. Now, just read one of yer books and relax.'

Lily tutted and shifted about under the quilt, then she stretched out as much as her stiff, useless legs would allow, causing Whiskey to whimper a protest. 'But my arms get too sore tryin' to hold the books,' she moaned, 'and anyways, I've nobody to play games with, my daddy and the boys are all at Mass.'

Lily had just discovered that she was missing bits of the busy hospital routine, where there was always somebody to talk to and some of the older children to read to her or play games with her. Even if she couldn't actually lift the pieces in games like snakes and ladders, the other person took her turn for her, so she could still take part and follow her own progress. She had physiotherapy sessions where she was wheeled up and down the corridors and then up and down floors in the big hospital lift. In between times, there were nurses and porters coming up to her bed asking her how she was doing and making jokes with her, and some of them even brought her the odd packet of sweets or toffees. The first quiet minutes she'd had in the house now alone with Whiskey and her mother had suddenly made her yearn for the hustle and bustle of the hospital.

'They'll all be back from Mass soon,' Mona said, 'and Heather and Kirsty will be callin' over with Sophie and Fintan.'

Lily immediately perked up. 'Good,' she said, 'I'll be getting my presents off them as well.' She frowned. 'I hope nobody else buys me another daft cookery set. Imagine buying me kid-on pots and pans and things, when I can't even get out of bed to use them! And it's not only that – they're not for a girl of ten. Things like that are for weans that think they're really *cookin'* things.' She gave an exaggerated, weary sigh. 'That was an absolutely useless present!'

'Now, Lily,' her mother warned, her hands on her hips, 'Mrs McLaughlin is an old woman, and it was kind of her to think of you at all. You should be more grateful. I think you're gettin' a bit too spoiled.'

Lily moved further down beneath the warm quilt. 'I don't

care if she's old,' she said in a muffled voice, 'it was still a stupid present to buy me.'

The much maligned goose was a good one. Tender, moist and full of flavour – packed with the traditional Irish potato-and-onion stuffing and surrounded by golden roast potatoes and the usual variety of plain vegetables that the Grace family liked. It was all so good that the girls forgot to make the usual connections between the dreadful, soggy parcel that had been so quickly dispatched to the cold depths of the garden shed, and the delicious, fragrant meat they were now tucking into around the kitchen table.

After the sherry trifle they all moved into the living-room where they listened to the radio for a while. Some time later, after a cup of tea with mince pies and slices of the Christmas cake that Mona baked for all the families every year, Fintan and Sophie moved themselves to go to Pat's for a game of cards.

'Are youse sure you won't come?' Sophie checked with the girls, feeling slightly awkward at leaving them to their own devices on Christmas Day.

Heather shook her head. 'I've been over twice today already, and Lily will be getting ready for bed soon.'

'Anyway, it's boring, and we only end up gettin' told off for laughing and wasting the game,' Kirsty put in. 'But you can tell Lily I'll come over and have a few games with her tomorrow morning.'

When their parents were gone, Kirsty went over to the polished wooden radiogram, took the crystal vase with the plastic roses on it from the top, and lifted up the lid. 'We might as well take advantage of the peace and play a wee bit of our own music,' she said gleefully, 'without havin' to listen to my daddy moaning about it all the time.' A few moments later 'The Yellow Rose of Texas' came belting out and that was followed by Bill Haley and the Comets singing 'Rock Around the Clock'. The sofa was pushed back and both girls got up to dance to the music until they were falling into chairs, breathless with the exertion and laughter.

A while later, as they sat listening to a radio programme, the front doorbell rang.

'Who could that be?' Kirsty said, checking the time on the clock. She got to her feet. 'It can't be my mammy and daddy back yet surely, it's only quarter to eight.'

'Maybe they want to collect something,' Heather suggested. 'Or maybe it's Liz, wanting to have a chat about the wedding again.'

'That'll be interesting,' Kirsty said, rolling her eyes to the ceiling. 'We'll all have to sit around again like stuffed ducks kiddin' on that we don't know Liz is expectin'. If it is her, I'm going into the kitchen to listen to the radio there, I couldn't be doing wi' listening to her yappin' on about how brilliant Jim Murray is.'

She went out into the hallway, and could see a tall, dark-headed figure she didn't recognise through the small panes of glass at the top. Surely it wasn't Larry Delaney again, she thought. She smoothed her hair down and took a deep breath before opening the door.

Standing on the doorstep, looking unusually dishevelled and obviously drunk, was Gerry Stewart.

'Is Heather in?' he said, supporting himself on the door-frame. 'I was out for a wee walk, and I thought I would call in to see her.'

'Well, I don't know how pleased she's going to be when she sees the state of you, and you're lucky my father's not in as well,' Kirsty said, folding her arms across her chest and shaking her head. 'Heather!' she called along the hallway, not knowing whether to laugh or be obviously critical of him. Still, she thought, it livened up a fairly quiet Christmas evening. 'You've got a surprise visitor . . .'

Chapter 34

❧❦❧

ona came back into the kitchen where the rest of the group were watching the last two left in a game of cards. Not wanting to disturb them, she looked back into the living-room where the lads and a few of their friends were sitting in the dark, engrossed in some sports programme on the television. She stood at the door looking at the black and white screen for a while, but not taking in anything that was happening on it. Then, when she heard a bit of cheering from the kitchen, she took it as a signal that the game was finished, and went back in to rinse out the few cups and glasses that were waiting to be washed in the sink.

'That room is that packed with lads, you'd swear you were in at the pictures,' Mona said to Sophie, thumbing back in the direction of the living-room. 'But at least it keeps them all quiet, and you know where they are.'

'It's great,' Sophie agreed, coming over to dry the things for her. 'I don't think it'll be too long until we get one ourselves. I can see Fintan getting more interested in it every time we come over to watch yours.' She lowered her voice now. 'How's Lily?' she asked. 'Has she settled for the night?'

Mona crossed her wet fingers and closed her eyes for a moment as though in prayer. 'Hopefully,' she said, giving a small strained smile. 'I hate to say it, but it's been a mixed blessing having her home. We hardly slept a wink last night, worrying about her – listening to her breathing and our hearts nearly stopping every time she gave a cough.'

'She looked tired when Pat lifted her up the stairs,' Sophie commented, 'so you'll probably all get a good night's sleep tonight.'

'I hope so,' Mona said. She suddenly stopped and then tears started to well up in her eyes. 'I think maybe we were all expectin' too much ... we built ourselves up, and then it's been hard to take it when she's complainin' about everything. She's been going on all evening about how she never got taken in to see Santie in his grotto this year. How could I take her into a big shop in Wishaw or Motherwell? We'd have had to carry her in, and then have everybody gawking at her as if she was some kind of invalid.'

'Sure, you couldn't,' Sophie agreed solemnly.

'She's too young to understand that she's just cross because she's still very weak and sore, and that she's frustrated at not being able to move.' Mona rummaged for a hanky in her cardigan pocket and then dabbed at her streaming eyes. 'We thought havin' her home for Christmas would mean that she was fine ... that she was back to normal. But she's not fine at all, Sophie. She's still a very sick wee girl.'

Sophie patted her sister-in-law's shoulder. 'Don't let things get on top of you, Mona. Lily has improved a hundred per cent since she first took bad, and we all see improvements in her every day.' She gave a little laugh. 'Sure, a few weeks ago she could hardly talk, and now she's chatting away like a wee budgie.'

Mona nodded, looking slightly mollified by the comforting words.

'Was Lily delighted with all her Christmas presents?' Fintan asked, as the game came to an end. 'She has some pile of stuff out there.'

'Oh, indeed she was,' Mona said, smiling now, 'especially when somebody played the games with her. The boys were good, they all took turns playing with her the whole day.' She laughed. 'Poor Patrick even sat playing scraps with her this afternoon, sorting out all her cherubs and angels into piles, and then she had him trying to do some kind of a crochet set. It came with the crochet hooks and wool and everything.' She sighed. 'I don't know who got it for her, but you'd think they'd have more sense than to buy her something fiddly like that when she can hardly lift her arms. She got all annoyed with it, and flung the basket with all the wool and everything across the room.'

'Ah, she'll soon be back to her oul' self,' Fintan said, patting Mona's arm.

'I hope so,' Mona said, 'because you begin to feel as if it's all your fault she's so miserable – as if you should be able to make everything all right.'

Wouldn't every parent like to make everything all right for their family?' Fintan said. 'Especially the little ones – but there's only so much we can do. After that,' he gestured towards the ceiling, 'it's up to the man above.'

'And there's times we'd feckin' well like to know what *He's* thinkin',' Pat cut in. 'Because I'm none too pleased with Him at the minute after what He's done to my poor wee lassie. I might as well tell ye, I'm none too pleased with Him at all.'

'Don't be saying things like that, Pat,' Mona snapped. 'And don't be lettin' the boys hear you either.' She shook her head despairingly. 'It's bad enough wi' all that's already happened in the Grace family to make them toe the line – if they heard you talking such blasphemy we'd have no chance.'

There was a little silence, as everyone pointedly ignored Mona's jibe about Claire.

'Listen, Mona,' Sophie said now, 'why don't you go and sit down at the table, and I'll bring you over a nice hot brandy?' Then, before her almost teetotal sister-in-law could argue, she said, 'It'll do you good, and it'll help you to sleep, medicinal like.'

There was a moment's hesitation. 'If I have one – will you have one as well?' Mona checked.

'I will,' Sophie said, smiling. 'Sure, isn't it Christmas night? If we can't let ourselves go a wee bit tonight, when can we?'

'I just thought I'd come down and have a word with you about Liz and Jim,' Gerry said, as he sat at the kitchen table, drinking the cup of tea that Heather had poured for him. 'I know we're not going out any more, and I'm not trying to get back in with you or anything . . . but you're the only one that knows them as well as me.'

Heather stood with her back to the cooker, holding her own cup of tea between both hands. She had tried to keep Gerry at the door, but he had ended up rambling on in such a loud voice that she felt it was easier to bring him inside for a few minutes. Despite pleading with Kirsty to stay in the kitchen with them, her sister had given a derisory laugh and gone back into the living-room saying, 'He's your visitor – *you* entertain him.'

'I think they're off their heads getting married,' Gerry stated now, his face a picture of misery. 'Jim Murray had no intention of getting tied down – I know that for a fact. He even told me that he was going to dump Liz after Christmas.'

'Well, that was obviously just big talk,' Heather said quietly. 'Fellas often say things like that to their pals, in case they look soft in front of them.'

'I don't care whether he was talking big or not, the fact is Jim's too young and they've hardly got a penny to their names.' He looked up at Heather. 'D'you know where they're going to have to live?' When Heather looked blank, he went on indignantly: 'His granny's spare room! What a start to married life. What do you think of that?'

Heather was silent for a few moments. Surely Gerry knew that they were *having* to get married? 'It's not up to me or you to think anything – that's Liz and Jim's business, and I'm not going to interfere.' She took a sip of her tea, wishing he would just hurry up and go home. 'By the sounds of things they've made up their minds what they want to do.'

'It's more a case of what Jim's being made to do,' Gerry muttered. 'She trapped him into this.'

So he did know. 'Well,' Heather said, picking her words carefully, 'it takes two to tango ... and Jim looked happy enough to me the other night when they were coming back from Glasgow.'

'He's a blidey clown,' Gerry stated. 'It's not what he wants ... he was in tears telling me the other night. He says it'll ruin his life. He said if I had still been going to Australia, he would have come along wi' me.'

'Well, he probably had a few drinks in him,' Heather said pointedly. 'The same way you have now ...'

Gerry pushed the mug of tea away from him, not even noticing that he had spilled drops from it onto the paper Christmas tablecloth. 'You can be awful hard-hearted, Heather Grace,' he said, standing up. 'Surely you don't want your pal to marry somebody that has no feelings for her?'

'It's to be hoped he has *some* feelings for her,' Heather snapped, 'when he's got her into the position she's in now. And anyway it's nothing to do with us.'

He shook his head. 'It's all a blidey mess – them getting

married when Jim doesn't want to. It'll never work out.' He ran a hand through his dark hair. 'If it had been me and you – at least we were suited. At least we would have made a go of it, once we got over this daft notion you have of needing a break.'

'Gerry,' Heather said through clenched teeth, and going over to open the door to the hall, 'get it into that thick head of yours that we would *never* have made a go of anything. It was only a teenage romance and now it's over, just like hundreds of other couples who finish up every week.' She paused for breath. 'And anyway, you have a new girlfriend. You shouldn't even be here talking to me – it's not fair on her. She's a lovely-looking girl and she doesn't deserve to have you visiting an ex-girlfriend.'

Gerry shook his head and muttered something under his breath that sounded like, 'She's nothing . . .'

Heather walked down the hallway ahead of him now, towards the front door. 'I'm going over to visit Lily in a few minutes,' she said, immediately feeling bad about lying, especially when it was about her sick little cousin, 'so it's about time you went home.'

Gerry came towards her, and then as he went to go out the door, he suddenly swung round and gripped her tightly around the waist. 'I love you!' he whispered fiercely, his blazing eyes piercing straight into hers. 'And if Jim Murray and Liz Mullen can make a go of it, then I don't see why we can't.'

'Because I don't love you!' Heather enunciated very slowly, pulling out of his grip.

'I might as well tell you,' he said, letting go of her, 'that I'm not going to give up. I'm going to keep waiting for you until you change your mind.'

'Well, you're wasting your time,' she called after him, 'and don't say I didn't warn you!'

She closed the door firmly, and sent up a prayer of gratitude that neither of her parents had been in to witness the unbeliev-able argument that had just taken place. She felt hot with embarrassment over the whole affair, knowing that Fintan would have disapproved of Gerry being allowed into the house with a drink on him to start off with. And God knows what he would have said and done when he heard the two of them arguing. Heather shook her head, hardly able to believe that it had happened herself. This definitely wasn't the Gerry who she had started going out with all those months ago. This Gerry was a total stranger.

'Did he not even bring you a Christmas present?' Kirsty said, affecting wide-eyed innocence as her sister came storming back into the living-room. She had obviously heard the exchange between Heather and her ex-boyfriend.

'It's not a bit funny!' Heather snapped, her dark hair flying as her head moved in temper. 'And I certainly didn't want any Christmas presents from him.' She strode over to the window, lifting the curtain to check if he was gone. 'I think that fella's gone off his head. You should have heard the things he was saying to me.'

'What kind of things?' Kirsty said, all interested.

'Aw, rubbish about loving me and never letting me go – all that kind of daft nonsense.'

'You should be flattered that he thinks so much of you,' Kirsty responded flippantly, then when she saw the enraged look on her sister's face she regretted not thinking first.

'You're no blooming help!' Heather said, throwing her arms up in the air. 'I'm beginning to feel almost frightened of him . . . I'm beginning to wish I was miles away from Rowanhill, because that's the only way I'm ever going to get rid of him.'

Kirsty's mind flashed back to that night weeks ago when she thought she'd seen Gerry hanging about outside the house, and she suddenly felt a cold chill run through her. But once again, she decided to say nothing to Heather, because it would only make her feel worse than she already did.

The men had been hunted in to join the lads in the living-room, leaving the women to clear up the kitchen in peace, and to allow Mona to get a few things off her ample chest out of their hearing.

'Another thing that Lily keeps goin' on about is Claire.' Mona said, up to her elbows now in hot soapy water at the sink. She kept her gaze straight ahead, although she could see nothing but winter shadows out of the darkened window in front of her.

Sophie continued wiping down the kitchen table, allowing her sister-in-law to approach this difficult subject at her own pace.

Although there had been a few shrouded remarks, this was actually the first time that Claire's name had been mentioned since the visit at the hospital.

'I'm well aware that everybody thinks I'm being too hard on her and that husband of hers, but I've got a family to rear.' Mona rushed on. 'And it's hard enough keeping lads on the straight and narrow with religion, without them having to watch Claire as she swans off disregarding all the Church's teachings and marries a non-Catholic in a public register office.' Mona's voice was now a little thick with the second brandy that Pat had made for her. Noticing that his wife had become that bit fraught, he had quietly replenished their glasses, hoping that it would relax her and help her to sleep when they went to bed that night.

She desperately needed a good night's sleep, but it was something that seemed to be getting more and more impossible to achieve with all the worry over Lily. At the best of times, Mona could be snappy and awkward, running herself into the ground, rushing backwards and forwards to the priest's house while trying to keep her own home up to her increasingly impossible standards of cleanliness.

But there was no telling her. She seemed to just work on her nerves – unable to let up. And she had been worse since Lily's illness, snapping at the slightest little thing or rushing upstairs in tears. And the only time she stopped was when she went to sleep at night, and now even that was being disrupted.

'Look, Mona,' Sophie said, folding the dishcloth into quarters and putting it back in the little bowl by the sink, 'there's no point in going over and over all this business with Claire. It's water under the bridge now.'

'Well, she needn't think she's goin' to worm her way back into our good books,' Mona stated. 'Landing in at the hospital like Lady-blidey-Godiva, with her fancy coat and her fancy presents.' She shook her head. 'After givin' Lily that locket, she sent her another present for Christmas – a charm bracelet. Pat got the post, so I had no option but to give her the present this year to keep the peace. But I might as well tell you, the minute I got his back turned, her Christmas card went into the fire as usual.'

'She sent the two girls charm bracelets as well,' Sophie

said, 'and they were delighted with them. There's nobody else in the family has the money to buy nice things like that, and I don't see why we should make things worse by refusing them. The girls are pleased that Claire thought of them ... and it makes her feel a wee bit better that she's had some contact with her own family. I know Fintan is happier that he's seen her, and it is Christmas after all.'

Mona whirled around now to look her sister-in-law square in the face. 'Tell me honestly, Sophie, does it not bother you what she's done? Do you honestly think you could be all pally with Claire Grace – taking presents from her – and then walk into the chapel, to receive communion, knowin' that we're condoning the fact she's living in sin?'

Sophie shrugged, feeling very uncomfortable with the conversation. 'Religion should be people's own private business. And it's not as if Claire is *our* sister. Live and let live, that's my motto.'

'That's all right.' Mona replied, 'until the problems come knockin' at your own door.'

'Well,' Sophie said, heading out towards the safety of the living-room and the men, 'there's no point in meeting trouble halfway.'

'With two good-looking girls like Heather and Kirsty,' Mona countered, 'trouble could be lurking around any corner.'

Chapter 35

'You're wearing the Chanel perfume,' Larry said, as he held open the car door to allow Kirsty to slide into the passenger seat. 'It smells lovely on you.'

Kirsty smiled to herself, wondering what he would think when he saw the black dress with the low neck and the pink fishtail that she was wearing under her good black swagger coat.

Apart from the night she had been singing in the talent contest, she had always been wearing ordinary, girlish clothes like Heather's suit or her own skirts and jumpers or trousers. This would be the first time Larry had seen her all dressed up for an evening out, and she wondered what his reaction would be.

'Hopefully, we won't have to queue,' Larry told her quietly as they walked towards the crowded doorway of the Trocadero. He tucked his hand under her elbow now, guiding her over to a closed glass door at the opposite side of the entrance from the queue. 'I know the owner and he'd give out yards to me if we pay to get in at the main door.'

'Hi, Larry!' a fellow in a black suit and bow-tie called to them from the head of the queue. He waved them over and then quickly ushered them in through the side door. As they went past the queue, Kirsty thought she heard her name being called, but when she turned around to see who had called it, she didn't recognise anyone in the crowd.

'This is lovely,' she said, taking in the dimly lit, glamorous surroundings, the polished dance floor and the white Christmas tree with the sparkly coloured lights that were all reflected hundreds of times in the mirrored walls. She moved across the thick-pile carpet that surrounded the dance floor with him, to a quiet corner table that would have been snapped up by someone else if they'd had to queue outside. 'Heather was saying she'd read in the paper that they'd just had this place renovated for Christmas. It really is the most beautiful dance hall.' It was definitely the sort of modern place she liked and secretly preferred to the old, very posh hotels like the one she would be singing in on New Year's Eve. The Trocadero gave her a feeling of anticipation – a feeling that anything could happen out of the blue.

This, Kirsty thought excitedly, *is exactly where I want to be. Before the night starts, I already feel happy.*

'Well, I want you to get used to it,' Larry said, pulling out a blue velvet-covered chair for her, 'because it's the sort of place you're going to be singing in often.' He helped her off with her coat, pausing for a split second as he caught sight of her sophisticated dress. 'My goodness . . .' His eyebrows shot up in surprise, then – before he got a chance to say any more – a bow-tied waiter came rushing across to take an order for drinks and then take their coats to the cloakroom for them.

While Larry's attention was taken up with the waiter, Kirsty turned to discreetly check her appearance in the rosy-lit mirror to the side of them. She studied the loosely pinned-up blonde hair that Heather had lightly sprayed in place for her, the ruby-cluster earrings that matched the pink fishtail at the bottom of her dress and the low neckline she had agonised a little over. All in all, she was satisfied with her reflection – more than satisfied. She thought the low lights made her look older and more sophisticated than she'd ever looked before – and tonight, she decided, that's exactly how she wanted Larry Delaney to see her. She glanced around her for a few moments, at the groups and couples starting to fill up the tables, then she turned back towards their own table and suddenly caught Larry gazing straight at her, an unusually serious look on his face. 'You're a fine-looking girl,' he said in a low, slightly hoarse voice, 'and tonight you've really excelled yourself.'

Kirsty smiled at him, delighted with the compliment.

'Of course, it's your voice that's the main thing,' he said, nodding his head. 'But when you're up on the stage, having a good appearance definitely helps ... whether you're male or female.'

'Well, it's quite obvious that you believe in appearances,' Kirsty said, his compliments and the atmosphere in the dance hall suddenly making her feel confident and unusually bold, 'because you're always immaculately dressed yourself.' She paused, studying him. 'You can tell just by looking at the way your hair's cut as well, that you're particular. None of the boys around our way would dream of goin' to half the trouble with their appearance.'

'Well, some young fellas don't—'

'Oh, it's nothing to do with them being younger,' Kirsty told him, her voice rising a little, 'it's just because they haven't got a clue about style and taste. And if they were your age they'd be even worse – sure, they're the kind that get worse with age, not better.'

Larry shook his head and started to laugh. 'You're some case, Kirsty ... some case.'

The waiter came across to them with a whiskey for Larry and a Babycham for Kirsty.

'Thank you,' Kirsty said, holding her glass up to her manager, then she took two big gulps of the drink.

'Go easy on that,' he warned her. 'I don't want your father blaming me for you drinking too much.'

'It's Christmas,' Kirsty told him, 'and anyway, I'm eighteen years old, so it's legal.' She held up the Babycham glass. 'It's not as if it's whiskey or brandy, it's only a light drink.'

Larry leaned towards her, half-amused by her attitude and half-concerned. 'Look, Kirsty ... I don't want to get on the wrong side of your family, it could spoil everything with our business plans.'

'Don't be daft,' Kirsty told him, giggling and taking a deliberately tiny sip from the drink. 'It's not business tonight – it's still Christmas and we're in a lovely place and we're out to enjoy ourselves.'

'OK,' he said, smiling wryly, 'have it your way, but just make sure I'm not held accountable for something I didn't do ...'

The band was good – very good. For a long while Kirsty just sat at the corner table opposite Larry watching the female lead singer – watching how she handled the microphone and how she moved – and listening to how she managed the difficult notes. They sat close together, listening, and when each song was finished, they discussed in great depth how well or not so well the singer had performed it.

A few times when a song she particularly liked started up, Kirsty felt like asking Larry whether they should get up to dance, but something held her back. She felt, really, that if he wanted to dance with her he would have asked. It wasn't her place to ask him. It was a strange kind of feeling, because she loved dancing and rarely missed a dance when she was out with her friends. They always had a stream of lads lined up to ask them to dance, and even on a quiet night she always had her girlfriends or Heather to dance with. Sitting down at the table all the time was a whole new experience for her.

In between watching the band, Kirsty enjoyed watching the girls coming and going to the ladies' room, which was within view at the top end of the hall. Their table was set at an angle, which allowed her to observe the groups of girls going back and forth without being too obvious.

Larry was quieter and more thoughtful than usual, Kirsty reckoned. A few times she tried to make conversation, asking him what he'd done for Christmas and whether he ever went back to Ireland for the festive period.

'Not at Christmas,' he'd said, shrugging. 'There's no point. When my father died my mother moved over to Manchester to live near her sisters, so there's nobody close back in Dublin.' He had elaborated no further.

'So what did you do on Christmas Day?' she asked.

'Friends,' he said, lighting another cigarette. 'I have very good friends in Hamilton.'

'And do you see your mother often?' she asked, intrigued that he would prefer to spend Christmas with friends as opposed to his family.

'Often enough,' he said. 'I'll have a few days down with her in the New Year.' He took a drag on his cigarette and then turned towards the band again.

Kirsty was just wondering whether it would appear very nosy if she asked him more about his family, when she heard her name being called. She turned around and there, waving across the dance floor at her, was Eileen Connor, a small dark-haired girl who used to work in the chemist's shop with her, until she got promoted to a bigger shop in Motherwell.

'I thought it was you!' the girl said, rushing over to her now. 'I hardly recognised you, Kirsty – you look fabulous!' She crouched down at the side of Kirsty's chair, taking in every detail from her hair to her shoes. 'What have you done to yourself? I can hardly believe it's you. That dress makes you look dead glamorous and far older.'

'D'you think so?' Kirsty said, happy because Eileen was actually three years older than her, and always used to talk to her as if she was still a schoolgirl when they worked together. Eileen was very career-minded and ambitious, so it was nice to impress her for a change.

'How's your Heather getting on?' the girl asked now, and a little note in her voice told Kirsty that she'd had a few more drinks due to the festive period than she normally would have.

Normally Eileen would be far more reserved, and unwilling to quiz another girl in so blatant a manner. 'Somebody was telling me she's moved to an office in Glasgow.'

'Oh, she's fine,' Kirsty said, and then went on to elaborate at great length all about the big shipping office and the important job her sister had, just to annoy the competitive Eileen. A few minutes into the conversation Kirsty felt a hand on her shoulder.

'I'm just heading out to have a few words in the office,' Larry told her, squeezing her shoulder and giving her a friendly wink. 'I won't be long.' He gave a nod in Eileen's direction, then moved out from the table in his easy, confident manner.

'Who is that?' Eileen asked in a shocked tone, her eyes following him as he strode purposefully out towards the entrance hall. 'He's like a film star ...'

Kirsty felt elated now, unable to believe how the tables had turned with her old workmate. 'His name's Larry Delaney. Actually he's my manager,' she said in a deliberately casual tone.

'So, you're still singing?' Eileen said, her voice high with surprise.

Kirsty nodded and finished off her second Babycham. 'It's all different now I'm with Larry,' she said, putting the empty glass back down on the table. 'All different venues, we're travelling a lot further out to the bigger places. Glasgow and Edinburgh and all that.'

'So, he's your *manager*,' Eileen said thoughtfully. 'He's not your boyfriend then?' She clasped Kirsty's arm, craning her neck to see over to the door. 'Oh, here he's coming, back – no, he's stopped to chat to another fella at the door.'

'Boyfriend?' Kirsty repeated vaguely, raising her eyebrows but saying nothing either way.

'He's gorgeous,' Eileen said. She put her head to one side thoughtfully. 'A wee bit old maybe – but still better than most of the fellas in here. And very well dressed.'

'D'you think so?' Kirsty said. 'I never really thought about it ...'

'He's not married, is he?' Eileen asked now, her eyes narrowed in suspicion.

Kirsty shook her head. 'Not a bit of him,' she said dismissively. 'Larry Delaney's not the marrying kind.'

'He looks the playboy type, right enough,' Eileen said, a dreamy look on her face. 'Expensive clothes, big car and everything.'

'Not at all,' Kirsty said, laughing. 'He's a right down-to-earth type.' She paused for a moment, for the right effect. 'Mind you – he does have a big fancy car, and it's lovely and comfortable. He picks me up in it regularly.'

'I might have guessed,' Eileen said, standing up. She gave Kirsty a long, knowing look. 'That's what the big change in you is all about, Kirsty Grace.' She thumbed in Larry's direction. 'Don't try kidding me – it's quite obvious he's your boyfriend. I could tell the minute he spoke to you. You can't fool me.'

'How d'you mean?' Kirsty said.

'The way he looked at you. Och, you know fine well what I mean!' the girl said, giving Kirsty a little friendly push on the arm. 'Anyway – good luck to you. You're definitely on to a good thing with him. If you get fed up with him, just let me know.' She went off in the direction of the ladies' toilet now, ever so slightly unsteady on her high heels. Kirsty sat for a while, gazing out over the dance floor and digesting Eileen Connor's words. It was funny, because her old workmate had definitely hit the nail on the head by saying all those things about Larry – the very things that had been going round and round in Kirsty's head since the night of the dream. But she had convinced herself that the sophisticated Dubliner Larry Delaney was definitely far too old for her – and in a very different league.

But now she wasn't quite so sure about that at all. If Eileen thought they were a couple then maybe it wasn't such a strange idea after all. Maybe young fellows just weren't mature and interesting enough for her. Maybe, Kirsty thought, she was like her Auntie Claire who was more suited to older men.

Chapter 36

❧

'You're very quiet, hen,' Sophie said, as she glanced across the fireside at her elder daughter. The radio programme they had been listening avidly to had just finished. 'Are you all right?' Fintan was outside with Pat and Michael in the surprisingly mild night air, tinkering with the car engine by the light of several torches. Sophie thought they were stone mad, and had wondered why they couldn't wait until the morning to do whatever tinkering had to be done. But, she concluded, that was men for you.

Heather gave a little sigh, and then put the back of the new red jumper she had just started knitting down on her lap. 'Och, I'm fine, Mammy,' she said, giving a tight little smile. 'I'm just a wee bit fed up ...'

'Is it about Liz?' Sophie asked, her voice gentle and low. 'It's bound to be a bit of a shock to you.'

The small effort of a smile drained from Heather's face now, and she wondered if her mother had heard something. 'D'you mean about her getting engaged?' she said lightly.

'I mean about her having to get *married*,' Sophie said firmly.

There was a painful little silence, as Heather realised that her mother must have been waiting all day for her to say something. 'Who told you?' Heather asked in a small voice, wondering if Kirsty had dared to say anything. She'd kill her if she had! Sometimes her younger sister let things slip, forgetting who she was talking to.

'Liz's mother,' Sophie confirmed. She looked her daughter square in the eye now, as this was a serious matter – as serious a matter as you could get when it came to young girls who were barely out of school. 'I met her after Mass this morning. There wasn't too many around in the chapel, and I saw her lighting a candle, so I went over to have a wee word with her and to wish her all the best for Christmas and the New Year.'

'And what did she say?' Heather asked, her brown eyes wide and fearful.

'She asked me what I thought about Liz getting engaged, and I just said that quite honestly, I hadn't heard a word about it.' There was a little pause, which indicated that Sophie knew that Heather had deliberately said nothing. 'So, I obviously gave her my congratulations, and said I must send down a wee present for Liz and Jim, when suddenly Mrs Mullen went into floods of tears.'

Heather's hands flew to cover her mouth, as she pictured the scene. Poor Mrs Mullen must have been distraught, because it was very rare for any woman in Rowanhill to show their feelings like that in public – especially in the chapel. 'Is she not happy about Liz getting married?' Heather ventured now.

'She's not happy about the circumstances,' Sophie said. 'There's not too many mothers would be.' She sat forward in her chair now. 'Mrs Mullen said they haven't two pennies to rub together. It's that bad Jim had to get a loan off his brother to buy the engagement ring. And neither Mrs Mullen or Jim Murray's mother has any room for them. They're going to have to rent a room off his granny.'

'Oh, God!' Heather said, remembering that Gerry had told her the same thing last night. Whether it was because he had been drunk and rambling on, or whether she just felt so awkward with him, the dire situation that Liz was now in had not really struck her. Now, listening to her mother, she realised that Liz and Jim getting married was not going to be the joyous occasion it should be.

For some reason Heather was feeling peculiarly guilty about the situation – and she knew it was daft to feel like this, considering it was nothing whatsoever to do with her. She supposed it was because Liz was her best and oldest friend, that people might think she had been behaving the same way herself. 'It sounds a right disaster,' she said now, 'the whole thing.'

'Well,' Sophie said, 'unfortunately that's what happens when two young people get up to things they've no business getting up to. They don't think that they might have to pay a price further down the road.'

Heather slowly nodded her head, her gaze turning to the orange coals in the fire.

'I'd no idea that Liz and him were up to things like that,' she said quietly. 'I'm as shocked as you.' She swallowed a lump in her throat. 'I feel as if I don't know Liz at all . . .'

'She's your friend and you do know her, Heather,' Sophie said kindly. 'And what's happened between them is nothing at all to do with you.' She hesitated. 'I had the very same thing happen to a good friend of mine.'

Heather looked up at her mother in surprise.

Sophie nodded her head. 'It's nothing new, hen. Girls and boys have been making mistakes since the beginning of time.' She leaned down to the scuttle to lift a few lumps of coal and throw them into the dying fire. She rubbed her hands together now, to remove any little bit of coal dust. 'In a lot of ways it's nature that takes over, and some people are too weak to fight against it. All down through the ages. In some creeds and cultures the girls get married off very young, for that very reason. Our Lady herself was supposed to have been a very young girl when she had Our Lord, and then she had to marry Joseph to make it look better – a man who was twice her age.'

Heather stared at her mother, amazed at what she'd just heard. She had fully expected Sophie to go mad about Liz, maybe even call her terrible names. That was the way mothers were supposed to react to these things. The way her Auntie Mona would definitely react when she heard – look how she'd gone on about Auntie Claire the other night. 'It's terrible, isn't it?' Heather said, tears suddenly coming into her eyes.

'They'll work it out, hen,' Sophie said in a soothing voice. 'And when the little one comes along, all the bad feeling will be forgotten. It'll be hard for the first few years and then they'll make as good a go of it as the next.'

'You're probably right,' Heather said, feeling much better about the whole affair. She picked up her knitting needles, ready to tackle the jumper again.

'Is that all that's wrong with you, Heather?' her mother probed. 'You don't seem yourself at all this evening.'

Heather sighed. 'Och, I suppose I'm just feeling a bit sorry for myself. I feel that I've nobody to go out with now this has happened to Liz. She was the one that organised all the nights out, gathered the rest of the crowd together, and I never realised how much I depended on her.' She stopped to disentangle a length of red wool. 'And Kirsty's all wrapped up in her singing at the minute, so she's not bothered about going out either. I don't think I'm going to have much of a New Year.' She held the knitting up. 'I'm turning into a right old maid – nothing more exciting to do than sit in every night doing my knitting.'

'It's not that bad,' Sophie laughed. 'You could be like me – stuck at a sewing machine for half the day every day.'

'But I'm only nineteen,' Heather moaned, 'and only a few weeks ago, I had the social life that a nineteen-year-old should have, and now everything's changed.'

'It's not just the business with Liz that's changed things,' Sophie gently pointed out. 'Don't forget you were going out with Gerry for quite a long time. You had him to go out with at the weekends, and you're bound to feel a difference now you're not. It can take a wee while getting back into a routine with friends.' She took a deep breath. 'Are you maybe havin' second thoughts about finishing with him?'

'Definitely not,' came the quick reply. 'We were never really that suited. For the last couple of months I was only going out with him to keep Liz and Jim company.' She halted, wondering whether to mention him calling to the house drunk last night. She decided against it. Her mother might just mention it to her dad, and there would be ructions if he knew that her ex-boyfriend had been drinking too much. 'I know it sounds daft, but I don't really want to go out to any of the local dances where I might bump into him, because he's still hoping we might get back together.'

'What about the girls from work?' Sophie suggested. 'You said they'd asked you to go into a show with them. Why don't you go?'

Heather raised her eyebrows, considering it. She'd had a great time out with them in Glasgow at the Christmas staff meal, and they had been keen on her joining them again.

'Maybe I should,' she said. 'I might give Sarah a ring tomorrow.'

Chapter 37

Larry came striding back to the table a few minutes later, just as the lights dimmed further and the band struck up the lively Dean Martin song; 'That's Amore'.

'D'you want to think of heading home soon, Kirsty?' he said, checking his watch and yawning.

'*Home*?' Kirsty said in a shocked tone. 'But we haven't even had a dance yet.'

'Did you want to dance?' Larry asked, as if the thought had never occurred to him. As if all the other couples dancing around the floor had just been brought to his attention.

'Not if *you* don't want to,' Kirsty said, all defensive now. She had presumed that Larry would want to enjoy the Christmas party spirit. She had presumed that's why he had brought her out. 'I just think it's a bit of a waste of a good band and a good dance floor *not* to dance. But I suppose you never brought me here for that ... even if it is Christmas.'

He looked at her disappointed, petulant young face. 'Come on, Miss Grace,' he said, in an exaggerated weary tone. He stood up and reached for her hand. 'Up you get.'

The first two dances were nice easy waltzes, and as Kirsty had presumed, Larry was an accomplished dancer who led her around the floor as naturally as if they'd been dancing together for years. Fellas were funny, Kirsty thought, you could never work them out. He was obviously enjoying dancing with her, yet he would have lazily stayed at their table on the edge of the floor watching while everyone else got up to dance.

They swirled past Eileen Connor and another girl who were dancing together now, and Kirsty deliberately moved in closer to the handsome Larry when she knew the two girls were watching. She was also smiling to herself, because it was quite obvious Eileen had not been asked to dance by any of the lads, otherwise she would have been up dancing with them instead of her pal.

'Who is that friend of yours?' Larry asked as they went past the girls for a second time, noticing the stares they were getting from them.

'I used to work beside her,' Kirsty said, looking up into his eyes. 'But she's not exactly a friend.'

'Well, she'll certainly know us the next time,' Larry said, 'because she's never taken her eyes off of us.'

Kirsty stretched up high on her tiptoes to whisper in his ear. 'I think she must be besotted by your good looks – she told me she thought you looked like a film star!'

Larry laughed out loud as though he had heard that one before, but he just shook his head and said nothing. The dance came to a halt, and they stood together on the crowded dance floor waiting for the next number to start. The lights gradually dimmed to a rosy glow and Kirsty felt a tingle of excitement when she realised it was going to be a slow dance. She listened to the opening bars, wondering which number it would be.

'Would you like a *last* drink?' Larry asked above the noise, emphasising the word *last*. He glanced over his shoulder towards the busy bar area.

Kirsty looked at her wristwatch. It was only quarter past ten. 'After this dance,' she said, putting her hands up on his shoulders. She was very surprised at how shy and backward Larry had suddenly become, because he had always given the impression of being a really confident man-about-town. He had seemed very confident with that older, sophisticated woman when they went for the meal in the hotel a few weeks ago. Kirsty struggled to remember the woman's name now, but it just wouldn't come into her mind. Larry hadn't seemed in the slightest bit awkward with her, and it was quite obvious by the way she had spoken to him that she definitely found him attractive.

Kirsty recognised the music now as one of her favourites, and one of the biggest hits that year – 'Unchained Melody'. The female singer was making a fairly good job of it so far, she noted, and then she suddenly felt Larry's arm sliding around her waist.

They moved around the floor very naturally to the rhythm, with Kirsty's arms loosely linked around Larry's neck. A few times, Kirsty drew back a little to look up at him, but he just smiled down at her and continued dancing in his relaxed, easy way. At one point, Kirsty laid her head on Larry's chest, the way she often did with other boyfriends, and she was confused when his whole body seemed to stiffen up and she felt him ever so slightly pull away from her. Again she wondered if he wasn't quite the playboy that people thought he was – and that he wasn't just as sure of himself as she had imagined.

She leaned in closer to him now, tightening her hold around the back of his neck and moving her legs that little bit closer to his. Being that close to him made her feel hot and tingly all over, and she wondered if Larry felt the same. She waited for some kind of reaction but again there was nothing to indicate that he had even noticed that she was almost clinging to him.

The dance eventually ended, and Kirsty headed off to the Ladies while Larry went to organise the final drink he had promised. She checked how she looked in the mirror, making sure her hair hadn't fallen down at the back and that her mascara hadn't ended up in black circles around her eyes making her look like a panda bear. Thankfully, it hadn't; all her make-up required was a little touch-up with powder and a fresh coat of the reddish-pink lipstick that matched her nail polish and the pink trim on the bottom of her dress. She gave a final glance at her reflection before she left. She definitely looked well tonight – the best she had ever looked.

And there was no doubt about it – Kirsty knew she was far better looking than that dark-haired woman in the hotel. And she was younger. It was only a matter of time and surely Larry would realise that despite the age difference, they were really suited. They wanted the same things out of life.

With that air of confidence wafting around her, Kirsty headed back to the dance hall, head held aloft, determined to enjoy the remainder of this glamorous night.

The man in the bow-tie who had been talking to Larry earlier was sitting at their table. He stood up when Kirsty arrived, beaming at her in admiration. 'So this is the latest new talent you were tellin' me about?' He nodded approvingly over at Larry. 'Well, if she sings half as good as she looks, you're on to a winner! You're a right cracker, hen!' He winked at Kirsty and gave Larry a thumbs-up sign and then headed back across the dance floor in a brisk, businesslike manner.

'He seemed really nice,' Kirsty said, flushing with pleasure. The man wasn't a lot younger than Larry, so if his opinions were anything to go by, she didn't come across as that young and silly. She sat down now, and reached for her fresh glass of Babycham, and as she took a drink from it, she felt the bubbly effect adding to the two drinks she'd already had.

'I think you certainly made an impression there,' Larry said quietly, giving her a long look. 'And when he hears you singing, he'll be even more impressed.' He motioned towards the stage. 'She wasn't a patch on you tonight. I was listening really carefully, weighing up the range of songs and watching how the band picked up certain numbers to give her a break every now and again. They were the songs that wouldn't have taken a flinch out of you. You've great stamina and energy on the stage.' He leaned towards her now, a contented look on his face. 'I'm delighted I was at that talent contest, it was just the right time for you to be discovered.'

'How d'you mean?' Kirsty asked, desperate for more praise.

'Well,' Larry said, considering his words carefully, 'any earlier and it wouldn't have worked – you would have been too young for all this. It's amazing the difference a few years can make.' He patted her hand now. 'Career-wise, you're very mature for a girl of your age. You've put a lot of work into these last few weeks.'

He paused, seeing the delight on her face at the compliment, and a small frown formed on his brow. 'But I think there might be one little problem, Kirsty . . . something I didn't think of.'

'What?' Kirsty said.

'Those girls on the dance floor, and the looks we've been getting from some other people. I have a horrible feeling that we might have been taken for a couple tonight . . . and that just might not look too good for either of us.'

Kirsty's blue eyes lit up, and she gave a girlish, tinkly laugh. 'That's surely not the end of the world, is it? People can think what they like.'

Larry stared at her for a few moments, then he reached into his suit pocket for his cigarettes and lighter. 'It's not as simple as that. Apart from anything else, I've got a business reputation to think of.'

'What do you mean?' Kirsty asked, suddenly confused by the conversation.

'Come on, Kirsty,' he said, raising his eyebrows meaningfully. He put the lighter on the table while he took a cigarette from the packet. 'You're not that naïve, are you? A man of my age out with a beautiful young girl in a dress like that . . .' His eyes moved very deliberately downwards to her breasts.

Kirsty looked down at her cleavage, and the dreaded pink flush she often got when nervous started to spread across her chest and neck. 'If you're sayin' that I'm not properly dressed . . .' she stuttered. 'If you're sayin' that you're embarrassed to be seen with me.'

She lifted her glass and took a big gulp of the fizzy drink, then she put the glass back down a little too hard, causing drops of the Babycham to spill onto the table.

'I'm certainly *not* saying that,' he said, reaching his hand across the table to cover hers. 'If anything, it's the opposite. I'm delighted to be out with you tonight, but I asked you to come out with me on a *business* basis . . . to check out the band and the singer.' He paused to light his cigarette. 'I'm also thinking about you, and how it looks for a lovely young girl to be out with an older fella like me. I wouldn't like people to get the wrong impression about you.' He sat back in his chair, blowing the smoke to the side, away from her.

'Your age doesn't bother me a bit,' Kirsty blurted out. 'I don't feel as if you're older than me . . . I think we get on really well together. I like you better than any fella I've gone out with . . .' She looked straight into his eyes now. 'I think we'd get on great together – there are plenty of couples that have an age difference.'

'Oh, dear . . .' Larry said, his face darkening. 'This is *exactly* what I was worrying about.'

A small, cold hand clutched at Kirsty's heart, as she suddenly realised that she was making a terrible fool of herself. 'You're not married or anythin' like that, are you?' she asked, thinking the worst.

'Kirsty, you don't know what you're talking about,' he said, sounding exasperated. 'You don't know the first thing about me or my life.'

'What d'you mean?' she stuttered out.

'If you *really* knew me – you wouldn't dream of saying such a thing.'

Chapter 38

L ater that night, Heather woke to the sound of her sister crying. 'What's the matter, Kirsty?' she called across the room in a startled whisper.

'Nothing . . .' Kirsty said in a croaky, muffled voice. 'Go back to sleep.'

Heather reached out her arm, feeling for the bedside lamp. She switched it on, and then covered her eyes for a few seconds to get used to the glaring light. 'What's wrong?' she said, sitting up. Although she was shocked at being woken in such a way, she wasn't altogether surprised that something was wrong. The way Kirsty had come into bed earlier on had made Heather think that her sister had been annoyed or upset about something, but at the time she'd been too tired to make any issue about it.

'What's wrong, Kirsty?' Heather repeated, throwing the covers back and getting out of her bed. She padded barefoot across the floor and came to the side of Kirsty's bed.

'Oh, I've made a terrible fool of myself . . .' Kirsty said, her voice faint and trembling.

Heather sat down on the side of the bed and placed a comforting hand over her sister's shoulder. 'It can't be that bad . . .' she said, suddenly alarmed as her mind flitted back to the scene with Liz the other night. *Oh, God,* she suddenly thought, *please don't let anything like that have happened to Kirsty.*

Kirsty moved now as though she was going to sit up, then it was as if the effort was too great and she slumped face-down into the pillow. 'I'll never be able to face Larry Delaney again,' she moaned. Then, her shoulders started heaving up and down as vicious sobs racked her body.

'Tell me what's happened,' Heather said, gently rubbing her sister's back and shoulders. 'Please, Kirsty . . .' But she just had to wait. Wait until her younger sister had exhausted herself sobbing and crying into the pillow. 'Are you OK?' she asked after a while, still fearful of what she was going to hear.

Eventually, the crying stopped and Kirsty came back up for air. 'I've made the most awful, blidey fool of myself,' she repeated, sniffling. 'I can't believe that I did it.'

'Did what?' Heather said, trying not to sound as impatient as she was now beginning to feel. 'I can't help you if you don't tell me . . .'

'I told Larry Delaney that . . .' She started off sobbing again. 'I told him that I thought we'd make a good couple . . . I more or less told him that I fancied him and wanted us to go out together.'

'Oh my God!' Heather said, unable to hide her shocked feelings. 'And is it true? Do you really like him?'

'Aye, I do like him,' Kirsty replied, a defensive note evident in her voice. 'Why? What wrong with him?'

'I don't believe it . . .' Heather whispered. 'He's absolutely *ancient* . . . he's nearly old enough to be your father . . .'

'Oh, fuck off!' Kirsty hissed, her voice trembling again. 'I might have known not to tell you – I might have guessed you wouldn't understand.' She shifted in the narrow single bed, turning towards the window, obviously trying to shrug her sister away from her. 'Oul' goody-two-shoes there – who passes her exams first time and never makes a mistake. Oul' Holy Mary who never puts a foot wrong . . .' Kirsty's face was now back in the comforting warmth of the pillow again.

'Shut up and don't be so childish!' Heather told her in the low, firm voice of an older sister. 'It's not my fault if you've lost all your sense and made a fool of yourself with that manager of yours.' She took a deep breath, realising that it was up to her to get things back onto an even keel. 'I don't know what you even see in him . . . you're far too good for him.'

Nothing was said for a few moments, signalling a truce.

'Do you really like him?' Heather asked again, this time in a softer, more understanding tone. She started rubbing her sister's shoulder again.

Kirsty gave a little sob and nodded her head.

'Well ... I suppose I've only met him once,' Heather conceded. 'Maybe there's more to him than meets the eye.' She halted. 'He's good-looking for his age, I'll give him that.'

Kirsty turned around now in the bed, her arms folded behind her head. 'If you knew him the way I do, you'd understand. I've never met anybody like him.' She gave a big sniff, prompting Heather to reach over to the windowsill for a paper hanky.

'He's dead clever, and really funny,' Kirsty went on, taking the proffered hanky. 'I've never felt like this about a fella in my life before ...' She dabbed at her eyes and then blew her nose.

'Maybe it's just infatuation,' Heather said quietly. 'Maybe it's just a kind of crush. You know, the way you might feel about a teacher at school—'

'No,' Kirsty said, rubbing her nose with the tissue. 'It's not anything childish like that. I'm not that stupid, I know the difference. I've had enough boyfriends to know ... Larry's totally different from them all.' She cleared her throat now. 'We've got loads in common. When I'm up there on the stage, and he's watching me, I feel on top of the world. I feel as if we were meant to be together.' She took a deep, shuddering breath. 'I think I might be in love with him.'

'What did you actually say to him?' Heather asked.

Kirsty slunk down into the bed again. 'I don't want to talk about it,' she whispered. 'I don't want to even *think* about it.' Then she covered her face with the sheet.

Heather stared down at the pink bedcover, wondering why all these terrible problems had suddenly plummeted into her life: poor Lily who wasn't getting better as quickly as everyone had hoped; then there was all the carry-on with Gerry, and of course Liz and now this bombshell with Kirsty.

Of the four, Liz's problem seemed the most serious – but it was likely to be the only one with a happy ending. At least Liz had got what she wanted: Jim Murray. She would get married and live happily ever after with her husband and her baby.

Long after Heather had gone back to sleep, Kirsty lay thinking about her journey home in Larry's car. Her face burned with shame at the memory. How could she have been so stupid? How could she have made such a terrible fool of herself? How could she have made such an embarrassing mistake?

She wondered now if it had been the Babychams. Had a couple of drinks loosened her tongue so much? Kirsty wasn't sure – all she knew was that it had seemed the right thing to say at the time.

Larry had hardly spoken two words for the first leg of the journey, then he had suddenly started talking and going over the whole excruciating situation again.

'Was it me, Kirsty?' he had asked in a low voice, his eyes focused on the dark road in front of them. 'Did I give you the wrong impression?'

Kirsty's head and shoulders had drooped as she sat cringing in the car seat beside him. She had eventually managed a shrug and a shake of her head.

How could she say that it had all started with a romantic dream about him? How could she answer him when she didn't know the answer herself? She supposed she had just got totally carried away with the whole idea of them working so closely together and him giving her the lovely dresses and then turning up at her house with the expensive perfume that night.

Had it been the perfume that had triggered off the dream? she had wondered.

'It's just that I never saw it coming,' Larry had said. 'I feel so dense that I never realised what you were thinking.' He had paused, concentrating on negotiating a tricky turn in the road that took them into Rowanhill. 'I suppose giving you perfume didn't help. I didn't think that you might read more into it – with you being so young . . .'

Kirsty had squirmed in her seat at the description of being *so young*, and wondering if he had read her thoughts about the Chanel No. 5.

'Was it that which confused everything? Me giving you the present?' he had asked.

'No,' Kirsty had said, in a small voice. 'I don't know what it was . . . I don't know what came over me. I should never have said anything, and I'm really, really sorry I did.'

They had driven down the main street of Rowanhill and then turned into Kirsty's street. He had pulled up outside the gate, turned the engine off and then turned towards her, his arm resting on the steering wheel. 'Do you think we can go on working together after this, Kirsty?' he had asked, his face solemn in the glow of the orange street lights.

Kirsty's chest had tightened and she had found she was almost struggling to breathe. 'I said I'm sorry, didn't I?' she had said, her voice like a child's – a bit like Lily's when she was in a bad mood.

Larry had looked out of the car window, his fingers drumming on the steering wheel. 'OK,' he had suddenly decided. 'We'll give it another go – we have to – we've got that New Year's commitment in the Clyde Valley Hotel in a few days' time.' He halted. 'We'll start all over again – just pretend this thing never happened. Make sure everything is on a purely business basis.'

'OK,' Kirsty had said, a huge wave of relief washing over her. 'That's fine by me.' *Thank God*, she had thought to herself. *Thank God he's not dropping me and my whole singing career.*

She turned her face back into the pillow now, wishing desperately for the sleep that had eluded her so far. She had to get up for work in the morning, and she needed a couple of hours at least to function any way normally.

Just as her eyelids started to close, she made a decision. Never again would she make such a fool of herself over a man. She would learn from this.

She would never, ever leave herself open to being hurt like this again.

Chapter 39

❧❦❧

Heather had the four penny coins ready in her right hand and the phone receiver in her left listening for an answer. She was all wrapped up in her old duffle coat and thick woolly scarf and gloves, as the temperatures had gradually dropped over the last few days into the more seasonal cold that they were used to. The sudden click on the line prompted her. She slid the copper coins one after the other into the dull brass slot to the side of the phone.

'Hello – can I speak to Sarah Fox, please?'

'Oh, ye'll have to wait a wee minute, hen,' a muffled, elderly female Glaswegian voice came over the line. 'I wis just passin' by when I heard it ringin, so I was.' There was a small pause. 'I'll just have to hang the phone up and then I'll gie her a shout. I shouldnae be too long, hen, for I just saw her mother at the windae.'

The phone receiver was laid down and Heather could hear what she imagined to be the creaking of the phone kiosk door and then the sound of an old lady's footsteps going off in the distance. She could then hear the rumble of city traffic passing by, and more muffled voices, and then eventually she heard the door creak open again.

'Hello, this is Sarah Fox,' came a familiar breathless voice. 'Who's speaking, please?'

'It's me, Heather.' She hesitated for a moment, suddenly unsure. Maybe her workmate had forgotten all about her over the Christmas holidays. 'It's Heather from the office.'

'Oh, Heather!' Sarah said in a high-pitched squeal. 'Ye decided to phone after all.'

Heather's heart lifted; she hadn't been forgotten. 'I was just wondering if it would still be OK if I came out for that Lex McLean show with you?'

'Of course it's still OK,' Sarah told her. 'They still have tickets left, because one of my mammy's friends got them today. I can go into the Pavillion tomorrow and get you one no problem.'

'Are you sure?' Heather checked.

'Definitely! Just give me a wee ring again at the same time tomorrow and I'll let you know I've got it all sorted out. You'll be stayin' the night at our house like we said, won't you?'

'Are you sure it's all right?' Heather asked, a sense of excitement running through her at the thought of a night out in Glasgow.

'Of course it's all right,' Sarah said, sounding almost insulted at being questioned. 'As long as you don't mind sharing my room.'

Heather laughed. 'Didn't I already tell you that I share a room with my dead annoying younger sister?'

After she hung up, Heather dug deep into her coat pocket for her small blue leather purse. She took another fourpence out and a small card she had tucked in the back. She sat the card up on the ledge and carefully dialled the second Glasgow number, then went through the same procedure with the coins.

'Hello,' a very crisp voice sounded on the line and then went on to recite the number.

'Hello ... Auntie Claire? It's me, Heather.'

'Heather?' Claire's voice was high with surprise. 'Hello, darling, what a lovely surprise.' There was a sudden silence. 'You're not phoning about Lily, are you?'

'No ... no,' Heather said reassuringly, 'she's coming on fine. Well, she's back in hospital for another wee while, but she's slowly getting better.' *A bit too slow*, Heather thought, but the hospital said she was definitely improving.

'I'm glad about that,' Claire said, the relief evident in her voice. 'Well, it's a lovely surprise to hear from you. Did you all have a nice Christmas?'

'Aye, we did, thanks,' Heather said, momentarily conscious of her local Rowanhill accent, but quickly reminding herself that she'd always felt comfortable talking to Claire and it was stupid to feel self-conscious just because they hadn't chatted in a while. 'I just thought I'd give you a wee ring to say thanks for the lovely charm bracelet ... and Kirsty asked me to say thanks as well.'

'Oh, that's really nice of you,' Claire replied. 'I'm delighted you both liked them. The minute I saw them I knew they would suit you.'

'Lily was wearing hers over Christmas as well,' Heather informed her aunt.

There was a slightly awkward little pause. 'Good – I'm delighted that your Auntie Mona let her have it.' Then, realising that the conversation was veering into uncomfortable waters, she changed the subject. 'So what have you been doing with yourself over Christmas? Anything nice?'

'Oh, I've been out and about,' Heather said, 'and we had a lovely day at home. Pat and Mona have a television set now, so we all went over and watched it a few times.' Then she quickly added, 'They got it for Lily really ... because she's not able to move about yet.' Some people thought television sets were only a fad, and didn't approve of them. She wasn't quite sure which side of the fence her aunt would come down on with regards to it.

'That was a great idea,' Claire said warmly, and obviously meaning it. 'Oh, I hope she's up and running about soon. I can't wait to see her back to normal. She's one of the brightest, liveliest wee girls I've ever known.'

'Oh, she is,' Heather agreed, 'and she is slowly getting back to her old self.'

There was a crackling silence on the line. 'Heather,' Claire said, 'does your daddy know that you were coming out to phone me?'

Heather felt herself going red, and was glad there was nobody to see her. 'I mentioned that I might ring you sometime to thank you for the bracelet,' she explained. 'And I was coming out to phone my friend from work when I remembered your card ... my friend lives in Glasgow as well.'

'Does she?' Claire asked. 'Whereabouts?'

'I'm not really sure,' Heather admitted. 'I think it's out near Govan or somewhere like that. I'll find out tomorrow, because I might be going to a show with her, and she's asked me to stay the night.'

'Oh, that's lovely!' Claire said. 'And you must come out and visit me and your Uncle Andy – we'd love to see you and Kirsty. We have two nice spare rooms, and we love having guests.'

'We will come some time,' Heather promised. She had a sudden thought. 'Maybe I could come out some Friday night, straight from work. It would be easier since I'm already in Glasgow.'

'That would just be wonderful!' Claire said, obviously delighted. 'You just give us a ring a few days before to check we're in, and we'll have everything all organised.'

Chapter 40

Heather had never been to a grown-up show in Glasgow on her own. She'd been to pantomimes at Christmas with the family, and she'd gone to comedy shows in Motherwell and Airdrie – but she'd never done anything like this on her own.

She had taken the train into Glasgow on the Friday afternoon, and then she had caught the bus from George Square that Sarah had told her would take her out to Govanhill – not Govan, she had stressed, laughing at Heather's mistake.

She had taken ages the night before deciding on what she would wear for this special outing. She decided on smart beige trousers and a black polo-neck with her camel three-quarter-length swing coat for travelling, and a lovely mid-brown suit with fur at the collar and cuffs. She had got this from Liz's mother's catalogue last winter, and was delighted that it fitted her so well, now that she had lost a little bit of weight. She also wore Claire's gold charm bracelet and a nice big cameo brooch that matched both outfits perfectly.

Even before she arrived at Sarah's house with her suit carefully folded in Sophie's brown leather overnight case, the trip on the train and bus during this festive time of the year had made her feel quite excited. The city looked lovely with all the Christmas decorations and coloured lights glittering, and people seemed chattier and cheerier. Heather had been very grateful to a well-dressed old couple she met in George Square who had shown her to the correct bus stop then insisted on waiting with her until the right bus came along. 'We're not in any rush, hen,' the old woman had told her. 'We've no family apart from ourselves, and we're just having a wee day out in Glasgow to look at the decorations and to pass the time. Christmas and New Year hangs long on yer hands when you've no family, isn't that right, Archie?' she'd said to her husband who nodded solemnly in agreement. 'We were never blessed wi' children, ye see,' she had whispered, 'but it was nobody's fault. Ye just have to accept these things in life.'

The couple had stood chatting to her for a good twenty minutes, giving her a run-down on their day from getting up at six o'clock in the morning until they went to bed after the news at half past nine at night.

'We live in a nice part of Bearsden,' the old man had told her. 'And we have good neighbours and a nice postman, Walter, who has a cup of tea with us nearly every morning. I used to work in the sorting office in the post office and Walter knew me from coming in to collect the post.'

'We're very lucky, really,' the old woman had said, her small bird-like face beaming. 'And we're involved with the church and everything; we had a lovely Christmas dinner out in the village hall with all the other retired members of the church.'

'Well, isn't it lovely you have each other?' Heather had said, feeling a bit strange when she realised that they were obviously Church of Scotland. Catholics would always have said with members of the *parish*.

Fleetingly, she thought of Claire and her husband, and wondered how people like Mona could take against nice people, like this elderly refined couple, just because they went to a different church. It was the same God after all. People were people, and it was how nice they were to others that counted.

'Here it comes,' Archie said, pointing his brass-handled walking stick as the Govanhill bus came into view.

Heather looked back at the helpful old couple as she waited for the bus to stop, thanking them profusely for all their help.

'It was a pleasure, my dear,' the woman said, linking her husband's arm now. 'It passed a wee while for us, and after you've gone on the bus, we'll walk back to Argyle Street and get ourselves a nice cup of tea in Lewis's tea-room.'

Heather felt almost tearful as she waved to them from the bus window, and then spent the rest of the journey thinking about her Scottish grandparents who had died about five years ago, only a few months apart, and then she thought about the Grace grandparents back in Ireland who she hardly ever saw. People like Liz who had grandparents who lived just around the corner were lucky, she thought.

By the time the bus reached her stop in Govanhill, she was glad to get off it and have her mind distracted from the sad thoughts of lonely old people by the chirpy Sarah who was waving and jumping about to make sure she didn't miss the stop.

It was exactly as Sarah had described it. A busy wide road, with cars and lorries running up and down it regularly and high, three-storey, sandstone tenement buildings on either side. A row of shops was just visible further on. It was obviously a good part of Govanhill, as all the houses had gleaming windows and letter boxes, and the small gardens were very well kept with small clipped box hedges.

At first glance, Heather found it strange seeing her friend in her casual clothes, her straight, brown hair tied back in a ponytail, as she was more used to seeing her in a formal skirt and blouse for the office, with her hair carefully waved and set. Sarah's narrow-legged black corduroy trousers looked really fashionable, topped with an oversized bright blue sweater with a big cowl neck. She was also wearing a lovely pair of two-tone black and grey ankle boots that were obviously a new style in the Glasgow shops.

'You look absolutely terrific – I'd hardly have recognised you!' Heather told her, eyeing her workmate up and down in open admiration as they stood at the bus stop. 'And what a fabulous jumper! Where did you get it?'

'Believe it or not, my mammy knitted it!' Sarah told her with wide eyes, in her high-pitched Glasgow accent. 'I saw the pattern in a magazine a few weeks ago and I showed it to her, but she said she was far too busy to do it until after Christmas. And guess what?' She put one hand on her hip for a bit of drama. 'She knitted it secretly while I was at work and gave it to me for part of my Christmas!' She shook her head, her ponytail swinging from side to side. 'I couldn't believe it ... Imagine going to all that trouble to have it ready for me – hiding it in the bedroom so's I wouldn't see it.'

'That was really nice of her and you look fantastic in it,' Heather told her workmate.

'And you look lovely too,' Sarah said, standing back to get a good look at Heather's outfit. 'That's a really posh coat you've got on, and the colour really suits you.'

Heather glowed at the description of her coat, and suddenly felt all sophisticated being in a different part of Glasgow with her fashionably dressed new friend. Rowanhill suddenly seemed a long way off.

'Oh, I meant to tell you,' Sarah suddenly said, 'Marie's got a bad cold and she won't make it. I wasn't talking to her myself, but she's not been too well all Christmas according to her mother.'

'Oh, that's a pity,' Heather said, genuinely disappointed. Marie, the other girl from Seafreight, was quiet compared to Sarah but very nice and friendly.

'Och, it doesn't really matter,' Sarah told her, 'because Barbara, my oldest pal from school, has brought a girl from her office who's nice enough, so there's still four of us going. They said they'll meet us in at the Pavillion as they're going into Glasgow early to get something to eat.'

'It's a shame that poor Marie is missing the show,' Heather said sympathetically. 'Maybe she'll make it out another night with us.'

'My mammy and daddy can't wait to meet you,' Sarah said, taking Heather by the arm. 'They love any of my friends coming, because the house is quiet since our John and our Mary got married. There's only me left, and my mammy still cooks and cleans as if there was the five of us.'

They started walking down the street now, linking arms, with Heather glancing this way and that at the houses and traffic, whilst listening attentively to Sarah's news. 'My mammy's made a steak pie with mashed potatoes and gravy, do you like that?'

'I love it,' Heather said, swinging her mother's overnight case as she went along. She felt so happy tonight that it wouldn't matter what Mrs Fox served up. Heather knew she would love everything.

Sarah's mother and father gave her the same warm welcome as her friend had, and Heather was amazed how similar the furniture and curtains were to her own family's. She hadn't been too sure about Sarah's religion as they had never talked about the subject, and Fox was one of those names that was hard to pin down as being Irish Catholic or Scottish Protestant. But the minute Heather spotted the pictures of the Sacred Heart on the walls and statues of Our Lady she knew they both had a Catholic upbringing in common.

The dinner was lovely, and Sarah's father made the two girls a beer shandy afterwards, which they drank as they were getting changed into their evening clothes.

Mrs Fox had been pink-faced with delight when Sarah told her how much Heather had admired her handiwork with the blue jumper. 'Do you or your mammy knit yourselves?' she had asked, as she cleared up the dinner plates.

'We all do,' Heather told her. 'Me, my mammy and my sister Kirsty. But it's more sewing my mother does, so she doesn't have a lot of time for knitting the more complicated things like the jumper. She only does baby things or something small like a tea-cosy.'

Sarah's mother looked thoughtful. 'Do you feel you could tackle that kind of jumper yourself, hen? It looks harder than it is. It's really only a couple of cables up the front and then it's all ribbing for the neck.' She paused, her head to one side, thinking. 'If you like, you can have a loan of the pattern, hen. And if you get stuck you can always send it home with Sarah and I'll help you out.'

Heather looked across the table at her friend. 'Would you mind if I had the same jumper? I wouldn't wear it to work or if we were out together or anything.'

'Not at all,' Sarah said, shaking her head. 'And anyway, you could do it in a different colour.'

Heather turned back to the older woman now. 'That would be great, Mrs Fox. I'd love to have a loan of the pattern.' The red jumper she was in the middle of knitting could wait, Heather thought. She would run into one of the wool shops in Glasgow on her way back for the train tomorrow and start on this new fashionable pattern straightaway.

'I'll look it out, and leave it on the sideboard for you in the morning,' the friendly Glasgow woman told her.

Sarah's bedroom was a bit bigger than Heather and Kirsty's room, but the fact she had it all to herself made it luxurious in Heather's eyes. The double wardrobe, the double bed with its nylon-padded bedspread and matching pillows, the dressing-table and the three big drawers – all to herself.

Apart from a slight reluctance to share the bed with her friend, Heather felt that her workmate had everything she wished for herself.

They had arranged to meet the others outside the Pavillion, and as they crossed the road towards the theatre, Sarah was all excited as she pointed out the two girls waiting for them. They were both quite small, the dark-haired one around Kirsty's height and the other girl, a curly red-head, was even smaller. 'Barbara's the one with the short dark hair, and she's absolutely brilliant,' Sarah told Heather as they walked towards them. 'She's a really good laugh when she gets going. That wee Patsy's not a close pal, Barbara only brought her to use up Marie's ticket.'

The introductions were quickly made but, unlike the glowing description Sarah had given of her old friend, Heather found Barbara to be a bit quiet and stand-offish. She put it down to the fact they had only just met and that some people took a wee while to warm up.

The other girl, Patsy, seemed very nice and friendly and she smiled a lot. They hadn't much time to chat as they had to find which part of the theatre their tickets were for, and then find their seats. There was one difficult moment when they stood at the end of the row of seats deciding who would sit where, but Barbara suggested that it would be best if Heather went in first followed by Sarah and Barbara and Patsy coming in last. Heather thought it didn't really matter since they were all together, but Barbara seemed to feel it was a very important issue.

The show was great. Heather laughed and laughed until tears streamed down her face and her sides hurt. It was the best fun she'd had in ages, and definitely the best fun she'd had all this Christmas. The bar in the Pavillion was packed at the break, so Sarah suggested that Heather and Patsy go and find a table while she and Barbara went to fight their way through the crowds to get them each a drink.

Patsy was nice but, if Heather was honest, the girl was a tiny bit boring when she went on about her work in a solicitor's office. She talked and talked in a low voice, going into a lot of detail about a new phone system that had been introduced, and Heather had to lean across the table to catch everything she said over the babble of noise. After a while Sarah and Barbara came pushing their way back from the bar, looking hot and flustered from queuing and pushing.

'Is gin and tonic all right?' Sarah asked, putting a drink down in front of Heather.

'For me?' Heather said, looking startled. 'I usually only drink bottled shandy when I'm out . . .'

Sarah shot a glance at Barbara. 'I told you she wouldn't want that.'

'It doesn't matter,' Heather said quickly, suddenly sensing a change in the atmosphere.

'It won't exactly kill you,' Barbara said, giving an irritated sigh. 'And if you don't want it one of the rest of us will have it.' She looked over at Sarah and rolled her eyes. 'I just thought it would be nice for us all to have the same drink and it was easier to order at the bar.'

'Barbara paid for the drinks herself,' Sarah blurted out, her face flushed and red. 'She got a Christmas bonus and she thought she'd treat us all. I thought since you'd had the few drinks at the office party, that you were game enough to try a new one out.'

An awkward silence descended on the group, and Heather suddenly felt responsible because she was a guest and an outsider. She had obviously put her foot in it by inferring that the girls hadn't checked what particular drink she wanted. She had only meant to say that she wasn't used to spirits, and wondered if she tried to explain it now, if it would help matters.

She turned to Barbara, a smile pinned on her face. 'Thanks for the drink, that was really nice of you, and honestly, it doesn't matter what it is.' She lifted her glass of gin and tonic up. 'Cheers!' she said, holding her glass out to the others and smiling broadly. She didn't want to be the cause of any dampener on this lovely, cheery occasion.

The others raised their glasses and clinked them together with hers, then they all took a sip of what Heather thought was a very dry bitter drink. But when she lifted her gaze back to the group, the look in Barbara's narrowed eyes told Heather that it was unlikely that they would ever be friends.

A bell rang to let the audience know that the second part of the show would recommence in five minutes, and Heather decided that she would rush to the Ladies before everyone started moving back into the theatre.

She came out of a cubicle to wash her hands, and a few seconds later Barbara emerged from one of the other cubicles. She walked over to stand by Heather at the sink, and then, in complete silence, washed her hands and then walked past Heather to dry her hands on the towel.

A feeling of embarrassment and anger began to build up inside Heather. She looked around the toilet now, checking there wasn't anyone else there who could hear. 'Barbara,' she said in a low, tight voice, 'I'm very sorry if I've offended you about the drink, I certainly didn't mean to . . .'

Barbara finished drying her hands, saying nothing for a few moments. 'It's OK,' she finally said. 'I suppose you can't help that you're different – that you're obviously not used to our Glasgow ways.'

Heather could feel the anger increasing inside her, and she knew without a doubt that if it had been Kirsty she would have given her a slap. 'What do you mean? What ways?'

Barbara looked directly at her, her green eyes narrowed into little slits. 'The ways that close friends behave with each other when they're out,' she said in a calm, even tone. She gave a quick glance in the mirror behind Heather, checking her hair was in place, as though they were having an ordinary, friendly conversation instead of this tension-filled exchange.

'You see, Sarah and me have been best friends since we were eleven – since we started secondary school – so we know each other inside out.' She gave a smug little smile. 'A thing like that drink business would never cause any problem with me and her. We know each other too well.'

Heather nodded, swallowing hard to relieve the tight feeling in her throat. 'That's lovely,' she said, trying to sound casual, as though Barbara's words and nasty attitude hadn't attacked her like little knives. She glanced in the mirror herself, affecting a relaxed and easy manner. 'I know what it's like, I've a best friend back home, Liz, that I've been going around with since I was five, and I've a sister only a year younger than me . . .'

Heather suddenly felt a sham as soon as the words left her lips, and she was shocked at the pangs of sadness she felt just mentioning Liz's name. Liz wasn't her best friend any more. She had totally forgotten Heather. She had thrown aside their special friendship as soon as someone else had come along. Liz Mullen only had time for one person now: Jim Murray, her husband to be.

Barbara lifted her handbag. 'So you and Sarah are only working pals then?' She give a funny little smile that was almost a sneer. 'A bit like that Marie lassie from her office?' she said, making towards the door. 'You're not likely to be coming into Glasgow on a regular basis, are you?'

The penny finally dropped. Barbara was making it very plain that there was no room for any close friendships in Sarah's life apart from their own long-standing one. Heather took a deep breath, determined not to let this girl get the better of her. 'I've plenty of things to do back home,' she said, raising her eyebrows, 'but I'm always game for a change if something more exciting comes up.'

The two girls walked back into the bar to join the others as though nothing had happened. The atmosphere lifted a bit, and by the time they went back in for the second half of the show, Heather felt that things had been smoothed over and the incident about the gin and tonic forgotten. But she noticed when they were all back in their seats that Sarah seemed to have angled herself so that she was leaning more towards Barbara and away from Heather. As the show went on, they leaned closer together, whispering and giggling, and not bothering to talk to either Heather or Patsy. Heather told herself not to let it upset her, but after a while she couldn't help it, and she realised that she felt very left out.

The same situation continued after the show when Sarah and Barbara linked arms to walk up to the nearest chip shop with Heather and Patsy trailing behind them, Patsy once again on her favourite subject of the intricate new phone system. They all walked to a bus stop together eating their chips, and then eventually Barbara separated from Sarah and she and Patsy went off to get the Govanhill bus.

'The show was great, wasn't it?' Heather commented as she threw over half of her bag of lukewarm chips into the litter bin at the bus stop. She had no appetite and had forced herself to eat as much of them as she could manage so as not to draw attention to herself.

'Aye it was,' Sarah agreed. 'Lex McLean is always brilliant.' She paused, finishing off her own chips then scrunching up the bag and throwing it into the bin. 'It was a pity a good night was spoiled by a bad atmosphere.'

'What do you mean?' Heather said, dreading what was coming next.

Sarah turned towards her now, her arms folded defensively over her chest. 'Well, you didn't exactly like Barbara, did you? You made it obvious to everybody.'

Heather tried to keep her breathing steady and even. 'If you don't mind me saying, Sarah, I think the opposite was true. Barbara most certainly didn't like me.'

'Well, I've never had anybody havin' a problem wi' Barbara before ... and she said you were dead off-hand to her in the toilet when you were on your own.' Sarah's voice was rattling out the list of accusations now and her face was red and angry. 'She said that you were even talkin' about me – sayin' that you only came out to Glasgow because you'd nothing more exciting to do back home.'

'I think you'll find that's not true,' Heather said in a stunned, quiet voice. What had she done to this Barbara that could have caused such a terrible situation to arise in just one evening? 'I really enjoyed being out at your house, meeting your mother and father, and I was grateful for the lovely dinner I was given.' She halted, desperate for her workmate to see what was plainly obvious. 'Can you not see, Sarah, Barbara's twisted everything around?'

'For your information,' Sarah suddenly snapped, her eyes full of rage, 'that's my best friend you're talkin' about.'

Then they stood together in silence waiting for their bus.

Heather lay in the strange room hunched up in the right-hand corner of the bed, well away from her workmate, wishing that the dark winter night would end and that morning would come quickly. She had often gone to sleep after an argument with Kirsty, knowing full well that they would make it up in the morning. But this was different. This wasn't Kirsty, the sister she knew inside out.

The girl in the bed beside her she now was a cold stranger.

They had made polite conversation on the bus going home and then during the short walk back to Sarah's house. They had sat chatting to Mr and Mrs Fox over a cup of tea and toast, telling them all the jokes they could remember from the show, but studiously avoiding each other's eyes.

Then, the girls had finally gone to bed and the frosty tension that had built up between them over the evening had grown into a solid, frozen silence.

In the morning, Heather made the excuse that she wanted to get off early to do a bit of shopping in Glasgow before catching the train back to Rowanhill.

'But won't you have a bit of ham and eggs?' Mrs Fox asked, a worried frown on her face. 'You can't travel all that way home in the winter without a decent breakfast inside of you.'

'The toast and tea was fine, thanks,' Heather said, gathering up her handbag and her mother's overnight case. 'And thanks again for having me.' Then she and the pale-faced and silent Sarah left to walk to the bus stop.

As they walked along, the unspoken accusations rumbling between them, Heather suddenly remembered the knitting pattern that Sarah's mother had left out for her. For a few moments she considered running back for it, but something held her back.

She didn't want a jumper the same as Sarah Fox any more. She didn't want anything to do with Sarah Fox any more.

Chapter 41

Larry Delaney was true to his word. He did not show any hint of awkwardness about what had happened that night in the Trocadero and he did not in any way refer to it. They met up in the empty function room that they used for rehearsals, and Larry greeted Kirsty as normal, with a big friendly smile. Then, after a few words, he went off to the bar at the front to get his usual Irish whiskey, a glass of lemonade for Kirsty and a pint of beer each for the band members who would be playing in Lanark on New Year's Eve.

Kirsty wasn't used to this. If she had an argument with any of her friends or with Heather, there would always be a very cool atmosphere between them afterwards. It was usually the same when she fell out with her mother and father. There would be a period afterwards where everyone was distant, and then some-one would make a move, the issue would be aired and someone would apologise or laugh and eventually it would all be forgotten.

But instinctively, Kirsty knew this was not the way things would be between her and Larry. The embarrassing incident where she had almost thrown herself at him would not be mentioned again. It was a strange way to deal with things, she thought, but as the evening wore on, Kirsty had almost forgotten the incident herself. And she was more than grateful that Larry Delaney had given her the chance to forget it.

By the time the end of the evening came, both the band and Larry agreed that there was no need for any more rehearsals.

'It's as good as it can be,' Larry said, as they picked up their coats and headed out of the function room. 'And I think you could do with giving your voice a rest, Kirsty. We don't want to strain it before the big night.'

'My voice feels fine. If you think another rehearsal might help, I'm happy to do it.' Kirsty said, but Larry cut her off.

'Do you *really* think another session going through all the songs is necessary?' he asked her, his brow furrowed. 'Are you saying that you don't feel confident enough to go on stage without another rehearsal? Surely you must feel OK about your performance by now?'

Alarm bells suddenly rang in Kirsty's head. Larry Delaney seemed to be losing confidence in her. Just because she was offering to keep practising to get it perfect, he thought it meant that she was saying her voice still wasn't up to standard.

Or maybe, she suddenly thought, he was suggesting that she was only using it as an excuse to see him. The thought made her feel all hot and flustered and she knew that the red flush would appear on her chest and neck at any minute. Her mind worked quickly as she lifted her scarf from the table, wondering how someone on a level with Larry might reply, wondering how someone like that dark-haired, sophisticated Fiona McCluskey might reply.

'Actually, I do feel OK about going on stage,' she said briskly, tying her scarf in such a way that it would cover her betraying red neck. 'I suppose I'm becoming too much of a perfectionist ... but if you want to get on in life, you have to do things right.'

Larry's face instantly lightened. 'No harm in that, Kirsty,' he said, smiling warmly at her.

'No harm at all.'

Kirsty smiled back at him, realising that she'd found the right way to communicate with her manager. Larry Delaney was a shrewd businessman, and he admired that trait in others. From now on she would make sure that every exchange with him would be carefully weighed up.

The young, impulsive Kirsty Grace had grown up.

That night in the dance hall she had learned a lesson – a very hard but very valuable lesson. It was a lesson she would never need to learn again.

Chapter 42

NEW YEAR'S EVE 1955

'Well, we're a right sad oul' pair with not a man between us,' Kirsty said, as the two sisters made their way up to Liz's house. 'Let's just hope that 1956 is luckier for us than this year has been.' She did up the toggles on her duffel coat as she walked along. 'I'm out working tonight in a right posh place where nobody will give me a second glance, and you're sittin' in with my mammy and daddy. That'll be a right bundle of laughs for you.'

'I'd much rather be on my own,' Heather told her, taking her fine black leather gloves out of her pocket, 'than be stuck with the wrong man. Anyway, Liz asked me to go with her and Jim to a New Year party in Motherwell, but I can't be bothered. You have all the carry-on with trying to get a taxi home, and if you do get one they charge double fare.'

'I wouldn't let that put you off,' Kirsty stated. 'There will be a few of you and you can all chip in together.' She stopped. 'D'you need a loan? Are you skint after Glasgow?'

'No,' Heather laughed, 'I'm fine for money, but thanks for the offer.' She smoothed one of the leather gloves between both hands as she walked along and then she started the same smoothing procedure with the other. 'Och, there's a good chance that Gerry Stewart will be there if Jim Murray's there – they always spend the New Year together. I really, really *don't* want to meet up with him on New Year's Eve.' She gave a big sigh. 'God knows what he might say and do. I just don't feel I could handle it if he started. I've had enough arguments recently to last me a lifetime. I'd far rather sit in with my mammy and daddy. Anyway, I think they're all going over to Mona's to watch the television because they've got some special Hogmanay shows on. Lily's being allowed to stay up late as well, so I'll be quite happy sitting yapping away to her or playing games with her.' Lily was on her second visit home and Mona had reported this morning that she was a lot more cheerful and amenable than she'd been over Christmas.

'I feel bad that I'm working or I would have gone out with you,' Kirsty said, tutting to herself.

'Well, you shouldn't feel like that,' Heather told her. 'This is your big chance. You're not saying you'd rather be at a New Year's party in Motherwell instead of singing in a nice posh hotel?'

Kirsty pulled a face. 'There's one half of me dead excited because it's the biggest thing that's happened in my singing, but there's another half of me dreadin' it.'

Heather looked at her sister. 'Are you over all that stuff with that Larry Delaney fella?'

They hadn't really discussed what had happened in any great depth since that night.

'Oh, definitely!' Kirsty said quickly, colouring up at the mention of his name. 'God, I'll never know what came over me that night to make me act so daft. I often think about it, trying to work it all out. I wonder if it was the couple of drinks? Surely it couldn't have been that?' Her brow wrinkled and she shook her head. 'If I thought that was the cause of it, I'd never let strong drink past my lips again.'

'Well, you weren't drunk or anything when you came in,' Heather said kindly, 'so I don't think it was that . . .'

'You didn't tell anybody else, did you?' Kirsty asked in a soft, fearful voice.

'Who would I tell?' her sister replied. 'Liz is interested in talking about nothing else apart from Jim Murray and the flaming wedding.' They were heading up to Liz's house now to give her the dates of the two Saturdays that Kirsty was available to sing with The Hi-Tones for Liz's wedding. Since it was now out in the open, and Liz had got over the awkwardness of telling people, she was full of plans for the smallish wedding she was planning.

'Would you normally have told Liz things like that? If she wasn't so busy with her own plans?'

Heather shook her head. 'No ... not when it's something serious about you. I'd only tell her daft things like when we'd had an argument or if you bought something new, or I might tell her about your singing – that kind of thing. I'd never tell anybody about anything that was really personal.'

'Good,' Kirsty said, a smile spreading across her pretty face. 'I used to think you told her everything – especially all the bad things about me.'

Heather looked at her sister now, irritation etched on her face. 'You've got a lot of faith in me if you thought that.' She halted. 'Do you talk to all your pals about me? I know you talked about me and Gerry at times.'

Kirsty looked vaguely injured, but knew she couldn't deny it as she'd been caught out on several occasions. 'Only the same daft stuff you've just mentioned. I'd never tell a soul about anything that was really serious.'

'Well, that's OK then, isn't it?' Heather said, feeling very heartened.

Things were looking up when she and Kirsty could talk in such a mature, grown-up manner. It made Heather feel better about not having Liz around so much, especially after the horrible episode in Glasgow with Sarah. She'd told Kirsty all about it, and Kirsty had said that Barbara was obviously jealous and there was no point in getting dragged into an argument that could affect her work situation. She'd told her to go back to work after the New Year and just pretend that nothing had happened.

'Has Liz said anything to you about a bridesmaid's dress yet?' Kirsty asked as they turned onto the main road in Rowanhill.

'No,' Heather said. 'I suppose she'll mention it when we're in the house now.'

'D'you think she'll have the nerve to get married in white?' Kirsty giggled. 'Or d'you think she'll go for a suit? I think her mother's the ould-fashioned kind that will make her go for a suit.'

Heather shrugged. 'I haven't the faintest . . . she used to talk about wanting to have a big white wedding when we were younger, but things have obviously changed.'

They sat in the Mullens' kitchen eating home-made shortbread and drinking cups of sweet Camp coffee, which Liz had painstakingly made with boiled frothy milk – telling the two Grace girls that it was just the way Jim loved it.

'I think we'll go for that second Saturday in February,' Liz said, looking at the brand-new holy calendar that someone had sent her mother for Christmas. 'I mean, we're not in that big a rush to have to make it the end of January.'

Kirsty didn't look near her sister, for fear of smiling at the wrong time and getting into trouble. 'You'll still have plenty of things to organise for February,' she told Liz, as though she organised weddings every day of the week herself.

'Well, it's not going to be a great big occasion,' Liz said cautiously. 'That's OK if you want to wait for years and save up for it . . . but I'd far rather get married now than have all that waitin' and savin'.' She held her hands out and shrugged. 'If you waited for years for these things – God knows what could happen in the meantime.'

'That's right,' Kirsty said, a mite too enthusiastically, 'Jim could meet somebody else and run off and get married to them!'

'Well, thank you, Kirsty Grace, for that vote of confidence in Jim Murray,' Liz said, rolling her eyes in exasperation.

Heather threw her sister a look that could have killed at ten paces.

'Och, I'm only kidding,' Kirsty said, pushing Liz's arm. 'Come on, Liz, don't lose yer sense of humour!'

'It's a good job I know you,' Liz said, smiling wryly in spite of herself. 'And it's a good job I can't get anybody else as good to sing at the wedding, or I'd be hunting you straight out of that front door.'

'Tell us,' Kirsty said, 'what about your dress? Have you decided on anything yet?'

'Plain empire-line,' Liz said in a definite tone. 'Three-quarter length with a matching coat . . . you know the kind of thing. Definitely not a suit – but something akin to it.'

'And will you wear it with a veil?' Kirsty enquired, taking a drink of her coffee.

Liz pursed her lips together and shook her head. 'I'm not bothering about all that palaver – a nice wee feathered half-hat is far more fashionable, and I can wear it again. You only get one wear out of a white dress and a veil.'

As she heard her friend's statements, Heather could hear Mrs Mullen talking instead of Liz. They had obviously hammered it out, and Liz had been forced to come down on the side of finance and practicality.

'Have you seen your outfit yet?' Heather asked, feeling obliged to show some interest, and that it would be better if she asked more tactful, ordinary questions than the kind of blatant things that her sister might ask.

Liz shook her head. 'Not yet. I'm waiting until the sales start. My mammy was saying that you never know what you could pick up in them. We're going to go into Glasgow next weekend and have a look in Lewis's and the other big shops.' She paused. 'If I don't see anything I really like, I thought I might ask your mammy to make it ...'

'Well, you'll still have about a month,' Heather calculated, 'so she should have time to do a nice job for you if you need her.'

'And what about your bridesmaid?' Kirsty asked, since there had been no mention of it.

Liz looked up at Heather. 'I'll see what there is in Glasgow, and if I see something that suits you, I'll ask them to put it aside for you. You'll be able to go in and look at it during your lunch break, won't you?'

'Aye. Of course I will,' Heather replied, suddenly feeling sorry for Liz and all this wedding organisation that had been thrust upon her and the unknown things that lay ahead. 'Just let me know as soon as you decide.'

The girls finished their coffee and chatted for a while longer about this and that. Heather didn't mention the fiasco with Sarah in Glasgow and just made out she had had a good time, and she was grateful to Kirsty for neither contradicting her nor laughing. Then Liz asked all about Kirsty's big hotel debut and they talked about that for a while.

'Listen,' Kirsty said, looking at her watch, 'I'll need to go. I've to be at May Ingles to get my hair done at half past three, and I'll have to get my bath first.'

'You're not going to go straight outside after a bath, are you?' Liz said, her face aghast at the thought. 'You could catch pneumonia.'

'Of course I am,' Kirsty laughed. 'I do it all the time.'

Liz turned to Heather now. 'Are you sure you won't come to that party in Motherwell with me and Jim tonight? There's a good crowd going.'

Heather shook her head. 'No thanks,' she said. 'I'm happy just staying in. I had enough gallivanting going in to Glasgow the other day.'

'But there's a minibus going from Rowanhill at eight o'clock,' Liz insisted, 'and there's quite a few girls and fellas going on their own.' She rhymed off the names of local girls they often went dancing with. 'Och, don't miss it, Heather, it should be a great night.' She suddenly halted. 'Is it because of Gerry?' She gave a big smile. 'He's not going – honest! That wee lassie he's going out with has asked him to go to a party out at her house in Wishaw.'

'Hey, less of the "wee" if you don't mind,' Kirsty put in, 'she's actually about the same size as me!' She rolled her blue eyes in mock indignation and they all laughed.

'What d'ye think?' Liz asked. 'I'd love you to go, because once Jim gets a few drinks in him he'll be off chatting to the other lads and leavin' me like a wallflower as usual.'

'He won't do that now that you're engaged . . . surely?' Kirsty said, knowing full well that Jim Murray was quite likely to do just that. If they were married for ten years he would probably still do it. He was the type that never changed.

Liz pretended not to hear Kirsty's comment as she waiting for her friend's answer.

Heather thought for a moment. 'Are you sure Gerry's not going?'

Liz nodded her head vigorously. 'Definitely – you know I wouldn't do that to you. Jim definitely said that he's goin' to that lassie's house.'

'You should go to the party,' Kirsty prompted her. 'You never know who you might meet.' Her eyes suddenly widened with delight as a great idea came to her. 'Ooooh, you can take a loan of one of those fancy dresses I have in the wardrobe – I don't have to give them back until next week! That black lace one would look brilliant on you.' She gestured towards her bust. 'You've got more to fill it than I have.'

'OK,' Heather suddenly said, picturing herself in one of the glamorous dresses. There was no point in sitting at home moping when she could be out having a good time. It might just make up for the big let-down she'd had last week. 'I think I will.'

Chapter 43

❧

Heather sorted her clothes out for the party while she waited for the water to heat up again after Kirsty had had her bath and rushed over to the hairdresser's house. Heather had picked out a few of the dresses to try on, but after she tried the black lace one on she knew there was no point in trying any of the others. It looked absolutely fantastic, and the small neat size fitted her to perfection.

'Good God!' Sophie had said, when Heather had called her mother up for her opinion. 'I hadn't realised you'd lost so much weight, that dress really shows off your lovely slim figure. You look like a film star in it.' She put her glasses on to look closer at the boned lace bodice and the thin spaghetti-style straps. It was all hand-sewn and must have taken ages to make – and cost a fortune.

'In fact,' Sophie said now, 'I'm sure that's the very same dress I saw Diana Dors wearing in one of the *Photoplay* magazines. If it's not the same dress, then it's as close as you can get.'

Heather turned around, looking at herself in the long wardrobe mirror. 'You don't think it's too low and tight for me?' she asked. 'I feel a wee bit self-conscious . . .'

'It's low right enough, but I don't think it's *too* low, and those dresses are all the fashion,' Sophie said. She smiled indulgently at her daughter. 'Och, it's New Year and it's a party, isn't it? All the girls will be dressed up to the nines.'

'I'll wear a stole with it,' Heather decided. 'There's a plain black satin one that goes with one of the other dresses and a pair of long black satin gloves, so they'll help to cover me up a wee bit more.'

'Just make sure you have your coat and stole on when you come down the stairs to go out,' Sophie said, winking conspiratorially. 'What your father doesn't know won't hurt him. I've heard him going on about Kirsty's stage outfits and there's no point in getting into a row with him over something stupid like that on New Year's Eve.'

Larry picked Kirsty up at seven o'clock. 'The outfit and hair are just perfect,' he said, looking approvingly at her.

'Thanks,' Kirsty said, giving him a bright smile that didn't quite reach her eyes. 'I thought the lights would catch the sequins on the dress, so I asked the hairdresser to put a few in my hair as well.'

'You're catching on,' he said, starting the car engine up. 'What counts is how it looks on stage. If you've got the right image *and* the right voice you have everything.'

Catching on, Kirsty repeated to herself. You'd think she was only a schoolgirl the way he was talking. She fought back a smart remark, determined not to cross swords with him. Tonight was too important to let anything get in the way.

The band members were already there, setting up the microphones and tuning their instruments. They greeted Kirsty with cheery smiles and a few light-hearted words, and she realised that after only a couple of times rehearsing with them, she felt relaxed and easy in the same way she'd had felt with The Hi-Tones.

When it dawned on her, Kirsty felt very good about it. Larry had explained that it was important for a solo singer to be able to adapt to the different bands in different places. The crowds started to come in to the beautifully decorated function room, to find their individual tables with their place-names, stopping to admire the very classy Christmas tree and decorations that still looking sparklingly fresh even though they'd been up several weeks by now.

As she watched the formally dressed men and women take their places, Kirsty decided that it was time for her to disappear into the dressing-room for a final run over the songs again.

When she came out on stage, the lights were dimmed very low, with candle-light flickering on each table. It was too dark to actually make out faces, but Kirsty was instinctively aware of Larry sitting at a table to the side of the stage – watching and waiting to see how she performed.

'I told you that Jim Murray would swan off with his pals,' Liz said with an indulgent smile as she watched him from across the crowded room. She was all dressed up for the evening in a pale pink strapless satin dress that suited her light colouring, and her fiancé was in his best suit. 'But you can't tie them down all the time, and as he said, he might as well enjoy this New Year as we don't know what situation we're going to be in next year.' She paused for a moment, her hand patting the back of her elegant, swept-up hair to check that it was all in place. 'We could have a baby or anything, and that would halt all the gadding about at the weekends.'

Heather slowly nodded her head in agreement, hardly able to believe that Liz had broached the subject of babies herself. She still hadn't come straight out and said, 'I'm expecting' or 'I'm pregnant', but she was obviously preparing people for the fact that they probably would have one in the next year.

Heather was glad she had dressed up, as everyone else looked very glamorous, the girls in lovely evening gowns and the boys in their best suits and one or two of them wearing bow-ties. When she arrived she had taken off her coat, but so far had kept the light stole around her, draped in such a way that it completely covered her bust. 'It's a gorgeous big house,' she said now, 'isn't it? It's obviously private and must be worth a fortune.' She gave a little giggle. 'How did we get invited? We don't usually go to parties in places like this.' She looked around the high-ceilinged sitting-room, admiring the intricate coving and the floral centrepiece that surrounded the fitting for a fancy crystal chandelier.

The downstairs hallway was beautiful, with very expensive-looking red velvet wallpaper, the kind Heather had only ever seen in the sorts of restaurants that her mother liked to visit on days out in the summer. The staircase was painted white with a dark wood banister, and the same patterned carpet that was in the hall below ran all the way up the stairs.

Both girls whispered how they would love to see inside the bedrooms.

'I bet they're gorgeous,' Heather had said, with dreamy eyes. 'All flowery and romantic. You can just tell – it's the type of house that it would just suit.'

'When you're upstairs in the bathroom later,' Liz said, 'look along the corridor and see if any of the doors are open wide enough to peep in.'

Heather had shaken her head. 'You must be joking, Liz Mullen – you know fine well I'm not brave enough. You'll have to do it yourself.'

'I will,' Liz grinned. 'I want to get ideas for when Jim and I eventually have our own house.' She'd glanced around her. 'Some day I'd like to own a house like this.'

'Wouldn't we all?' Heather said, and then the two girls looked at each other and went into childish fits of giggles, drawing inquisitive looks from the others around them.

Earlier on they had been shown into the dining-room where an expensive radiogram was playing jazz music, and the polished mahogany table and chairs had been pushed into the large bay window to give room for dancing later on. An older kitchen table had been piled up with bottles of beer and lager that people had brought along with the usual drinks for the girls like Snowballs, Babycham and Cherry-B. There was also a bottle of whiskey that someone had brought and a bottle of gin. Dishes with crisps and nuts were dotted about the place and Liz had reported that she'd heard someone say that there would be sandwiches and more substantial food later.

Heather had grimaced to herself at the thought of the gin and tonic she'd forced herself to drink at the Pavillion in Glasgow, and had happily settled on a glass of lemonade. She decided she'd see how she felt later, but she might have one of the fancy little bottles of something when it was time for the bells.

'Who's actually giving this party?' Heather suddenly asked Liz in a low whisper. 'I feel funny being in here and not even knowing them.'

'I don't know the people at all,' Liz whispered back now. 'As far as I know it's a sister and brother who're having the party. Mark and Katherine somebody . . . I can't remember the name. Jim said they're a wee bit full of themselves wi' all the money, but quite nice considering.' She halted. 'The mother and father are away to a big posh do at a hotel in Edinburgh and they're not coming back until tomorrow night.'

'That's very handy,' Heather said, taking a sip from her glass of lemonade. 'Although I'd be terrified to have anything at home in case things got broken or damaged, and if I owned a place as nice as this I'd be even more terrified.'

'Seemingly they're a very decent family, so there won't be any rough ones here or anything. Jim knows the fella through work,' Liz explained, 'and he just told Jim to bring a few friends with him since you never know who'll turn up, because a lot of people like to see the New Year in at home.'

'Well it's a nice change to see some new faces,' Heather said quietly. 'I know it's terrible if you don't know a soul, but we've got the best of both worlds tonight because there's the wee group that came from Rowanhill with us in the minibus if we've nobody else to talk to.' She gestured over to a corner where the other six were chatting animatedly, three lads and three girls – none of whom were going out with each other.

'D'you not fancy any of them?' Liz asked her now. 'Michael Heggarty's a nice fella – I had a couple of dates with him before I started goin' out with Jim.'

'No thanks,' Heather said, shooting her friend a warning glance. 'I think if I'd fancied him you'd have known by now.'

An hour later there was a nice-sized crowd in the house and Heather and Liz had met quite a few of the people they didn't know. Jim had come across to introduce Mark McFarlane who was the fellow who lived in the house. He was very friendly and well-spoken, with smooth brown hair and glasses.

'This is Liz, my fiancée,' Jim had said, and Heather noticed the glow that came to Liz's cheeks at being described in such a way.

'And this is my friend, Heather,' Liz had said, almost pushing her forward. 'And she's single before you ask – and she's got a good job in an office in Glasgow!'

Everyone laughed at Liz's pointed introduction but Heather found herself cringing as she shook Mark's hand. Her friend had made it sound as though she was trying to flog her off at a cattle market. She wouldn't have been surprised if Liz had pointed out that she had good hair and nice white even teeth.

Later, when the dancing started up in the dining-room, Mark McFarlane came across to ask Heather to dance. He was very friendly and chatty, asking her all the usual questions about where she lived and what schools she'd gone to. He then went on to tell her how his father owned several bookies' shops and that he was now managing the biggest one. He'd previously worked with Jim, not wanting to get involved in the family business, but his father had made him several offers that were much too good to refuse.

'Let's be honest,' he'd told Heather as he swept her around the floor in a waltz, 'how many fellas my age are driving brand-new cars and going to Italy for their holidays? And it's just as easy working for my father as it is for any other boss ... and there's a lot more perks.'

Heather had nodded her head in agreement, wondering what it must be like to have such a glamorous lifestyle. 'Well, there's no fear of me following my parents into anything,' she'd laughed at one point. 'My father's a school janitor and my mother does sewing – but I'm happy enough with my job in Glasgow.' She twirled around the floor and ignored the sinking feeling that came into her stomach at the thought of returning to work on the fourth of January and facing Sarah.

Mark McFarlane had shrugged. 'Och, women shouldn't have to worry about finding decent jobs. What they need to do is find a decent man with a decent job.' He gave a little smile. 'By the time the family comes along they're far too busy keeping the house to do anything else.'

'I think,' Heather said, giving him a surprised look, 'that

maybe your views are a wee bit old-fashioned these days. A lot of women like to have their own careers.'

'Maybe,' he'd said, smiling down at her. 'But there's a lot who would jump at the chance of a nice house and a nice car.' He nodded in the direction of Jim and Liz. 'There's a pair who would jump at that. They must be mad getting married so young . . . or maybe they don't have much choice.'

'They seem happy enough about it,' Heather said, wondering if he knew the reason for the sudden rush.

The next time they circled around that part of the floor, Heather noticed that Liz and Jim seemed to be in a heated discussion – or maybe even an argument. She was quite taken aback since it was a fairly public place to be arguing, but when she got a good look at them she deduced it was Liz giving Jim a good telling off about something.

Possibly, he'd already had a bit too much to drink, Heather thought. Then she scolded herself for being so nosy. It was normal for couples to have the odd row – and they could have been rowing about anything.

Mark's very attractive sister Katherine came over to them at the end of the dance, and said she thought it was about time to put the food out, otherwise people might get a bit too tipsy to enjoy it.

'I'll come back to you later,' Mark McFarlane told Heather. 'So don't go too far away.'

'I think you've made a good impression there,' Liz whispered as they piled small sausage rolls and a variety of sandwiches on their plates. 'And he's a good catch. If you leave the stole off at the next dance, you've as good as got him.'

'Heather made an apologetic face. 'He's not my type, Liz,' she whispered back.

'You hardly know him,' Liz countered, sounding a bit irritable. 'God, you're never going to meet anybody if you keep being so fussy.'

Having picked their choice of the food, they turned to cross the beautifully carpeted hallway and head back to the comfortable chairs in the sitting-room.

Heather suddenly felt Liz tug at her elbow. 'Oh, my God!' she gasped. 'Look who's just walked in!'

Heather turned to look and there, standing at the front door chatting to Jim, was Gerry Stewart. 'Oh, no!' she said, moving quickly across the hall and into the large sitting-room. She made for a dimly lit corner of the room, away from the other groups of people milling around chatting, and put her bag and drink and food on a sideboard next to their chairs. 'I thought you said he definitely wasn't coming here!' she hissed, turning accusingly to Liz. 'You promised me. You know I would never have come if I'd thought he'd be here as well.'

Liz put her handbag and plate of sandwiches down next to Heather's and then she crossed her heart with her thumb. 'Honest to God I didn't know he was coming tonight. He wasn't supposed to be here ...' She halted. 'You know I wouldn't do that to you ... don't you?'

'Well, how do you think it looks?' Heather said sharply, hurt and betrayal staring out from her eyes.

'It was Jim,' Liz stated weakly. 'He told Gerry you would be here ...'

'When?' Heather asked. 'I only decided that I would come this afternoon.'

'Jim called in after you left and I told him,' Liz explained calmly and in a low voice, desperately hoping that it would encourage her friend to respond in a similar manner. 'And when he went back up home Gerry was sitting in the house waiting for him.'

Heather took a long deep breath.

'I gave Jim hell for telling him,' Liz said, sounding on the verge of tears now. 'I only found out about ten minutes ago. We were just standin' chatting when Jim just said casually that he wouldn't be surprised if Gerry called in.' She held her hands palm-up. 'He came out with it, just like that – as if there wasn't a problem in the world about him coming here.'

'And what did you say?' Heather said in a flat, resigned voice. She knew her friend well enough to tell that she had not been involved in any deliberate betrayal.

Just like herself, Liz had underestimated Gerry Stewart.

'I went absolutely mad,' Liz said. 'But it's as if you can't get through to him.' She stopped, swallowing back the tears.

It dawned on Heather now that this is what they had been arguing about when she saw them earlier on.

'Jim's just terrified that Gerry might go to Australia and he'll never see him again,' Liz continued. 'He thinks that you might change your mind and take Gerry back, and then everythin' will be all hunky-dory the way it was before. He keeps goin' on about the four of us going out together at the weekends, or if you and Gerry got married then us takin' turns to visit each other's houses – all that kind of rubbish.'

Heather nodded, her lips pressed tightly together. Eventually she looked up at her friend. 'Well, there's nothing can be done about it now, it's just a case of getting through the night.'

'Oh, I'm really sorry this has happened,' Liz whispered. 'I feel terrible . . .'

'It's OK,' Heather said, attempting a smile. 'There's no point in everybody getting upset about it. I suppose worse things could happen.'

'D'you know something, Heather?' Liz said now. 'Men are really, really stupid, aren't they?'

Heather nodded. 'I'm beginning to think they are.'

Liz reached over for the drinks, handing Heather hers first. 'I don't suppose Gerry had that wee lassie with him, did he?'

'I didn't look at him long enough to see,' Heather replied.

A while later Jim came into the sitting-room on his own, obviously looking for the girls. He gave them a big cheery wave and then came over.

'Enjoying yourselves, ladies?' he asked, his face red and beaming from the bottles of beer he had already drunk.

'We were,' Liz told him, 'until we saw your companion at the door.'

'Oh, d'you mean Gerry?' he said, pulling a chair in beside them. 'He said the other place in Wishaw was dead, full of oul' grannies and everything, so he told them he'd a sore head and he needed to go home.'

'Very nice,' Liz said, rolling her eyes disapprovingly.

Heather picked at a sandwich she didn't want, saying nothing. The last thing she wanted to do was cause a row between Liz and Jim. Especially since it was obvious he'd had a bit to drink. Besides, he wasn't going to see things from her point of view, no matter what. Gerry Stewart was like an idol to him, and he wasn't interested in hearing anything derogatory about his pal. Keeping quiet seemed her best option, enduring the next couple of hours until it was time to go home.

'You're not going to believe it,' Jim said laughing. He thumbed in the direction of the hallway. 'That nut Gerry walked all the way from the bottom of Wishaw to get here. He said all the taxis were packed wi' people headin' home for the bells, so he was quicker hoofing it.' He shook his head, but was obviously impressed with his friend's effort. 'Daft or what?' Jim continued. 'He said he wanted to have a good New Year in case he takes up that job in Australia, and he definitely wasn't going to have a good night with all the oul' ones in the other place.'

Mark McFarlane suddenly appeared through the crowds, and chatted to Jim for a while. Then he turned towards Heather. 'D'you fancy another turn on the dance floor?'

A wave of relief flooded through Heather. An escape route, which would keep her well out of Gerry's way for a while. 'I'll see you later,' she told Liz, then she slid her small handbag over her wrist and followed Mark out towards the darkened room where all the couples were now dancing to a Glenn Miller tune. Her flimsy black stole slipped off one shoulder as she crossed the hallway, but she didn't dare stop to fix it in case she found herself face-to-face with the cause of her anxiety.

'I thought I'd never get back to you,' Mark said, taking her into his arms. 'I'd to see to a few things, but I think everything's under control now. I can relax and enjoy myself.'

They moved around the floor nice and easy. Mark was obviously an accomplished dancer, and something about the way he moved and held her made Heather guess that he had probably gone to dancing lessons.

That was the sort of thing he would do, she imagined. He wanted to give a good impression with everything he did – he didn't come across as the sort of person who would be content to be second-best at anything.

'You're a nice mover,' he told Heather as they went into a

quick-step for the next lively number. He gave a big warm smile. 'I take it you like dancing?'

She suddenly caught sight of Gerry at the edge of the floor, staring across at them. She turned her head away, deliberately ignoring him. 'I love it,' Heather told him, smiling back in a friendlier manner than she really felt. Hopefully, Gerry would presume they were together and head off into one of the other rooms to find Jim or some other fellow to chat to. He might even find another girl.

They whirled around the floor, occasionally bumping into other couples and laughing good-naturedly about it and sometimes getting a nice space where they could really do the dance justice. Liz and Jim waltzed up beside them, Liz tapping Heather playfully on the shoulder and obviously checking she was OK.

As the fourth dance together came to an end, Mark caught her around the waist tighter now, obviously feeling more confident and sure of himself. 'You're a very good-looking girl,' he complimented her. 'And obviously intelligent. I like a woman who knows her own mind.'

Heather laughed, throwing her head back. She was trying to keep things friendly and light, not wanting to encourage him too much, yet happy to look as though she was occupied with another fellow as far as Gerry was concerned. 'You weren't saying that earlier on when you were talking about a woman's place being in the home!'

'In your case,' he called above the music, 'I'd definitely be prepared to make an exception. You can lay down the terms and I'll agree to anything!'

Heather laughed along with him, enjoying the light-hearted banter, but she was very careful to make sure that she didn't lead him on in any way.

The record came to an end now, and they moved to the side of the dance floor, waiting for the next record to drop down onto the turntable. As they stood chatting, Heather suddenly became aware that the stole had slipped down from her shoulders leaving her voluptuous frontage uncovered. As she turned in a fluster to catch it, the fine satin material slithered out of her reach and floated down onto the dark depths of the floor.

She stood back for a moment, checking to see exactly where it had landed, then, just as she bent down to pick it up, Gerry Stewart seemed to appear out of nowhere and in a second he had quickly retrieved it for her.

When she saw him, Heather's face visibly stiffened and she descended into a hostile, stony silence.

'Sorry, but this is *my* dance, Mark,' Gerry said, cutting in between them. 'I think you've had Miss Grace long enough for one night.' Without a word he handed her the stole back and – grateful to have the security of it back again – Heather clutched it against her chest.

Mark stepped back, his face dark and serious. 'I don't think so . . .' he blustered, looking at Heather now, not quite sure how to react. 'We weren't actually finished . . .'

'Well, I think you are now,' Gerry told him.

Heather felt a hot rush of anger. 'You can't just cut in like this,' she hissed, not wanting to make a scene. The last thing she wanted was a row over her in Mark McFarlane's lovely house. Only cheap, conniving girls had lads fighting over them, and even though she didn't fancy him, she didn't want Mark to think badly of her. 'Don't be so damned rude!'

It was quite obvious that Gerry had been drinking heavily again. She thought the Christmas episode had been a one-off. What had got into him now? The old Gerry she knew neither drank too much nor would ever have behaved in public in such a way. She knew he was still upset about them breaking up, but his behaviour had gone beyond a point that any girl would put up with.

'Well, I think it's time someone else got a chance to dance with Heather,' Gerry said to Mark, completely ignoring what she had just said. He reached out, and very firmly took her hand in his. 'So I think you'd be better off just finding yourself another partner.' He gave a little smile. 'I'm sure you won't have any trouble, you being the host with the most tonight and everything.'

'I'm still dancing with Mark,' Heather said, pulling out of his grasp.

'Look, you've been told,' Mark said, suddenly squaring up to him, his shoulder pushing against Gerry's. 'Just bugger off and leave us alone!'

Gerry stopped for a second, his eyes narrowing, then he turned his head to the side.

'Touch me one more time,' he said in a low, threatening voice, 'and you won't live to see the New Year in!'

Heather looked around now with wide, frightened eyes, hoping that Jim might have seen what was happening and come over to cool his friend down a bit – but there was no sign of him and Liz. They must have gone back into the sitting-room. Thankfully, nobody else seemed to be reacting to it.

Mark stared at Gerry for a few moments as though considering the situation, then he suddenly backed off, his hands held up in a conciliatory manner. 'OK,' he said in a resigned tone, 'I'm not going to ruin things for everybody else by getting into a stupid fight. It's the wrong night for that.' He adjusted his bow-tie then he looked at Heather. 'I'll come back for you later . . .' Then he disappeared off through the other dancers.

Heather took a long, deep breath. 'I hope you're well pleased with yourself,' she said, her brown eyes glinting and angry.

Gerry stared at her now, as though searching for something in her face. 'I'm sorry . . . I didn't mean for that to happen.'

'Well, you shouldn't have started the argument then,' she told him.

'I couldn't help it,' he whispered. 'I've never seen you look as lovely . . . that dress is beautiful on you.'

Heather looked down at herself and realised that she was holding the flimsy stole by her side. Her cleavage was now very evident over the top of the low-necked lace dress and her shoulders were almost bare, apart from the narrow straps. She had never worn anything as daring as this before, and certainly not while she was going out with Gerry. Heather was suddenly conscious of his eyes taking in every tiny inch of her bare skin.

She turned away from him, adjusting her hair, and then started to put the stole back on, but his hand came out to gently catch hers and prevent her from covering herself up again.

'Please dance with me, Heather,' Gerry said, in a small, pleading voice. 'Just one dance? Surely you don't hate me that much that you won't have a dance with me at New Year?'

She looked past him now to see Jim and Liz coming back in to join the other dancers and she gave a sigh of relief. Jim would be able to handle him. He wasn't that drunk that he wouldn't listen to his friend. Then, as she watched them start dancing together, she suddenly felt that it wasn't fair on them to have to mediate between her and Gerry. They wouldn't have too many party nights for a while. By the time they got the wedding organised and settled into where they would live, they would have very little money. They would also have very few nights out together before the baby came. And certainly not in a nice house like this.

'Please dance with me . . .' Gerry said again, and the broken tone of his voice suddenly touched something inside her.

'If I do,' she bargained with him quietly, hoping that no one was listening, 'will you promise to leave me alone?'

Silently Gerry nodded his head. He opened his arms and she moved towards him.

Kirsty stepped back on stage after the break, brimming over with delight and confidence. Apparently the manager of the hotel had approached Larry after only a few numbers to ask if he could book her immediately for some events he had coming up. There was a big football event, a charity night and a business-men's dinner, to name a few off the top of his head, and the manager told Larry that he was sure Kirsty would go down a bomb.

'She's a wee star!' he'd said. 'In fact, she's rarer that that – she's a wee diamond!'

When she had finished the first half and gone backstage, Larry had come rushing through to tell her the news. 'It's not just the bookings I'm delighted with,' he had told Kirsty excitedly, looking more like a handsome film star than ever in his tuxedo and fancy bow-tie, 'it's the reaction to your performance – your voice and the choice of songs.' Then he had leaned forward and very gently put the tips of his fingers on either side of her face. 'You're going places in 1956, Kirsty Grace! Mark my words.'

Kirsty's heart had soared at the touch of his hands and at the things he had just said – but she hadn't let it show. 'That's great,' she had said, smiling back at him – a very careful smile that went nowhere near her eyes.

'And I have to tell you,' he had carried on, 'that you look just exquisite up on that stage.' He had held his arms up as though searching for words. 'Everything about you is just fantastic tonight – just as I knew it would be.'

Kirsty had nodded her head, taking it all in. 'I'm delighted it's all going down so well – it's a great start.' She'd paused for a moment. 'Now, I don't mean to be rude, but I just want to touch up my make-up and sort my hair, so that I look fine for going back on stage.' Then without once looking him in the eye she had swung around in her swivel chair to face the gilt mirror again.

It was the longest dance of Heather's life. She could feel Gerry Stewart's warm, beery breath on her face and neck and she was sure she could feel and hear his heart beating through his shirt every time he tried to press closer to her.

She didn't know whether it was better when he was quiet, although the intensity of him almost frightened her. When he spoke, she had difficulty hearing him, and it meant he had to bend closer to her and almost touch her ear with his lips.

Eventually, the music stopped and as soon as it was decently possible, Heather extricated herself from Gerry's arms. 'Thank you,' she heard herself say. 'But now I need to go to the bathroom.' And before he could stop her, she walked out of the room and up the stairs as quickly as her legs would carry her. She had hardly closed the bathroom door when she heard a loud rap on it. She took a long deep breath.

'It's me!' Liz's voice came from outside. 'Are you all right?'

A cool wave of relief washed over her and she rushed to unlock the door.

Liz came in quickly, making sure she secured the door after her. 'Are you all right?' she repeated. 'I could see your face when you were dancing, and I was worried sick about you.'

Heather nodded her head, sinking slightly inelegantly in her tight lace dress to sit on the side of the bath. Liz put the toilet seat down and sat on that. Normally, the two friends would have spent a good five minutes discussing the lovely wallpaper and the fancy towels, but under the circumstances they took in nothing of their surroundings.

'Och, I suppose I'm OK,' Heather said, with a quiver in her voice. 'I just wish this night was ended and I was tucked up and fast asleep in bed.'

'We haven't long to go until the minibus comes,' Liz said encouragingly, 'just another hour or so.' She paused. 'My God – it's ten to twelve! It's nearly the New Year. We better get back downstairs.'

'Look,' Heather said, 'you go on down and find Jim. Just give me a couple of minutes to wash my face and freshen up and then I'll be down.'

'Are you sure?' Liz checked.

'Positive,' Heather said, giving her a reassuring smile.

It was strange. The night had been the most successful one in Kirsty's singing career so far and yet she hardly felt a thing. She had imagined almost floating off the stage in a cloud of elation if she had ever got the sort of response from an audience she had got tonight.

And yet, here she was – half an hour into 1956 – standing in front of hundreds of strangers, bowing to their thunderous applause and whistles and calls for more songs. As she stood smiling and waving at the crowd, she was surprised to find that she was able to distance herself from the moment, thinking how very odd it was to feel so very, very calm in the face of such enormous appreciation.

She had never felt terribly nervous singing with the The Hi-Tones, but they were an easy band who sang in easy-to-please places. She had always learned her words and made sure she could hit the notes, but that had never been too difficult, for often the volume of the band and the crackly microphones had drowned her voice anyway.

She'd never worried too much, thinking that nobody would be too hard on her if she had the odd off-night. But thankfully, it had never happened. But she had quickly realised that the easy-going regime with the boys was all over. She was now singing to a different tune career-wise, and she was silly to think it would have been any different.

It had definitely been hard work over these last few weeks, getting ready for this big night – rushing out in the dark winter evenings to catch the bus into Wishaw for her singing lessons: all the hours practising her scales upstairs in her bedroom or lying in the bath; the time spent learning the words of the new songs, and then the evenings spent rehearsing them with the band.

But tonight she had reaped the rewards. The applause and the appreciative look in Larry Delaney's eyes when he had come to wish her a happy new year and give her a glass of champagne proved it.

Heather came downstairs to find that everyone had assembled in the sitting-room and were now listening intently for the bells that signalled the end of the old year and the start of the new.

A figure moved out from the edge of the crowd towards her as soon as she came in. It was Mark McFarlane. 'Are you all right?' he asked in a low, concerned voice.

Heather nodded, embarrassed to look him straight in the face. 'Yes, thanks. I feel terrible . . . this happening in your house. It nearly ruined your party.'

'Och, don't worry about it,' he told her. He nodded over towards the window. 'Jim spoke to me, then he went over and had a word with that Gerry fellow. They were outside for a good while and he seems to have managed to calm him down a bit.'

'Good,' Heather said, looking relieved. She touched Mark on the arm. 'You go back to your sister and friends – I'm fine, honestly.'

When the bells rang out the room erupted into a big cheer and then everyone gathered into a wide circle to sing *Auld Lang Syne*. At one point Heather made herself look across the room and there was Gerry looking straight back at her. He was in between Liz and Jim, linking hands with them both and singing.

For an instant, Heather felt she was looking at an old photograph – a photograph that had been torn and damaged, a photograph with a person missing from it. And that person was Heather Grace.

Just a few months ago it would have been the four of them laughing and happy. Jim and Liz, Gerry and Heather. And she would have preferred it if her feelings hadn't changed towards him, because up until recently he had been a decent, dependable fellow. But her feelings *had* changed. And there was not one single thing she could do about it. It suddenly made her feel frightened and uncertain of the future.

What if she always ended up feeling like this? What if she always went off the boyfriends she once had liked and fancied?

Heather told herself not to be so silly, that it was much better to be on your own than to be with somebody you no longer fancied or felt you had anything in common with. Imagine being *married* to someone like that. And yet Heather knew there must be countless people going out with or married to people they no longer loved or found attractive. She knew that from her own short experience with Gerry and she knew that she could never go out with anyone like Mark McFarlane.

Being stuck with someone you didn't love or fancy for life was like a death sentence. Heather gave a tiny shudder at the thought. She was still young and had plenty of time to worry about such things. She could still meet someone.

And yet as she looked around her now at the couples all kissing and cuddling and wishing each other a happy new year, she wondered what if she *didn't* meet someone ever again? What if she ended up alone?

Kirsty was relaxing in the dressing-room with a Coca-Cola, waiting for Larry to take her home. The tall thin glass of champagne sat neglected beside a vase of seasonal red flowers with huge leaves. Kirsty had only taken two mouthfuls from it, terrified in case it might have a peculiar effect on her and loosen her tongue – and that she would start saying all those embarrassing things to Larry Delaney again. She couldn't possibly take that chance.

Besides, the champagne didn't have quite the sweet fizzy taste that the Babycham did, and she was quite disappointed at the bitter dry taste it had. If Kirsty was asked which she preferred, she decided she'd have to be truthful and say she far preferred the cheaper drink.

She was just contemplating how often things you looked forward to in life were disappointing when you actually experienced them, when a knock came on the dressing-room door.

'Come in!' she called in a cheery manner, presuming it was one of the band members heading off, or someone bringing her another drink, as she had already turned down several drinks sent through to the dressing-room for her tonight.

The door opened and, to Kirsty's enormous surprise, in walked Larry's friend, Fiona McCluskey, and a slightly younger dark-haired woman who looked very like her. They were both dressed very glamorously, Fiona draped in the rows of pearls she seemed to favour and the other woman in lots of sparkly jewellery.

Kirsty sat bolt upright in her chair, a feeling of foreboding about her. She'd had no idea that this old friend of Larry's was in the audience, but then she'd hardly seen any of the people who were at the show due to the subdued lighting.

'I hope you don't mind us barging in, dear,' Fiona said, her eyes wide and bright, 'but I just had to come and say how wonderful your singing was and how much we absolutely loved it.' She paused. 'Larry certainly got it right on *this* occasion.'

Kirsty stood up now, not quite sure what to do with herself. She linked her hands together, resting them on her flat stomach. 'Thank you, that was very kind of you,' she said, her voice sounding strangely formal to her own ears. 'I'm glad you enjoyed it ...'

'Your voice is really excellent,' the other woman said, sounding sincere enough, but there was something in her tone that made Kirsty feel very wary.

'Oh, sorry,' Fiona said now, laughing and not sounding really sorry at all. 'How very rude of me – I haven't introduced you.' She turned towards her companion. 'This is my sister, Helen, who is actually a *professional* singer.'

Kirsty wasn't a bit surprised they were sisters as there was a strong resemblance, not like her and Heather. Both these women had dark, blackish hair with olive skin and high cheekbones. Fiona was slim, bordering on thin; her sister was slim but more curvaceous. 'Oh, really?' she asked. 'And what kind of singing do you do?'

'Light opera and the better class of musicals,' Helen said in a clipped tone. 'I travelled abroad quite a bit with it – but I've more or less given it up. Much too time-consuming.' She smiled at Kirsty now. 'There's better ways to enjoy life than singing for your supper.'

Kirsty nodded, not quite knowing what to say next. She had never met anyone before who had been in proper musicals or who sang opera professionally. She knew a few girls and a fellow who were in an operatic society in Hamilton, but that was only amateur. She decided it was best to keep quiet rather than speak up and show her ignorance.

'We were just admiring your dress,' Fiona said, moving closer to have a really good look at it. 'Do you mind me being awfully cheeky and asking where you bought it from?'

Kirsty suddenly felt very uneasy. What should she say? Should she just come straight out with the truth or try to bluff it? Should she pretend that the dress was her own? By the looks of their own dresses and jewellery, these women were obviously the type of people who could easily afford to buy a dress like this and would know all the shops and designers.

'Actually,' she said, 'Larry organised the dress for me.' She managed a little smile. 'I hadn't much time to go out and buy a suitable dress, so I asked his advice and he brought this out for me.'

'How very, very helpful of him,' Fiona said, glancing at her sister. There was a pause, then she turned to look at Kirsty with narrowed eyes. 'This dress came from Fraser's in Glasgow, and Larry Delaney actually picked it for Helen.'

Kirsty stared at both women, not quite sure if she'd understood. The red flush started to announce itself on her chest and throat as it always did at the worst possible time. She swallowed hard, her throat suddenly feeling tight. 'Are you saying that this dress belongs to *you*?' she asked Helen, her voice a little croaky now.

'I am,' Helen said quietly, but there was no accusation in her tone or attitude. She didn't look happy but she wasn't blaming Kirsty in any way. 'And no doubt he produced some others for you? A black lace dress, a green satin?' She went on to describe several of the dresses that Larry had loaned her.

Kirsty slowly nodded her head. There was no point in

denying it. 'Yes,' she said, 'Larry loaned me a few . . . he said to pick which one I'd like for tonight.' She halted. 'I'd no idea who they belonged to. I thought maybe Larry kept a stock of them for any of his stage acts.'

'You're not too far off the mark,' Fiona told her, with a slight sneer in her tone. 'But no doubt you'll learn. The longer you know Larry, the more you'll find there is to know about him.'

'Like what?' Kirsty asked, suddenly wanting to hear more. She wanted to hear the very worst about him now, so that she knew exactly what she was dealing with.

The dressing-room door opened and Larry Delaney walked in. He halted when he saw Kirsty's visitors, obviously taken aback to find them in chatting to her.

'Fiona . . . Helen . . .' he said, coming towards them. He stopped a few feet away from the sisters, not wishing them a happy new year as Kirsty had expected him to do. 'Is there something I can do for you?'

'Oh, I think you've done enough for us already,' Fiona told him with a throaty laugh and eyebrows raised in a knowing manner. She put her arm through her sister's. 'We must get back – we have important people waiting for us.'

'Helen?' Larry asked as they swept past him. 'How is David?'

'Marvellous!' Helen said in an airy, light way.

'It's been quite a while,' he said, following them towards the door. 'I'd really like to see him again soon . . .'

Fiona opened the door and let her sister out first. Then, without a backward glance, she closed the door tightly behind her.

The noise of the door closing was still an echo in the silence of the large dressing-room as Larry came back towards Kirsty, distractedly running a hand through his perfect hair.

'What exactly did they want?' he asked her, his eyes narrowed in thought.

Kirsty was silent for a moment, debating what to say. 'They said they came in to tell me how much they enjoyed my performance . . .'

'And?' He looked at her now, waiting. He obviously knew they had said far more than that.

Kirsty shrugged, hating the thought of saying something that would insult or anger him, something that might hurt him. Then, she suddenly decided that he had had no difficulty whatsoever in telling her how things were last week. When it had come to telling the truth Larry Delaney had not held back one single inch. He had not considered how hurt she had felt.

Why should she care about him?

Kirsty looked up at him now, her eyes steely blue. 'Fiona McCluskey's sister said that the dress I'm wearing belongs to her. She said all the dresses you gave me were hers.' Then for good measure she added, 'She could describe every one of them.'

The hand came down now to cover his mouth. He moved his head from side to side and gave a weary sigh. 'Not again,' he said quietly, more to himself than Kirsty. 'You'd think they'd have better things to concentrate on than muck-raking about me. And this is neither the time nor the place for them to be doing it.'

'What do you mean?' Kirsty asked, curious now.

'Helen and I had business dealings a few years ago. It didn't work out for a variety of reasons and she's never forgotten about it – or forgiven me.' He looked at Kirsty now. 'There were other people involved and it was a lot more complicated than a few dresses she left behind.' He pressed his forefinger in the middle of his chest. 'A few very expensive dresses that I paid for.'

'So you don't get on with them?' Kirsty stated, rather unnecessarily.

'Well,' he said, smiling wryly, 'I suppose that's one way of describing it.' He turned towards the door. 'I'll just have a last word with the hotel manager about these other bookings and then we'll head off.'

'Larry . . .' Kirsty said, suddenly realising that she didn't want this personal conversation to end quite so abruptly. There was so little about him that she really knew, and she wanted to get every bit of information out of him while he was in this more open, communicative mood. She told herself she was no longer interested in him from a romantic point of view, but she just wanted to know the kind of man she was dealing with on a business level. 'Were you just acquainted with Helen McCluskey on a business basis?' She took a chance now. 'Both her and her sister gave the impression that there was more to it . . .'

'They would,' he said in a flat voice, his fingers clasping the door handle.

She hesitated before asking one final question – then she went for it. He could only tell her to mind her own business. 'Who's David? You mentioned him the last time we met Fiona McCluskey as well.'

There was a silence. Kirsty held her breath, thinking that this was the sort of silence that people often described as deafening. She wondered if she had gone too far.

Eventually, Larry Delaney turned back round to face her. 'David,' he said in a quiet, grim voice, 'is my son.' There was another smaller silence. 'Helen McCluskey and I have a son together.'

When Jim came rushing in to say the minibus was waiting outside for them, Heather heaved a sigh of relief. It was quarter past one, which wasn't bad for New Year. She pulled her coat on now, which she had been holding beside her for the last ten minutes, and then she lifted her bag.

It was a pity the way the evening had turned from being so pleasant to suddenly being so awkward. It was a pity Gerry Stewart had ruined it by turning up. Thankfully, he seemed to have totally quietened down after the bells signalling New Year. He had come over to give her a kiss and wish her all the best for the next year, but he hadn't made the fuss she had been dreading. He had gone back to chat to Jim and a few fellows in the hall, and a while later when she went through to dance with some boy from Hamilton, she saw him sitting in a chair. It dawned on her then that he was now very drunk and sleepy, and hopefully incapable of causing any more trouble. Several times already she had witnessed Jim trying to wake him up, and presumably he'd have to do that now to get him in the minibus home.

'You ready?' Liz said, smiling but looking a little tired around the eyes. The party hadn't turned out as well as she had hoped for either. Not for a last New Year as a single girl. Jim had been back and forward between her and Gerry – his loyalties totally divided between best friend and fiancée.

'I want to say goodnight to Mark . . .' Heather said as they walked out into the hall. It would have been much easier to just

257

sneak out while he was occupied with another group, and hope she never saw him again. But Heather knew it would also have been cowardly and rude. She wanted to be able to speak to him if she bumped into him unexpectedly, without feeling awkward and embarrassed about the episode earlier. It had also dawned on her that he might be asked to Liz and Jim's wedding next month, and she didn't want the thought of meeting him again hanging over her.

It was best to make a polite, quick exit now and end on a pleasant note.

She popped her head quickly into the dining-room but couldn't see him anywhere, then she went down the hallway towards the kitchen, and there he was, leaning against the jamb of the door, chatting to another fellow in a bow-tie.

'I just wanted a wee word with you,' she said, smiling apologetically for interrupting them.

'You're not going now, are you?' Mark said, looking very disappointed. He left his beer glass on a small table in the hall. 'I was just going to come back in to see you . . . I thought we might have another dance.'

'The minibus is outside, so I've got to go,' Heather explained, trying to look as though she was disappointed herself.

He reached a hand out to her shoulder. 'Can I see you again?' he said, looking directly into her eyes.

Heather's stomach tightened. 'I'm not sure, Mark . . . after all this business with Gerry.' She was telling the truth now. Even if she had been attracted to Mark, she wasn't ready to start courting another lad. 'I'm not sure if I'm ready to go start seeing anyone else . . . not just yet.'

'OK,' he said quietly, his head moving up and down. 'Maybe in a few weeks?'

'We'll see,' Heather said, not wanting to hurt his feelings.

He reached forward now and took her face gently in his hands and then he kissed her gently on the lips. 'It's a pity,' he said. 'I think we would have hit it off really well. I've never met anyone like you before – you're clever and funny and beautiful. You're a really special girl, Heather.'

For some reason she couldn't understand, tears suddenly rushed into Heather's eyes. Tears about what, she didn't know.

Maybe it was because he was being kind to her after what had happened. 'Thanks, Mark – your party was lovely . . .' Then she turned away and rushed down the hallway.

The minibus was freezing and it was a smaller one than the one that had brought them. It should only have held eight, but eleven of them – including Gerry Stewart – had to squeeze in. Heather sat on the edge of Liz and Jim's seat, steadying herself by holding onto the seat in front. Gerry was up at the back of the bus, slumped in a single seat and looking fast asleep again.

Larry's car pulled up outside the Graces' darkened house, which signalled that Sophie and Fintan had already retired for the night. If they had still been at Mona and Pat's they would have left the living-room light on.

'Thanks for the lift, Larry,' Kirsty said as she gathered her things around her to get out of the car. She hadn't chatted much on the journey home as she felt sleepy, but a number of things had been flitting around in her mind. Most of them were questions that she couldn't ask. Questions about Helen McCluskey and Larry's son. Questions like whether they'd been married or whether it had been an affair. And lots and lots of questions about what had gone wrong between them, and why he wasn't seeing much of his little son. At least Kirsty supposed he was young – he could be at school for all she knew.

She didn't ask him any of the questions that were rattling around inside her head.

'I was just thinking that you having to drive me places is a bit of a bind for you,' she said, her hand on the handle of the car door. 'It's not like being in the band, when everyone was going to the same places anyway. You're having to drive to Rowanhill to pick me up and then go on to wherever we're going, and then bring me back again. It's a lot of driving around for you.'

'I don't mind,' he told her in a surprisingly cheerful voice. 'It suits me fine at the minute. If and when it changes, we can sort out some other arrangement.'

'You never know,' she told him, thinking of the envelope of money that he'd given her tonight. 'Maybe I'll save up enough to buy a car . . . I was thinking of asking my daddy to take me out for a few lessons.'

'Good girl!' he said, obviously impressed with the idea. 'It's something you'll definitely have to consider when your career takes off – and by the way things went tonight, it looks as if it's going in the right direction.'

'I'm really glad,' Kirsty said quietly.

She looked up at him now and caught him staring straight at her in a deep, very thoughtful way. She wondered what he was thinking. Probably about those two McCluskeys, or maybe he was thinking about the little son he didn't seem to see much of. Whatever it was, it had dampened down his usual confidence and ability to give the impression that he could handle everything. 'Thanks again, Larry,' she said, turning to fiddle with the car handle in the dim light of the orange street lamp.

'Kirsty,' he said in a low, almost hesitant voice, 'I'm sorry about last week . . . I hope I didn't hurt your feelings too much. Sometimes I can be a bit brisk . . .'

Kirsty's heart sank like a stone at the mere mention of it. 'I'm fine,' she said, in as chirpy a voice as she could muster, hoping to cover her embarrassment. 'I was just being stupid . . . I don't know what got into me that night. I think those Babychams must have gone to my head . . .'

'So, it wasn't serious?' he checked.

'No,' she said quickly, opening the car door. 'And you don't need to worry – there's no fear of it ever happening again.'

The minibus stopped in the main street in Rowanhill and the tired, very quiet group started to get off. Heather moved first so that she wasn't left near the end when Gerry was getting off. She'd also given her share of the minibus fare to Liz, so that she wasn't standing there with the rest of the crowd sorting out money when it stopped.

A few minutes before turning into Rowanhill, Jim had moved to the back of the bus to rouse his drunk, almost comatose friend, and was still coaxing him to waken up as the others filed off.

'You're not walking home on your own, are you?' Liz checked as they got off. 'Is there anybody else who lives down your street?'

This would never have been an issue before, as the two lads

had always made sure the girls were seen right home to their doors.

'I'll be fine,' Heather said, glancing back anxiously at the bus. She wrapped the satin stole around her neck several times now, like a big scarf, and then she buttoned her coat up to the neck. 'Sure, it's only a few minutes walk.'

'But you never know who could be around with it being New Year – there could be any drunken eedjits around.'

'I'll be absolutely fine,' Heather reassured her friend. She went over now and gave Liz a hug. 'I hope it's a good New Year for you and Jim, and I can't wait until your wedding.'

A big smile spread on Liz's face. 'Thanks ... although I'm gettin' a wee bit nervous about it all as the time gets nearer. You're a great pal and I can always rely on you.' She lowered her voice. 'And I hope the right man comes along for *you* this year as well.'

Heather laughed and raised her eyebrows. 'I won't be holding my breath.' Then, hearing Gerry's slurred voice coming from the front of the minibus, she moved. 'I've got to go. Why don't you drop down to see me tomorrow afternoon?'

'Fine,' Liz agreed, 'I'll see you then.'

Heather walked away briskly, almost running as she crossed the main road to be out of sight by the time the last two had dismounted from the minibus. A short while later she turned off the main road, then went quickly down the silent streets that led to her home.

Kirsty had just arrived home, and had thrown a handful of kindling sticks and some small bits of coal on the living-room fire to liven it up. She knew she and Heather would sit up for a while discussing their evenings and thought they might as well be warm and comfortable while they were chatting.

She took her shoes off downstairs and then padded upstairs to change out of Helen McCluskey's dress into her fleecy pyjamas, dressing-gown and slippers. She was back downstairs with the grill on for toast and waiting for the kettle to boil when Heather's key sounded in the door. She moved out to greet her.

'How did it go?' Heather asked as she came along the hallway, stopping to take off her coat and hang it up.

'Brilliant,' Kirsty said, her eyes sparkling with the memory. 'I went down really well. We've got more bookings at that hotel, and a few other people came to Larry to ask about me as well.'

'That's great,' Heather said, truly delighted for her sister.

'Here,' Kirsty said, coming towards her with outstretched arms, 'I think we should at least say "Happy New Year" to each other! Especially since there's not another skull around to say it!'

They hugged each other, laughing, then Kirsty stood back to admire Heather's black lace dress again. 'You look fantastic in that,' she said. 'A million dollars.' Then she gave a little laugh. 'And it probably cost that if the real owner is anything to go by . . .'

'What d'you mean?' Heather asked, her brow furrowed in confusion.

'Listen,' Kirsty whispered, pointing upstairs, 'you run up and get into your pyjamas an' I'll have tea and toast ready for you when you come down, then we can sit and have a good oul' chat about our nights. You're not going to believe half the things I found out about that Larry Delaney tonight.'

Heather nodded and took off her shoes – exactly as her sister had done – draped the black stole over one arm and tiptoed upstairs in her stocking feet.

The girls were sitting on either side of the fireplace in their night-clothes, their feet tucked under them, drinking their second cup of tea, when the loud, desperate rapping came on the front door.

'Heather!' a voice was calling. 'Heather! You'll need to come quick.'

The girls looked at each other with shocked, frightened eyes. It was half past two in the morning and they'd been home for nearly an hour. What on earth could it be? The last, and only, time anything like this had happened was when Lily was taken into the hospital. They both got to their feet at the same time and rushed out into the hall.

They could see two figures silhouetted through the glass in the door as they approached it. Then the loud banging came again, startling them as they were so close to it.

'My God,' Kirsty said, 'I think that's Jim Murray.'

'Don't open it!' Heather suddenly said, flattening her back against the coats hanging in the hallway. Her eyes were wide with fear. 'That must be Gerry Stewart with him and I don't want him coming in – he's dead drunk!' She halted, now hearing a noise upstairs. 'Oh, God! That's my daddy up – he'll go stone mad if he sees any of them drunk outside.'

'Heather!' a distraught voice called from outside the door. 'It's Liz – open the door!'

Kirsty pushed forward now, bending down to lift the flap on the brass letter box. She'd soon sort out this blidey business, she thought. And if it was that Gerry Stewart carrying on again, he would take what he got from her – no doubt about it.

'Who's there and whiddye want?' she called in an unusually aggressive voice.

Heather stood statue-still watching her younger sister, with her hands clasped over her mouth. Her father's slow and steady footsteps were approaching the bottom of the stairs.

'It's Liz an' Jim!' Liz called back in a screechy voice, crying now.

'And who else is with you?' Kirsty demanded.

'Nobody,' Liz said, 'just us.'

'That Gerry Stewart better not be with you!' she warned. 'Or I'll brain him over the head with a poker.'

'For God's sake, open the door,' Jim said in a strangled voice. 'We've got some terrible news to tell you.'

Chapter 44

❧❧

NEW YEAR'S DAY 1956

Gerry Stewart was pronounced dead at four o'clock in the morning on New Year's Day. Waking up to the news, Rowanhill was in a state of shock.

Heather Grace had been awake all night since Jim and Liz had come banging on the door to tell her he was in hospital fighting for his life.

She had gone to bed ages after they left, but not slept, instead running the scene over and over in her mind like a film. She could picture everything that had happened – minute by minute – right up until Liz had come back to the Graces' house at eight o'clock that morning to tell her that Gerry had died. He had never regained consciousness after the accident. He had gone into some kind of coma and never come out of it.

After Kirsty had let them in in the early hours of New Year's Day, Jim Murray had sat on the sofa, holding his head in his hands and breaking his heart crying. 'I can't believe it,' he sobbed. 'One minute he was standing beside me . . . and the next minute he was lying in the middle of the road covered in blood.'

Heather was seated, white-faced and shivering, in one armchair with Kirsty perched on the arm of it, while Liz was sitting on the other armchair at the opposite side of the fire. Fintan and Sophie hovered behind the sofa in their dressing-gowns, not quite sure what to say or do, but feeling they had better stay downstairs until they'd heard the worst.

Heather looked at Liz with wide, startled eyes, afraid to ask what had happened.

'It was a taxi,' Liz explained at last in a horrified whisper.

'It was my fault!' Jim cut in, punching a fist onto his knee. He hadn't drunk as much as Gerry had, but it was obvious that he'd had a good few drinks. 'If I hadn't argued with him, he would be all right instead of lyin' in the hospital in intensive care . . .' He shook his head vigorously, as if trying to shake the horrible images away, the images that had haunted him since he saw Gerry being taken away in the ambulance.

Jim had wanted to go with Gerry, but the police who had arrived on the scene and the ambulance men said he'd had too much to drink, and anyway, his family were following straight behind the ambulance. He advised them to give it an hour or so then phone the Law Hospital to see if there was any news.

'So what happened then?' Kirsty asked. 'What had the taxi to do with it?'

Liz glanced anxiously at Fintan and Sophie, then back to Heather. It was too terrible not to tell the truth, no matter how shocked the older people were. 'Well, you see . . .' she said to Heather, then stopped for a moment to clear her voice, 'after you left, Jim got Gerry off the bus, then he started to insist that he was going to catch up with you. He said he wanted to walk you home the way he always did. He said he was worried about you goin' home on your own.'

Heather looked over at her friend with tortured eyes, feeling desperately guilty. She knew that everyone was thinking that it was all her fault for finishing with him in the first place. If they'd still been going out, Gerry would not have been so drunk and upset to carry on in such a way.

Liz looked over at Jim now, anxious in case he reacted badly to the events being discussed – but he was now sitting quite still. 'Jim gave me his and Gerry's money for the minibus, and I went over to give it to the others, so I didn't know what was going on. Anyway,' she continued, rubbing a tear away, 'Jim told him that you didn't want to see him . . . and that you'd probably be in bed by the time he reached your house – but he wouldn't listen.' She glanced again at Jim, then she went on. 'They had a bit of a fight – an argument – it was all at the back of the minibus and the rest of us didn't see it because we were at the front with the driver.'

Jim got to his feet now, and went to stand in front of the dying fire. 'That's the mistake I made – I should have left him alone and he'd still be alive. The worst he would have done was come down here annoying you . . . but you'd have got over that.'

Heather's head drooped and she covered her face with her hand. Kirsty rubbed her back, trying to comfort her.

'He would've just made one last eedjit of himself with you,' Jim continued, 'and then he would finally have accepted that you didn't want him. He would have eventually got used to it . . .'

'So what happened after the argument?' Kirsty prompted, confident that her parents would say nothing about the drunken row given the circumstances. Anyway, she thought to herself, they might as well get all the gory details out tonight in one go. It would be hard enough over the next few days without trying to second-guess the missing parts of the jigsaw puzzle.

'I was tryin' to hold him back,' Jim went on, his voice wavery and strained. 'I didn't want him to make a complete fool of himself. He was the cleverest fella I know – but he could be dead pig-headed at times.' He halted, gathering himself together again. 'And then we fell against the minibus, and I tripped and landed on the pavement.' There was a weary sigh from Fintan as he pictured the drunken brawl, which everyone either didn't hear or ignored.

'It all happened really fast after that,' Jim said, shrugging his shoulders and scraping his fingers through his tousled fair hair. 'By the time I got myself up off the ground, he was out in the middle of the road . . . he wasn't fit to walk, he was staggering all over the place. And then this taxi must have come flyin' around the corner – none of us even saw it comin' – and the next thing there's this terrible bang . . .' He turned away now, unable to finish. Liz got up and went over to stand beside him, her arms wrapped around his right arm.

'It was his head,' Liz said gravely, taking up the story where her fiancé had left off. 'The ambulance men said his head had got the worst of it. It wasn't just the car hitting him. He got thrown up in the air and then he landed at the kerb on his head.' She gave a long sad sigh, but struggled on with the story. 'There was a lamp-post inches away from where he was lying, so we're not sure if he was thrown against that.'

'Oh my God!' Heather groaned, sobbing and rocking backwards and forwards in the chair. 'Poor, poor Gerry! What a terrible thing to happen to a young fella . . . I can't believe it.'

Sophie rushed over to comfort her.

'I still can't believe it!' Jim said, his eyes red-rimmed and looking as if they had sunk in his head. 'I feel as if it's all just a bad dream . . . I feel as if I'll wake up in the mornin' and me and Gerry will be laughing at this when I tell him.' He looked around at all the people in the room now. 'He's my best pal . . . and I might never see him alive again.'

'It mightn't be as bad as you think,' Fintan said in a comforting, reassuring voice. 'When they get him into hospital now and check him over – he might not be as bad. A bit of spilt blood can look far worse than it is.'

Jim closed his eyes and shook his head. 'I know he's not goin' to make it . . . I could tell the minute I looked at him lyin' there on the road . . .'

When he phoned the hospital at half past four on New Year's morning, Jim Murray's worst fears were confirmed.

Gerry Stewart had died at exactly four o'clock with his mother and father by his bedside.

Chapter 45

❧❦❧

'I've never seen Jim in such a state,' Liz said when she came around to tell Heather the terrible news later that morning. After leaving the Graces' house, she and Jim had gone back to Liz's to wait for a while, then Jim had phoned the hospital from the phone box in the main street at half past four to be told that Gerry had died.

Neither of them had slept. Jim had sat in a daze on Liz's mother's couch until around six o'clock and then he decided he would walk on up to Gerry's house before going home.

'It was only starting to hit him by the time he left me,' Liz said, taking a cup of tea from her friend. She poured a good bit of milk in from a chunky blue jug, and added two spoonfuls of sugar. 'I suppose the few drinks were wearing off him, and he could see what had happened.' Her voice dropped. 'He keeps blamin' himself . . . saying that Gerry would still be alive if it wasn't for him.'

'I keep thinking the very same thing myself,' Heather confessed, her face chalk-white and with faint dark circles now forming around her tired brown eyes.

'It was nobody's fault,' Liz said, taking a sip of hot sweet tea. 'Not yours and not Jim's. Something in Gerry just snapped and he wasn't thinking straight. Drink, I suppose.' She tutted at the thought. 'And who would have expected another taxi to be around Rowanhill at that hour? You hardly see a taxi around the place from one week to the next.' Liz shrugged. 'Still, it was the new year, and I suppose there's more traffic on the roads then than at any other time of the year.'

'It was the most terrible, terrible coincidence,' Heather whispered, both hands clasped around the mug of black tea that sat untouched in front of her. 'An unbelievable coincidence that

Gerry was in the middle of the road when a car came flying around the corner. There probably hadn't been anything on the road for the half-hour before or the half-hour after. I know I never saw one single car when I was walking home.' She reached for the milk jug and poured a small drop into her mug, and then she put the jug back down on the table, almost spilling it in the process. She could hardly see the jug she was so tired, and yet when she'd tried to sleep for a couple of hours, her brain wouldn't stop going over and over the images of Gerry Stewart lying in the road.

Liz was tired too, after staying up all night and then walking through the dark New Year streets to tell Heather what had happened. She knew she would be waiting anxiously – and she didn't want Heather to hear the bad news from anyone else.

'I didn't want to come bangin' on the door just in case I woke the whole house up again,' she explained. 'But I knew that folk like Mona would maybe be up early for eight o'clock Mass . . . and I didn't want you to hear it from anybody else. They're bound to have called his name off the altar, and everybody in the place will be talkin' about it, especially with it being New Year.' She raised her eyes to the ceiling. 'This is when I wish we were all rich and could afford phones – it would make life an awful lot easier, wouldn't it? Instead of having to trail up and down streets and stand in freezing phone boxes that don't work half the time or that won't take the blidey pennies that they should.'

Heather nodded her head. She'd never had to use a phone box for anything terrible like that, and certainly not in the middle of the night. But then Liz and Jim had probably never had anything like this happen to them before either.

Maybe that's what happened in life as you got older, she thought. Unimaginable things started to collect around you – like Lily getting polio.

And Gerry Stewart getting killed because of her.

'I'll go now before the whole house wakes,' Liz said, as the kitchen clock showed that it was coming on for half past eight. 'My mammy was going to the early Mass, so I'll go home and see her before going to bed for a few hours.'

'You must be exhausted,' Heather said. She halted, wary of

saying anything that might just allude to her friend's unspoken condition. 'How do you feel?'

'Tired,' Liz said, giving a lopsided, weary smile. 'And a bit sickish . . .'

Heather looked up at her and unconsciously bit her lip, stopping herself from saying anything that Liz might take the wrong way.

'There's no point in me kiddin' on about this, after what's happened,' Liz said in a low whisper. 'You know I'm expectin', don't you?'

Heather took a deep breath. 'Well . . . I wasn't really sure. I didn't know what to think.'

'I didn't know what to think either . . . I got the shock of my life.'

But still, she'd had the guts to come right out with it, which said a lot about her. A lot of girls would have said nothing until the baby was born, and then just made out it was a couple of months premature.

'But you're happy about it,' Heather said, feeling relieved that her friend had decided to confide in her. It made her feel better somehow about everything. 'You are happy, aren't you?'

Liz's head drooped a little; it was obvious she was embarrassed. 'I am – and I'm not, if you get what I mean,' Liz said. 'I love babies, and I always wanted me and Jim to get married . . . but in some ways I'm terrified.'

Heather nodded. She knew she would feel exactly the same.

They walked to the front door together, just as they had done a few hours ago. Only tiredness and sadness made them walk a little bit slower.

'Heather,' Liz said, as she stood on the doorstep, the cold morning air sweeping in past them and down through the hall, 'there's something you need to know about Gerry.'

Heather felt as though something had just wrapped itself around her throat, wrapped itself around her throat very tightly. Her legs felt weak and shaky.

'What is it?' she whispered.

Liz shook her head very slowly from side to side. 'He never told his mammy and daddy that you'd split up . . . they thought you were getting engaged soon. He'd showed them the ring and everything.'

Heather pressed the back of her hand against her mouth. 'Oh, dear God . . .' she whispered. Lots of things came into her mind, but she couldn't seem to get them out. How could they have thought she was still seeing him when she wasn't around at Christmas? And what about the other girl he'd been seeing from Wishaw?

'He said you were just concentrating on your new job,' Liz said, as though reading her thoughts, 'and he never brought that lassie to the house.'

'But she was at Mass at Rowanhill on Christmas Eve,' Heather finally said. 'They must have seen her then, surely?'

'No,' Liz said, pulling a face. 'I knew that even at the time, but I didn't want it to put you off him. He'd told Jim that the girl came out with two pals in a car. They went straight back to Wishaw after Mass, they never went near Jim's house.' She put her hand on Heather's arm. 'He told Jim he only brought her there to give you a shock. He wanted to make you jealous . . . he had no interest in the girl at all.'

'And what about the New Year party he went to in Wishaw with her?'

'Same again,' Liz said. 'Everything was to make you jealous.'

Heather shivered, suddenly aware of the early morning chill.

Chapter 46

M ona wasted no time. It was as quick as her surprisingly shapely legs would carry her without breaking into a run that she came down from the church and straight to her brother-in-law's house. Who would have thought it? Heather's old boyfriend killed in an accident last night.

She'd no idea who would have the latest news – whether it

would be herself telling them, or whether they would have heard already. Either way, she would enjoy a bit of a chat with them over a cup of tea, finding out every detail that she possibly could.

Mona had seen Liz Mullen's mother at the other side of the church, but decided that Mrs Mullen was too tight-mouthed about things, and it would probably take ages trying to get anything worthwhile out of her. Liz would have been a better bet herself, but like all the young ones, she'd likely be in her lazy bed this morning, and not shifting until it was time for the half-eleven Mass.

Sophie was at her disorganised best, lighting the gas under the kettle and then the grill while trying to give Mona attention at the same time. 'We've had very little sleep,' she explained to Mona, 'and I don't think our Heather's had any at all. She's in a state of shock with it all. Thank God she wasn't around when it happened ... Thank God she didn't see him after he'd been knocked down.'

'Dear, dear, dear,' Mona said, her mouth grim. She was thinking that it was a pity in a way that Heather or Kirsty hadn't been around when the accident happened, because they might have had more details. You could never rely on Sophie, she always got a story back to front. For some reason she never seemed to listen properly, she never got all the tiny wee details that made a story worth telling.

'I've made her go back to bed for a few hours,' Sophie said, 'and if she goes into a deep sleep I won't even waken her for Mass.'

'But she's not *sick*, is she?' Mona asked, her voice high with disapproval. 'Surely she can go back to sleep when she's been to Mass? It's a double commitment today with it bein' New Year's day on a Sunday. If you miss Mass the day it's like missing two ordinary Masses.' She shook her head in exasperation, watching Sophie now as she placed four slices of bread on the toasting pan, and then slid it under the lit grill.

'I'll see how she is when it's time for Mass,' Sophie said in a quiet, firm voice, indicating that she and not Mona would decide. She went into the cupboard for the tea caddy.

'That's a dangerous game to start,' Mona told her. 'You'll build up trouble for yourself if you start gettin' lax about Mass wi' young ones.' She pursed her lips together. 'It could lead to the Claire business happenin' all over again in your own house.'

'How's Lily?' Sophie asked. 'Did she enjoy herself last night?'

'Grand,' Mona said, knowing that she had been deliberately blocked. 'We couldn't get the wee devil to bed after you and Fintan left. She kept saying that she wanted to stay up to see Kirsty and Heather coming home, but Pat lifted her up the stairs at one o'clock.' She smiled now in spite of herself. 'Isn't it great to see her taking a few steps on her own now?'

'Oh, it is, Mona,' Sophie said, her eyes glistening with tears. 'It's nearly a miracle, when you think how she was only a short time ago.'

'I've a feeling they'll let her out for good soon,' Mona said. 'Another couple of weeks at the most.' She halted. 'And did Heather say how Gerry Stewart was at the party? I wonder was he drunk or what? It seems awful strange that a bright young fella like that would get knocked down in Rowanhill . . . I mean, who would believe it? There surely must be more to it?'

'I don't know how it happened myself,' Sophie replied, 'but no doubt all the facts will come out. People love to know all the gory details.' She set about buttering the hot toast and putting it on a plate in the middle of the table.

'Oh, don't be talking,' Mona sighed, 'people would sicken you with their talking about others.' She sighed. 'Of course, it's different when it's a member of your own family. I'm only interested in what's happened because of Heather . . . otherwise I wouldn't bother. How is Heather in herself? Is she takin' it bad?'

'I'd say she's numb with shock,' Sophie told her. 'She used to be very fond of him, and he was good to her. I always found him a nice young fella, myself.' She got the mugs out for the tea.

'I expect she had her own reasons for finishing with him,' Mona mused now. 'Reasons you'll know nothing about . . . there could have been a side to him only Heather saw.'

She sat on for another while, going over and over the same information, hoping that one of the girls might come down with a morsel more news than she'd managed to get out of Sophie.

Eventually – tea drunk and toast eaten – Mona gave up and

went home to get her own crew up, fed, washed and out to Mass.

Chapter 47

'Come in, hen. It's awful good of you to call up to see us,' Gerry Stewart's mother said in a thin little voice, when Heather was shown into the living-room by the auntie who had answered the front door. There were a few women in the kitchen already, and the auntie went back to join them, leaving the bereaved mother alone with her visitor.

Heather went across the room to where Mrs Stewart was sitting in a high armchair by the fire. Her grey hair was in the tight little permed curls she'd had done for Christmas, and she was dressed in her Sunday-best clothes – a navy skirt and cardigan with a neat string of pearls that her dead son had bought her for Christmas.

Heather had finally got to sleep around nine o'clock on New Year's Day. She had gone up to bed after seeing Liz off, and lain awake for a while across the room from the lightly snoring Kirsty. She had heard Mona's quick steps coming in the front gate, and moments later her voice had echoed up from the kitchen.

Eventually, Heather had drifted off into a heavy, dreamless sleep.

She didn't wake when Kirsty got up and dressed and went out with her parents to Mass. In fact, she had slept until Sophie came up to call her at two o'clock in the afternoon.

'I hate waking you ... but you might not be able to sleep again tonight, hen,' her mother had explained. 'And I thought you might want to take a wee walk up to see Mrs and Mrs Stewart ...'

Heather had turned her head towards the window, dreading the thought of all the difficult things that she must face.

After much discussion with her parents and Kirsty, and

another hour's serious talking up at Liz's house, Heather had decided to go and see Gerry's family on her own. The family would expect her to be there, and would be upset if she wasn't. For six months she had been in and out of the house on a weekly basis. She had never stayed long, just popping in and out, but the Stewarts had made her welcome, and she owed Gerry's family the greatest of respect under these horrendous circumstances.

She decided she should go this afternoon, before the body was brought back to the house, before the crowds of people from Rowanhill and beyond descended upon the house. Heather had put on her plain black coat and hat. As she lifted it out of the wardrobe, she glanced at the lace dress and the satin stole that she'd worn to Mark McFarlane's party the night before.

From Kirsty's story of the dress she'd worn the previous night, it would seem that the dresses were jinxed. In one short night they had brought nothing but aggravation and bad memories to both girls. She would tell Kirsty to pack them up and give them back to Larry Delaney the very next time she saw him.

Looking at the dress now, she felt the party was a lifetime ago instead of only hours. Things would never be the same again. Heather Grace would never be the same again.

Mrs Stewart was a good bit older than Sophie, a matronly looking woman, probably into her sixties. Gerry – named after St Gerard Majella, the patron saint of childbirth – had been a surprise after his two older sisters, and arrived when his mother thought she had finished with all that. And she certainly hadn't expected the rush of delight and love she suddenly felt when this afterthought was thrust in her arms by a big rough midwife from Shotts. She'd found herself cuddling him into her, instinctively protecting the tiny little bundle from the loud nurse.

From that day on, she had protected her youngest child and only son. The son who had brought her so much pleasure in life. And she had been successful up until four o'clock this morning.

'I'm so sorry,' Heather said, tears streaming down her face. 'I can't believe it's happened.' She put her arms around the older woman's neck and kissed her on the cheek.

'And I never will, hen,' Mrs Stewart said, patting Heather's arm as she embraced her. 'They might as well put me into my own grave now . . . I'll never be the same after this.' Her voice faltered. 'I can't believe God would do this to us . . . do this to poor Gerry.' She shook her head. 'What did he ever do to deserve that terrible accident? What did he ever do to deserve such a terrible death?'

A pain came into Heather's chest, making it hard to get a deep breath. She moved back now to sit on the couch opposite the stricken woman. 'I don't know what to say . . .' she whispered, searching for the fresh hanky Sophie had tucked in her coat pocket.

'I know you're upset, hen,' Mrs Stewart said, nodding her head. 'I know you were both fond of each other. I know what you thought of him. Jim Murray was the very same, they've been pals since they were wee boys.' She shook her head. 'We used to call them Mutt and Jeff. You never saw one without the other.' She made a small sighing noise. 'Aye, poor Jim is in an awful state . . . he broke his heart cryin' here not two hours ago. He says he doesn't know what happened, one minute Gerry was standing talking to him and the next minute he was lying in the road. That taxi must have been going at an awful speed not to see him.'

Heather lowered her head and moved the hanky up to her streaming eyes. *Oh, my God* . . . she thought, *this is the most terrible nightmare.*

Mrs Stewart told her in a halting fashion all the tragic events that had happened in the hospital last night, and then she went on to relate the details of the funeral that had been arranged so far. Gerry's father and his two sisters were down with the priest at that very minute and they would know more about the actual day and time of the Mass later. The older woman then went on to say that Heather was welcome to come and sit up beside the female members of the family at the front of the church if she wanted.

'For all we know, hen, you could have ended up being part of our family.' She had nodded her head slowly. 'If Gerry had had his way – you certainly would have been.'

Heather attempted another deep breath that still didn't go down as far as it should have. She was beginning to feel a little bit light-headed now.

'Thanks very much for asking me,' she said in a quiet, respectful tone. 'But I don't know if that would be right, Mrs Stewart, you see . . .' She searched desperately for the right words. She didn't want to be hypocritical and deceitful just because there was no one around who could expose her. 'Me and Gerry had had a bit of a falling out . . . We hadn't really been going out together as a proper couple for a wee while.'

'Well, hen,' the older woman said, with the tiniest of smiles at the corner of her sad mouth. 'He told me about you concentrating on your new job right now, but he was hoping that things would get back to normal in the New Year.' She halted for a moment. 'Young folk always have ups and downs . . . but you were the only girl for Gerry. I knew that from the first minute I saw you together. He loved you very much.'

Heather said nothing. There was nothing to be said. And there was nothing to be gained from saying it.

A short while later she got up to leave. 'I'll be back for the rosary,' she told the heartbroken mother.

'A wee minute before you go,' Mrs Stewart said, suddenly getting out of her chair. With great purpose she went down the hallway and into her son's bedroom. Seconds later she came back into the living-room holding a small blue leather ring box. There was no mistaking it. The tiny cube shape with the rounded top could not have held anything else.

Heather's whole body stiffened.

'I wanted to give you this while we were on our own,' she said, handing the box to the younger woman. 'Gerry bought it for you – he would have wanted you to have it. It couldn't go to anybody else.'

Heather took the little box from her and held it between her hands for a few moments. Then, with fumbling hands she pushed the lid back and her eyes looked down at the diamond solitaire ring.

'He had been planning to give it to you for Christmas . . .' His mother's voice faded away.

It was as though everything seemed to be fading away now, Mrs Stewart's voice, her strength, her brave smile.

Heather looked at the frail older woman and knew that she

could not hurt her by refusing it. 'I don't know what to say . . .' Heather said, choked with tears and regret for the way things had ended up between her and her old boyfriend.

'Just take it, hen,' Mrs Stewart said, patting Heather's hand. 'It was you it was meant for.'

If only she could have been left with just the pleasant, cheery memories of their courtship. If only Gerry had accepted that her feelings had changed, that she didn't fancy him any more. They might have ended up as friends, agreeing that it was the right thing to part, where they could both go on and meet someone else more suited to them.

If only Gerry hadn't spoiled it all at the end by refusing to let go. But he had. He had become ridiculously obsessed with wanting her. And he had died still wanting her.

Nothing Heather could do now could change that end. She knew she would just have to live with it.

But that didn't mean his mother and family had to live with the pain of knowing how difficult he'd become – not on top of all the other pain they would have to endure. They didn't need to know it and she wouldn't be the one to tell them.

Chapter 48

'This is brilliant!' Lily Grace said, grinning up at the female physiotherapist who was rubbing some sort of oil into her arms and legs and then massaging it into the muscles. 'D'you like it?' the physiotherapist – Marjorie Clarke – asked, amused by her chatty patient. Lily had been a pleasure to work with from day one. In all the weeks she had been lifted from her bed and then wheeled down a warren of corridors to the physiotherapy unit, she had never once complained or said she didn't want to go.

Of course there had been odd days when she was a bit off and quiet, but she always bounced back.

'Like it?' Lily said, looking up at the hospital room ceiling with all the metal lights. 'I absolutely love it.' She closed her eyes now as Marjorie worked on the muscles at the top of her left arm, gently kneading and massaging in turn. 'I could lie back and get this done to me every single day.' She paused. 'That's what some posh folk get done to them, isn't it?'

'How d'you mean?' Marjorie asked.

'Well, when I was tellin' my big cousin Kirsty about gettin' the oil massaged into my legs and arms, she said that I'm really lucky because all the posh folk have to pay a fortune to get it done – and I'm gettin' it for free!' She halted for a moment, her brow wrinkled. 'What do posh folk get it done for? They haven't all got polio, have they?'

The physiotherapist sucked in her breath. Lily sometimes asked the most difficult, almost unanswerable questions. 'No, not everybody that gets massages has had polio,' she explained. 'People just like getting massaged because it's good for their muscles and things, and because it makes them feel relaxed.'

'Is that right?' Lily mused. 'I think I'll have massages for the rest of my life – when the polio is all gone.' She lay rigid on her back now as her arm was lifted up straight and then gently bent in across her chest. The procedure was then repeated a number of times, and then the physiotherapist moved over to massage the oils into her right arm and repeat the same physical movements.

'Tell me if I hurt you or if I'm going a wee bit too hard,' Marjorie offered.

'You're not hurting me a bit,' Lily said. 'An' the best thing is it's helpin' me to get right back to normal, isn't it?'

'Definitely,' Marjorie Clarke said. 'Your muscles are getting stronger every day. Oh, we'll soon have you up and about – there'll be no stopping you.'

'Well, I'm walkin' a lot better for a start,' Lily told her, 'and I'm able to hold my books now for a good wee while.'

'And what else can you do that you couldn't do a few weeks ago?'

'Well, I can put on my own pyjamas and dressing-gown,' Lily said proudly, 'and yesterday I was able to wash myself in the bath.'

'Och, you're a wee star, so you are!' Marjorie said, sounding very impressed. 'You're definitely one in a million.' The

278

physiotherapists were always gratified to see improvements in all their patients, but Lily Grace had been a very special case. Even at her worst, when she could hardly move, it was obvious from her lively eyes and her voice that she had always been a bundle of energy. An energy that refused to be dampened down by the insidious germ that had done its best to snuff the life-flame from the little girl. A physical energy had transferred itself into a total belief and determination.

During the darkest and most hopeless hours of her illness, Lily knew that one way or another she would get back to what she had been before. Even when the adults felt the odds were insurmountable, Lily had not lost faith in herself. And that had made all the difference.

Twenty minutes later both patient and physiotherapist were exhausted from all their efforts.

'I'll ring for Matt to come and fetch you,' Marjorie said. 'It'll be time for your lunch shortly.'

'I hope it's not that tapioca again,' Lily said, shuddering at the thought. 'It's like frogs' eyes all done in milk.'

Marjorie shook her head and laughed. 'I'm just going to the office for a few seconds and then I'll be back.'

Lily lay back on the exercise table, thinking about school and wondering when exactly she'd be back. She'd hoped it might be Easter, so that she would be back in time for all the nice summer things – especially visits to the swimming baths in Airdrie, the school trip and sports day.

She thought about Mrs McGinty and the country dancing and wondered when her legs would be strong enough to dance again. She could hear the Scottish tunes in her head now, and instinctively her legs and feet started to move to the imagined music. The movement in her skinny but dead-weight legs was minimal, but they could definitely move and so could her arms, as she pretended to conduct the orchestra that was playing the music.

The door of the physiotherapy room opened and Lily attempted to move into a sitting position.

'And how's wee cheeky-face the day?' the porter called as he manoeuvred the trolley through the door.

'Frankie!' Lily giggled as he wheeled the trolley over to the side of the exercise bench she was lying on. 'I thought it was that Matt that was comin' for me . . .'

'Och, he had to go out and help the ambulance drivers wi' somethin'.' He winked at her. 'He's probably off havin' a wee skive somewhere, chattin' up the nurses. Did you not know he's a right Casanova wi' the ladies? Oh, aye,' he joked, 'he's a right ladies' man.'

Lily giggled at the thought of the dour-faced, balding Matt having the nerve to approach any girl. Then, as she watched him put the brakes on and sort out the pillow and blankets, her face became serious. 'Have you got a girlfriend yet, Frankie?'

'Me?' he said, his voice high with amusement. He ran a finger under the high-buttoned round collar of his starched white tunic.

'Aye, you,' Lily said, studying him closely. She was checking his hair, his height and his weight.

'Not me, hen,' he laughed. 'I wouldn't go near women, they're far too dangerous.'

'No, seriously,' Lily said. 'You see . . . I've got two big cousins, and they're dead nice-lookin' and everything . . . but they haven't got boyfriends at the minute.'

Frankie shook his head, trying not to laugh. 'If they're that good-lookin', you're not tellin' me that they haven't got plenty of boyfriends?'

'It's true!' Lily said, her voice high with indignation. 'It's just that they're a bit fussy . . . but I think you would suit one of them fine.'

'Which one?' Frankie said, leaning his elbows on the trolley, his face cupped in his hands.

Lily raised her eyes straight to the white ceiling, giving the matter very serious consideration. It would be just perfect now if she could match up Kirsty or Heather with Frankie, that way she could get to see him every day, like she did in the hospital. It was a pity she was far too young herself for a boyfriend, but her cousins having him would be the next best thing.

'Kirsty!' she suddenly decided. Heather was a bit too serious and crabbit at times for somebody as nice as Frankie. Anyway, she remembered, she probably wouldn't be in the mood for a new boyfriend since that other one got killed. She'd probably be a bit upset and bad-tempered for a few more weeks. She looked now at the porter, thinking how he would keep Kirsty in stitches laughing all day, the way he did with all the patients in the hospital. He would make a great boyfriend, and every time he came to visit Kirsty he would call in to visit his old patient, and probably bring her sweeties or even a wee present. Lily wondered if hospital porters were well paid.

'Well,' Frankie prompted. 'Whit's this Kirsty like?'

'Lovely,' Lily said. She paused, a rare shy look appearing on her face. 'Actually, everybody says she looks a bit like me.' Her eyes grew wide. 'She's got the same blonde hair and everythin', *and*—' She paused for dramatic effect. 'She's a dead famous singer!'

'Is she now?' Frankie said, looking at the watch he had pinned on his tunic and not really listening. He had a young boy to pick up from theatre in quarter of an hour – an appendix case – and he didn't want to get into trouble for being late again. The surgeon that was on this afternoon was particularly bad-tempered and had shouted at him in front of the nurses the other morning.

'I'm tellin' the truth,' Lily said with a slightly huffy tone to her voice, being very sensitive to people not taking her seriously. 'She sings on the stage in really posh places now.'

Frankie nodded his head distractedly. 'Did Marjorie say how long she would be?' he asked.

'No, she didn't,' Lily replied. She stopped for a moment. 'When are you on a late shift again, Frankie?'

'Tomorrow night,' he said, whistling a tune in agitation. That impatient surgeon would really take the head off him this afternoon if he was late again.

The door swung open now and Marjorie came striding through. 'All ready, Miss Grace?'

She went around the other side of the bed to help Frankie lift their little patient.

'You don't need to lift me. If you just hold the trolley,' Lily told them, 'I can easily slide across.'

'Go on then,' Frankie told her, intrigued as to whether she actually could move herself.

Very carefully, Lily got up into a straight sitting position then, with her arms supporting her on the bed, she gingerly swung her legs around and onto the trolley. After a couple of shuffling movements of her bottom, she was sitting straight in the middle of the trolley. 'Well,' she said, a little breathlessly, 'whiddye think of that then?' She lay down, tired from this final exertion.

'Like I said before,' Marjorie told her, 'you're just a wee star!'

Chapter 49

❦

'**A** re you sure you're up to going in tomorrow?' Sophie checked. It was Tuesday night and they were all sitting around the fire, drinking tea after their evening meal. Fintan was in the kitchen with the table covered in newspapers, cleaning shoes. 'You've not slept properly since Sunday night.'

'I'll have to go in,' Heather said in a flat voice. 'I've no option, I won't get paid otherwise. I'll probably lose the day's pay for the funeral on Thursday anyway, and I can't afford to lose the two days.' All the shops and offices had been off the Monday and Tuesday with New Year's Day being on the Sunday.

'It would be a lot easier to just say you were sick,' Kirsty piped up. 'One of us could ring in for you and say you weren't well enough to go to work, and then you could go to the funeral and get paid for it. If you need a doctor's note you only have to say that you've not been feelin' well.'

'I wouldn't like to,' Heather said, shaking her head. 'It would be telling a lie.' She suddenly thought of having to face Sarah back in Seafreight and she felt even more tired. She would dearly love the couple of extra days off to catch up on her sleep and just hide away from everything.

'Och, how are they going to know any different?' Kirsty asked, twirling a strand of her curly blonde hair around her finger. 'As far as they know you could be lyin' in your bed dying with flu.'

'I think Kirsty has a point there,' Sophie said. 'You've not had much sleep these last few days, which can't have done you any good.'

'I'm not sure if they'll pay me,' Heather said. 'I might be too new to get paid for being sick.'

'You don't need that much money now Christmas is over,' Sophie said gently. 'And you can always pay us two days less dig money if you're off. Your father won't argue with that . . . he'd rather see you back to your old self.'

'And I can give you a few pounds if you're stuck,' Kirsty offered. 'I haven't had much time over Christmas and New Year to spend anything.' She laughed now. 'I'm going to go mad at the January sales at the weekend.'

'I'll think about it,' Heather said, 'and thanks for offering about the money. It's good of you both.'

Fintan appeared at the living-room door holding a heavy black shoe in one hand and a polish brush in the other. 'Have ye all decided who's going to the rosary at the Stewarts' tonight?'

'I'm going,' Sophie said, looking at the clock. It was twenty to seven and the rosary was scheduled for half past. The actual prayers would only take about half an hour, but people would stay on, having a cup of tea or a small drink with plates of sandwiches and cakes being passed around.

'I thought I'd go into the hospital with Michael and Sean tonight,' Kirsty said. 'Lily was complaining that I've not been in to see her as often, so I'd better show my face or she'll be giving me a right telling off.'

'That's good,' Sophie said, 'because I know Mona and Pat are going to the rosary tonight as well.'

Kirsty gave a sigh. 'I'd better get going, Michael said he'd toot the horn for me at twenty past seven.' She laughed. 'D'you know what that cheeky wee bizzim said to Mona about me last night?'

'I wouldn't be surprised at anything she said,' Fintan laughed.

'She said to tell me to make sure I looked my best! Can you believe it?' Kirsty was shaking her head in disbelief and laughing. 'She said she was tellin' some of the nurses that I was a famous singer and they wouldn't believe her, so I've to make sure I'm all dressed up in my best things and they might believe her then. She said I'd not to come into the hospital with my old duffel coat on or she'll kill me. I've to do my hair up and I've to wear something fashionable.'

Sophie threw an eye across at Heather who was the only one not laughing. She didn't even seem to be listening. She was just starting into the fire, lost in her own thoughts.

'You might be glad of your duffel coat tonight,' Fintan said, nodding towards the dark window. 'It would freeze the lugs off you out there. The weathermen on the radio were right, the mild spell is gone and the temperatures have dropped.' He tapped Sophie on the shoulder. 'I'd be careful what shoes you put on tonight, for it's going to be frosty later and you could have a fall like last year. You were all black and blue with bruises after it.'

Sophie looked startled. 'It was my pride that was more hurt than my legs,' she said, remembering. 'Imagine falling outside the church after Sunday Mass – I was pure mortified.' She suddenly decided, 'I'll wear my black leather boots, the ones with the good rubber soles.'

'If you dig them out, I'll give them a quick polish for you,' Fintan said, going back into the kitchen.

Sophie got to her feet, a small frown on her face. 'Have you decided what you're doing about tonight yet, Heather? Are you coming to the rosary with me and your daddy or are you going to the hospital with Kirsty?'

There was a silence. 'Neither,' Heather finally said, 'I'm just going to go to bed.'

'And what about work in the morning?'

Heather took a deep shuddering breath. 'I'll go in,' she decided. 'If I get a good night's sleep I'll feel a lot better.'

Kirsty felt she knew every stone on the road into the hospital, she'd been there that often over the last month. At least things were a lot brighter and cheerier now than they'd been when they first started travelling. Michael and Sean Grace were two nice lads, and she enjoyed the journey over with them, chatting about music and work. Sometimes they were shy and quiet with her and Heather – especially if there was a crowd around – but she could tell it was because they weren't that confident and quite easily embarrassed.

Kirsty sat in the back seat, all dressed up in a pair of fitted navy trousers that showed off her slim waist and hips and a pale blue twin-set that she only wore on special occasions. She'd put rollers in her hair and given them a good spray with lacquer while she was getting dressed, and it had given it the more glamorous wavy look that she knew Lily would approve of.

She'd finished putting on a final coat of mascara, combed out her long blonde hair and was just stepping back to admire herself in the wardrobe mirror when her cousin tooted the car horn.

Heather had been downstairs in the kitchen filling a hot-water bottle to take up to bed.

'Will you be all right?' Kirsty had asked in a concerned voice as she pulled on her short blue swing coat. 'I'm still not convinced you should go into work.' She stopped. 'What about that bitchy Sarah? Are you up to facing her the way you're feeling?'

Heather had looked up at her with dark-ringed eyes. 'I couldn't care less about Sarah,' she'd said. 'I was just thinking about it earlier and I realised that after what's happened, stupid childish things like that don't matter.' She'd given a little shrug. 'If she doesn't want to talk to me then that's her hard luck. There's plenty of other people in the office I can be friendly with.'

'Good for you!' Kirsty had said, her voice full of admiration. She had been delighted to hear her sister sticking up for herself. Heather was always too worried about keeping on the right side of people so this was a definite improvement.

The car horn had tooted again.

'Well, get yourself a good night's sleep.' Kirsty had said, making for the hall. Then, just as she went to open the front door, she'd turned on her heel and walked quickly back into the kitchen. She'd walked over to her sister and put both arms around her neck.

'You'll be fine, Heather,' she had said, hugging her. 'You'll feel much better in the morning.' She'd given a little laugh. 'And if that Sarah so much as looks as you the wrong way, tell her your wee sister will come in and batter her!'

The lads chatted about a new engine they were going to put in the car that would make it even faster. Kirsty chipped in now and again, but her conversation was token and gradually she slipped back into her own thoughts about the events of the last few days. Gerry Stewart was her main thought. It was hard to think of anything else, because apart from the fact that his death had been the most terrible shock, she still found it impossible to imagine that someone her own age could actually be dead and gone for ever.

Someone she had laughed and had a joke with was now going to be put in a coffin and buried under the ground, never ever to be seen or heard from again.

When she pushed the dark, disturbing thoughts out of her mind, pictures of Larry Delaney took their place. And Kirsty didn't quite know what to do with those thoughts except push them away. They were pointless and stupid.

Larry Delaney had once told her that she knew absolutely nothing about him. And he was right. And the little bits she had come to know about him didn't make any sense to her. All they did was tell her that he lived in a very different world from hers. A world filled with people like Fiona and Helen McCluskey.

Kirsty had so many questions that she wanted to ask him. But the more she knew of him, the more she was afraid of the answers. The things she had already found out made her think that the clever Larry Delaney she knew and liked – and had even fancied – was really a total stranger. A stranger who had a lot of secrets.

She knew now that he had a young son by Helen McCluskey, but she knew nothing about the relationship or what they had meant to each other. It was quite possible, Kirsty thought, that they had been married. For all she knew they might still be married. She looked out of the car window as the bright lights of Motherwell approached, feeling young and foolish and very naïve.

There were so many things that she didn't know and didn't really understand. Like this terrible nightmare with Gerry. Like the situation with Larry and Helen McCluskey – how they could still speak and be polite and civil to each other even though something terrible had happened between them.

Kirsty wondered how people like those dark-haired McCluskey women could go about talking and acting in such an uppity way when Helen obviously had either an illegitimate child or a broken marriage behind her. She and her older sister showed no signs of embarrassment or shame at the situation she was obviously in. The girls and women she knew from Rowanhill who had made mistakes like that tended to keep a very low profile. They didn't want to draw attention to themselves and their mistakes by parading themselves around the place.

Take Liz Mullen for example. Now she was pregnant, Liz wouldn't be out and about so much, she would go to work and come home and concentrate all her spare time on the plans for her small wedding and her future home. She wouldn't mention her plans unless directly asked, and she certainly wouldn't be bringing up the subject to anyone she happened to meet.

If it had been the big white wedding that was saved and planned for, the whole Mullen family would have been talking loudly and proudly about it from the day the engagement was announced. When it was quiet and hushed and the bride-to-be and her family wouldn't meet their eyes when they were congratulated on the forthcoming nuptials, people would quickly realise that there was something more than romance and love hastening the event. And then they would say no more.

Everyone had someone in their family who had let the side down one way or another. Kirsty thought now of her beautiful Auntie Claire who had caused all the gossip in Rowanhill by going her own way. She hadn't been pregnant but she had done something that was probably deemed worse as far as the more pious parishioners were concerned. She hadn't made a mistake of the flesh that any silly girl or woman could make – she had made a cold, calculating decision to turn her back on her religion and her class. And that wouldn't be forgotten, not in Rowanhill. The rejection was a black mark on Claire and the family that would never be forgiven.

But Kirsty instinctively knew that the mistake Claire had made would not be held against her where she lived in Glasgow. The people there would only see her lovely clothes and nice big house and car and her unbowed, proud ways. The kind of people Claire mixed with would probably be like that Fiona and Helen who would still feel so superior and above everyone else that nothing anyone could say would bother them.

As the car turned into the hospital grounds, Kirsty suddenly came to a startling conclusion. It was only people in small, parochial villages like Rowanhill who kept those rigid, judgemental views where everyone had to behave the same as everyone else, and where it was demanded that everyone toe the Church and community line.

Kirsty had thought it was the same everywhere. But now she suddenly understood that it was only Rowanhill's way, and the way of other small claustrophobic villages. There was a bigger, wider world outside where people were far too busy getting on with their own lives to waste time scrutinising the shortcomings of their neighbours.

The more she thought about it, the more Kirsty realised that the big world outside Rowanhill was the one she wanted to belong to, where people could do what they liked and it was nobody else's business.

When the time was right, Kirsty Grace wanted the freedom of the bigger world.

Lily's eyes lit up with delight when she saw Kirsty coming through the ward doors, all dressed to kill like a model out of a fashion magazine, and she was gratified to notice all the nosy-parker visitors at the other beds were having a good look at her too.

When they were having their evening meal earlier on, Lily had told the other children in the ward that she was expecting her big cousin to visit her tonight, the big cousin who was a famous singer and who wore only the most fashionable and expensive clothes.

And Kirsty hadn't let her down. She had followed the instructions – passed on through Mona – that she must look her best.

'Well, you came,' Lily said, folding her arms and giving a satisfied little sigh. She was sitting there resplendent in a pair of fancy pink pyjamas that someone had got her for Christmas, and a bright pink hair ribbon that one of the young nurses had tied in her curly blonde hair just before visiting time. She had loads of nightdresses and pyjamas to choose from now, and Mona had brought her in hair ribbons in a variety of colours.

'Aye, I did, cheeky-chops,' Kirsty said, coming over to give the little girl a peck on the forehead. She lowered her voice. 'And I didn't wear my scabby oul' working duffel coat, I put on my best clothes just like you said.'

'I'm glad to see you did,' Lily said, glancing around the ward to see who was still watching. Disappointingly, most of them had gone back to their own conversations. She looked up at her two brothers, her brow furrowed. 'Is it only youse two that are comin' tonight?' she quizzed.

Michael nodded, handing her a brown paper bag. 'My mam and dad have gone to the rosary for that Stewart lad that got run over by a taxi – did you hear about it?'

Lily nodded, her eyes flitting between her brothers and the unopened bag in her lap. 'Aye, it was Heather's old boyfriend. I knew him really well. We used to have a laugh when he was in her house, and when his dog died in the summer he gave me the dog's fancy collar for Whiskey. The red one with the studs. Did you not know that?'

'I think I remember something about it now,' Michael said, smiling over at Kirsty.

'Talkin' about Whiskey,' Lily said in a serious tone now, her eyes narrowed and looking from Michael to Sean, 'I hope youse are all keeping him well fed. He looked a bit skinny to me when I was home for New Year.'

'That's because he's missing you,' Sean told her. 'He wouldn't eat a bite for days when you went into the hospital at first, and every time you come home and go away again, he does the same thing.'

A big smile broke out on her face now. 'Aw ... poor Whiskey. He must be really missin' me.'

The boys looked over at Kirsty and then they all rolled their eyes and tried not to laugh at their bossy, temperamental young sister.

Lily opened the brown paper bag now and took out the latest

copy of *The Beano* and an Enid Blyton book called *Welcome Mary Mouse*. She had asked her mother to look in her bedroom for the book, as she wanted to give it to a little girl in the ward who got hardly any presents at Christmas.

'Brilliant,' she murmured to herself as she scanned the cover of the book, then she shook out a Bounty Bar and a packet of Rowntree's Fruit Gums from the bottom of the bag.

Welcome Mary Mouse was a book she had grown out of, and one she would be able to read aloud when they were in the day-room together, and practise what it would be like when she was grown up and a teacher.

She had decided that the other day. She would be a dancing teacher with her own dancing school if her legs got back to normal, and if they didn't then she would just be an ordinary primary school teacher. Either way, there was no harm in practising her teacher's voice for when she was older.

'So what's all the news?' Kirsty asked her now. 'Have they told you when you're getting' out yet? And what's happened to what's her name – your wee specky pal? I noticed she's not in her usual bed any more.'

Lily put the book down in her lap and tried hard to look disapprovingly at Kirsty's description of her ward-mate. 'For your information,' she said primly, a little smile sneaking around the sides of her mouth, 'Margaret got home last week. She said she's going to write to me every week, and that we can be pen-pals.'

'Where's she from?' Sean asked.

'Holytown,' Lily said.

'That'll be excitin' for you,' Michael laughed. 'A pen-pal that lives only a few miles away. You're supposed to get pen-pals from America and Australia and places like that. You don't get pen-pals wi' people that only live up the road from you.'

'Shut up, you,' Lily said, tutting at him. 'It's only because we're not well and can't walk or get on the bus to see each other. We've said when we're older that we'll visit each other's houses and we'll stay with each other during the summer holidays.' She sniffed. 'You can't do that if you live in America or Australia, can you?'

'So what's this about me havin' to get all dressed up to visit you?' Kirsty asked in a high, indignant voice. 'My oul' duffel coat wasn't good enough, I hear.'

'Well,' Lily said, 'it's just that some people in here didn't believe me when I said my cousin was a singer, so I wanted to make sure you looked like a real singer when you came in. There's nothing actually wrong with the duffel coat, it's just that it makes you look like somebody that only works in a chemist's shop.'

Kirsty's heart lifted as she suddenly noticed that Lily was using her hands now the way she always used to. She was pointing and moving them when she wanted to make a point. Not as flamboyantly as she used to, perhaps, but she was definitely using her hands again. She decided not to make any issue of it, as she didn't want Lily to become all self-conscious as she sometimes did.

'Oooooh ... that would be absolutely terrible, wouldn't it,' Kirsty teased, 'havin' a cousin that looks like she works in a chemist?'

Lily ignored her now, having spied one of the nurses coming up the ward. 'Veronica!' she called to the heavy-set elderly woman. 'Is Frankie on tonight?'

'Yes, Lily,' Veronica smiled. 'Did you want him for something?'

'Aye,' Lily said, trying hard to conceal her excitement, 'I just wanted a wee word with him.'

'I think he's in the office. I'll tell him when I go back down.'

'Who's Frankie?' Kirsty asked for something different to say.

'Oh, he's the porter for this ward.'

'And what do you want him for?' Sean asked.

Lily sighed as though she was weary of answering daft questions, as though she was the adult and the other three were the irritating nosy children. 'I just want to check wi' him what time I've got physio in the morning.' She raised her eyebrows disapprovingly at her elder brother. 'Is that OK with you?'

Sean shook his head and laughed. Mona would soon knock all the uppity-ness and cheek out of Lily as soon as she was well enough. The four of them sat chatting for a while, Michael and

Sean giving Lily a run-down of what had been happening in her favourite television shows, and then they all took turns telling jokes. Then the two lads said they were going to visit a local man they knew who was in another ward with a broken leg, and they'd be back in ten minutes.

Lily went on to ask Kirsty all about Gerry Stewart being killed and what had actually happened to him. She listened carefully as Kirsty told her a diluted version of events, then she looked up at her big cousin. 'He was a bit funny at times, wasn't he? I don't mean funny as in a good laugh – I mean he was a bit peculiar at times.'

'What do you mean?' Kirsty asked curiously.

'Well, you know when they finished up?'

Kirsty nodded.

'Well, he used to meet me up the road at the chip shop and that, and ask me all about Heather. He would ask me what train she got in the morning, and what time she got in from work. Then he would ask me to find out what she was doin' at the weekends, and he would sometimes come into the library in the evenings to see if I was there and find out what she had planned.'

'Did he?' Kirsty gasped. 'And did you tell him all about Heather?'

Lily nodded her head. 'Nothing dead private, like. I only told him boring things like what trains she caught home from Glasgow.'

Kirsty cast her mind back to Heather's first day at work. 'Did you tell him when Heather was starting her new job and what time she'd be home the very first day?'

Lily's brow wrinkled as she tried to remember. 'Probably,' she said shrugging. 'It was ages ago ... before I got sick and went into hospital. I can't think that far back.'

'That wasn't very nice of him, asking a wee girl loads of questions about an adult ... I'm surprised you didn't tell Heather.'

'Och, I felt a bit sorry for him at first,' Lily explained. 'But I went off him a bit when I saw him actin' strange.'

'What did he do?' Kisty asked, growing more and more worried at this news.

'Well, one night I was up at the bedroom window, and I saw him hidin' at the side of your house,' she whispered. 'But he didn't see me. He was tryin' to look in the window to see if Heather was there.'

Kirsty's blood suddenly ran cold as she remembered the night she thought she had seen a man's figure in the back garden. 'How d'you know that it was Gerry Stewart?' she checked. 'Did you see his face?'

Lily shrugged. 'Because I know his dark wavy hair and his height and everything. He's not as tall as my daddy or my Uncle Fintan, and who else would be creepin' about your house at night?'

'Did you not say anything to anybody?' Kirsty asked. 'Did you tell your mammy or daddy?'

'No,' Lily replied. 'I felt sorry for him because I knew he still liked Heather – and anyway, he used to give me a shilling every time I found out anythin' about her.' She grinned now. 'I was savin' up for Christmas and the money was very handy.'

'I don't believe it,' Kirsty said, aghast at the news, and even more aghast that Gerry had been prepared to use an innocent girl in such a way. He must have been really desperate. She shook her head now, thinking that Heather had had a narrow escape. Turning up at the house drunk, causing fights at parties – God knows what he might have done next.

Lily saw the medium-sized figure coming up the ward now in the white tunic and smiled to herself. He came to stand at the end of the bed.

'I believe you wanted a wee word with me, Miss Grace?' he said, running a hand through his Brylcreemed quiff.

'Aye, I did,' Lily said, beaming from ear to ear. 'I just wanted to check what time I had to go to Marjorie in the mornin'?' She glanced over at Kirsty to see what impression the porter had made on her so far, but Kirsty was just looking at him with a strange look on her face, as if she was studying him closely.

Frankie's brow furrowed. 'Did she not tell you when you were there this afternoon?'

Lily looked all innocent. 'I forgot ... Och, it doesn't matter anyway. I'll find out tomorrow.' She paused now, then indicated towards the silent Kirsty. 'This is my big cousin, the one I was tellin' you about. The singer.'

Frankie looked across the bed at Kirsty, and his eyes lit up when he saw the pretty, well-dressed blonde. 'Don't I know you?' he asked, trying to work how they'd met before.

Kirsty looked back at him, then she realised that he was in fact familiar to her. 'I think so,' she said nodding. 'I definitely know your face . . . but I can't remember where from.'

'Maybe you've seen him around the hospital,' Lily interjected, not wanting to be left out of the conversation. That often happened with adults, she'd discovered. She'd start off on an interesting subject, and before she knew it, they were all talking to each other and ignoring her. 'Frankie's one of the best porters here and he wheels me up for my physiotherapy when he's on the day shifts.'

Kirsty shook her head. 'No, that's not it . . . I've definitely not seen him in the hospital before.'

'Maybe we met at the dancin'?' Frankie suggested.

'Which dances do you go to?' Kirsty asked, her mind ticking over. She definitely knew this Frankie but there was something different about him now.

'Och, me and my pal Terry go to dances all over the place,' he said airily, 'Wishaw, Motherwell—'

'That's it!' Kirsty burst out. 'I know where I know you from now! It's the hospital uniform that confused me.' She went into peals of hysterical laughter, unable to speak.

Frankie looked at Lily, mesmerised. 'Is she all right?'

Lily shrugged, her mouth in a tight pout of disapproval. This wasn't going the way she'd expected at all. She'd expected Kirsty to be shy and impressed with Frankie's good looks – she hadn't expected her to go into fits of laughing at him.

'I don't believe it!' Kirsty said, slightly more composed. She bent for her handbag to search for a hanky to dab at her eyes. 'Are you Terry McGinn's pal?' she giggled. 'Terry the secret Teddy boy? You're the one that keeps the Teddy-boy suits in his house, aren't you?'

Frankie went beetroot red, realising that he was being mocked. 'Aye,' he said, touching a hand to his trademark quiff. 'Terry's oul' boy won't let him wear the gear at home.'

'D'you not remember dancin' with me and my sister at Motherwell Town Hall a few weeks ago?' she said, trying not to laugh at the memory of the two young lads trying to act all tough and cool.

Light suddenly dawned on Frankie, and his face turned even redder as he recalled how Terry had persisted to the last minute, trying to walk the two sisters home. 'Och, Terry's a right clown at times,' he blustered. 'He'd do or say anythin' for a bit of a laugh . . .'

'I've known Terry for years,' Kirsty told him now, 'and he's always been a nice fella.'

She decided now that she'd had enough fun out of the situation and she didn't want to hurt Terry's friend's feelings. She hadn't really meant to laugh as heartily as she had, it was just the shock of realising that this very professional-looking porter, in his white tunic and nurse's watch, was the self-same person as the hard-looking Teddy boy she'd met at the dancing.

They chatted generally for a few minutes, Frankie now so relaxed and easy that Kirsty had given up on the teasing. Then he asked her all about her singing and where she went and that kind of thing. After a bit, he glanced down towards the office at the bottom of the ward. 'I suppose I'd better get back to work, they'll be lookin' for me. You never get a minute at this job.'

'Well, according to this young lady here,' Kirsty said, indicating towards her cousin in the bed, 'you do a very good job. She speaks very highly of you.'

'Are you goin'?' Lily asked him, looking disappointed.

'Aye, I've a few more things to do before I clock off,' Frankie said, winking at her.

Lily took a deep breath. 'Are you not goin' to ask Kirsty for a date?' She looked at her shocked cousin, all dressed up in her beautiful blue twin-set, and her blonde hair all done up in waves. 'I thought you might like to take her out to the pictures or somethin' like that . . . She hasn't had a boyfriend for ages.'

'You cheeky wee article!' Kirsty gasped, unable to believe her ears. This time it was her turn to blush and she certainly did. She took a deep breath as she felt the customary red rash start to spread all over her neck. 'Don't you dare ask anybody to take me out ... I'm certainly not that desperate.' She looked at Frankie now, who suddenly looked amused.

'Sorry to disappoint you, girls,' he said, suddenly looking all puffed-up and full of himself, 'but I'm afraid I'm already spoken for. I've been goin' out with a right lovely-lookin' girl for the last five weeks.'

'And I'm not lookin' for a boyfriend either,' Kirsty said indignantly, shooting daggers in her interfering cousin's direction.

'Aye,' Frankie said, as if Kirsty had never spoken, 'I think I've landed on my feet there, she's actually training to be a dental nurse.'

'Aw...' Lily groaned, folding her arms in annoyance and shaking her head. He was probably just saying that because Kirsty had laughed at him. She wished she'd never said anything about Frankie and Kirsty going on a date now, because she'd be too embarrassed to ask him to come out and see her at the house when she left the hospital. That Kirsty had ruined everything.

'I'll have to go now, girls,' Frankie said, giving them both a flirtatious wink. 'Duty calls.' He went off down through the ward with a renewed swagger in his stride.

'I'll blidey well kill you!' Kirsty hissed as soon as he was out of earshot. 'What did you think you were doing?'

'I was only tryin' to get *you* a date,' Lily said, equally annoyed. 'He's a really nice fella and you were killing yourself laughin' at him.'

'No wonder!' Kirsty said. 'He's nothin' but a blidey wee nyaff, and I wouldn't be seen dead goin' out with him or his stupid pal.' She shook her head. 'You don't half land me in the predicaments, Lily Grace!'

Lily gave a big disgruntled sigh now. 'Well, I just hope you're happy with yourself now, for you've ruined *everything* for me. I really liked Frankie and I wanted him to keep being my pal when I left the hospital.' She halted, her eyes narrowing. 'You'll be sorry when you're an oul' maid all on your own and nobody wants you.'

'Well, for your information,' Kirsty retaliated in the same childish manner, 'I'd rather end up an oul' maid than be stuck wi' a wee nyaff like him! So keep your match-making to yourself.'

There was silence for a few moments. 'Maybe Heather would like him,' Lily ventured.

'Don't even think about it,' Kirsty hissed.

Chapter 50

Heather got off the crowded train and started the familiar walk through the station and out into the streets of Glasgow. There were still traces of frost in at the kerb and the parts of the pavement that had not been trodden on. It was the coldest morning she had experienced since working in the city, and as she climbed the hill to her office she could feel the chill wind irritating her eyes and pinching at her nose and cheeks.

A lovely wave of warm air hit her as she entered the swing doors on the ground floor and helped to thaw her out as she mounted the building in the lift with the other office workers.

As she walked across the office to hang her coat and other outdoor things, she heard various calls of 'Happy New Year, Heather' coming from all corners of the office. She turned towards those nearest, a fixed smile on her face and repeated the same greeting back to them. Then, when she had combed her hair and discreetly checked her lipstick in her compact mirror, she smoothed down her straight tweed skirt and went into Muriel Ferguson's office to check if Muriel wanted her to start on the filing of any documents that had come in during the period the office had been closed. She knew that the meticulous spinster would have been in bright and early this morning and got a head start on everybody else.

'If you could make a start on this lot it would be great,' Muriel said, handing her a stack of documents in all shapes and sizes. 'I think it's going to take us days to catch up on it all. And when that Danny Fleming comes in, maybe you could ask him to check up on any bills of lading that need to be typed up as well.' She stopped for a moment, and then gave Heather a long look. 'Are you all right, Heather? Did you have a nice Christmas and New Year?'

'Fine,' Heather said, nodding her head, her gaze fixed on the top document in the pile she was carrying. 'When I've finished these, I'll come back for more.' She turned and went out into the main office to get started on them.

A few minutes later the sound of laughter and banter signalled the arrival of Danny and his workmate Maurice, and then Sarah Fox's voice joined in with the laughter. Whether she had just arrived with the lads or whether she had been in the office already, Heather neither knew nor, she suddenly realised, cared. She did not feel in any way awkward or angry or anything. In fact, she had no feelings at all regarding Sarah Fox.

Heather ignored all the muted laughter and chat and kept her attention focused on the filing cabinet, carefully scanning the top of each document then searching for the appropriate folder.

'Are you not even goin' to wish us a Happy New Year?' Danny Fleming asked in an exaggeratedly hurt tone. He was now beside her and leaning a hand on top of the filing cabinet. 'I called across to you twice and you just ignored me.'

'Oh, I'm sorry, Danny,' Heather said, giving an apologetic smile. 'I really didn't hear you . . . I'm trying to get all this stuff sorted out.' She indicated the pile of letters and documents and bills waiting to be filed.

'You're surely feelin' all keen and businesslike,' Danny said in a surprised tone. 'Sure, it's hardly nine o'clock yet. What's up wi' you?'

Heather shrugged and affected a little laugh. 'I just feel like keeping myself busy,' she told him. 'I'm not in a very chatty mood this mornin' . . .' Then she remembered. 'Muriel said can you check out if there's any bills I need to type out . . .'

Danny saluted and clicked his heels, Gestapo-like. 'If Miss Ferguson requires me to check out bills – then I will check out bills!'

Heather laughed more naturally now, but as she did so, she

felt unexpected tears in her eyes. She took a deep breath and fixed her attention back on the pile of paper.

'Did you have a good Christmas and New Year?' Danny asked, reluctant to make a start on his actual work. He shuffled through some of the papers on the top of the filing cabinet.

'Fine,' Heather heard herself say again.

'I don't think you ate too much,' Danny said now. 'I'm sure you've lost weight – even your face looks thinner.' He stepped back to get a good look at her, and then he moved to the side to get a good view of her rear end and legs. 'You've definitely lost weight, Heather ... what have you been doing to yersel?'

'Nothing,' Heather said quietly. 'I had a wee bit of a cold over the New Year ... and I didn't feel like eating much. I'm OK now.' In truth, she had no appetite at all. Since cutting down before Christmas, she found her stomach had shrunk and she couldn't eat half as much as she used to. And since the New Year ... food almost choked her. And whilst weight was the last thing on her mind, she knew that Danny was right because the skirt she had put on this morning that was usually tight around her hips and waist, now swung around easily with room to spare.

Danny shook his head. 'Well, we'll need to start feedin' you up at the break-times.' He turned now to his tall thin pal who had just sidled up alongside. 'Won't we, Maurice? We can't have Heather losin' her nice curvy figure, can we?'

'Definitely not,' Maurice agreed, straightening up his tie. 'We need all the buxom women we already have in the office,' he joked. 'We don't want all these skinny-malinkies taking over.'

Danny made some retort about Maurice being the biggest skinny-malinky in the office and then they waited for her to put in her tuppence-worth as she usually did. But Heather said nothing. She felt a peculiar tightness in her chest and however she racked her brain, she found she couldn't think of one funny or smart remark to say back. Eventually, the boys drifted off, looking confused and slighted by her attitude.

At the back of her mind Heather knew she wasn't behaving the way that people were used to, but she didn't seem able to help it. She felt tired and fuzzy and everything seemed a greater effort than normal. The only thing for it was to do one job at a time and concentrate wholly on it, even if it meant not being able to chat and laugh with her work-mates.

Mr Walton appeared in the office around ten o'clock, having had some banking business to attend to in town earlier. After he settled in, he went around the various desks wishing everybody all the best for the coming year. He halted at Heather's desk, complimenting her on the work she had got through already, and asking her how she had enjoyed the festive period.

Again, she made a suitable if faltering reply and eventually what should have been an ordinary light-hearted conversation crumbled into an awkward embarrassing silence, and Mr Walton went back to his office scratching his head.

The morning gradually crept in with Heather going back and forward to Muriel's office every so often to replenish the pile of filing and then walking back to disperse it amongst the steel grey drawers and green cardboard hanging files. As the eleven o'clock break approached, Sarah Fox – who Heather had been vaguely aware of flitting around – suddenly appeared at her side.

Heather kept her attention on the filing cabinet, and didn't look up.

'Could I have a wee word with you when the others have gone down to the canteen?' she asked in a hesitant voice.

'Is it about work?' Heather said in a cold tone, not making any attempt to look at her.

'No,' Sarah said, 'it's actually personal . . .'

'In that case,' Heather said, looking her straight in the face, 'the answer is *no*. Apart from work issues, I don't have one single thing to say to you.' Then, as the buzzer sounded in the distance for the morning break, she put the file she was working on back in its place and banged the metal cabinet drawer shut.

Sarah reeled backwards against a desk, shocked by both Heather's attitude and the sudden movement of the big heavy drawer. Her usual confident demeanour had suddenly deserted her in the face of this cold, steely stranger who was nothing like the girl who had started working here a few weeks ago. The girl who Sarah mistakenly felt she had the upper hand with. 'I'm sorry . . .' Sarah said now, her voice stuttering and uncertain. She lifted her handbag and almost ran down the office in the direction of the Ladies'. Heather turned away, looking for her own handbag. Then she passed the little groups who were still loitering around the office and went downstairs. She joined the queue to get herself a cup of tea, which she brought back and drank sitting alone at her desk.

The rest of the morning passed in a fog of filing, weighing and stamping mail and typing out the most urgent letters and bills. Heather got through it all, applying the same tactics she had used for the first part of the day – doing one job at a time and not looking up from it until it was time to move onto the next.

Just before lunch, Mr Walton came across the office to speak to her.

'Heather ... would you mind stepping into my office for a wee minute, please?'

'Not at all,' Heather said. 'I'll just put these files back in place and I'll be straight in to you.' At the back of her mind Heather felt vaguely aware that it was unusual for Mr Walton to bring members of staff into his room at lunchtime. He usually went out on the dot for his own lunch. She wondered if there was some kind of a problem, but couldn't imagine anything that it could be. He had been fine with her earlier on this morning and gave no indication of anything being wrong.

She shrugged to herself, unable to summon up enough curiosity or interest for it to worry her. Like the way she had worked all morning, she would deal with the situation when it arose.

The buzzer went again, signalling that it was one o'clock, and everyone started lifting jackets and coats and heading in the general direction of the door.

'Are you coming with us for lunch?' Marie Henderson, the quiet girl that Sarah always sat with, asked as Heather was lifting her handbag. 'We're going down to the Trees.'

Heather looked down at the floor. 'Mr Walton wants a word with me, so I could be a wee while ...'

'We'll wait if you want,' Marie offered, looking back anxiously at Sarah, Danny and Maurice.

'No,' Heather said, cutting her off. 'If I feel like coming I'll catch up with you.'

Heather tapped on Mr Walton's office and walked in.

'Sit down, sit down,' he said warmly, motioning to the comfortable leather chair facing his own.

Heather did as she was told and sat down in the chair. Then she waited.

He sat forward in his chair, resting his arms on the tooled-leather table, the fingers of both hands linked together. 'I've asked you to come in because I'm a little bit concerned as to how you are ...' He halted. 'Is there anything wrong, Heather? You don't seem quite yourself.'

Heather looked up at him blankly, vaguely knowing she should say something – but quite, quite unable to find a single word.

'Are you feeling ill?' he asked now, in a concerned, fatherly way. 'You don't look yourself at all ... several of the staff have said they're a wee bit worried about you.'

Heather took a deep breath and finally found a small wisp of a voice. 'I wanted to ask you if I could have the day off tomorrow ... to go to a funeral. It doesn't matter about the day's pay ...'

'Of course,' Mr Walton said quickly. He sat back in his chair. 'Is it somebody close, Heather? A relative?'

A picture of Gerry suddenly swam into her mind and she felt all light-headed and strange.

'It's a boy,' she whispered, vaguely wondering if she should have said man or lad. 'He was my boyfriend up until I started work here.'

'What happened?' Mr Walton asked. 'Was he sick?'

Heather shook her head. 'It was a road accident ... he got knocked down early on New Year's morning.'

'Good God ...' the office manager murmured. 'That's very tragic.'

Heather suddenly felt all dizzy; she took a big gulp of air, trying to steady her breathing.

'You see,' she went on in the strained stringy voice, feeling that she should explain it fully for some reason, 'he was trying to catch up with me. He wanted to see me home ... He was crossing the road and then a taxi came flying round and didn't see him ...' She felt immediately guilty, telling it as though it was the taxi-driver's fault – but she couldn't tell him that Gerry

302

was drunk and that in all probability it was his own fault. That just seemed too cruel an explanation to voice.

Mr Walton's head was bobbing up and down, indicating that he understood. 'Of course you can have the day off, Heather,' he said, standing up. 'It's perfectly understandable that you'd want to go to the funeral . . .'

Heather stood up quickly now and the dizziness suddenly increased along with a whooshing noise in her ears. She bent down to retrieve her handbag from the floor and suddenly the green flowery carpet seemed to be moving up towards her.

'Are you all right, Heather?' Mr Walton said, moving quickly around the table towards her.

'I'm fine,' she replied. And then everything suddenly went black, and Heather Grace keeled over in a dead faint on Mr Walton's office floor.

Chapter 51

Looking back on it, Heather could never really remember the journey out to her Auntie Claire's house in the taxi or how it was decided that she should actually go there instead of going home.

When she came round in Mr Walton's office, Muriel Ferguson and some of the older women were standing around her, talking to her in encouraging, gentle voices. She had tried to sit up, but as soon as she did, the dizziness and the spinning in her head started again. This went on for quite a while until she was able to sit up and drink a cup of sweet tea and force down two digestive biscuits.

She had a vague recollection of people coming in and out of Mr Walton's office to see how she was. Danny had stood at the office door with a shocked look on his face, asking her if she was feeling OK and Sarah had come over and knelt beside her, saying she hoped she felt better after she got home and how sorry she was about the stupid argument they'd had. She'd also gone on to say something about Gerry and the funeral, and Heather had felt suddenly sick when she realised that the whole office must have been talking about it.

She remembered Mr Walton asking her if any of her family had a phone, and how long did she think it would take her father to drive out and collect her. Then he had asked her if she knew anyone nearer, maybe someone related to her, who lived in Glasgow. Sarah had butted in then, suggesting that Heather might like to come home with her, she explained how Heather had stayed a night over Christmas and how her mother and father would be delighted to have her.

Mr Walton thanked Sarah for her kind offer, but said they would have to let her family know and then decide what to do. It had been decided from the onset that, whatever happened, Heather was in no fit state to go home on the train or the bus alone.

Heather knew she must have given somebody the little card she had tucked in the back of her purse with Claire's address and phone number on it, because Muriel Ferguson had given the card back to her in the taxi after she'd shown it to the taxi-driver.

'This looks like it!' Muriel announced in a high, almost excited, voice, as the taxi came to a stop outside a detached granite two-storey house on a tree-lined avenue. It was set back off the road on a rolling incline, with several sets of steps running up through neatly trimmed gardens on either side. She turned to Heather. 'You did say you've never been out to your aunt's house before, didn't you, Heather?' she checked again.

How strange she's never visited here, Muriel thought, but deduced the aunt and uncle had only recently moved into the area. But as she looked at the fine-looking house and all the others around it, she found it even stranger that Heather hadn't bragged to everyone in the office about her aunt who lived in the big house in Glasgow.

Heather nodded – her head still fuzzy and sore from where she'd banged it on the office floor when she fainted. 'I've never been out here before,' she confirmed. 'So I'm sorry I can't direct you.'

The door of the house opened and a slim dark-haired figure in a sweater and neat jeans came rushing down the steps.

'I'm Heather's aunt – is she all right?' she called out in a clear Irish tone.

Muriel Ferguson had got out of the back of the black cab first when the driver had come to open it. 'She's improving,' she said, nodding her head gravely. 'But she's not been at all well at work.' She stepped away from the vehicle and lowered her voice so that Heather wouldn't hear her. 'She's fainted several times . . . kept going in and out of consciousness.'

Claire stood there listening with a very concerned look on her pretty face. 'She'll be fine now, we'll get her straight into bed.' She moved towards the taxi, and then got into the back of it beside her niece while Muriel spoke to the taxi-driver, checking that he would wait a few extra minutes to allow them to get Heather safely into the house.

'How are you, Heather?' Claire asked gently, patting her niece's hand. 'Are you feeling a wee bit better? Are you well enough to walk up to the house?'

Heather nodded her head very carefully. 'I'll be fine,' she told her aunt in a weak voice. 'I walked out to the taxi from the office.'

'Come on then,' Claire said, smiling encouragingly at her niece, 'we'll get you out now and into the house.'

'I'm really sorry for being a nuisance,' Heather told her as she followed her aunt out of the low taxi door. 'I feel really silly for fainting in the office.'

'You're not the first, my dear,' Muriel told her in a chirpy voice, 'and you won't be the last.'

Five minutes later Heather was propped up on the cream and wine and blue paisley-patterned velvet sofa in her aunt's house with the deep-buttoned back and arms. She had two blue-tasselled cushions under her head and a fluffy eiderdown on top of her.

'And you don't need to worry about a thing, I'll let them all know back at Seafreight that you're safe and sound,' Muriel said in her officious voice. Then, when Claire ran out to the kitchen to bring in some logs to brighten up the fire, the secretary glanced around her, taking in the expensive but discreet furnishings and the tasteful cream and beige walls, hung with a mixture of classic Glasgow and Edinburgh prints and several original watercolour and oil paintings. There was also a large framed photograph of what looked like a family standing at the front of a simple, white-washed farmhouse out in the country.

Muriel's gaze flitted to the white marble fireplace, which had a coal fire burning in the grate, and then at the mahogany table at the window, with the large oriental vase filled with cream and orange lilies. To one side of the vase there was a silver-framed wedding photograph of Heather's aunt and her older-looking husband and on the other side a small religious statue. On closer inspection, she recognised it as the Sacred Heart – a well-known Catholic symbol. Muriel Ferguson was Church of Scotland herself, and didn't have any close friends of any other denomination, but she did have an aunt in a nursing home in Paisley with a Catholic friend who had lots of these kind of statues.

Muriel was most impressed by Heather's relatives living in such an elegant place and more than a little surprised. It was quite obvious from her respectful attitude that Heather came from a very decent hard-working family, and Muriel presumed from the things that she'd heard the girl say about her mother sewing and the father being a school caretaker that they were fairly ordinary. But this particular strand of the family were not quite so ordinary. They were obviously of a different standing – they had to be to be living in this particular part of Glasgow.

She was amazed that Heather hadn't let it be known that she was so well connected – Muriel certainly would have. She had learned the importance of status long ago. What was the point in keeping social advantages like this to yourself? People only treated you as they saw you, Muriel thought, so it was most important that they should know all the facts. Claire came back in carrying a basket of small logs. She sat it down at the side of the fire then, after giving the glowing coals a good poke, she proceeded to throw half a dozen logs into the middle of it.

'I've turned the radiators up as well,' she told Heather. 'I don't want you getting cold on top of everything else.'

'It's lovely and warm in here already,' Heather said, thinking how luxurious it was to have central heating in your own house. Apart from small electric fires for emergencies, they only had coal fires back in their house and if you didn't keep your eye on them in the winter, it was absolutely freezing.

Claire offered Muriel tea or coffee, but the secretary declined, saying she would love nothing better than to sit down and relax in such a lovely room, but unfortunately work and the taxi at the front door beckoned. Another time, she told Claire, when she wasn't under pressure from work.

She followed Claire out into the magnolia-painted hallway with a high decorative ceiling and as she shook hands with the sophisticated Irishwoman at the front door, Muriel reckoned that the old granite house must be one of the most expensive in the location.

After she'd seen the middle-aged secretary off in the taxi, Claire came quickly back up the steps and into the house. She lifted a good-sized footstool, which was covered in the same paisley-pattern velvet as the sofa, and plonked it down on the floor beside her niece.

'You're a very sensible girl,' she told Heather, pushing the sleeves of her jumper up to her elbows. 'You were right to come out here rather than travelling all the way home on your own.'

'I'm really sorry ...' Heather said in a low, cheerless voice. 'Causing all this fuss at the office ... and then disturbing you.'

'Of course you're not disturbing me!' Claire said in a warm reassuring voice. 'I·was doing nothing apart from raking up a few leaves and tidying around in the garden. I'm really sorry you're not well, but I'm delighted to have you as a visitor.' She smiled now and patted Heather's arm. 'Didn't we talk about you and Kirsty coming out after Christmas anyway?'

Heather nodded and managed a little smile. 'It would have been far nicer if I wasn't sick ... I feel a bit stupid. Imagine fainting in my boss's office ...' She closed her eyes and shook her head.

'I wouldn't worry about that,' Claire told her. 'I'm sure plenty of people have fainted in offices over the years.' There was a little pause. 'Now, you're welcome to stay here on the sofa,' she said, patting the quilt, 'or we can take you through to one of the spare bedrooms. The beds are all made up so it's absolutely no trouble. It's your decision.'

'I still feel a wee bit dizzy,' Heather said, 'so maybe I'd be best staying here for a while.'

'Grand,' Claire said. 'I think a sleep would probably do you the world of good – you look very tired.' She paused. 'Did you feel sick before you went to work this morning?'

'I felt funny,' Heather admitted. 'And I've not really slept much the last few nights ...'

Claire looked at her now as though she was going to say something, but then thought better of it. 'Have a wee sleep now, we can chat later.'

While Heather slept, Claire went out into the hallway to the phone. She dialled Directory Enquiries and got the number of the parish priest in Rowanhill. It was the last place she wanted to phone, but apart from phoning the police or the doctor, she didn't know anyone in Rowanhill who actually had a phone. She would just pretend to herself that she was making a call from an office and this was just a stranger on the other end of the phone. She dialled the number and then took a deep breath. After a few rings a man's voice came on the line.

It was the parish priest, Father Finlay – the priest that Mona worked for.

Very politely and precisely, Claire explained the situation to the priest and asked if it were possible that a message could be relayed to Sophie and Fintan that Heather was safe and being looked after at her Aunt Claire's house.

'Could I ask asking who's calling?' the priest asked.

'Claire ... Claire McPherson.'

There was a pause. 'Would that originally have been Claire Grace?'

Claire's heart started to beat quicker. She might have known she wouldn't get away with things that easily. 'Yes, Father – I was Claire Grace,' she replied, 'and now I'm Claire McPherson.'

There was a longer pause. 'The Chapel House isn't a telephone service,' he said in a curt voice, 'but given the circumstances ... we'll try to do our best.' His voice rose now, to the familiar one used in the pulpit. 'The Catholic Church try to look after their own, and the other members of the Grace family have always followed the correct religious path.' He stopped again. 'Mona Grace should be in here shortly, I'll pass the message on to her.'

'Could I just give you the house number, please?' Claire asked, struggling to keep her voice steady. 'So they can speak to Heather themselves.'

'Go on,' the priest said curtly.

Claire recited the number and as soon as she came to the last figure the line clicked off.

Chapter 52

Sophie and Fintan sat on either side of the kitchen table.
'I think we should go out to Glasgow and collect her,' Fintan said in a quiet but definite tone. When Mona had come down from the Chapel House with the message, young Patrick had been quickly dispatched to get him at the school boiler house. The children weren't due back in school until next week, but the boilers still had to be checked regularly. 'We can't have Andy McPherson coming in from work at seven o'clock and then doing a double journey out to here . . .'

Sophie nodded her head. 'But what about the chapel?' she asked. 'The body's being brought to the chapel tonight.'

'Oh, Jesus, I forgot,' Fintan said, clasping his broad hand over his mouth in thought. The business with Heather had taken over everything else. 'Look, you go to the chapel tonight, and when Kirsty comes in from work her and me can go into Glasgow then. I'd rather have her with me to sit in the back with Heather when we're coming home, just in case she's not feeling too good. We can all go to the funeral in the morning then, depending on how she's feeling. If it's only a faint, she could be as right as rain in the morning.'

'I'm not sure Heather is fit enough for the funeral, whatever she says,' Sophie said in a low voice. 'I'm worried about her . . . I didn't want her to go into work this morning but she insisted.' She sighed. 'When Mona came rushing down here I knew there was something wrong . . . I felt it all day.' She pressed a finger and thumb on the bridge of her nose now, trying to ease the tension that was building up.

'Well, you spoke to her, and she sounded fine,' Fintan said, coming around to where Sophie sat to put his arms around her. He kissed the top of her head. 'Didn't you say she sounded fine?'

'I suppose so . . .' Sophie agreed in a half-hearted way. 'Claire wanted her to stay the night, but Heather's insisting that she needs to be home for the funeral.' She looked up at Fintan. 'She does need to go to the funeral, doesn't she?'

'I think so,' Fintan said. 'It would look awful bad if she didn't.'

Kirsty sat in the front seat reading out the directions to her father, as it was the first time he'd ever driven into a strange part of Glasgow in the dark and he didn't want to get lost – especially on a foggy, frosty night. It was a long drive into Glasgow from Rowanhill and over to Bellshill, then they followed the long road out towards Calderpark Zoo and then straight into the city.

Claire had given clear and precise directions and Fintan was relieved when he saw the signs for Giffnock coming up.

'You've been a good navigator,' he told his younger daughter. 'I wouldn't have managed as well without you.'

'Och, it was easy enough,' Kirsty said, 'and doing a journey like this has given me a feel for driving myself.'

'You?' Fintan said, glancing over at her. 'You're thinking of learning to drive?'

'Why not?'

'Well, for a start it's an expensive business, and you're very young.'

'Michael Grace is driving,' Kirsty told him, 'and he's younger than me.'

'But he's a lad,' Fintan said, laughing at the idea now, 'and he's training to be a mechanic. There's not many young girls your age learning to drive and nobody I know in Rowanhill.'

'Maybe I could be the first,' Kirsty said quickly. 'I want to be more independent, and I don't like Larry having to pick me up all the time.'

Fintan negotiated a corner. 'How could you pay for driving lessons and afford to run a car?'

'I've got quite a bit saved up in the Post Office,' Kirsty reminded him, 'and I'm going to be earning quite a bit more at the weekends now. The hotels I'm booked into pay over double what I was getting with the band.'

'True enough,' Fintan said, 'I hadn't thought of that.' There were far worse things she could do with her money, he thought.

'I was wonderin' if you might take me out for a few lessons . . .'

'I might have guessed there would be a job in it for me,' he laughed.

They came into a very quiet, residential area now.

'I think we're nearly there,' Fintan said. 'It must be one of these roads here or hereabouts.'

He drove on for another little while then eventually pulled up in front of the granite house. 'Well,' he said giving a little sigh of relief at having eventually reached the right destination, 'it looks like this big mansion thing is Claire's house.'

Kirsty thought her father's voice sounded as though he was proud of his sister having the house mixed with a tinge of apprehension. 'Do you feel nervous going in here,' Kirsty asked quietly, 'seeing as it's the first time?'

'Not really,' Fintan said, turning off the car lights. 'Maybe just a wee bit awkward . . . the way things have been.'

'Are you happy to see Claire again? D'you feel you've missed her?'

'Of course I've missed her,' Fintan said in a low, slightly hoarse voice. 'She's my young sister . . . how else could I feel?'

'Well, I'm looking forward to seeing her again, because it's been over two years since I last did,' Kirsty stated, 'although I suppose I'm just a wee bit nervous about meeting her husband.'

'Well, don't be,' Fintan said, opening the car door. 'He's a very nice man – he's a real gentleman.'

They both got out of the car.

Kirsty looked at her father in the half-light of the yellow street lamp. 'He's a good bit older than her, isn't he?'

'I suppose he is,' Fintan said, nodding his head.

'Does that bother you?' Kirsty asked.

He thought for a moment. 'Not really,' he replied. 'He's a nice fellow, so I don't think the age makes a whole lot of difference – it was the religion that caused all the trouble.'

Then father and daughter walked up the steps to the house, both wrapped up in their own private thoughts.

Heather was sitting up in the corner of the sofa, tired and pale-looking but feeling much better than she had earlier in the day. After a two-hour sleep she'd wakened to find Claire sitting in an armchair opposite quietly reading. When she woke properly they sat and talked for a little while, then Claire went into the kitchen and brought her back a tray holding a bowl of home-made chicken soup and two slices of thick, crusty bread.

'Eat it all,' Claire told her. 'You'll feel much better when you've got something inside you.'

When she started eating, Heather felt surprisingly hungry. Both the soup and the bread were lovely, and she sat quietly eating until it was all finished. Claire indicated that she should just put the tray down on the low coffee-table in front of the sofa.

'Well done,' her aunt said, smiling at the empty bowl. 'That will do you good.' She looked up at Heather now. 'What's happened? I've got a feeling that you're upset about something. When you came out of the taxi this afternoon you looked as though you'd maybe had a bit of a shock . . . as if something had happened.'

Heather looked back at her aunt and suddenly her eyes filled up with tears. 'Everything's gone wrong,' she said, shaking her head. 'And I think a lot of it's my fault.' Then, she laid her arms down on the side of the sofa and put her head on top of them and started to cry in earnest.

'Nothing can be that bad,' Claire said, coming over to comfort her. 'I'm sure it will all get sorted out.'

'But it can't be sorted out,' Heather sobbed, taking the clean handkerchief that her aunt had retrieved from her jeans pocket. 'You can't sort things out when somebody is dead.' The torrent of tears came again until finally she had exhausted them.

For the next two hours Heather sat and talked and talked,

while Claire sat beside her on the sofa and listened – offering the odd word of comfort here and there where it was appropriate.

'You've had a tough time,' Claire told her when she had finished the whole story. 'But it's not your fault.'

'I feel in some way it is,' Heather insisted. 'I feel as if I could have handled it better, tried to get through to him in a way that would have left him feeling all right about it.'

Claire squeezed her hand. 'You did everything exactly right, and you need to believe that. It's not your fault if an ex-boyfriend became obsessed about you – it's entirely *his* fault. And it's certainly not your fault if he got drunk and wandered out in the road in the middle of traffic.'

For a moment Heather thought she should perhaps remind Claire that Rowanhill didn't have enough vehicles on the road to be worthy of the term *traffic*. That it was quite an unbelievable coincidence that a taxi should appear as Gerry Stewart was in the middle of the road – but she decided against it. Claire was obviously so used to city traffic that she just presumed if you walked out in the middle of the road a car would eventually hit you.

'I feel so bad about Gerry's family,' Heather whispered now. 'About the ring and how they were hoping we'd get engaged . . .'

Claire had looked her square in the face. 'Do you want my advice?'

Heather nodded.

'Keep the ring and say nothing.' She gave a little shrug. 'What's the point in hurting them any more? Let them think what they want to. Let them think you were going to get engaged if it gives them any little bit of comfort.' She took both Heather's hands in her own and squeezed them. 'That poor, poor woman has lost her son . . . her heart will be broken. You and I will never know how that feels.'

'I feel so sorry for her,' Heather said, dabbing the hanky to her eyes. 'They're a very nice family, that's why I felt they deserved to know the truth.'

'Look, Heather,' Claire said gently, 'you've done your best to tell the truth about the break-up and it sounds as if the poor woman doesn't want to hear that. She just wants to feel that everything was fine in her son's life right up until the minute he died.'

'And I want her to feel that too,' Heather said. 'I don't want her to know that Gerry went a bit weird because I know it would just make the whole tragedy worse.'

'If you feel well enough tomorrow, do the dignified thing and just go to the funeral,' Claire told her now. 'If you don't, you'll regret it when it's all over . . . and there won't be a single thing you can do about it then.'

There were some minutes of tension when Fintan entered his sister's house for the very first time. All the awkwardness and difficulties that had caused the family estrangement seemed to suddenly swim in between them, demanding some sort of acknowledgement.

'I'm grateful to you for looking after Heather today, and I'm delighted to be out visiting your home at long last,' Fintan said as he embraced her. Kirsty had already greeted her aunt and had gone on into the sitting-room to see her sister, leaving them to talk in private.

Claire was immediately on the defensive. 'I'm glad I was able to help Heather, but I wish that you'd come to visit me just for the sake of it. I wish it hadn't been a duty call for you.'

'Now, Claire,' he said, taking his young sister's hand, 'things aren't that simple . . . and shouldn't we be grateful things have moved forward?'

'Why did we have to wait until this happened for you to see me or until Lily was in hospital?' she asked, hurt staring out of her piercing green eyes. 'You had no excuse not to come to my house, Fintan. You were always invited – you and the rest of the family.'

Fintan bowed his head. Like all the Grace men he hated these kinds of family confrontations and avoided them at all costs. It was only when there was a fear of any harm coming to his own girls that he was forced to come down with a heavy hand. 'I don't want to row with you, Claire . . .' he said in a low voice. 'There was no deliberate decision not to come to your house . . . it was just the way things happened with the wedding.'

'Andy's a good man,' she said, a tremble now evident in her

voice. 'He's never done anybody any harm in his life . . . it wasn't his fault that we weren't able to get married in the Catholic Church.'

'It's all in the past and forgotten,' Fintan told her. 'We don't need to go over it all now.'

'But it's *not* in the past,' she insisted, 'and it won't be forgotten until we sort this out properly.'

Fintan sighed now. This had not been the best of days. 'I'm heart sorry about the way this all happened . . . but all families have their difficulties over things like religion. It would eventually have changed one way or another and we would have sorted it out.' He shook his head. 'There wasn't a day that went by that we didn't miss you . . .'

Claire cleared her throat. 'Well, it's nice to hear you saying it . . . but I might not have known it if it hadn't been for Heather taking sick at work.'

'Well, maybe we can all learn from the situation,' Fintan said, 'and try to make sure these things don't happen again.'

'She's welcome to stay the night – or stay for as long as she likes,' Claire said, bringing in a tray with cheese and cold-meat sandwiches and warm sausage rolls. She went back into the kitchen and came back the second time with homemade apple tart and slices of cherry cake.

'What do you think?' she asked her brother, putting the plates down. 'Do you feel she's well enough to travel home with you tonight?'

Fintan looked across at his pale-faced daughter, his brow furrowed. 'It's up to you, Heather – whether you feel up to it or not.'

'I'm a lot better,' Heather decided, 'and I do need to go to the funeral in the morning. Whatever happens, I couldn't miss it.'

'If you just make it to the chapel for the Mass,' Kirsty said, 'that will be all you need to do. You can go home and go to bed after that.'

Heather closed her eyes and nodded, unable to bear even the thought of it. She made herself eat a quarter of a ham sandwich and a small piece of the fruit cake even though she still had no appetite. If she fainted again, at least she would know it wasn't through her own stupidity of not eating.

After they had finished eating and drinking a second cup of tea, Claire took them all on a guided tour of the house before it was time to leave.

'It's beautiful!' Kirsty breathed, taking in the double spare room with the white furniture and the matching coloured glass lamps at either side of the satin-covered bed. The other spare room was a twin with similar furnishings. 'It's like a hotel – a really lovely hotel.'

Claire laughed embarrassedly but looked delighted at the compliments.

'I'm very lucky to have all this,' she said as they walked back downstairs to the sitting-room. 'And I suppose that's one advantage of marrying an older man. They have things like houses and cars organised by the time you come on the scene.' She waved her hand around the hallway. 'I only had to pick the colours for the decorating and add a few more womanly items in the sitting-room and bedrooms. Most of the things were already there.' She looked at the girls now. 'I have to say that the spare bedrooms were decorated with you two in mind ... I kept hoping some day that you might start coming out to stay the odd weekend.'

Kirsty and Heather both nodded in agreement.

'Now we know our way out here, you won't be able to get rid of us,' Kirsty laughed.

Just as they went to sit down again for a last few minutes, Andy McPherson came rushing through the front door in a smart pin-striped suit and carrying a dark overcoat and a leather briefcase. He beamed with delight to see his wife's relatives.

'I got held up at the office and I thought I might have missed you all,' he said, shaking hands with Fintan and smiling warmly at the two girls. 'And how's the patient?' he asked. 'Feeling a wee bit better, I hope?'

'A lot better, thanks,' Heather said, feeling herself blushing. The whole situation of her fainting and causing all this fuss was now becoming very embarrassing and she knew more of it lay ahead when she got home to Rowanhill. There would be her mother all worried and telling her that she shouldn't have gone to work in the first place and then there would be Mona, dying to know every detail about what happened. That's, of course, if she was still speaking to Heather for having gone out to Claire's house.

'A drink, Andy – Fintan?' Claire asked the men.

'A gin and tonic would be lovely,' Andy said. He turned to Fintan. 'There's whiskey and brandy or there's a few bottles of beer there.'

'I'm opening a bottle of sparkling wine,' Claire stated, 'so if anyone else fancies a glass?'

Fintan thought for a minute. One wee drink would do no harm driving and it just might help them all to relax. 'A glass of beer would be lovely, thanks.'

'What about the girls?' Claire said, looking straight at Fintan. 'Are they allowed a glass of the wine? It's not very strong.'

Fintan shrugged then smiled. He only worried about them getting into situations that they couldn't handle because of drink – but he knew they couldn't be in safer hands at the moment. 'Och, I suppose a wee glass won't do them any harm . . .'

Kirsty got to her feet, delighted that her father hadn't shown them up. 'I'll give you a hand to carry the drinks in,' she told her aunt, trying to suppress a childish, delighted smile.

After a few moments, Heather followed the two females in, feeling a bit self-conscious at being left with the two men.

'The glasses are in the cupboard over there if you don't mind getting them,' Claire told Kirsty, then she went into the fridge to get the wine. 'Will you have a glass of wine?' she asked Heather when she appeared at the door.

'Maybe just a small one, thanks,' Heather said. She looked around the bright, modern kitchen. 'You've everything in this house, haven't you?'

Claire paused, the wine bottle in her hand, peeling the crinkly gold paper off the top of it. 'I suppose we have a lot of nice things . . . but Andy works very hard.'

'You don't work now, do you, Claire?' Kirsty asked, putting three wine glasses on the worktop.

She shook her head and smiled. 'Not since I got married. I keep busy around the house and the garden and I meet up with girlfriends in the city a couple of afternoons, and then we have people out at the weekends or we visit them.'

'Oh, it sounds really glamorous,' Kirsty sighed. 'It's just the kind of life I would like.'

Claire smiled. 'From what I hear, I think you have a very exciting life already, Kirsty. Heather was telling me all about your singing career – you've done very well for a young girl so far.' She turned to the side now to carefully pop the cork from the wine, and then she quickly poured some into each of the three glasses and let the first bubbles settle down before filling them up to the top.

'Oh, would you get a bottle of beer from the fridge please, Kirsty?' she asked now, reaching into the cupboard for a beer glass and a tall chunky glass for Andy's drink. She went into another cupboard for the gin and a small glass bottle of tonic. She mixed the drink then added ice cubes and slices of lemon which were already cut and wrapped in the fridge.

'If you girls would put the drinks on a tray from the bottom cupboard,' she said, 'I'll just sort a few bowls of crisps and nuts for us to have with them. Some evenings Andy enjoys relaxing with this then we have our dinner a bit later.' She laughed. 'He particularly likes it when we've got pleasant company like this.' She halted, an anxious look coming over her face. 'You will come back out to see us again, won't you?'

Chapter 53

The village of Rowanhill poured into the church on the first Thursday in January to pay their last respects to Gerry Stewart. Heather had been up since eight o'clock although the Mass didn't start until eleven. She'd sat up talking to her mother and Kirsty about the Gerry situation again until eleven o'clock the night before, and then she went to bed feeling exhausted. She'd slept fitfully, but had definitely had more sleep than she'd had the last few nights. The long chat she'd had with

Claire had somehow made her feel a little bit better, and she knew that if she could just get through the next few hours things might start to get back to normal.

Kirsty had had to go into work in the chemist's, but they said she could have the time off for the funeral and go back in after lunch, which was decent of them. She said she would leave half an hour before the Mass to give her time to get changed into her best black clothes and walk down to church with the rest of the family.

Around nine o'clock Mona appeared at the door with her arms folded high over her chest and her jaw set in stone.

'I thought I'd call round to see how you were feelin'' after yesterday,' she said when Heather answered the door. 'I wasn't sure if you'd still be in your sick bed.'

'I'm a bit better, thanks,' Heather said as they walked into the kitchen. 'I'm still a wee bit shaky but I'm a lot better than yesterday.'

'So what exactly happened?' Mona asked, although there was more of an agitated angry edge to her voice than concern.

Sophie, hearing the voices, came downstairs in her dressing-gown. She knew that Heather wouldn't be up to dealing with her aunt's awkwardness this morning. She'd hoped to be up and in her funeral clothes before her sister-in-law came round, but Mona's disapproval about her state of undress was the last thing on her mind this morning. Sophie had also had a bad night, going over all the things the girls had told her last night about Gerry and his carry-on. She'd had no idea what Heather had been putting up with, and how Christmas and New Year had been wasted for her with the strain of worrying when he would turn up and in what state.

'Why on earth didn't you tell your daddy?' she'd asked Heather in a shocked voice. 'He'd have gone up to see him and sorted it all out.' She paused, thinking. 'Maybe none of this would have happened if you'd—' And then she stopped, seeing the pained look on Heather's face.

'It wasn't my fault ... I tried everything I could,' Heather whispered.

'I know, I know,' Sophie said. 'I didn't mean that the way it sounded. Anyway, a lot of these things are down to fate . . . and an accident is an accident.'

Heather looked at Mona now, and tried not to feel all defensive. 'I just wasn't feeling well – I was all dizzy and weak and then I fainted in the office.'

'So it was really just a *faint?*' Mona said, her eyebrows raised in surprise. They were all standing in the kitchen now, as though they were somehow afraid to sit in the chairs as they usually did. 'I thought it was somethin' far more serious, with the emergency phone call and all of that.'

Heather went over to the sink and started washing the mugs and plates that had been used this morning. She needed to concentrate on something because she could feel that the conversation was heading in the wrong direction. She really was not in the frame of mind for Mona's interrogation and her head was still fuzzy and achy from yesterday.

'She banged her head when she fell,' Sophie chipped in quickly. 'And it wasn't just one faint, she kept going in and out of it. Her boss and all the people at work were very worried about her. She definitely wasn't fit to be in work or to travel home on the train.'

'Well, we all thought it was something a lot more serious,' Mona repeated, her jaw getting tight again. 'It all seemed very dramatic, especially with the phone call to Father Finlay . . .'

Heather felt herself becoming more and more annoyed as she listened to her aunt. She was scrubbing the mugs so hard that the painted flowers that decorated them were in fear of being completely scrubbed away.

Sophie knew that the bit about the priest was rankling most with Mona and she was prepared for it. 'We needed to be told and there was no one else Claire could phone,' she stated, watching Mona flinch as she said Claire's name. 'In cases like that most people phone the Chapel House. The alternative would have been the police or the doctor.'

'I would have preferred if the doctor had been phoned,' Mona said. Her arms were still folded tightly, her fingers digging into the fleshy part at the top of her arms. 'I would have preferred anybody bein' phoned instead of Lady Muck usin' the priest and me as an answerin' service . . .' She took a deep breath, determined to have her say. 'If it had been me, I'd sooner have walked it home from Glasgow to Rowanhill than set foot in her Protestant house. I wouldn't have gone near it supposing I'd had to crawl home on my hands and knees.'

Heather whirled around, unable to listen to any more. 'Well, that's the difference between us, isn't it?' she said, her eyes burning with rage. 'I was grateful to go out to Claire's house and it was just common sense for me to go there because I was already in Glasgow. There was nobody else I knew that I could have gone to.' She fleetingly thought of her fair-weather friend Sarah who had offered to have her out in her house in Govanhill, but there was no way that Mona was going to find out about that.

Mona's face was stony-grey. Never had either of Sophie's girls dared to answer her back in such a manner. They had occasionally disagreed with her, but they had done it in a polite and inoffensive way – or in Kirsty's case, she would have turned the disagreement into a joke.

'Claire was more than happy to do whatever she could to help,' Heather went on, deliberately not looking at her mother. She knew Sophie would be making faces and trying to quieten her down. 'It made sense for me to go out to Claire and Andy's, and I'm very grateful to them for making me so welcome.' She paused, looking Mona straight in the eye. 'And she made my daddy and Kirsty welcome too.'

'Well,' Mona said, making for the hallway now, 'ye're all easy pleased and ye all have short memories. I'm surprised at your father . . . but then I suppose that Pat would have been the same. No backbone.'

'As far as I'm concerned,' Heather continued, her tone and manner defiant, 'I think something good came out of me fainting yesterday. It gave me and Kirsty a chance to get to know our Auntie Claire and her husband – and we both think they're lovely. They're nice decent people who wouldn't be the kind to run other people down or stick knives in their backs. And they have a beautiful big house that Andy works very hard for – and Claire has it spotless and perfect.'

Mona made a loud snorting noise, almost like the sound a horse would make. 'I'm surprised that one would dirty her hands with housework, and I'm sure she was delighted getting the chance to show off her ill-gotten gains. To show off all that she got for marrying an oul' relic nearly twenty years older than her.'

Heather turned back to the sink, her hands squeezing and twisting the dishcloth tightly under the soapy water. She couldn't believe what she was hearing, and yet she shouldn't have been surprised because when she was riled, Mona was capable of anything.

'Now, you know the age gap's not that big,' Sophie said in a low voice, terrified in case a full-blown row broke out this morning of all mornings, 'and there's nothing to be gained from running them down like that. They were very good to Heather yesterday, and the way everybody had cut them off, we had no right to expect anything.'

'Oh, they'll be glad to creep back into the good books, I can see it all now,' Mona said, raising her eyes to heaven. 'And Claire Grace has been very clever – very cute – trying to get back in with the younger more innocent ones. She did the very same comin' to the hospital to see our Lily.' She pulled a face now, the way children did when they were arguing. 'Oh, she came into the hospital all dressed to the last with her la-di-da ways of goin' on, and handin' out expensive presents that she hoped would impress us all.'

Heather half-turned around, feeling that Mona's rantings didn't deserve her complete attention. 'Well, I think Claire was just being generous and kind,' she said through gritted teeth. 'It was really nice of her, and Lily was pleased with the present – it really cheered her up.'

'Oh, ye're all easily codded,' Mona said, looking very sceptical, 'especially all the young ones among ye . . . It's Claire this an' Claire that.' She looked at Sophie now. 'She's some company for your daughters – she's a fine one to be held up as an example. You can take my word on it, Sophie – if she gets accepted back into this family with her Godless husband we'll all rue the day. We'll never be able to say a word to our families again. If we condone what Claire Grace has done we'll answer for it later.'

'I don't think you should be saying things like that,' Heather

322

snapped. She was fed up with this bossy interfering aunt who felt she could say whatever she wanted and that everyone would just take it.

'That's enough now,' Sophie warned in a firm tone, looking from her daughter to her sister-in-law. Things were getting very out of hand. She'd never heard Heather standing up for her views like this before. 'Today's not the day for this kind of talk. We have a funeral in a short while . . .'

But Heather couldn't stop herself now. She whirled right around to face her aunt again. 'Well, I think the trouble *you're* causing is far worse!' she threw at Mona. 'I think stirring up all this spite and holding grudges is far worse than anything Claire has done.'

Mona gave a big sigh and shook her head. 'Now, d'you see what I mean, Sophie? It's startin' already and that's after only one visit.'

After Mona had left, there was an uneasy silence between mother and daughter, both wishing that Mona had never come round. They had been handling things reasonably fine this morning until she came on the scene.

At twenty to eleven Fintan came downstairs in his dark suit and black tie and Sophie, Heather and Kirsty Grace put on their black coats and gloves and pinned their black lace mantillas on their heads, then they set off for the church.

On the way up, Sophie took Heather's and squeezed it tightly. 'You'll be fine,' she told her. 'And you've done all the right things – nobody can say a word about you.'

Heather looked at her mother and gave a sad weary sigh.

Kirsty gripped her other hand. 'My mammy's right, just keep going the way you have and you'll be fine.' She gave a little teasing smile meant to gee her sister up a bit. 'And we've all made sure you've had plenty of toast this morning, so you've no excuse for fainting.'

'And if we come across Mona,' Sophie advised, 'just keep your ears and your mouth closed. Don't let her upset you in any way. I've already told her I don't want to hear anything more today.'

'Was she in this morning already?' Kirsty asked. She had come rushing in at the last minute with just time to get changed and out.

Heather nodded her head but said nothing.

Our Lady's Catholic Church was a sea of black suits on the men's side and black coats and hats or mantillas or headscarves on the other. Fintan spotted Pat and the boys in a centre pew and went to join them while the three females slid into a pew up in the front third of the church.

Heather kept her gaze straight ahead, knowing that people would be looking at her and talking and saying that she'd been Gerry's girlfriend. They would be watching to see how she reacted or didn't react at various points throughout the proceedings.

She felt she had no more tears left as she had cried her heart out the last few nights and then again with Claire yesterday afternoon. But the tears hadn't helped. She still felt shocked to the core about Gerry's death. The untimely death of a young fit man. The death that was so, so unnecessary.

Liz and Jim came in with Jim's parents and went up the centre of the aisle to sit just behind the immediate family on either side. Whether they spotted Heather or not, they gave no sign of having seen her as they passed by her pew.

From where she was sitting she could see the front row and the back of Mrs Stewart's head as she sat in her dark coat and hat between Gerry's two sisters. His father was on the opposite side, looking as if he had somehow shrunk inside his heavy black woollen coat. The priest came out on the altar and after that things went into automatic pilot as she joined in with the rest of the congregation in the ritual of the Latin Mass she had attended with her family since she was a baby.

When the Mass and the funeral service were all over the mourners crowded in the churchyard and waited in silence while the coffin was lifted into the hearse, and the wreathes and flowers were all placed around it.

As the crowd started to fall into place behind the hearse, Heather saw Mrs Stewart looking around and knew instinctively that she was looking for her.

'I'll be back in a minute,' she told the others and went over to the stricken woman.

'Will you and your mammy and daddy come back to the chapel hall for a wee cup of tea with us when the men go on to the graveyard?' Mrs Stewart said in a croaky voice. Her eyes looked dark and hollow, evidence of the sleepless nights since New Year's Day. The tradition in the village was that the men followed immediately behind the hearse with the women coming after them. They would walk for half a mile or so after the hearse and then the men would get into cars and go to the graveyard while the women went back home or to the chapel hall depending on the size of the crowd expected for the customary tea and sandwiches.

Heather and Kirsty had planned to slip away from the crowd as the funeral group passed the top of their road, but now Gerry's mother had asked them all back she couldn't possibly refuse. 'Thanks for asking us,' she said, squeezing the older woman's hands.

'He would have wanted you there,' Mrs Stewart said, her voice crumbling away in sorrow.

Even with the most enormous effort to hold them back, two great tears slid down Heather Grace's face.

The church hall was set out with several large trestle tables laid out end to end at the top of the hall, covered in white paper tablecloths and laden with the usual fresh sandwiches and rolls cut in half and hot sausage rolls, bridies and traditional Scottish mutton pies. There was also heavy fruit cake slices and a variety of cakes and meringues for afterwards. Several of the Catholic Mothers' Union were on hand to man the tea urns and replenish the food when necessary. Two men from the St Vincent De Paul were in the small ante-room at the side serving whiskey and sherry, and because of the cold day they were offering to make cups of hot sweet toddy for anyone who needed warming up.

There were smaller tables along the sides of the hall where people could take their plates and cups of tea and sit in the warmth and relative comfort of the wooden hall chairs. Kirsty had decided at the last minute to accompany her parents and Heather to the chapel hall. 'Och, I might as well if you're all going,' she told Heather. 'I'll only have to go home and make myself something to eat anyway before going back to work.'

Whilst in a way it did suit her, Kirsty also felt that Heather could do with a bit of back-up just in case anybody said anything to her. She wasn't sure who might actually *say* anything, but she supposed Mona was a likely suspect given the snippets of the conversation that Heather had told her this morning.

'Have you seen Liz about?' Heather whispered to Kirsty as they went to sit down at an empty table. Sophie was over in a corner chatting to a couple of women from Cleland she hadn't met up with for ages, while she waited for Fintan to come back from the graveyard with the other men. 'I haven't seen her since we were in the chapel.'

'No, I haven't seen her either,' Kirsty said, looking around now. She scanned the groups at the tables and those coming in the door then she shrugged. 'Maybe she went straight home.'

'I was sure she was taking the full day off work,' Heather mused. 'Maybe she's gone off somewhere with Jim and his mother and father, although I'm sure Jim will have gone to the graveyard.'

'They're like flamin' Siamese twins at the minute,' Kirsty said, rolling her eyes. 'Liz isn't lettin' him out of her sight. I think she's terrified he might change his mind.'

'Shush, you!' Heather told her, her eyes glinting with annoyance. 'Somebody might hear you.'

'They know already,' Kirsty said. 'Some of the women were asking me in the chemist's this morning about them getting engaged. They were hinting the way they usually do when they think there's more to it – asking did I know if they'd set a date and that kind of thing.'

'Did you say anything?'

'What do you think?' Kirsty said, sighing and raising her eyebrows. She turned away, shaking her head, then she turned back quickly hissing, 'Don't look now, but here comes Mona like a ship in full sail with that big black hat.'

Normally Heather would have tittered and laughed along with her sister, but she could find precious little to laugh about at the moment. She just wanted this awful day to be over and done with, and then she might be able to think about normal things again.

'Well, girls,' Mona said, coming over to them now, carrying a cup of tea and a plate of sandwiches and sausage rolls, 'isn't this a terrible sad business? A young fella in the prime of his life as well.' She put her things on the table and then pulled out a chair to sit beside them, obviously having put the morning's disagreements behind her.

'It's terrible,' Kirsty said, taking a bit out of a warm bridie. 'I feel really sorry for poor Mrs Stewart ...'

'God love her, the poor woman,' Mona agreed. She stirred her tea now, looking very thoughtful. 'It was maybe just as well you'd broken up with Gerry,' she said to Heather, 'it would have been terrible if you'd been in the same boat as your good pal, Liz.'

'How d'you mean?' Heather said, keeping her voice as ordinary as she could. The row from this morning had really upset her and she was not in the frame of mind for more of it.

'Well, the position she's in,' Mona said, taking a sip of her tea. 'With her organising a quick wedding ...'

Heather shot Kirsty a glance.

'Don't look at me,' Kirsty hissed. 'I've not said a word.'

'No, don't be blaming your sister,' Mona said, almost sweetly. 'I didn't hear it from her. I didn't have to – the whole place is talking about it. It seems Jim Murray got a bit drunk last night and let the cat out of the bag in the pub.' She shook her head, looking directly at Heather now. 'He's took it awful bad about his pal ... awful bad altogether. Seemingly, he was blaming himself for not being able to hold on to him when he wanted to follow you home ...' She halted. 'There's some even sayin' that Gerry Stewart threw himself in front of the taxi deliberately ... suicide like.'

Heather pushed her plate away and stood up. She hadn't been hungry to start with, but she suddenly felt that another bite of a sandwich would choke her. She'd expected Mona to say *something* – that would only have been typical – but she hadn't expected to hear the very worst slant that anyone could possibly put on it. She hadn't even considered that extreme slant herself.

Surely Gerry Stewart had not been that desperate? Drunk and

upset, yes. But suicide? Heather couldn't even contemplate the thought.

'I'm just going to have a word with my mammy,' she told Kirsty. 'And then I might head back home.' She lifted her bag and without a word or a backward glance to Mona she went across the hall to where Sophie was standing.

'Poor Heather,' Mona whispered now to Kirsty. 'She's not at all herself. The whole thing's got the girl in an awful state. She doesn't know half of what she's sayin' and we won't hold anythin' she does say against her at this terrible time.'

'She'll be OK,' Kirsty said, reaching for a beef and mustard sandwich. 'Anybody would feel upset at the funeral of a young lad – especially when he used to be her boyfriend.'

'She's probably feelin' very bad about her finishing with Gerry Stewart, and then this happening. She's probably wondering now if she had been a bit hard on him.'

'Well, she shouldn't be feelin' that,' Kirsty stated, 'because she's nothing to feel bad about.'

Mona nodded, taking a bite of a chicken sandwich. 'I agree wholeheartedly with you, Kirsty,' she said now. 'Heather has nothing to blame herself for at all.' She sat for a few moments in silence, looking around her, checking who was there. 'I hear you were out at the house in Glasgow last night?'

Kirsty took another sip of her tea. 'My daddy and me went to collect Heather,' she said, deliberately giving very little away.

'I believe it's lovely,' Mona said. She knew she'd have to tread very carefully here if she wanted any information, because much as Kirsty was the easiest going of the two girls, she had the Grace bit in her and could clam up when she liked. 'According to what your father told Pat. He said it's like one of those old mansions.'

'It's beautiful,' Kirsty said, brightening up. 'It's got all the modern things like a fridge and a toaster and a fancy cooker, that kind of thing.'

'And did she cook you a dinner or anything?' Mona said lightly.

'No, no – we'd already had our dinner earlier,' Kirsty said vaguely. She'd just spotted the men coming in the door now, back from the graveyard. 'She did us lovely sandwiches, and then when Andy came in, we all had a drink and some nuts and crisps.'

'And did you have that while Andy was havin' his dinner?' Mona asked.

'No,' Kirsty said, only half-listening. She was watching Jim Murray coming through the door on his own. There were a lot more people coming in, but there was no sign of Liz Mullen.

'So he came in from work and sat and had a drink before eating?' Mona said, trying to picture it all.

'The three of us had this nice sweet sparkling wine,' Kirsty said, watching Jim now as he made for the bar in the little ante-room. She thought he looked very strained and agitated. 'And Andy had a gin and tonic and my dad had a bottle of beer.'

'Not a lot for a man coming in from a hard day's work,' Mona said, her eyes wide with shock. 'A drink and a few nuts and crisps!' She repeated the list again to herself, as though learning it off by heart.

Heather felt a gentle tug on her coat sleeve. 'Have you a wee minute, hen?' Mrs Stewart asked. 'I'm awful sorry to bother you, but I have a few people here I'd like you to meet . . . I was tellin' them about you and Gerry and they said they'd like to just have a wee word.'

Heather looked at her mother now, hoping she might just say something that would rescue her. But Sophie didn't seem to notice; she just put her hand out to Mrs Stewart and offered her heartfelt condolences. After they had spoken, Heather followed the bereaved mother back to the group of women who all offered her their sympathies and told Mrs Stewart how lucky Gerry had been to have had such a lovely fiancée.

'Well, *nearly* engaged,' Mrs Stewart had said, tears welling up in her eyes, and Heather simply did not have the heart to correct her.

Jim Murray came out of the ante-room with a large glass of whiskey in his hand, taking great gulps out of it.

'I'll just go and have a word with Jim,' Heather told Mrs Stewart, 'if you don't mind.'

Jim's suit looked sort of ruffled and his black tie was loosened around his neck.

'Where's Liz?' she asked him. 'I haven't seen her since we were in the chapel.'

Jim shrugged. 'I don't know,' he said in a disinterested manner. 'She said she was goin' home when I went to the graveyard and she'd come back later.'

'Well, if I don't see her, will you say I'll call up to her house either tonight or tomorrow night? We said we'd meet up to talk about the wedding dresses—'

'Can you believe this is happening?' Jim suddenly said, cutting Heather off. His eyes were darting around the hall. 'I feel it's all like a dream ... as if he's going to walk in the door at any minute.'

'I wish he would,' Heather said, her voice cracking a little. 'I'm sure everybody does.'

Jim took a big swig out of the whiskey glass. 'Who are you kidding?' he said, his tone changing and his eyes narrowing. 'I bet you're just glad he's out of the way ...'

'Don't be so stupid!' she told him, horrified at what he'd just said. 'We were just like a lot of couples – we broke up, that's all.'

'Aye, right,' Jim said, taking another mouthful. He started to cough, almost choking. 'Well, I'll tell you something, Rowanhill will never be the same place for me after this ... Nothing will ever be the same now my mate's gone. What's the future going to be like for me now?' He shook his head dolefully. 'Everything's changed ... everything's changed.'

Heather glanced around her, hoping no one could hear him. She wondered where Liz was now. 'You shouldn't be talking like that,' she said quietly. 'You've got a lovely girlfriend and you're due to get married.'

'A noose round my neck, more like,' he said in a low voice.

Gerry's father came over to ask Jim something, and gradually he moved away from her, towards another group. Heather heaved a sigh of relief, deciding that she'd done everything she needed to do and she would go now and get Kirsty and they would go home together. All she could think of was going home and upstairs to bed, where she would pull the covers over her head and blot out the whole world.

The two girls walked up the Main Street, both weary with the weight that funerals bring and relieved to leave the mourning group behind. Then, just as they came up towards Liz's house, the door opened and Mrs Mullen came rushing out, still wearing the good Sunday blouse and skirt she'd put on for the funeral.

'Oh, thank God!' she called, her breath coming in great gulps. 'I was just watching out the window to see if any of you were passing – and my prayers have been answered! Will you run up to the phone box and phone an ambulance for Liz? Something's happened and she's bleeding.'

'Where is she?' Heather asked anxiously, her pale face turning even whiter.

'She's on the couch,' Mrs Mullen said, pointing in through the open door. 'The bleeding started off in the church and it got worse when she came out. She's in an awful state.'

'I'll go and phone the ambulance,' Kirsty said, looking at Heather. 'Then I'll run back to the hall and tell Jim. You go on in and stay with Liz.' Then she took to her heels in the direction of the phone box.

'Oh, thank God it was you and Kirsty,' Mrs Mullen said, as they rushed into the house. 'I didn't want to go asking just *anybody* and Liz said to watch out for you. She didn't want the whole place knowing. By rights she should have gone into the hospital a good hour ago, but she wouldn't let me call anybody else to make the phone call.'

Twenty minutes later the whole of Rowanhill knew something was happening as the ambulance drove down the main street with the emergency siren blaring and came to a halt outside the Mullens' door.

Hours after being admitted to hospital, the doctors told Liz Mullen that she had indeed lost her baby. Having noticed the absence of a wedding ring on her finger, they had been more muted in their condolences than they would have been had she been a married lady.

After Kirsty had discreetly alerted Jim Murray as to what had happened, he had gone running down the road to be with his fiancée and he was with her in the hospital when they were both told the sad news.

Heather had waited with Liz until Jim and then the ambulance came, and then she walked slowly down the main street where Gerry Stewart had been killed, wondering what else could go wrong.

At her mother's insistence Heather agreed to give work a miss on the Friday. It didn't really take a lot of persuasion as she knew she still wasn't back to herself. While she didn't feel as bad as the day she had fainted, she knew she wasn't up to doing a reasonable day's work. Sophie pointed out that Heather had been through more than enough with all the funeral business without having had the shock of Liz's miscarriage as well. Heather felt a bit anxious about not going in to work, but when Sophie made the phone call and Mr Walton had said he hadn't expected Heather in and she wasn't to come back to work until she was fully recovered, she felt a bit better.

Chapter 54

'It's freezing tonight,' Kirsty said as she slid into the passenger seat of Larry's car. She made a loud shivering noise. 'Thank God the car's warm.' She leaned over the seat to put a carrier bag into the back. 'It was too cold to come out in an evening dress so I decided to wear my trousers and jumper and change into the dress when I get to the hotel.' She gave a little giggle. 'I hope the heating's working or I'll be going on stage wearing my big woolly jumper over my dress! I'd look very glamorous then.'

Larry laughed. 'You should be toughened to the cold, living in Scotland,' he told her. He put the car into gear and pulled off.

'It's supposed to snow tomorrow,' she told him. 'It's lucky it's tonight and not tomorrow night or we'd be in trouble. The roads up in Lanark often get snowed in.'

'This has been one of the mildest winters I've ever known in Scotland,' Larry said now, as they drove out into the darker roads beyond the village street lamps. 'I've never known a Christmas and New Year so mild.'

'Well, it's definitely changed tonight, the temperatures have gone right down. Was Dublin ever as cold as this?' she asked him as they drove along. 'What kind of heating did you have?'

He went silent for a moment – his light-hearted mood suddenly disappeared as though she had asked him something very serious. 'I suppose it was coal ...'

'*Coal?*' Kirsty said in a surprised voice. 'I thought it was always turf they used in Ireland. Where my daddy's family come from in Offaly, it's all turf. I never knew they used coal in Dublin.' She halted, thinking. 'D'you ever miss Dublin? You said your mother was in Manchester, so I suppose you don't have much family back in Ireland ... do you?'

'None that I know of,' he said. 'Or maybe none that I want to know about.'

Kirsty looked at him strangely, but he just kept his eyes on the road, staring straight ahead.

Light flakes of snow had started falling by the time they arrived at the Clyde Valley Hotel.

'It looks lovely, the garden all covered in white,' Kirsty said as they walked across the car park and into the welcoming warmth of the hotel.

'I don't think it will come to anything much until tomorrow,' Larry remarked. 'It'll be all melted by the time we finish.'

As she walked through the foyer, Kirsty mused that this was now her third time in the place, and she was quietly pleased with herself for not being in the slightest bit nervous about it now. She was already used to the plush surroundings and felt almost the same coming into the fancy hotel as she had felt with the clubs. It was part of her job and she had come to realise that the other people who worked in the hotel were only doing their jobs too – from the hotel manager to the waitresses and bar staff and cleaners. She would remind herself of that from now.

Larry was obviously used to grander things back in Ireland and it probably had never bothered him coming into a place like this, and it would be the same for people like those two

McCluskey sisters – the kind who went to very posh places and played golf in exclusive clubs.

Kirsty felt a little pang of something she couldn't quite describe when she thought of the dark-haired women, especially now that she knew that there was – or had been – something very serious going on between Larry and that Helen.

She doubted if she would ever know the story behind it, because any time she broached his personal life, Larry just put up a barrier, a barrier she just could not get through no matter how hard she tried.

She felt a bit foolish now, thinking back to how she had imagined that Larry was this single man who had just been a quiet Irish bachelor up until she met him. She couldn't have been more wrong. He certainly hadn't been living a bachelor's life if Helen McCluskey had had a son by him.

Just recently Kirsty had started to realise that people were not always what they seemed. Helen McCluskey definitely didn't seem like a woman with a chequered past. Her confident, uppity manner didn't give the impression of a woman who had anything shameful to hide.

And then there was Claire, who Mona had been painting as this cold, snobby woman, who lived in a show-house rather than a real home. As soon as she had walked into her aunt's house in Glasgow, Kirsty had realised that all the stories about Claire and her husband had been nonsense. Claire lived in the kind of beautiful house that Kirsty would absolutely love to have when she was older and married. If she ever got married.

She still worried that she never seemed to meet anyone who she liked or vaguely fancied. Apart from that daft notion she'd had with Larry Delaney, there hadn't been anything else that remotely resembled romance in her life.

The dinner-dance evening went much the same as the dance at New Year. Kirsty had sung the same songs and felt very comfortable and easy as she slipped from one song to the other through her performance. The audience were every bit as enthusiastic as the one on New Year's Eve which really delighted her as she had half-thought that the celebratory night had been something to do with it, and that they might have cheered on any singer. Kirsty had also felt easy enough about wearing another one of Helen McCluskey's dresses tonight. She had suggested to Larry that she might as well get a couple of wears out of each dress before having them dry-cleaned and giving them back to him. Larry had just shrugged, saying she was more than welcome to the dresses. They had only been hanging in a spare room in his flat. Kirsty thought it made sense. And she wasn't likely to come across the owner again. By the time she'd got her wear out of the borrowed dresses, she'd have picked up a few glamorous stage dresses of her own.

'I was wrong about the snow,' Larry told her when he came into the dressing-room at the break in the show. 'It's got quite heavy and it's lying on the ground. As soon as you're finished we'll head off, because we might have to take it very easy going home if the roads are bad.' He thought for a moment. 'And don't worry if you see people leaving early, it's not because of your singing, it'll be because they want to get home before the snow gets worse.'

'Wasn't I sensible that I brought my jumper and jeans?' Kirsty said, laughing.

'You're a very sensible girl,' Larry said, smiling warmly at her. 'And one of the most down-to-earth women I know.'

It was only when she was on stage later on that it dawned on Kirsty that it was the first time Larry had used the word 'woman' when he was referring to her instead of 'girl'.

Larry knocked on the changing-room door a few minutes after Kirsty came off the stage. He came striding across the room to her, his brow furrowed. 'I think we might have a bit of a problem tonight, Kirsty.'

Her heart sank. This was it. This was the night when the bubble would burst. This was the night when she would discover that she had got it all wrong about people thinking her singing was good. Quite a few people had gone before the final part of the performance, so it was quite possible that they hadn't enjoyed it.

Kirsty took a deep breath. 'Did the manager not like me? Does he not want me to do the other bookings?'

Larry shook his head, laughing in amazement at her suggestion. 'He loved you – the audience all loved you. How could you not know that?'

Kirsty shrugged, feeling all awkward and embarrassed.

'I wasn't talking about the performance,' Larry said, shaking his head. 'I was talking about the weather – about the blizzard that's blowing outside.'

'What?' Kirsty said, her voice incredulous. 'You're not serious, are you? It can't be that bad.'

He took his jacket off and put it over her bare shoulders and Kirsty caught the lovely smell of the expensive cologne he wore. He then put his hand out and caught hers.

'C'mon outside and see for yourself,' he told her, pulling her to her feet.

As their hands locked, Kirsty felt as though a little electric shock had gone through her body. A little shock that told her she had been kidding herself for the last few weeks. A little shock that told her she still had very strong feelings for Larry Delaney. When they reached the door he dropped her hand, as though he had just realised he was still holding it.

A hefty breeze took Kirsty's breath away and whipped up her blonde hair when she stepped outside. She looked around her with wide disbelieving eyes. How could things have changed so much in five hours? The hotel garden was now a thick white carpet of drifting snow, and the shrubs and bushes looked like dazzling white sculptures through the lace curtain of snowflakes that were still falling.

'All the roads outside Lanark are completely blocked,' Larry informed her. 'The police called in to tell the manager to ask anybody who was travelling locally to take it easy and anybody travelling further afield to stay where they were until morning. Apparently the forecast is even worse for tomorrow.'

'What are we going to do?' Kirsty asked, pulling Larry's jacket tighter around her shoulders. 'How will we get home?' She gave a little nervous giggle, as a feeling of silly girlish excitement started to bubble up inside her at the thought of being stranded. As though it were some kind of adventure – the sort of adventure she used to read about in her Enid Blyton books. The sort of adventure she would have loved to happen to her and her friends when she was a young teenager.

But she wasn't a young teenager, and she wasn't with her friends. This could be more like a romantic novel. Being stranded often happened in those. And she was with a handsome older man.

Except that the older handsome man didn't have the slightest interest in her.

Larry drew his breath in, weighing up the situation. 'I honestly don't think we're going to be able to make it home,' he told her. 'It would be really dangerous on those narrow, winding roads. We could end up sliding back downhill and off the road.' He nodded back towards the building. 'The manager has said we can stay in the hotel for the night as they're not too busy. They have a couple of spare rooms.' He put his arm on her shoulder. 'We'd better go back inside or we'll get be soaked through.' He guided her back into the hotel.

Kirsty felt a small but intense pang of alarm running through her. She'd never stayed in a hotel room before, and she didn't have a change of underclothes for the morning. What would she do? And, more to the point, what would her mother and father think? They would be worried sick when they got up in the morning and she wasn't in her bed. 'It's too late for me to phone anybody in Rowanhill to let my mother and father know,' she said anxiously as she walked alongside him, holding on to the lapels of his jacket. 'I'll have to wait until the morning. Hopefully they'll not miss me until then . . .'

'They'll understand,' Larry said, 'and they'll be glad you didn't take the risk of going home in this weather. It's just a case of getting a message to them as quick as you can in the morning so's they're not panicking.'

'I suppose you're right,' Kirsty said, brightening up. She would have time to think who she could ring. The priest was definitely out after the call Claire had made earlier in the week. 'I suppose I could always ring the post office,' she suddenly thought. 'The people live in the flat up the stairs, so they'll be in to sort the mail out around eight o'clock as usual. The postman will let them know when he's passing the house around nine.'

'Good thinking,' Larry said, as they walked into the bar. It was half-empty now as most of the people who had attended the dinner dance had left to make their way home through the snow. 'Don't be worrying about anything now, relax and enjoy the chance to stay in a nice place.'

'You're right,' Kirsty agreed, 'there's no point in getting all worked up about it, when we can't do anything to change it. Worrying isn't going to make the snow go away.'

'It would be a hell of a lot worse,' Larry reasoned as they sat at a table, 'if we set out and got stranded in the dark somewhere.' He shook his head. 'It doesn't bear thinking about, and I don't think we've really got any option. We'll have a nice warm room here in the hotel—' He suddenly halted. 'A nice room *each* here in the hotel,' he said, emphasising the word 'each'.

Kirsty felt her throat tighten a little. 'This is an absolute disaster . . . isn't it?' She looked up at him, at his white shirt and black bow-tie, and she suddenly remembered she still had his jacket around her shoulders. 'And you've no change of clothes, have you?' she asked, taking his jacket off and handing it to him. The hotel was lovely and warm and she didn't need it now anyway.

He nodded thanks and then put the jacket back on. 'I've a zip-up bag in the back of the car with a sweater and a few bits and pieces of toiletries in it.' He shrugged. 'In case the car ever broke down . . .'

'Thank God I've at least got my jeans and jumper and my boots,' Kirsty said, 'but I've no pyjamas or toothbrush or anything like that . . .'

'Don't worry,' he said in a soothing voice. 'The hotel will probably have some stuff you can borrow.'

'D'you think so?' Kirsty said, raising her eyebrows in surprise. 'Do they have nightclothes and things like that?'

'I'm sure they have bits and pieces in the lost property . . . things that guests leave behind.'

'Lost property?' Kirsty repeated indignantly, her brow wrinkling at the thought. 'I'm definitely not wearing anythin' that a stranger has left behind.'

Larry looked at her shocked face and laughed. 'I'm sure they will have laundered anything they have . . .'

'I don't care,' Kirsty said, trying not to laugh along with him.

'It's not a bit funny ... I'll be freezin' in the room with no pyjamas.'

'They'll have radiators in all the rooms,' he told her, 'and if you're really stuck, you can wear my shirt or jumper if you like.'

'Lovely,' Kirsty said, rolling her eyes and laughing.

'Right,' he said, standing up, 'I'm going to get us a drink now and see if they have anything left for you to eat. I had a meal with the manager when you were on stage, but you must be starving ...'

Kirsty shook her head. 'I'm not hungry, I only have a bit of toast when I go home. I'm never really hungry when I'm singing.'

'I'll see what they have,' he said. 'Now, what are you having to drink?' He grinned. 'You can go mad now since you're not going home!' The look in his eyes and his tone of voice told her that he was only joking.

Kirsty paused for minute. 'Anything but Babycham.' She was terrified to have the bubbly drink again when she was with him, after what had happened the last night she'd drunk a few.

'OK,' he said. 'I'll see what there is.'

Kirsty looked around at the other groups of people while she was waiting. Most of them were older than her, but there were a few who looked roughly her own age, who gave her curious glances as they passed by. Several people came across to say how much they had enjoyed her singing, and one young girl sat down in the seat next to her to ask her what it was like to be a famous singer and how hard was it to become one. She explained that it was her eighteenth birthday and her parents had brought her and three friends out for the dinner dance, because they'd heard that this wonderful new singer was on that particular night.

Larry had come back with the drinks, but had gone to the empty table next to them, not wanting to interrupt. He sat drinking his whiskey and listening to the conversation with great interest.

'Och, I'm not really famous,' Kirsty told the girl, laughing at the idea. 'I'm only really starting out.'

'You're a brilliant singer,' the girl said, looking at her with adulation. 'And it must be really hard learning the words to all those songs. Some of them are really new, so that must mean you've to constantly learn new words to keep up to date.'

'I suppose that's the bit you do need to work at,' Kirsty agreed. 'But it's just like when you had to learn poetry or tables at school. You just sit down and make yourself learn it, because if you forget the words when you're on stage it would be a right disaster.'

'I never thought of that,' the girl said, biting her lip at the thought.

'It can be hard work at times,' Kirsty admitted. 'but it's really, really worth it. Especially when nice people like you take the trouble to come up and tell me.' She gave a little shrug. 'The rest of it is a bit of luck – being in the right place at the right time.'

'I think you're absolutely great,' the girl said, in a breathless, overwhelmed voice. 'You're so modest and down-to-earth when you have such a powerful, fantastic voice . . .' She halted. 'And you've got such lovely blonde hair and a beautiful figure. That dress is gorgeous on you – it makes you look like a movie star. There's not many singers around here who look like that.'

'Oh, thanks!' Kirsty said, almost embarrassed with the compliment. 'That's really nice of you.'

The girl stood up now. 'I'll make sure I tell all my friends and their families to come and hear you when you're back here again.'

After she'd gone, Larry moved across to join her at the table. He carefully slid a tall thin glass over to Kirsty. 'Compliments of the manager – it's champagne.'

'Oh my God!' Kirsty said, her voice high with excitement. 'Up until this New Year I'd never had champagne in my life before.' She looked at the champagne flute now and laughed. 'You'd think I was a right seasoned drinker – I should have said I've hardly had *any* kind of drink before, never mind champagne.' She suddenly remembered the wine at Claire's house. 'Now I seem to be getting offered it more and more.'

'Well, enjoy it,' Larry said, clinking his whiskey glass against hers. 'You deserve a celebratory drink, and there's no harm in it as long as you keep it in moderation. We can all fall by the wayside when we've had one too many.'

Kirsty looked away from him now, wondering if he was

referring to the night she'd been stupid. He'd never given any indication that he'd held it against her, so she hoped that he was just talking generally.

He took a mouthful of his whiskey. 'That girl was right – your singing was just fantastic tonight. It was the best I've heard yet.' He looked at her and then shook his head. 'Your voice just gets better and better.'

'Well, the hotel band is really professional,' she said, 'and I think that makes a big difference. I used to think The Hi-Tones were good but you can tell the difference when you're working with really good musicians who do it for a living.' Kirsty felt embarrassed now, so she took a sip of the champagne for something to do.

'There's only one thing wrong though, Kirsty,' he said, 'you're going to have to stop knocking yourself down when people give you compliments.'

'What d'you mean?' Kirsty asked.

'I mean you should believe what people tell you . . . you are a wonderful singer, and it's got nothing to do with the band. They're just good, competent musicians – but you're in a different league altogether.'

Kirsty looked over at Larry now now, and he was staring at her in a kind of strange way, as if he had just met her and was studying her so he would know her again.

'Thanks,' she said in a quiet voice. 'I'm grateful for you telling me that . . . it means a lot.'

'Good,' he said, smiling warmly at her now. Back to the old Larry. 'I'm glad to hear you saying that, because your success up to now has been through your own hard work – don't be saying that it's down to luck. Your success is all down to you.'

'I don't agree with all of that,' Kirsty said, sipping at her drink. 'Because it was good luck that I met you . . . if I hadn't met you then I wouldn't be here tonight.' She waved her hand around the hotel lounge. 'If it wasn't for you I wouldn't be singing in a lovely place like this, I'd be in a wee fleapit of a freezin' church hall . . .' She held up her glass. 'And I certainly wouldn't be drinkin' champagne! I'm just an ordinary girl from an ordinary village, and it's because of you that I'm gettin' the chance to better myself.'

The strange look was suddenly back in his dark greenish-brown eyes. 'It was good luck for both of us, Kirsty. Taking you on my books was one of the best moves I've ever made.' He reached across the table and took her hand. 'I've been meaning to say this to you before now . . . that night we were in the Trocadero . . .'

Kirsty's stomach lurched. *Oh no*, she thought, *he's going to remind me of what a fool I made of myself again. He's going to mention that really embarrassing night . . .*

Then, a young waitress in a black dress with a little frilly white apron suddenly appeared at the table with a tray with sandwiches and a silver rack of buttered toast.

'Lovely!' Kirsty said, reaching out for a piece of toast. She looked up at the waitress, overwhelmingly grateful at the diversion from Larry's conversation, and determined to make the most of it. 'That's really good of you making me toast. Have you been working all night?'

The girl glanced over towards the bar, and when she saw no sign of the manager, she sunk down into one of the chairs at the table, grateful to steal a few minutes away from her work. 'Aye,' she said, rolling her eyes to the ceiling, 'and I'm on again first thing in the mornin'. You're not goin' to believe it, but I'm goin' to have to stay the night in the staff quarters of the hotel because of the snow. I usually get a taxi home to Carluke, but they're all off the road tonight.'

'It's terrible, isn't it?' Kirsty said, taking a bite of the buttered toast. 'We're havin' to stay the night as well.' She nodded over at Larry, who was now happily sipping his whiskey, his bow-tie loosened and the top button of his white shirt undone. Then she added rather unnecessarily. 'Of course we've got a single room each.'

They chatted for a few minutes longer, the waitress asking Kirsty about her singing and then Kirsty asking her more questions about her job in the hotel – all light-hearted, ordinary talk that kept Larry safely off the more sensitive subjects.

The manager suddenly appeared behind the bar, and a glance in their direction got the waitress to her feet and scuttling off to attend to the last hour of her duties. He came across to the table with two more flutes and the remainder of the bottle of champagne that he'd opened for Kirsty.

'Blidey awful night, isn't it?' he said, grinning at Larry. 'I can't get home either . . . but I suppose we might as well make the best of the night.' He leaned over and refilled Kirsty's glass then filled one for himself and Larry, then he held the bottle of champagne up to the light to check how much was left. 'That was a wee bonus tonight,' he explained. 'A big group of solicitors that were at the dinner dance. They told me to put a dozen bottles on ice and they only used eleven.' He held his glass up to Kirsty. 'After your sterling performance tonight, I thought you were the one that most deserved to have a wee glass of Moët et Chandon.' He winked at Larry. 'Those solicitors are nothin' but a crowd of robbing gets – we're far more entitled to drink the champagne than they are.'

Kirsty laughed heartily along with the two men, and then, feeling relaxed for the first time that whole evening, she sat back in her chair and enjoyed the luxury of the hotel and the expensive champagne.

The bar was empty now and so was the champagne bottle. The manager had gone off to get the keys for the bedrooms leaving Kirsty with the last half-glass from the bottle and a night-cap of a large whiskey for Larry.

Kirsty had been very, very careful with the alcohol. She had drunk it slowly, and found herself constantly checking the effect it was having on her. Apart from feeling nice and relaxed and a little tired, she knew she was still her normal self. And she knew that there was no way she would say or do anything tonight that would cause her to make a fool of herself. She had definitely learned that lesson.

Larry checked his watch; it was quarter past one. 'Are you OK, Kirsty?' he asked her in a concerned tone. 'I know this has been a bit of a shock to you . . . staying out all night when you hadn't planned it.'

'I'm absolutely fine,' Kirsty said quickly, giving him a reassuring smile. 'And I've enjoyed myself. The dinner-dance went well and I've enjoyed sitting here chatting to everybody.

It's a lovely place and I'd be daft not to enjoy it.' She halted. 'I know it's no big deal to you – you've obviously been brought up used to all these nice things – but our family are just ordinary and wouldn't be used to this kind of thing. Not that I'm ashamed of my up-bringing or where I come from or anythin',' she hastily added. 'My mammy and daddy are really decent hard-working people and I'm actually very proud of them and my sister.'

The hotel manager reappeared, and handed them both a key. Kirsty's had ten on it and Larry's nine. 'You're across the corridor from each other,' he told them, 'on the ground floor. There are toilets at either end of the corridor and breakfast is on until ten, so you can get a long lie-in if you want since it's Saturday.'

They both thanked him then, when he left, Larry suddenly remembered. 'You wanted to check about nightclothes, didn't you?'

Kirsty looked back in the direction the manager had gone and then she shrugged. 'Och, I'll be all right . . . it's a bit late to have him running about looking.' She laughed. 'If the rooms are cold, I might just borrow your shirt.'

'Fine by me,' he said, 'but I'll go after him and check it out if you want.'

Kirsty reassured him she would manage then Larry came back to the subject they had left earlier.

'Your sister seemed a very nice girl,' Larry said, leaning forward now, his arms resting on the table, the whiskey glass cupped between his hands. 'Different from you – but just as nice in her own way.'

Kirsty nodded. 'Heather's great,' she told him. 'I suppose we are different, but we get on really well. We used to fight like cat and dog when we were younger – and sometimes we still do – but underneath it all, I think the world of her.' She stopped. 'She's not had it easy recently with one thing and another, but I know she'll be fine. She's always been more sensible than me in a lot of ways.' She gave a little sigh. 'When I think of all the terrible things that have happened to other people I know . . . I should be counting my blessings.'

Larry looked at her now. 'D'you mean the young fellow that got killed? The funeral you were at yesterday?'

Kirsty nodded. She'd mentioned it very briefly to him in the car when they were driving over, but the subject had got changed somehow and they'd gone on to something else. She'd thought of bringing it up again, but then she decided it was the sort of thing that Larry might find a bit too personal – or worse – the emotional chatter of a young woman about her equally young friends.

'I don't want you to think I'm prying into your business,' Larry said now. 'Maybe you don't want to talk about it?'

'No, I don't mind talking about it at all,' Kirsty said, surprised that he was interested. 'It was Heather's old boyfriend who got killed . . . or got himself killed through stupidity.'

'Christ!' Larry said, shaking his head. 'And was he only a young lad?'

'Aye,' Kirsty said. 'I don't think he was twenty-one yet.'

'What happened?'

And then she poured the whole story out, while Larry Delaney listened intently.

'Your sister has really been through the mill, hasn't she?' Larry said, when she finally finished. 'That's really rough about her friend losing the baby on the same day that her old boyfriend gets buried.'

'Terrible,' Kirsty agreed. She took another sip of the champagne then shrugged. 'I feel very sorry for Liz, but she more or less got herself deliberately pregnant so's that Jim Murray would marry her. He had no intention of marrying her up until that happened. There had been no mention of engagements or anything like that.'

'There's plenty of situations that happen like that,' Larry said, staring down into his whiskey glass now. 'I know from my own experience . . .'

Kirsty decided to take a chance. 'Are you talking about your little boy?'

He nodded. 'I suppose I am.'

'Do you mind me asking what happened?' she probed, very tentatively.

'I wish I could answer that, Kirsty,' he said. 'I wish I knew what happened myself – how the shrewd careful businessman that nobody would get one over on, suddenly made the most basic mistake of all.' He took a long drink of his whiskey and then the story poured out. 'Have I told you that I own a bit of property around Hamilton and Motherwell?' he asked her.

Kirsty couldn't remember if he had mentioned it. She paused, dredging her memory. Larry continued without waiting for an answer. 'The two McCluskey sisters came looking to rent a house I owned out in Motherwell, and that's how I first met them. Their parents were moving to Australia to live beside a brother and they didn't want to go, so they needed to find a place of their own. They seemed nice enough and everything – and obviously they're smart, good-looking women – so it was easy enough to become friendly with them.' He ran his fingers through his dark hair. 'Helen was very interested when she discovered I was in the music business, with her being a singer, so she got me to introduce her to people involved in musicals.' He shook his head now, obviously not enjoying reliving the story. 'I used to run her back and forward to rehearsals, help to organise her costumes, that kind of thing.'

'The same way you're helping me and running me around in the car?' Kirsty said, raising her eyebrows.

Larry nodded. 'I suppose you could say it was a similar kind of arrangement.' He looked her straight in the eye now. 'Except the people involved were very different . . . I've discovered over the months that you're not a bit like Helen McCluskey.'

Kirsty sat up straight in her chair now, not sure how to take his comment. She knew of course the two sisters were very different to her, but she didn't know if this meant that she was better or worse.

'You're a much more honest, direct person,' he said, as though reading her thoughts. 'And when we started going out together, I didn't realise she already had somebody else.' He sighed now. 'A married man that she'd been seeing for years.'

'What happened?' Kirsty gasped. She pressed her fingers to her mouth.

'I was totally stupid,' he said, giving a wry grin. 'Your typical thick Dubliner who didn't see what was staring him in the face. She got me over to the flat for a meal one night and persuaded me to stay – not that I needed a lot of persuasion.' He shrugged. 'I was never in love with her. She wasn't bad-looking and she was nice enough – but she wasn't the kind of girl you could talk to, and she definitely wasn't the kind of girl I had envisaged ever being seriously involved with. She was just OK . . .'

'But you were obviously *very* involved with her,' Kirsty pointed out. She wanted to know more, even though it was painful listening to it all. She had to know *exactly* the kind of person Larry Delaney was.

'I'm not denying it,' Larry said, shrugging. 'And it was stupid of me not to imagine where it might lead. I'm not blaming her entirely, but the next thing I knew she was pregnant and she was declaring me the father.' He shifted his gaze now, as if he was talking to a spot about a foot above Kirsty's head. 'The last thing I could handle was the thought of abandoning a poor kid. So I offered to marry her and we set a date and all the rest of it . . .'

Kirsty finished the last mouthful from her glass. 'Did you actually get married?' she asked in a low flat voice.

'No.'

Kirsty felt a flutter of relief. At least she hadn't been making a fool of herself over a married man. That would have been the very worst.

Larry gave a deep, weary sigh. 'She suddenly said that it wasn't fair to me, that she knew I didn't love her in the way that I should to get married, and she suggested that we leave it for a while – wait until the baby was born and then see what happened. So it went on and on. I moved her into a bigger place of her own before David was born, and I sorted her out with a car and everything she needed for the baby. All the things I'd dreamed that I'd do if I was ever lucky enough to have a family of my own.'

'It sounds as though you couldn't have done any more,' Kirsty whispered. 'She was blidey lucky compared to a lot of girls.'

'I know I shouldn't really be telling you this, Kirsty,' he said now, his voice rough and croaky, 'but I feel you might understand things – understand me – a small bit better if I do explain it. It just feels important to me that you should understand it . . . I don't want you thinking bad of me.'

'I don't think bad of you . . . and I appreciate you telling me all this,' she said. Then, before she could stop herself, she suddenly stretched her hand out to cover his. As though he was the young person and she the older, experienced one. And he didn't move. He actually moved his hand so their fingers were entwined tightly together.

'We only slept together a couple of times ... we both could feel we had nothing in common apart from the baby. And even after David was born, there was still something huge missing between us.' He halted. 'Maybe if I'd been brought up differently I might have had different expectations of family life – I might have realised that we would never have made a decent couple no matter how hard I tried. The only good thing about it all was David – from the very first minute I saw him, I loved him completely. So I just kept waiting and waiting, thinking that things would change and we'd all somehow manage to be a happy family together.' He gave a small, bitter laugh. 'But of course it never happened. It never could have happened. You can't make things happen just by wishing for them.'

'So when did it all finish?' Kirsty asked in a low voice, squeezing his hand in encouragement.

'When David was about three years old the married man came out of the woodwork,' Larry said now, rubbing a hand across his face. 'He'd left his wife, and the next thing I knew was that Helen was sitting me down and telling me that she wasn't sure if I was really David's father or not. That there was just the tiniest chance he was the other fellow's.'

'Oh my God!' Kirsty said, biting her lip. 'That's just absolutely terrible ...'

He let go of her hand now, and then he looked at her. 'I suddenly don't seem all that smart and businesslike now, Kirsty, do I?' He gave the same bitter laugh. 'I think you're probably shocked to know that older, supposedly mature men can make complete eedjits of themselves, aren't you?'

'I'm not thinkin' anything like that at all,' Kirsty said softly. 'I'm just sorry to hear you've gone through all that ... I really am.'

'I was a bloody fool,' he told her. 'And there are times when I'm still a bloody fool.'

'How d'you mean?' she asked.

'Well, David's nearly four now,' he said, 'and I've never found out whether he's rightly mine or not. Helen's moved in with the other fellow now, and they're supposedly getting married as soon as his divorce comes through.'

'So where does that leave you?'

'Nowhere, I suppose,' he replied. 'I haven't seen the little lad for ages, and maybe I should just give up . . . maybe it would be better for him if I just faded off the scene and let them get on together. He doesn't need anything from me now, the other fellow has plenty of money and they won't go short of anything.'

Kirsty gave a shiver now, suddenly realising that the heating had gone down in the bar, and also that they were the only two left sitting in the entire place. She shifted in her chair, feeling achy and stiff from sitting in the one spot so long. 'I think I'd better move and find this room.' She got to her feet, then ran her hands over the blue satin dress that Larry had bought Helen McCluskey, straightening out the creases.

Larry drained his glass. 'Let's go, Miss Grace,' he said in a surprisingly cheerful voice. 'Or the next thing we know I'll be pouring out the early part of my life to you as well, because I've just discovered something about you that I didn't know . . .'

Kirsty's heart leapt. 'What?' she said eagerly. At last he was treating her like a grown woman. She swept her blonde hair back over her shoulder and waited.

'I've discovered that you're a very, very easy person to talk to, and a very good listener. Many people are good at talking but few are good at listening.'

'Well, that's nice to hear,' Kirsty said, although she wasn't quite sure if it was the kind of compliment she'd dreamed about getting from him. Being an easy person to talk to wasn't exactly the sort of thing that a girl wanted to hear. She would by far have preferred him to tell her how lovely she was and how devastatingly attractive he found her.

Larry went out to the car to retrieve his hold-all while Kirsty went across to the dressing-room to get her own things. He was standing in the foyer waiting for her, bag in hand, his black hair and suit liberally sprinkled with melting snowflakes.

'It's worse, if possible,' he told her. 'The car's completely covered over; I'm going to have to shovel it out of the snow in the morning.' He laughed and pointed to her bag. 'I'm glad you brought your ordinary clothes with you, you would have looked a bit silly helping me to dig out the car in an evening dress and high heels!'

Kirsty made eyes at him to signal her annoyance and then she swung the carrier bag in his direction and they both went down the corridor towards their rooms, trying to laugh quietly so they didn't waken the other guests.

Kirsty looked at the numbers on all the doors, wondering who the well-off people were who could actually afford to pay for a dinner dance *and* a hotel room in the financial dip that always hit everyone she knew after Christmas.

Rooms nine and ten were the last two rooms at the bottom of the corridor, just before it veered off to the left where there was another longer corridor.

'I presume the rooms are all the same,' Larry said in a low voice. 'But if there's any difference you get to choose. Women always need the bigger spaces.'

Kirsty smiled and held out the carrier bag holding her jumper, jeans and boots. 'Well, I'm not exactly prepared for a big hotel room. I think one wee chair will hold everything I've got.'

He stopped at number nine and put the key in the door. A waft of warm air hit them immediately.

'Thank God it's not cold,' Kirsty said, walking in. 'At least I won't need to go to sleep in my jumper and jeans.'

She looked around at the big double bed with the wine and blue bed cover that matched the curtains and the fabric on the dressing-table stool and lovely old-fashioned chair that re-minded her of the sofa in her Auntie Claire's. 'It's gorgeous!' she said, putting her bags down on the floor. She went over to peek out of the window to see the snow-covered main gardens at the front of the hotel then she moved over to sit on the bed and gently bounce up and down on it. 'I bet you've stayed in loads of hotel rooms, haven't you?'

Larry inclined his head. 'I suppose I have stayed in a good few over the years ...'

'Are they all like this?' Kirsty asked, waving a hand around the room.

'Some are,' he said shrugging, 'and some are different.'

Kirsty got to her feet. 'Let's see your room then,' she said in a businesslike manner, putting her hand on his shoulder to turn him around towards the door.

The other room had twin beds with green bed-covers and curtains and a view of the white-covered car-park and back gardens from the window.

'I think I'll keep the room across the way,' she told him. 'It'll be a change for me to stretch out in a nice big bed.'

Larry lifted his bag up on top of one of the beds then he unzipped it and checked the contents. 'Brilliant!' he said, smiling over at her. 'I've got two clean shirts in it and a new toothbrush and toothpaste – so, Miss Grace, you can pick what you want.'

Kirsty put her hands on her hips. 'Let me see the shirts,' she said in a mock-suspicious manner.

Larry lifted out a perfectly ironed and perfectly folded smart white shirt with a pale blue pin-stripe running through it, then he dipped back into the bag and produced a much thicker plaid shirt in cream with brown and green – the sort of good casual shirt he would wear under a heavy woollen sweater.

Kirsty reached for the plaid shirt, recognising the expensive label from one of the Scottish tartan shops in Glasgow. It felt cold from having been in the boot of the snow-covered car. 'This looks the cosiest,' she told him, hugging the soft shirt tight to her chest to warm it up. 'And I'll take the toothbrush and toothpaste if you don't mind? I couldn't go to sleep without brushing my teeth.'

'Take it, take it,' he laughed. 'I'm sure I'll sort one out in the morning.'

She turned towards the door now, suddenly reluctant to leave him. Even though she knew he had no interest in her apart from her being a good listener. 'Well . . .' she said, hesitating at the door. 'I'll see you in the morning then . . .'

A small silence fell. 'Will you be OK?' he asked in a low voice, his eyes studying her.

'I'll be fine,' she told him, in as bright a tone as she could muster at this hour of the morning.

Kirsty went across the hallway deep in thought. This had been a strange, strange night. She had heard things she did not want to hear and she had stifled all her instincts and feelings. And although she knew that Larry Delaney saw her as little more than a younger sister, this strange night had probably been the best night of her life.

After she had been down to the bathroom at the end of the corridor to brush her teeth and wash her face, and after seeing the bottles of bath foam and dish of white bath-cubes Kirsty decided she would run herself a nice hot bath. It just might help her to relax and sleep better in a strange place. She turned the taps on and poured some of the rose-scented bubble bath into the steaming water.

She came padding back up the corridor to the bedroom in her bare feet to collect her things. When she got into the room she shook Larry's plaid shirt out of its careful folds then undid all the pearly-white buttons. Then, she slipped the straps of the evening dress down, unzipped it and let it fall to the ground.

She took off her matching white satin bra and cami-knickers and pulled on the plaid shirt, wishing she had a fresh change of underwear for the morning. She took a few kirby grips from her make-up bag and quickly pinned her hair up so that it wouldn't get wet in the bath.

Then, as she looked at the carefully folded underwear for a few moments, an idea came into her mind. She went over to feel the long, thick radiator under the window. It was boiling hot. So hot she couldn't hold her hand on it. She smiled to herself, deciding that she would soak and rinse out her little things in the bubble-bath and have them clean and dry and smelling lovely for the morning.

Then, like somebody from the comedy films she had seen in the pictures, she stuck her head out of the bedroom door, looked either way to check there was no one around, and scurried along the corridor to have her bath and carry out her illicit laundry. The bath was lovely, hot and relaxing, and Kirsty lay back and pondered over all the things that Larry Delaney had told her, wishing that she was older and more sophisticated.

She came back into the bedroom a short while later with the knickers and bra rubbed into dampness by a large bath towel, then she went over to the radiator and spread them out. She was just turning back the covers on her luxurious bed when a small knock came on the door.

Kirsty's hands flew to her throat. 'Who is it?' she called in a short sharp whisper – trying not to sound as startled and frightened as she felt.

'It's me,' the unmistakable rich Dublin voice came from the corridor. 'I could hear you going in and out and I just wanted a little word with you before you went to sleep.'

She flew across the room to the door, her heart thudding. 'Is there something wrong?' she asked, opening the door to him.

He stood there looking down at her, his face white and serious. He was also in his bare feet, his white shirt loose over his dark trousers with only a couple of the buttons done.

'Yes,' he said in a low whisper, 'there is something very wrong . . .'

And before Kirsty knew what had happened, Larry Delaney had swept her up in his arms and his warm mouth was crushing hers in exactly the same way it had happened in her dreams.

When that first breathless kiss eventually came to an end, Larry tilted Kirsty's chin up to look into her eyes, then he led her by the hand across the floor to the bed.

Chapter 55

L arry threw the covers back on the bed and then quickly and easily lifted Kirsty off her feet and laid her on it. He stretched a hand to switch off the bedside lamp, and then he lay down beside her and kissed her once again. A kiss that lasted a long, breathless time. A kiss that Kirsty had been waiting for for months.

When the kissing finally stopped, she moved back on the pillow to look at him. Her heart was still racing and she had the funniest warm feeling down low in the pit of her stomach that made her want to reach out for him to kiss her again. To kiss her all over in places she'd never dreamed she'd want a man to kiss. Places she hardly knew about.

But she didn't reach out to him. She wasn't ready to go beyond this stage yet. There were things she needed to know first.

'What's happened?' she asked him. 'What's made you change your mind? That night in the Trocadero—'

'You mean the night you frightened the life out of me?'

'I don't understand . . .' she said, propping herself up on one elbow. 'And I think I need to . . . to know where this is all leading.'

Larry bent down now and lifted her free hand to his mouth and kissed her fingers one by one. 'I thought it was going to be another terrible mistake,' he told her, his voice weary. 'I thought I might be heading down the same path I went down with David's mother . . . but then I realised tonight when we were talking, that it was completely different. I suddenly realised that I was actually on the verge of making the biggest mistake of my life. A monumental mistake I might never be able to put right . . .'

Kirsty waited, her breath coming in short bursts, terrified he might stop and not tell her all the things she so desperately wanted to hear. She closed her eyes, trying to still her rapid breathing, then she felt his warm breath on her face and then she felt his wonderfully soft lips kiss one of her eyelids and then the other.

'Oh, Kirsty . . .' he whispered, his voice ragged and heavy with feeling. 'I love you with every single bone and breath in my body. And if it's a huge, terrible mistake telling you this, then I'm afraid I've already gone and done it.' He stopped. 'That first night I saw you on the stage, something happened to me, and things have never been the same since. I know you're younger than me, and that will probably cause us big problems, and I'm also very aware of all this trail of trouble behind me. But I really feel that I'm going to be in much, much bigger trouble if we don't at least give it a chance.'

Kirsty opened her eyes and looked up into his. 'I don't know what's going to happen either,' she said in a low, fearful voice, 'and there's a lot of things I'm frightened about. But I know one thing for sure – I love you too, Larry . . . I love you with all my heart. I think I've loved you since the second we met.'

And then without the slightest warning, a huge sob suddenly rose up in Kirsty's throat and salty tears started to spill down her face. She wrapped her arms around his neck and buried her damp mascara-streaked face in Larry's perfectly white shirt and she cried and cried as she clung to him.

Eventually, the crying quietened down and Kirsty came to rest her cheek against Larry's slightly rough, stubbly unshaved cheek. Then they stayed like that in the dark silence of the hotel bedroom for what seemed like a long, long time.

Larry kissed the side of her head. 'I want to talk to you about something, Kirsty,' he said, 'if you're up to it . . . if you're awake enough to take it in.' He tightened his arms around her. 'I'd feel better about everything if I could explain this one last bit.'

'I am wide awake,' Kirsty said, cuddling into him. 'Tell me . . .' She wanted him to talk and talk for as long as he liked, just as long as they could stay wrapped around each other. It was the best feeling she had ever had in her life. None of the boyfriends she had danced with and even canoodled with over the years had prepared her for what it would feel like to lie in the arms of a real mature man. For all Kirsty Grace's confidence and sharp tongue with males, she had very little physical knowledge of them, simply because the real attraction had never been there before.

But now – with Larry Delaney – a whole new exciting world had suddenly spread itself out at her feet.

'It's all this business about David,' he said, 'why it made me wary of getting involved with another woman. That whole episode of my life was the one thing I'd been trying to avoid.'

'Well, I can assure you I'd never do that!' Kirsty cut in, her voice high and indignant. She struggled to sit up so she could look at him properly. 'That's one thing you'll never need to worry about,' she said earnestly. 'I would never, ever get pregnant before I was married and ready to start a family. Even if I'd never met you, I would never want that to happen – I'm not like Liz Mullen. I want more out of life than to be running after a man. I have a career and I have ambitions ... and I've more pride in myself than to let that happen to me.'

Larry smiled down at her – the 'trying hard not to let her see he was amused' smile – then he kissed her again. 'I know that about you already, Kirsty, and it's one of the reasons I fell in love with you. I love the fact you have such pride in yourself and such high principles.' He took a deep breath. 'But there's a few things I need to put you straight about – I'm a bit worried that you have the wrong impression of me. I'm not this middle-class, well-heeled businessman cum playboy that you seem to think I am.'

Kirsty waited, intensely curious now.

'I have worked very hard and I admit I've done well enough financially – beyond what I'd ever hoped or expected.' He was struggling now. 'But I got a very bad start in life. My mother wasn't married and she left me in one of the children's homes in Dublin ... I was brought up early on with the nuns and then I was fostered out to various places.' He shook his head. 'I never knew what it was like to grow up in a real family until I was finally fostered at eleven years of age by a nice, decent family – the family whose name I took, and who now live in Manchester.'

'Oh, Larry ...' Kirsty said, her arms tightening around him. 'That must have been terrible for you.'

'It's all I knew,' he told her. 'And you just get on with it. The nuns were nice enough, I didn't have any major problems, and I was good at school – I learned easily, which helped.'

'How did you come to be fostered by the family?'

'It was an older couple who were too late to adopt a baby,' he explained. 'They were visiting the home and I was asked to show them around. They started visiting me and taking me for days out – that kind of thing ... and gradually they asked if I'd like to go and live with them.'

'Was it OK?' Kirsty asked curiously.

Larry nodded. 'They were great, they gave me a whole new start. If it wasn't for Tommy and Nora Delaney I would not be in the position I'm in now. Tommy was a building engineer and Nora had been a teacher before she got married. Tommy used to take me fishing and golfing and he often took me out to work with him on the building sites when I was a teenager. I suppose that's how I got interested in the property business myself.' He sighed. 'Tommy died about five years ago, and Nora moved over to Manchester to be beside her sister and her nieces. I still visit them all regularly and I always will – they were very good to me. They were the nearest I've ever had to a real family and I'm grateful to them.'

'You would never believe that you had that kind of background,' Kirsty said. 'You come across as a really confident person ...'

'I've always worked hard to be like that,' he told her. 'But I failed badly getting into that situation over David. It was the one thing I'd always vowed I'd never let happen – that I'd never be responsible for bringing a child into an unpredictable situation. I'd always hoped I'd be married and settled and give the kid everything I never had myself.' His voice dropped. 'I wish to God I'd never met Helen McCluskey ... she was my biggest nightmare come true. I'd decided I'd never get tied down until I was totally secure in jobs and money, and that I'd be really picky and choosy about the woman I got serious about.' He halted. 'I don't want to get embarrassingly personal here ... but I was sure we'd been careful – that there was no way a child could have been conceived.'

'Do you honestly think that David is your son?'

Larry shrugged and gave a tired-sounding sigh. 'I just don't know ... there's every chance he's the other fellow's. And because of that, I think I'm going to have to give up and let him settle into the real family his mother wants now. I've got to give him the chance that I never had, to have a proper family life.'

Kirsty had a sudden uncomfortable thought. 'Did Helen McCluskey know all that about your background? Did you tell her all about it?'

'No,' Larry said, shaking his head. 'Not at all. She thought Nora was my real mother, and anyway, she had no great interest in things like that. She was only interested in having nice clothes and a nice place to live.' He squeezed her tightly. 'You're the only person I've ever told that to. In all the years since I left Ireland, I never trusted anyone enough to tell them the truth. I always felt it was a ... I suppose a vulnerable part of me. A part that I didn't want people have access to. I wanted them to just see the confident, capable Larry Delaney that you first met.'

Kirsty's heart soared. Larry Delaney loved her and trusted her enough to bare his soul to her in a way he had never done with one other person.

At this very moment in time the whole world was suddenly perfect.

Kirsty woke up in the silent white January morning, still wrapped in the warmth and security of Larry Delaney's arms – exactly the same way she had fallen into a deep sleep around four o'clock. She looked at his peaceful sleeping face, trying to resist the urge to kiss his lovely full lips or to trace a finger over his eyes and mouth.

Just looking at him now brought that strange new feeling back into her stomach, the feeling that made her want to get even closer to him. But Kirsty knew she wouldn't. Not yet.

They had a long way to go before anything more serious happened. They had months of kisses and cuddles and hand-holding to do before it reached the next stage. As she looked at the bright sunshine peeping around the wine and blue curtains, she thought how it had been the most unexpected and beautiful night. How they had come to be stranded in this hotel together, and how the snow had given them this wonderful opportunity to sort things out, to sort out the feelings they had both been hiding. She was still wearing Larry's big soft shirt and he was still in his rumpled white shirt and suit trousers. Thank goodness he had plenty of other suits, she thought, because the ones he was wearing would have to go into the dry-cleaners to achieve the sharp pressed look that all his clothes had.

Larry suddenly stirred, and after a while his eyes opened. He stared at her for a few moments and then he drew her close to him again and kissed her on the lips. 'Thank God it wasn't all a dream,' he told her. Then he just held on to her tightly – breathing in her warm feminine smell and delighting in the feeling of her small neat body tucked closely into his.

They both appeared in the dining-room at nine o'clock, dressed in casual jeans and jumpers. Neither had great appetites for the full Scottish breakfast that was put down in front of them, so they only picked at the sausages, bacon, black pudding and eggs on their plates. They took in very little of the hotel surroundings or the other guests. All that mattered was that they were together at this moment, and the plans they would have for the future.

When they wandered out to the car park to check how bad the weather situation was, they were both amazed to see that the strong winter sunshine had already started a quick thaw, and the car looked as though it could be moving fairly soon.

Chapter 56

'Have ye heard?' Mona came bustling in through the front door, hardly giving Fintan a chance to open it properly. Having been up and about for hours, the downstairs windows wide open for fresh air and to let the breakfast smells out, she was now ready to relax into a Saturday-morning chat with her neighbours and relatives. 'Have ye all heard about the murders? It's just been on the ten o'clock news again.'

'No,' Fintan said, following his brother's wife down the hallway towards the kitchen, as if it was her house rather than his. 'We haven't heard anything this morning. You don't mean the girl that was murdered in the golf course in East Kilbride?'

'No, no,' Mona said emphatically. 'This is much closer to home – the family are from Uddingston. Seemingly they lived in a lovely bungalow as well.'

'What's wrong?' Sophie asked, coming to meet them at the kitchen door, clutching the front of her dressing-gown. As always, she was conscious at being caught out in her nightwear by the gimlet-eyed Mona, who she knew would have done half a day's work so far. 'Is Lily all right? Have you any more news on her?'

'Bright as a button last night,' Mona said, 'and hopefully due out next week.'

'We were going to take a run in to visit her tonight, if there's not too many others going.'

Mona folded her arms high up on her chest, for once more interested in talking about another subject than her daughter. 'I came around to see if any one of ye might know that family that was murdered in Uddingston.'

'A family murdered?' Sophie repeated, clasping at her throat. 'Mother of God! It's only a couple of days since they found that young girl's body near Glasgow.'

'Well, there's more, and it might even be the same killer,' Mona said dramatically. 'This time he used a gun.' She pointed to the middle of her forehead. 'Shot all three of them stone dead through the head. They went by the name of Smart, according to the news – the man in the house was a Peter Smart.' She shook her head in disbelief. 'Did not one of youse hear it on the news? It was on at nine o'clock then again at ten.'

Sophie's hand flew to cover her mouth. 'Oh, dear God . . . I never thought to listen to the news yet. I had a music programme on – it's nice and relaxing in the morning.'

Mona gave a sigh of exasperation. 'You should keep yerself more up to date on things, Sophie,' she chided. 'There's more important things going on in the world than music and books, you know. Especially when you think of young girls being murdered and raped and whole families bein' shot dead only miles from us.'

'You're right,' Sophie said, looking as contrite as an errant schoolgirl. 'I must make myself listen to the news and read the papers more often.'

Mona stared at her sister-in-law for a moment, always amazed that Sophie could admit to her faults so easily – and yet do nothing most of the time to change them. Mona certainly wouldn't feel so comfortable owning up to faults, but she supposed that in her own way, she tried hard not to have any.

'I wonder how long that'll last for!' Fintan joked. 'The only paper she likes is the *Sunday Post* because it has all the nice wee stories in it.'

Mona threw a look of despair in Fintan's direction, wondering how he put up with such a vague, disorganised wife. Pat Grace wouldn't stand for it, that's for sure. He was a man who appreciated the ship-shape way things were run, where meals were ready on the dot and things were cleared and washed up the minute they were finished.

Mona glanced around the busy, cluttered kitchen now. 'I suppose Kirsty's gone off to work?'

'Not this morning,' Sophie said. 'It's her Saturday off . . . and anyway she stayed the night at the hotel she was singing in up in the Clyde Valley. Seemingly, they got a very bad fall of snow out there last night, and the roads weren't safe to travel on.'

'It's amazing that the weather can be so bad only an hour away,' Fintan said. 'We only had a light fall of snow last night, and you'd hardly know it this morning. There's only the odd wee bit at the side of the roads.'

Mona looked from Sophie to Fintan, her mouth gaping open. 'You say Kirsty stayed the night in a *hotel*?' she repeated.

Sophie nodded, suddenly beginning to feel uncomfortable. 'Oul' John the postman came to let us know just after nine o'clock. Kirsty phoned the post office to ask them to tell us she was safe. She didn't want us finding her bed empty this morning,' she explained. 'But I probably wouldn't have looked in anyway, because I always leave her and Heather sleeping in on a Saturday if they're not working.'

Fintan looked up at the round wooden clock on the wall that had come as a wedding present from Ireland over twenty years ago. 'She said that the roads were a lot clearer this morning and they'd be setting off as soon as the smaller roads had been gritted.'

Mona's head moved from side to side in thought. 'I'd be wary letting a young girl go off on her own for the night,' she said, 'now there's murderers and rapists on the loose. Who else was with her?'

Sophie glanced at Fintan. 'I suppose that Larry fellow was still there, he picked her up as usual . . . and then there would be the band.'

'All men?' Mona asked, her voice high.

'All working men,' Fintan said. 'Men that would look after Kirsty, the same way the local band looked after her when she was out with them.' He went over to the back door now and lifted a galvanised bucket and a small shovel, and then headed into the living-room to attend to his morning task of emptying the cold ashes from the grate, and then relighting the fire with paper and thin wooden sticks and any hot cinders that were left.

'Will you have a cup of tea?' Sophie asked, holding the teapot up. 'I just made a fresh one for Heather. She's just getting washed, she'll be down in a minute.'

'Go on,' Mona said, pulling one of the chairs out from the table. 'I might as well. The lads have all had their breakfast, and there's only our Patrick left. He can sort himself out.' She smoothed down the skirt of her apron. 'We're all going to have to be more vigilant now, with a madman on the loose. God knows when or where he could strike next.' Mona tutted several times to herself, a tortured look on her face. 'Ye'll have to keep a close eye on them girls now. You wouldn't want them to be travelling around too late at night, or walkin' home in the dark or anythin' risky like that.'

'Oh, we'll be keepin' an even closer eye on them,' Sophie assured her. 'Who would believe that we'd ever have to worry about murderers near Rowanhill?'

Heather came down the stairs now and into the kitchen. 'Who's been murdered?' she asked, her eyes moving from her mother to her aunt. She was grateful that Mona wasn't still going on about Gerry's funeral or making sly digs about Liz being in hospital. Although she'd had a good night's sleep, she still felt very fragile over the whole thing.

'Did I hear somebody saying there's been another murder?'

'A whole family!' Mona stated, delighted to have someone who was as interested in the shocking story as herself. She would have preferred Kirsty to chat it out with, but since she wasn't available, Heather would just have to do. And at least she would have a better grip on what was happening in the world than the feather-headed Sophie.

Chapter 57

❧❧❧

When they heard Larry's car pulling up at the gate, Sophie and Fintan had gone rushing to the door to make sure it was Kirsty home safe and well. The talk of the nearby murders had circulated all around the village, and was now the main thing on people's minds. Larry had come out of the car to assure them that Kirsty had been well looked after by the hotel and that no harm had come to her.

'The weather is something you'll have to take into account from now on,' Fintan said, his face dark with worry. 'And if you'd set off and got stuck in one of those back roads you could have been frozen to death by the morning.'

'That's exactly why we didn't set off,' Larry agreed. He then reiterated Kirsty's point about the staff having to stay the night as well, and how it was a case of being sensible and practical about the situation.

'It's different for a man being out all night,' Fintan continued, 'but anything could happen to a young girl in these hotels. You don't know who could be watching what room she went into, especially now we have that madman on the loose.' He shook his head. 'We'll have to think carefully about the singing until he's caught, or until the long dark winter nights are over.'

Kirsty's stomach clenched at the thought of their nights out together coming to a halt. She bit her lip, terrified of saying something that might antagonise her father any further. Most of the time Fintan was fairly placid, but she knew he was more than capable of putting his foot down if he thought it was necessary.

'We'll certainly be very careful about the bookings after this episode,' Larry agreed in a low, serious voice. 'And I'll warn the more remote places that we'll be cancelling if there's any threat of severe weather.'

'Fair enough,' Fintan said, brightening up now, 'fair enough.'

'Will you come in for a cup of tea or a bowl of home-made hot soup or something?' Sophie offered. 'You'll need something to warm you up.'

Larry paused. Then, without looking at Kirsty, he said, 'A bowl of soup would be lovely, Mrs Grace, and it might just give me the chance to tell you both how well your daughter is doing.'

Kirsty caught her breath. This was the first time Larry had got involved with her family. He had just had a few polite words with them before, letting them know where Kirsty was going and assuring them she would be seen home safely. But coming in for a plate of her mother's soup was a different matter, and Kirsty wondered if they would be in any way suspicious.

There had only been the four of them around the kitchen table, and as they all sat enjoying the soup and bread, Fintan asked Larry about what part of Dublin he was from and all the things that people from the same country who live in another country ask. Then, they moved on to chat more generally about the weather and the murders and the terrible tragedy that had happened to Gerry Stewart.

Kirsty had been terrified to look Larry too closely in the eye, in case they gave anything away, but any time she did look across the table at him, she was amazed at how easy and relaxed he was with her parents. She wondered just how they would react if they knew how their business relationship had suddenly changed into something much more. She wasn't too worried about her mother, but she had a feeling that her father wouldn't take to it too well – especially if his attitude towards her staying in the hotel was anything to go by.

When the meal was finished they sat for a few more minutes and then Larry got to his feet.

'That lovely soup was just perfect for a cold winter's day,' he said to Sophie, bringing a pink tinge of delight to her cheeks. Then he shook hands with Fintan and said he must head home and get things sorted out for the evening, as he had a new band playing in Glasgow and he wanted to take a run out for a couple of hours to see how they got on.

'As long as you don't hit snow again this evening!' Sophie laughed. 'You wouldn't want to be stranded two nights in a row, and definitely not out in Glasgow.'

Then Kirsty had walked with him out to the car on her own. 'I can't believe that's just happened,' she whispered as they walked along. 'You didn't say you wanted to meet them.'

'It had to happen sooner or later,' Larry said quietly. 'I want them to get used to me, and get to know me. And they seem like lovely people, which isn't a bit surprising since they have such a lovely daughter.'

'Oh, you know all the right things to say.'

'We'll go for that meal on Tuesday night, and I'll pick you up around seven,' he said to Kirsty as he got in the car. 'Although I haven't a notion how I'm going to get through the next two days without seeing you . . .' He halted, then he reached into the glove compartment. 'I'll give you my business card, it's got my address and phone number on it. Maybe you might give a ring . . . or even if you could get away for an hour or two tomorrow afternoon or something, we could meet up?'

A broad smile broke over Kirsty's face. 'I'll definitely ring you tomorrow – are you in all day?'

Larry nodded and laughed. 'My one day of rest, I sit in all day reading the Sunday papers and listening to the radio.' He raised his eyebrows. 'I can even watch the telly now in the evenings since I treated myself.'

'And will you cook for yourself?' Kirsty asked, her voice high with surprise.

Larry nodded. 'It was one of the things they taught me in the home . . . I can cook more or less anything.'

'I'm impressed,' Kirsty whispered, looking into his eyes. 'Even more impressed.'

'Weren't you terrified staying in a big old hotel room all on your own?' Sophie asked when she came back into the house.

Kirsty shook her head, trying to answer the question without telling a direct lie. 'I wasn't a bit frightened,' she said. 'The hotel was lovely and we were well looked after. I was more worried about you and my daddy thinking I'd done a bunk or something – and then when we heard the news in the hotel about the murders I raced to the reception to ask them to let me phone a message through to the post office.'

'Well, luckily the postman came before we knew you hadn't come home,' her father said now. 'But even though we got the message we were still worried about you being out all night with people we don't know very well. And especially with the

365

majority of them being men – men behind the bar and men in the band and that kind of thing. It's no place for a young girl to be out on her own.'

Then, when she could just imagine the awkward questions forming in her father and mother's minds, she went quickly on, trying to fill in the answers for them, 'Och, there was actually plenty of girls and women,' she told them. 'I got chattin' to this lovely young waitress from Carluke, and she ended up having to stay the night as well. Quite a lot of the staff couldn't get home because the taxis were taken off the road. I think they have to do that regularly in the winter – it's because a lot of the roads are narrow and on severe slopes. The slightest bit of ice or snow makes them very dangerous for driving.'

'Well, it's a place you'll have to think twice about going to again,' Fintan warned.

Sophie nodded her head. 'That's true,' she said. 'The Clyde Valley is very high up. And you say you had a room all to yourself?'

Kirsty nodded. 'A lovely big double bed, and the cover of it matched the curtains and chairs.'

Her mother looked very impressed. 'When I do the bedrooms up again,' she mused, 'I must have a go at matching things up.'

Kirsty heaved a secret sigh of relief. She had got away with it. But she and Larry would have to be very careful from now on, until they picked the right time to tell everyone about them. They had driven very carefully from the hotel down into Lanark and then taken it very slowly out into Carluke and then Wishaw. When they got there and realised they would be parting from now until a rehearsal on Tuesday night, Larry suggested that they stop off somewhere quiet for a cup of tea or coffee.

'I want us to go out properly, Kirsty,' he had told her earnestly, holding her hands across the café table. 'I want to take you for nice meals or to a show or the pictures . . . all the things that couples do. I want to make up for all the things we could have done at Christmas . . . all the time we've wasted.'

Kirsty's heart had just soared and soared. She had not the slightest doubt in her mind that Larry Delaney was the man for her. The man she would spend the rest of her life with.

'Maybe we could cut the rehearsal short and go out some-where for an hour on Tuesday night,' Kirsty had suggested.

'Maybe we could just cancel the rehearsal completely,' Larry had said, laughing, 'and have the whole night to ourselves. You don't even need to rehearse, Kirsty. Your singing comes so naturally to you, and you learn the new songs easily.' He raised his eyebrows. 'You didn't need half the rehearsals we did – I only organised them so I could keep seeing you regularly and hear that fantastic voice.'

'Are you serious?' Kirsty had asked, thrilled with this little piece of news. It made her feel a lot better because she still felt embarrassed thinking back to the night she had let all her feelings out.

'I'm very serious,' Larry had said. 'And I'm determined that we'll see each other more from now on.'

They had crawled back at a snail's pace into Rowanhill – dreading parting from each other – and the only two people in the village not talking about the murders.

'Where's Heather?' Kirsty asked now. She had decided she would let Heather in on her unbelievable secret, and was anxious to relive every minute of it all telling her sister.

'Liz came out of hospital today and Heather went up to visit her half an hour ago,' Sophie said. 'You might want to take a wee walk up to see her yourself. The poor girl's bound to be in a terrible state. People are saying that it might have something to do with the shock of Gerry Stewart's accident. She was there when it all happened.'

'D'you think it might have had anything to do with it?' Kirsty asked in a quiet voice.

Sophie shrugged. 'It could well have . . . but then miscarriages can happen at any time.'

Liz was sitting up in bed in her pink nightdress, with several pillows propping her up, and a bottle of Lucozade and the usual bunches of grapes and boxes of chocolates that people give to a sick person, on her bedside cabinet.

'I don't know what's going to happen about the wedding now,' she said to Heather in a thin, frail voice. 'I'm just hoping and praying that Jim will want to carry on with all the plans we've made.'

'Of course he will,' Heather reassured her pale-faced friend. 'He was all caught up in the plans as much as you were. I'm sure everything will be fine once he sees you up and about and on your feet again.'

Tears suddenly rushed into Liz's eyes and Heather reached over to the box of tissues to get her some paper hankies.

'I didn't think I'd be this bothered about losing the baby,' Liz sobbed. 'I hadn't really had time to think about it . . . I just kept putting it out of my mind. I didn't want to believe I was expectin' a baby before we got married. I thought that if I got the wedding all sorted first, that I'd have plenty of time when we were married and on our own to sit down and get myself all organised.' She shrugged. 'The poor wee thing . . . I lost it before we even had the chance to get used to having it. Before I'd even got happy about having it.'

'And does Jim feel the same?'

Liz nodded, dabbing the hanky to her streaming eyes. That was the one thing I was sure about – he loves kids and always wanted his own.' She stopped for a few moments, trying to catch her breath and blink back the tears. 'He's not been down to see me since I got home . . . he must have got held up at work or something. He sometimes goes in on Saturdays.'

'He'll be down soon,' Heather said in a soothing tone, thinking that he really should have been in to the hospital this morning to bring Liz home.

'And he's been spending a lot of time up at the Stewarts' house,' Liz said, 'helpin' them sort out Gerry's things.'

Heather's stomach tightened at the mention of his name.

Her face softened. 'D'you know he even phoned Gerry's uncle out in Australia from work for them? They never thought about telling the uncle until the day after the funeral. Mrs Stewart was in such a state and with not sleeping too well, she wasn't thinkin'. Anyway, as soon as Jim knew she wanted to let her brother know, he said he'd give him a ring from the office.' She shook her head. 'The uncle was really upset. He was very fond of Gerry from when he was a wee boy, and he said he'd been hoping that Gerry would be out to stay with him later this year.'

'It's a pity he didn't go at Christmas,' Heather whispered. 'And maybe the tragedy might never have happened.'

They chatted for a little while, but all the conversation seemed very dark and heavy, about the terrible snow some places had got and the local murders. Heather told her friend all about Kirsty getting stranded up in the Clydeside area and having to stay the night in the hotel.

'Trust your Kirsty to land on her feet,' Liz said, managing a faint smile. 'The rest of us would get stuck havin' to walk miles in the snow or havin' to knock on somebody's door for help. Trust your Kirsty to get stranded in a big fancy hotel for the night where they give her a room and bed and breakfast. That would be a dream come true for me. It's the only way I would get to see the inside of a place like that.'

The baby of course dominated most of the talk, as Liz told Heather that she was the only one she could really be open and honest with. 'I'd only told my mother and you about it,' she said, 'and I don't know what my mammy even said to my daddy. I know everybody else was guessing, but I never actually came out with it and told them that it was true.' She rubbed her nose with a tissue. 'And I've no intentions of getting into big discussions with anybody about it. I'm just going to say I collapsed and I don't know what caused it.' She looked up at her friend. 'That's what happened to you at work last week, and nobody accused you of being expecting, did they?'

'No,' Heather said, wrinkling her brow in confusion. 'And I didn't think for a minute that anybody would jump to that conclusion, because I was never pregnant.'

'Exactly,' Liz said, brightening up a little. 'Maybe I could just say the same kind of thing, and eventually they'll all stop talking about it.'

'I think people are too busy talking about these murders now,' Heather said, changing the subject. And although the subject of murder was not any cheerier, at least it had nothing to do with anybody they knew.

Just then the front doorbell rang and Mrs Mullen's quick footsteps could be heard rushing to answer it.

'That might be Jim,' Heather said, looking expectantly towards the door.

A few moments later Kirsty was shown into the bedroom and Heather saw the look of disappointment on her friend's face.

Apart from the fact that she was disappointed that it wasn't Jim, Liz had just remembered that Kirsty had been there the other day when it all happened, and it was she who had phoned the ambulance and then run for Jim. Kirsty was bound to know what had really happened. And if she hadn't guessed, then no doubt Heather had told her.

'How are you feelin'?' Kirsty asked in a genuinely sympathetic voice. She felt very sorry for the poor girl and all she'd gone through. Then she looked across the room at Heather, who still wasn't back to her old self. Gerry Stewart's death and all the drama surrounding it had really hit her hard. Kirsty suddenly felt very grateful that she'd not had anything terrible like that befall her. And she felt very lucky when she thought of the magical night she'd just had with Larry Delaney.

'Och, I suppose I'm OK,' Liz said, not meeting Kirsty's eyes. There were times when she felt that Kirsty Grace could just be that wee bit flippant and sarcastic, and she wasn't taking any chances on her being like that today. She definitely wasn't in the mood for any of her old nonsense. Heather Grace was a different kettle of fish. She was far more serious and you always knew where you were with her. 'I'll be fine,' Liz said, rubbing her nose again. 'I'm just a wee bit run down and tired . . .'

'You'll be up and about soon,' Kirsty said, 'and things will seem different . . .' She looked at all the grapes and chocolates on the bedside. 'I'll be up at the shops later if there's anything I can get you.'

'Thanks,' Liz said, sniffing into her hanky, 'but I think I'll be OK.' Then she looked up at Kirsty. 'What's all this about you gettin' stuck in the snow and having to stay out all night?'

Then the conversation lightened up a little as Kirsty told the story with great gusto, embellishing the bits that would make them laugh and missing out the wonderful bits about Larry Delaney.

'What a bloomin' shame,' Kirsty said as she and Heather walked home together, coats tightly buttoned and scarves high up around their necks against the winter chill. 'It just seems like absolutely everything has gone wrong for poor Liz. And what I'd like to know is where was that Jim Murray? He should have been there beside her, holding her hand after all she's gone through.'

'I don't think he knows what he's doing at the minute,' Heather said. 'He's lost his best friend and now he's lost the baby him and Liz were expecting. All the plans they were making seem to be falling apart.' She halted now as they passed a neighbour to nod and say 'hello'. 'I think Liz is worried about the wedding now . . .'

'D'you mean that he won't want to go through with it?' Kirsty gasped. The thought hadn't struck her. 'Surely he wouldn't let her down now?'

'I don't really know what to think,' Heather said, sighing wearily. 'I'm guessing that she feels Jim was only marrying her because he had to and now she's worrying that he'll feel trapped into having to do it.'

They walked along the main street in silence for a while, passing the church and the chemist's shop where Kirsty spent her working days. Then they turned off down towards the street they lived in.

'How are you feeling?' Kirsty asked, glancing at her sister. 'You're still very pale.'

'Och, I'm OK,' Heather told her, pulling her scarf more tightly around her neck. 'I slept a wee bit better last night . . . but I still keep thinking about everything that's happened. Thinking that if I hadn't finished with Gerry maybe everything and everybody else would be OK.'

'That's a stupid way to think,' Kirsty said. 'Things just happen. Look at Liz. She would have lost that baby anyway, and she'd still be in the same position whether you were still going out with Gerry or not.'

'I've had a few people making digs at me about Gerry,' Heather told her sister in a low voice. 'When I was up at the paper shop earlier this morning, I was getting wee comments from two women about how broken-hearted he was when we split up.' She shook her head. 'And there's the crowd from Rowanhill that were on the minibus that night, they must have seen us arguing at the party earlier on . . . then they heard Jim and Gerry arguing. I feel the whole place is talking about me and blaming me for what happened to him.'

Kirsty thrust her arm through her sister's and pulled her closer. 'Don't listen to them, it'll be all forgotten in a few weeks' time,' she advised. 'Even today, they're only interested in hearing about the murders on the radio and reading about them in the newspapers.' She paused. 'Just keep yourself to yourself for a few weeks and they'll all forget about it.'

'But it's hard to keep a low profile in Rowanhill,' Heather said in a flat voice. 'You meet people everywhere, at the shops, at Mass on Sunday—'

'Why don't you go to Claire's next weekend?' Kirsty suddenly suggested. 'It would give you a wee break. You could go straight from work on the Friday and then stay until it's time to go back to work on the Monday morning. She would be absolutely delighted to have you – it was one of the last things she said before we left.'

Heather's eyes clouded over in thought. 'That's not a bad idea,' she said. 'I might think about it.'

'And if anybody says a word to me in the chemist's shop about you,' Kirsty told her, 'I'll take the nose off them, and they won't ask again.'

Heather smiled now. 'Thanks. I know I can always rely on you, and it's a really big help.'

'Well,' Kirsty said squeezing her arm, 'I might have to rely on you as well.'

'Why? What's wrong?' Heather asked, slowing down.

'There's nothing wrong as far as I'm concerned.'

'Tell me!' Heather insisted.

'It's Larry . . .' Kirsty's voice was a low whisper, but there was just the tiniest note of excitement in it.

Heather came to a standstill. They were too close to their own house to finish the conversation walking quickly. 'What's happened?' Her heart was sinking now, dreading what her sister might tell her.

Kirsty looked around her to check there was no one about

who might overhear them. 'It's a big long story . . . but he's told me that he feels exactly the same about me.' She paused.

'But I thought you said you weren't bothered about him anymore,' Heather said in a shocked tone. 'After that night in Hamilton, where he was horrible to you . . .'

'It was only because he was worried about me being younger,' Kirsty explained. 'And he's already had a bad experience with women and didn't want to get involved with me.'

'So, what's made him change his mind?' Heather asked, her brows knitted together.

Kirsty hesitated, trying to find the right words to explain this wonderful turn of events. 'It just happened. We were talking in the bar for ages last night . . . we talked and talked about everything and it gave us the chance to get to know each other really well.' She halted, almost breathless with emotion just talking about Larry. 'He's not from the well-off background that I thought. In fact, there were loads of things I'd assumed about him that were wrong. The more we talked, the more we discovered we had in common.'

Heather's voice dropped. 'Did anything happen when you were in the hotel on your own?'

A little smile came on Kirsty's lips at the memory. 'He kissed me . . . and it was brilliant!'

There was a silence. 'Are you sure that's all he did?' Heather asked, her eyes narrowing in suspicion. 'He wasn't trying to take advantage of you or anything? Look what happened to Liz.'

Kirsty's smile disappeared. 'No he was not!' she hissed. 'For your information, he was quite the opposite – a real gentleman. He's nothing like that flamin' Jim Murray, and I'm not that stupid that I'd go with somebody if I knew he didn't care about me – and I certainly wouldn't be goin' around havin' sex with him!'

'Good,' Heather said, but she still didn't look at all relieved or happy. 'I'm glad nothing serious has happened to you, because you and him are not at all suited. It would be worse than the way things went for me and Gerry Stewart.' She shook her head dismally. 'He's far too old for you for a start—'

'Shut up!' Kirsty said, her eyes wide and glaring with anger. She couldn't believe that Heather could be like this towards her, when she'd been so supportive about the funeral and Liz and everything. 'Larry's age doesn't matter a bit, and anyway, it's not that huge a difference. It's only about ten or eleven years – nothing like the difference between Claire and her husband.'

'I don't care,' Heather said, starting to walk on now. 'It's a total disaster, and my mammy and daddy will go mad about it. They haven't the slightest clue that there's anything going on between you. If they find out they'll stop you going out singing with him and everything. They'll be really mad to think that they've trusted you with him, and all the time he had his lecherous eyes on you.'

'I thought you'd understand,' Kirsty said, catching up on her sister. The anger she felt was now slowly dissolving into hurt. 'I thought you'd be the one that would stick up for me . . .'

Heather's head moved from side to side, her dark wavy hair swinging as she did so. 'The fact that I don't understand shows you that it's all a load of nonsense. It sounds to me as though that Larry Delaney has suddenly realised that he's on to a good thing with a young girl who's easily impressed. And he's not stupid either, he's probably told you all that rubbish about other women just to make you feel he's a really good catch – that women are falling over themselves to get him.' She paused. 'He might just be saying all those things so that he can keep you on his books now that your singing career is taking off, and if you get loads of bookings it'll make more money for him.'

Kirsty looked at her sister now, devastated at her words. 'I have never heard you saying such terrible things before,' she said slowly, 'and you've got it all completely wrong. Larry loves me and he told me that last night.' Her chin tilted defiantly. 'And whatever you say, I know that I definitely love him.'

Heather raised her eyebrows, a sceptical look on her face. 'I think you're being totally naïve and stupid and you're only making a fool of yourself over that man – and I don't want to hear another word about it.'

Hot, angry tears sprung into Kirsty's eyes. She took a deep, shuddering breath. 'I don't care if you are my sister – that's the last time I'll ever trust you again, Heather Grace.'

Saturday evening was very quiet in the Grace household. Too quiet for Sophie, who had noticed the strained atmosphere between the two sisters.

'Have you two had an argument?' she asked Heather as they dried and put away the dishes that Kirsty had washed. 'You don't seem to have too much to say to each other this evening.'

'No,' Heather replied, rubbing the tea-towel hard across a dinner plate. 'I think we're both just a bit tired.'

Kirsty appeared at the kitchen door with a used glass that had been left on the table in the sitting-room. She went over to the sink and after dipping it in the soapy water in the basin, she ran it under the hot tap to rinse it.

'Your father and I were thinking of taking a run in to the hospital to see Lily tonight,' Sophie told both her daughters. 'So if either of you want to come with us . . .'

'I'll come,' both girls replied at the same time, each thinking they might avoid having to stay at home with the other.

Chapter 58

❦

There was still a palpable tension between the sisters as they walked behind their parents going to half past eleven Mass the following morning, Heather in her black and white checked coat and white hat, Kirsty in her camel coat with a brown angora beret. Things had thawed a little the night before as they all sat around Lily's bed, laughing and joking, and it had been hard for them to openly ignore each other.

There had been a slight awkwardness when Lily asked Kirsty all about being snowed-in at the hotel. 'That's dead funny,' the young girl had said, shaking her head. 'Because the snow wasn't that bad here.' She'd motioned to the window behind her bed. 'I was watching the snow all day yesterday, and I was moaning that it was melting too fast for it to be really white.'

'Well, it was really white up in the Clyde Valley,' Kirsty told her, 'and really, really deep.'

'And you had to stay the night in the hotel?' Lily had said, her eyes wide with interest. 'That must have been great!'

Kirsty had felt her neck flushing as all eyes were on her at that point, and she'd begun to feel guilty, as if she had made the whole thing up. The snow certainly hadn't been as bad in other parts as it had been where they were, but she and Larry had told the truth and anyone in the hotel could verify for them. She had glanced over at Heather to see whether she had a disbelieving look on her face, but she was flicking through a *School Friend* magazine that Lily had given her.

Later, the two girls played a game of Scrabble with Lily and managed to make it look as if they were the best of friends, arguing and joking over words, but their smiles did not reach their eyes. Both of them knew that it was all an act, and that a lot of work was going to have to be done to repair the damage.

They walked into the church together on the Sunday morning, and sat side by side in the pew going through the motions as they had the previous night for the sake of their parents. When the priest came out on the altar and started the Mass, they stared down at their Sunday missals, each lost in their own thoughts and not seeing a single holy word. Kirsty Grace prayed with all her heart to God that he would let things work out between her and Larry. That he would forgive Larry for the sins he had committed with that Helen McCluskey and that everyone would understand about their relationship when it finally came out into the open.

Heather Grace sat beside her, praying that Kirsty would see sense over this ridiculous, unsuitable romance, that Liz Mullen would be OK, and that people would stop blaming her for everything that had happened to Gerry Stewart.

When they came out from Mass, Heather told them that she was going to call in at Liz's for half an hour. 'I just want to check if she's feeling a bit better,' she said, not looking at Kirsty, and obviously not inviting her to come along with her. 'I'll be back in plenty of time for my dinner.'

'We're having it earlier today,' Sophie reminded her, 'because your father and I are doing a run over to Wishaw to see his cousin Betty along with Pat and Mona this evening.'

376

Kirsty's heart suddenly leapt. If her mother and father were out, it might just give her an opportunity to see Larry. She said nothing until Heather had gone into Liz's house, and they were walking towards the phone box. She started to rummage in her pockets and purse for change for the phone.

'I'll catch up with you in a few minutes,' she told her parents. 'I want to make a phone call to a girl from school that I should have rung over the New Year.'

'Who's that?' Sophie asked curiously. She knew most of the girl's friends.

'Nancy Brennan,' Kirsty said, naming one of her old school pals. 'You've met her a few times, she's been out to the house. She lives over in Carfin and I promised her I might take a run over some evening.'

'Have you change for the phone?' Fintan said, holding out a handful of coppers.

'Thanks,' Kirsty said, feeling guilty as she took the money from her father.

Kirsty didn't need to check the number on the little card she had in her pocket, as she already knew it off by heart. It rang out several times, and then Larry's lovely Irish voice came on the line.

The pips for the money sounded, then Kirsty hurriedly shoved four of the pennies into the slot. 'It's me . . .' she said in a slightly anxious voice. Then she added, 'It's Kirsty . . .'

She could hear the big, deep sigh on the other end of the line.

'You must have read my thoughts,' he said. 'I was thinking about you all morning and hoping you might phone.'

Kirsty's heart lifted. She closed her eyes, saying a quick, silent prayer of gratitude to God for listening to her earlier pleas in church. 'Well,' she said, trying to sound casual, 'I was just passing the phone box and I thought I would give you a wee ring.'

'I'm missing you, Kirsty,' he said now, in a serious voice. 'I haven't stopped thinking about you since yesterday afternoon.'

Kirsty glanced around her now, to make sure there was nobody outside the red public phone box who might be listening to her. It wouldn't be the first time that people had listened into other people's private conversations in Rowanhill. 'And I'm missing you,' she said in a low voice. *Missing* didn't even begin to describe what she felt. It was so deep and serious she couldn't find words for it.

'Is there any chance of us meeting up?' he asked. 'Maybe going out for a couple of hours tonight?'

'I could probably meet you for a while this afternoon,' Kirsty suggested. 'I could get the bus to Newarthill, and then if you met me there, maybe we could go for a run somewhere.'

'That would be brilliant. When?' he asked.

A knock suddenly came on the glass of the telephone box, and Kirsty turned to see two girls she knew, waiting to use the phone. She motioned to them that she was nearly finished. 'Would half past four suit you?' she asked him.

'Kirsty, darling, any time would suit me,' Larry laughed. 'I've just been punching in the time until I heard from you, and was dreading that if you didn't phone I might have to wait until Tuesday night.'

'Well, you won't have to wait until Tuesday,' Kirsty whispered. 'I'll meet you at Carfin Cross at half past four.'

'He called in shortly after you and Kirsty left yesterday,' Liz told Heather as they both sat on the edge of her bed. She was up and dressed today, in dark trousers and a white knitted jumper, but she still looked pale and drawn under her make-up and pink lipstick.

'And how was he?' Heather asked, deliberately keeping her voice low as she knew Liz's parents were in the sitting-room and might hear them.

'Still not himself,' Liz said, biting the nail on her thumb. 'He said he was going to have an early night last night, so he didn't come round.'

'Are you seeing him today?'

'I'm not sure ...' Liz said, glancing towards her bedroom door. 'I was going to go up, but my mammy says she doesn't think I should be out and about for the next week.' She rolled her eyes. 'I suppose she's right; I'm still bleeding fairly heavy.'

'He'll probably come down later,' Heather said. 'He's maybe

giving you time to get back on your feet . . . until you can go out to the pictures or the dancing together.'

'I just wish we could get a bit of time on our own,' Liz complained. 'If he comes down here, there's always my mother and father around, and it's the same if I go up to his house. The only way around it is to get married. That's the only way couples get to spend any time on their own.'

Heather nodded as though she agreed, thinking that she would by far prefer to be on her own from now on. Look where Liz had landed herself because of her boyfriend, and now she and Kirsty weren't talking all over boyfriends again. It just wasn't worth it.

Later, as she walked back to her own house, Heather mused over the situation again, unable to understand how a girl could get into such a state over a lad. She'd met a few nice boys over the years, but none who had made her feel she'd want to get married or even engaged to them. Gerry was the closest she'd ever come to anything like that.

None of the feelings she'd ever had came close to what she had imagined real love was like. She'd never felt all excited and romantic about them. A good night's dancing and a good laugh was the most she'd ever had with any of the boys. And she certainly had never felt like going to bed with any of them.

Not that she ever would – even if real love suddenly struck her down. The thought of even seeing a man naked made her shudder, and she certainly couldn't imagine letting any man see her without clothes.

Yes, Heather Grace decided, she would stay quite happily on her own. Friends for her nights out and home with her mother and father for the rest of the time would suit her very well, for the foreseeable future.

After all she had seen and experienced recently, she didn't need or want any man.

Chapter 59

❧❧❧

It was just as well she and Heather weren't really talking, Kirsty reasoned to herself. It meant that she didn't have to explain herself or tell a white lie as she had done to her parents.

Sophie and Fintan had gone off to Wishaw in Pat's car twenty minutes ago, so Kirsty waited until they were safely out of the way and then she got herself ready to catch the quarter past four bus over to Carfin.

She didn't have to waste time deciding what to wear, as she had spent the last hour or so thinking about it. Larry usually saw her dressed for rehearsals in casual clothes or in really glamorous dresses for the stage. For this first date together, Kirsty wanted to wear something that would make her look really nice – not anything that would make her look as if she was trying *too* hard, or not hard enough.

She settled on a fine black woollen sweater that had a collar and three pearl buttons, and a pair of fitted black slacks, which slipped nicely into her black suede ankle books with the grey fur trim. A pair of pearl earrings picked up the buttons on her sweater and her charm bracelet finished the outfit off perfectly.

As she examined herself in the mirror, turning this way and that to check herself from every angle, Kirsty decided with some satisfaction that she had achieved exactly the look she had wanted. It was the sort of outfit that she often saw film stars wearing in *Photoplay* or one of the other magazines, when they were photographed out shopping or waving to their fans. They usually wore mink coats draped over their shoulders, but Kirsty decided that her three-quarter-length camel coat and black scarf would look just fine. She left her blonde hair loose and long, the way that Larry liked it. She had brushed it thoroughly first to loosen the curls, then with the help of some setting lotion, she had coaxed it into a more fashionable, wavy style. A few dabs of

Chanel No. 5 gave her that special little lift, knowing that he had chosen it especially for her.

Heather was in the sitting-room reading a book when Kirsty looked in.

'I'll probably be back before my mammy and daddy,' she said, pulling on her gloves, 'but if I'm not back, you can say I won't be late.'

'Fine,' Heather said, not lifting her head from her book. Then, just as Kirsty went out into the hallway, she called in a softer voice. 'Be careful about coming back in the dark ... they still haven't caught whoever murdered all those people.'

Kirsty stopped in her tracks. She had forgotten about the murder business. 'Thanks for reminding me,' she called back to her sister. 'I'll make sure I keep to the streets that are all lit up.'

As soon as she stepped off the red double-decker bus, Kirsty could see Larry's car waiting for her just up from the bus stop. She walked smartly towards the car, looking neither right nor left at the bus she had left behind or the other passengers who were still getting off, as she didn't want to draw any attention to herself.

The door was partly open waiting for her, and the engine of the car was running so they could move off quickly.

'This is just how I imagined it would be,' Larry said as she slid into the cool leather of the passenger seat. He leaned over to take her face in his hands and kiss her gently on the lips. 'Just seeing you walking along there made me feel the happiest man alive, and having you in the car beside me like this is just indescribable.'

'Well, that makes us two very happy people,' she said, kissing him back, 'because I feel the very same about seeing you.'

He kissed her once again, then he put the car into gear and they pulled away, little knowing that the bus driver had watched Kirsty's movements with great interest and had taken particular note of Larry Delaney's expensive car.

'Where do you want to go?' Larry asked, as they drove along on the main road that led to Motherwell. 'We can turn off now in any direction that you want.'

Kirsty shrugged. 'I don't mind . . . but there's not going to be much open on a Sunday evening.' She halted. 'You live in Motherwell, don't you?'

Larry nodded. 'We could go to a café or we might even catch the pictures if you like.'

'Why don't we go to your place?' Kirsty suggested.

There was a little silence as he got the car into top gear, then he turned his head to look at her. 'Are you sure?' he asked.

'Yes,' she told him. 'I'd really like to see where you live . . . I keep imagining it, and I bet it's all wrong. I keep wondering if it's big or small, tidy or untidy . . . that kind of thing.'

Larry laughed now. 'You never cease to surprise me, Kirsty Grace. You're so honest and open about even the smallest details, and I think that's one of the things I first liked about you.'

'I've actually not been very honest this afternoon,' she admitted in a low voice. She tucked a strand of blonde hair behind her ear. 'I decided to say to my mother that I was going over to visit an old school friend of mine . . . it just seemed easier than explaining about us.'

Larry's forehead creased in concern. 'I really don't like putting you in the position where you're having to tell lies. It means we're getting off on the wrong foot with your parents.'

'It's no big deal,' Kirsty said, wishing she hadn't said anything now. The last few days seemed to have been fraught with misunderstandings and disagreements with everybody, and she didn't want that interfering with her and Larry.

'Was there anything said after I left you yesterday? Were there any problems with your mother and father?' he asked now.

'No . . . not at all,' Kirsty said. 'They thought you were great, and they were delighted with all the things you'd said about my singing. I think it was just the worry about me being stranded up in the Clyde Valley with the snow, and obviously with the dramatic things that have been in the news recently.' She gave a little laugh. 'It's unbelievable really, because nothing ever happens around this area, then suddenly we have a mass-murderer on our hands.'

'Well, it's understandable that they should be worried,' Larry commented. 'I'll be worrying now every time I think of you out on your own.'

'I'll be perfectly fine,' she told him. She didn't want to spoil the precious time they had together now going over her father's comments about them staying in the hotel, or mulling over Heather's funny attitude to their romance. Anyway, she thought, there wasn't anything that serious to tell him, and hopefully it would all sort itself out in good time.

The house that Kirsty had imagined Larry living in wasn't anything like the house he actually owned. In fact, it wasn't a house at all. It was an upstairs mansion flat – or spacious apartment if you were using the language of the estate agents in the newspaper adverts. They had driven down through the town centre of Motherwell, past the Town Hall – where Kirsty and Heather and their friends often went dancing – down the long hill that led towards Hamilton.

They passed a mixture of old two-storey houses in grey and red sandstone and similar ones painted in white, then they passed rows of smaller one-storey houses in red sandstone. About halfway down the hill, Larry turned the car off towards the right and they drove along a tree-lined avenue until they came to a stop in front of a tall, well-kept red-stone building that was divided into a number of apartments.

'This is it,' Larry said, turning the engine off. 'This is where I hide away when I'm not working.'

Kirsty stepped out of the car, closed the door and stood staring up at the very smart building for a few moments. It had something of the appearance of the hotel up in Lanark with similar bay windows and perfectly maintained stonework, and there was a uniformity to the heavy curtains and pelmets, as though one design had been used throughout.

'It looks really lovely from the outside,' Kirsty finally said, as she walked around the car towards him, her blonde waves bobbing on her shoulders. She was relaxed and smiling, and in a funny way she felt proud on his behalf that he owned a flat in this very smart place. And she knew it was all because Larry had told her all about his background, and that he had worked so hard to achieve it.

'Good,' he said, smiling brightly at her. 'I hope you like the inside as much.'

Larry Delaney's flat had everything that a modern home could need or want: television, fridge, fancy radiogram, vacuum cleaner – all the things that Kirsty had read about in magazines, and the sort of things that she had seen in her Auntie Claire's house in Glasgow. The sorts of things that she had never imagined herself owning in a million years. And yet here she was now, going out with a successful businessman who owned all these things.

'It's beautiful,' Kirsty breathed, looking around the big, airy sitting-room with the bay window that looked out onto the street. The room was furnished fairly simply, with a dark three-piece suite and a long coffee-table in the centre, and a television, radiogram and a dark wooden table with four chairs pushed against one of the walls. Wine and cream Regency-striped curtains with matching tie-backs and a pelmet decorated the windows. A black-and-white ink sketch was framed above the fireplace, and on close inspection Kirsty recognised it as O'Connell Street in Dublin.

As she walked around the room, Kirsty felt there was something missing and after a few minutes she realised what it was. It needed some sort of colour – the sort of colour that a woman would introduce in the way of flowers and cushions and maybe a few colourful pictures. The sort of colour that Kirsty knew she could bring to this lovely apartment. The colour she knew she could bring to Larry Delaney's whole life.

Kirsty took off her coat and outdoor things and then Larry gave her a guided tour of the very modern kitchen and the bathroom, which even had a shower. Then he led her upstairs to the two large bedrooms that were on the floor above.

'I'm not always as tidy as this,' he confessed as they stood at the door of his spacious bedroom, which was the exact shape as the sitting-room downstairs and with the same tall bay window and wine striped curtains. From first glance Kirsty thought it was so obviously a man's room, with the heavy Victorian wardrobe and chest of drawers with a man's ivory brush and shaving set, and a large carved dark wooden chair with a similar striped fabric to the curtains. The high, wide, wooden bed with pale blue sheets and pillow-cases and a navy top cover took up most of the main wall. 'I have an older woman who comes in to tidy up for me on a Friday,' Larry explained, 'and with us being away until yesterday afternoon, I haven't had a chance to untidy it all yet.'

'I think you keep this very well,' Kirsty told him, looking around the high-ceilinged room. 'I think you keep it all very well.'

Then there was a silence as they stood opposite each other on the threshold of Larry's bedroom. Kirsty looked up at him; their eyes met and she saw the same look in his eyes as she had seen in the hotel the night he came to her room.

He reached for her now and drew her into his arms, and she could feel the warmth of his heart beating through the fine wool of his sweater. Then he kissed her long and deeply, and a hot wave of desire shot through her, leaving her weak and breathless.

She reached up to her full height and wrapped her arms tightly around his neck, feeling his lips hard on hers and then his kisses became slower and deeper as his tongue gently probed her mouth.

Kirsty Grace had been held tightly and kissed many times before now by young boys, but it had never ever felt the way that it felt with this handsome older man. And her body had never responded in the way it was responding to him now. The feelings she had were new and wonderful and exciting – but there was also a little edge to all the feelings that was frightening.

Then, Larry's kisses slowed down until he eventually stopped, then he took her hand and led her across the room to the big high bed. He didn't lift her this time as he had done a few days ago in the hotel – and he didn't need to. There was no question that Kirsty Grace was willing. They lay down on the bed together, their arms wrapped around each other as though they were the only two people in the whole building and in the whole world.

They kissed and talked and then kissed again – and each time the kissing became more passionate until Larry had somehow moved to lie on top of her and she was suddenly startled when she felt his male hardness pressing close against her lower stomach and hips. Within moments she felt herself instinctively moving against him and the little darts of desire were now growing into an overwhelming passion she had never ever imagined. As their kisses grew deeper Kirsty found her hands were moving under Larry's sweater as she wanted to feel and touch and breathe in so much more of him.

Eventually, through the silent encouragement from Kirsty and the heat that had now generated between them, Larry moved into a sitting position and pulled his sweater over his head. Then, as he lay back down again and Kirsty ran her hands across the fine hairs on his chest and then over his bare shoulders and back, she thought how his body looked even more attractive than she had ever imagined. He looked even more handsome now than he had in the sexy dreams she'd had about him.

Passion escalated between them until Larry's hands gently brushed over Kirsty's breasts and then came to seek them under her sweater, and at that point she did exactly as he had done. She sat up and pulled the sweater up and over her blonde hair, and came to lie beside him again wearing only her little white bra.

Larry's arms came around her again and they hugged and kissed and moved against each other until at last Larry pulled himself away from her. 'We've got to stop, Kirsty,' he said in a low, reluctant voice. He moved to sit on the side of the bed, his fingers running through his thick dark hair.

'Do you want to stop?' she whispered, leaning over to stroke his back again.

There was a silence. 'No, I really *don't* want to stop,' he said quietly, pulling his sweater back on.

'I don't want to stop either,' she told him.

Larry turned back to kiss her lightly on the forehead. 'I think that we're going to have much bigger problems if we don't.'

Chapter 60

Heather went back into work on Monday morning. The weather was milder again, all signs of snow having disappeared with the small but significant rise in temperature.

'Make sure you keep well wrapped up,' Sophie had said as she had seen her off at the front door earlier in the morning. 'It's this changeable weather that catches people out. Keep your scarf and gloves on at all times when you're outside, and make sure you have something decent to eat at your lunch break.'

Heather had assured her mother that she'd do everything right, and went walking up to Rowanhill train station, sighing to herself as she went along. It would be a long time before she was allowed to forget the fainting episode.

Everyone was very nice to her, saying they hoped she felt much better and discreetly not mentioning the funeral, and Mr Walton told her she should take things easy around the office for the next few days. Danny and Maurice came up to her, making good-natured jokes about her fainting at the boss's feet and then saying very kindly that she should look after herself.

Then, halfway through the morning, Sarah came up to her while she was typing out a letter. Heather had spotted her coming across the floor, and deliberately turned her head to the side as if she hadn't seen her.

Sarah stood for a moment, hesitating, then she plunged in. 'I'm really sorry about what happened to your old boyfriend . . . and I'm sorry about the night we went to see the show.'

'Thanks,' Heather said, staring straight at her typewriter. She lifted the file from her desk and proceeded to thumb her way through all the documents, pretending she was looking for something.

'That night,' Sarah continued in a wavery voice, obviously very embarrassed and awkward, 'it was all a big misunderstanding.'

'Forget about it,' Heather said abruptly, still not looking at her workmate. She lifted out one of the documents, pretending to scan it closely.

'Marie can back me up . . .' Sarah attempted once again. She bent down towards the desk, her face close to Heather's.

'Go away!' Heather whispered in a heated voice. 'I don't want anything to do with you. You had your chance to be friends with me over Christmas and you ruined it.' She looked straight up into Sarah's face now. 'You don't need me to be friends with you, you've got that wonderful Barbara. You should just stick with her because you make a lovely pair.'

'I made a mistake,' Sarah said, her eyes filling with tears. 'And I just came to say I was sorry, but if you're not interested in listening, then I'll just leave it.'

At the morning break, Marie Henderson came to stand beside Heather in the queue at the canteen.

'Could I have a wee word with you while we're having our tea?' Marie said in a quiet but friendly tone.

'Of course you can,' Heather said, handing her money to the assistant for her cup of coffee and a chocolate biscuit. Although she still wasn't that hungry, she was making sure that she ate something at all the breaks. Besides, she had lost enough weight now to fit into even her smallest clothes, and she didn't really want to go any thinner. Things hanging off you were just as bad as having clothes that were too tight.

They went to sit at an empty table by the window.

'It's about Sarah,' Marie said, putting her cup and saucer down on the table. Then, when she saw the set of Heather's jaw, she reached across the table and touched her arm. 'Look, I was in the exact same situation as you.'

'What do you mean?' Heather asked, her brow furrowed in confusion.

'I went out to stay at Sarah's house a couple of times, and then that Barbara came out with us, and it caused a big row.' She halted. 'That's why I didn't go to the show at Christmas.'

'But I thought you weren't well . . .'

'I made it up,' Marie told her, taking a sip of her tea. 'I decided after the last time I stayed at her house that I'd never go there again. When we went to the dancing Barbara was horrible to me, making snidy remarks about my hair and clothes, and she kept trying to leave me out of the conversation all the time.'

Heather's eyes narrowed as she remembered how she had felt when she got the same treatment. 'What did Sarah do about it?'

'Nothing. She couldn't seem to see anything wrong in what Barbara said or did.' She paused. 'But she's had her eyes opened . . . she knows now what a big mistake she's made by taking Barbara's side. She came in crying to me the first day we came back after New Year. She said she couldn't believe that she'd been so stupid.'

'What happened?' Heather asked, intrigued now.

Marie looked over her shoulder, checking there was no one listening. 'She'll probably tell you herself if you ever get back speaking again . . . but she doesn't want Danny or any of the lads in the office knowing about it.'

'Knowing about what?'

'That Barbara . . .' Marie whispered, '. . . is *queer*! She got drunk at a New Year's party and made a pass at Sarah – and Sarah nearly died!'

Heather's hands flew to her mouth. 'Oh my God!' she whispered. 'I don't believe it!'

'Well,' Marie said, opening her Kit-Kat biscuit, 'they had a big row, and Barbara told her that she'd deliberately insulted all Sarah's friends so's they could just be together on their own. She told her that she's known she was a lesbian for the last couple of years.' She looked up at Heather now. 'Sarah's really sorry about what's happened between you and her, and she's already said she's sorry to me.'

'So what did you say?' Heather asked, shocked at the news. She'd never have guessed in a million years that Barbara was that way inclined. But then she'd never known anyone who was a lesbian before.

Marie shrugged. 'There's no point in making things worse for her, is there? We've all got to work together and nobody wants to work in a bad atmosphere every day, do they?'

Heather thought for a few moments. She supposed she'd got used to bad atmospheres what with all the rows over Gerry and the big row she'd had with Kirsty. The worst row they'd ever had. 'I suppose not,' she said, giving a little sigh. 'But I've no intention of being *really* good friends with her again, and I definitely won't be going out to stay at her house.'

'I don't blame you,' Marie said, smiling now. 'But I think she's more than paid for her mistake. That Barbara was her oldest friend, and now they're not even talking.' She paused, her head on one side in thought. 'Although there's one thing I will say for Sarah – she's a loyal enough friend. She made me promise not to tell anyone apart from you about Barbara, and she said she's not going to tell anyone herself. She said that Barbara had made a big enough fool of herself trying it on with her, and she didn't want everybody else talking about it. She said that even if she was a lesbian, that she was still a nice person underneath it all.'

Heather took a sip of her coffee now, and mulled the situation over. 'Well,' she said after a while, 'I suppose Sarah can't be that bad if she's prepared to forgive Barbara for all the trouble she's caused and for . . .' She raised her eyebrows. 'And for making such a big mistake as to think Sarah was the same as herself.'

Marie swallowed the last of her Kit-Kat and smiled. 'That's exactly what I thought.'

Muriel Ferguson came across to Heather's desk just before lunchtime to give her a fresh supply of luncheon vouchers. 'I'm glad you're feeling so much better,' she said, giving her an unusually friendly smile. 'And I must say how much I enjoyed meeting your aunt – she's such a lovely refined person.'

'Thank you,' Heather said, putting the vouchers into her handbag. 'And thanks again for looking after me when I wasn't well – it was really good of you.'

'Not at all,' Muriel said, still smiling. 'It was nice to know that we had more things in common than I thought. Your aunt definitely has all the signs of good taste and a good education.' She sighed and waved a hand down towards the area where Danny and Maurice had their desks. 'It helps to know there are other people on the same wavelength as yourself . . . especially when you have to mix with the other kind day in and day out. How they let the lowly working-class types into these white-collar jobs is beyond me.' She leaned forward now, and lowered her voice. 'I'm afraid if you educate certain people beyond their station, you usually end up having to pay the price.'

Heather stifled a smile at Muriel's pompous observations, but managed to nod vaguely and say nothing. It was quite obvious that she had decided that all Heather's family must be tarred with the same wealthy, middle-class brush as Claire and her husband.

At lunchtime Heather rushed to collect her coat and scarf to get out of the office before the others, and then she headed down into the city centre on her own. She really wasn't in the mood for company and she still wasn't quite sure what she was going to do about Sarah. Like the situation with Kirsty, she knew it couldn't go on for ever, but she wasn't ready to hold out the olive branch just yet.

She bought a *Woman's Weekly* magazine from a news-stand outside the Central Station and then she walked the few yards down to The Trees restaurant. As usual it was pretty busy, and she had to queue by the door until a table became vacant. She was just looking at the small menu deciding what to have, when she heard Danny's voice over in the queue.

'That good-looking, dark-haired girl,' she could hear him telling the waitress, 'she won't mind us joining her, because she works in the same office as us.'

A few moments later, Heather had the two lads seated beside her, and after she'd listened to their latest jokes and heard everything that they'd got up to over the weekend, she relaxed and began to enjoy their light-hearted company.

When they'd finished their main course, Maurice went off upstairs to the Gents, leaving Heather and Danny on their own.

'I wanted to ask you something,' Danny said, both his voice and face unusually serious. 'I've been asked to a wedding out in Rutherglen in a fortnight's time, and the invitation is for me and a partner . . .' He paused, then cleared his throat. 'I wondered if you would like to come with me? I'll buy the present and everything, so it won't cost you anything. You just need to come looking your lovely self.'

Heather felt her throat tighten. 'Do you mean me to come as a friend . . . or as a girlfriend?' she asked.

Danny's face suddenly reddened. 'I'd love it if you were

actually my girlfriend ... but then you already know that, Heather, don't you?' He halted. 'Maybe we could go to the wedding and see how we got on after that. What d'you think?'

Heather was silent for a few moments. 'I'm sorry, Danny,' she said, tears suddenly pricking at the back of her eyes, 'but I really don't think I'd be very good company for you the way I am at the minute.' She swallowed hard on the lump that had formed in her throat. 'I think you should ask somebody else ... somebody who would enjoy a nice day out with you.'

Heather felt terrible refusing this lovely, friendly little fellow, but she knew she would only be leading him on by accepting his invitation. She'd already been down that road with Gerry – and she wasn't prepared to go down it again with another lad who she knew really liked her when she wasn't sure herself.

Danny nodded his head and managed a brave smile. 'Och, it was worth a try anyway,' he said, trying to sound light-hearted. 'I've a few girls on my list ... but you were the one at the very top.'

'I'm really sorry,' she whispered. 'But I'm not ready to get friendly with another boy for a while ...' A tear suddenly dropped on the tablecloth and Danny quickly handed her the paper napkin that was by the fourth, unused set of cutlery.

'It's OK, it's OK,' he told her, patting her hand. 'My timin' was never very good with these sorts of things ... but it's not worth gettin' upset about.'

Then, right on cue, Maurice appeared back at the table, and after a wink from Danny he launched straight into the joke they had both planned if his workmate had been given the big knock-back that he had feared from Heather Grace.

Chapter 61

❧❦❧

The following Friday afternoon Lily Grace was discharged from hospital. A small party was organised for her that evening, and all her school friends and neighbours gave a great cheer as they watched her step out of the ambulance and then walk very carefully down the path and into the house on the arms of her mother and father.

The journey back home was only the beginning of another road that would take months going backwards and forwards to the physiotherapy department in the hospital, and daily exercises at home. But as always Lily Grace was determined.

She was already back up on her feet and walking around – albeit painstakingly slowly – and her arms were now strong enough to hold her books and write and draw. It had been a long and difficult journey for everyone involved, but she had been one of the lucky children who had survived the polio scourge and not one of the thousands who had been wiped out by it.

She sat laughing at *Mr Pastry* and then she watched a new game show on the television, then Mona helped her upstairs to get changed into her fancier clothes.

Around seven o'clock aunties and uncles and cousins and one or two neighbours arrived at the house to welcome Lily home for good and she sat up in the corner of the couch, with Whiskey curled up in her lap. She was all dressed up in new jeans and a bright pink jumper that Mona had knitted for her during the cold winter nights when she despaired of her only daughter ever coming home again. She had her curly blonde hair tied up in two pigtails, decorated with pink and white checked ribbons.

Her four brothers hung about the house for a while, and when it started to get a bit crowded Michael and Sean went outside with a cousin to have a look under the bonnet of Pat's car. They stood chatting in the cold, fiddling around with points and plugs to see if they could work out what was causing the rattling noise when the car started.

The younger brothers, Patrick and Declan, went backwards

and forwards with cups of tea and tiny glasses of dark-red, sweet sherry and bottles of beer for the guests, while Mona bustled around with plates of sandwiches and apple tarts and slices of the Christmas cake she had kept especially for this occasion.

Sophie and the girls appeared around half past seven after Heather had got in from work and had eaten and changed into more casual clothes. They came carrying iced buns that Sophie had baked that afternoon and a big cream cake that Kirsty had bought at the baker's shop next door to where she worked.

To all intents and purposes, it looked as though Heather and Kirsty were just the same as always as they laughed and chatted with everyone. Only they knew that they never spoke directly to each other if they could help it, and they never met each other's eyes. Kirsty was very hurt at her sister's attitude to her relationship with Larry, and she couldn't understand it. Apart from the fact there was a bit of an age difference, there wasn't anything else wrong with him.

Kirsty hadn't mentioned the connection between him and Helen McCluskey to Heather – or to anyone. She had decided early on that there wasn't really any point. As Larry had said, David was now living with his mother and the man who was more likely to be his father, so there was no need to dredge that all up. There were bound to be plenty of other men going around who had been accused wrongly of being fathers – and what was the point in advertising it?

Even if Heather had known about David, Kirsty would still have expected her sister to stand by her, to listen to her and to sympathise with her and maybe advise her. But the thing that Kirsty missed most about her sister was sharing the wonderful, exciting bits about Larry with her.

At this delicate stage in the romance – where neither her parents nor her friends knew – Kirsty would have loved to have sat in the kitchen or lain on her bed upstairs chatting with Heather, telling her how it felt when Larry Delaney kissed her and held her and whispered in her ear that he loved her. Instead, she would have to keep all those special things to herself – and that hurt very much.

It hurt that her only sister had distanced herself from her when she needed her most.

There was a great buzz around Mona Grace's house, almost like a birthday party, and it was exactly what Lily needed to bridge the gap between her coming out of the busy hospital to the relative quietness of her home. It also helped to distract her from missing all the friends she'd made in hospital between the nursing staff and the other young patients, the friends she'd made in a dire and adverse situation, the friends who had helped to get her through the dark, early days when the polio was doing its worst.

Heather sat beside her mother and father on the kitchen chairs that had been lined up against the wall, and shortly afterwards Fintan's brother Tommy and his wife Janey from Wishaw brought chairs over to sit next to them. Kirsty sat over on the couch beside Lily and Whiskey and Patrick.

Mona came over to Sophie's group carrying slices of Kirsty's cream cake on side plates, and after dishing them out, she went back to the kitchen to get her own plate to join them.

'Have you all had enough sandwiches and everything?' Mona asked through a mouthful of cream, looking gratified whenever everyone told her that they had. She finished her cake then turned to Heather. 'And are you back to your old self now?'

Heather nodded. 'I'm fine thanks. I went back to work on Monday.' She picked at a few stray crumbs on her plate.

'You haven't been back out to Glasgow since?' Janey Grace suddenly asked. She was one of those small, bland, mousy-haired Scottish women who you would hardly notice most of the time, but who was quite capable of stirring things up – especially when she was coupled with the fiery-tempered Mona. Both women were more ardent in their love of the Catholic Church and in discussing the rudiments of their housework than Sophie was, and when there was a family gathering they tended to gravitate towards each other. Their conversation usually ran along the lines of the health of their respective parish priests and the disgraceful way that certain parish members let the side down.

'Oh, I'm in Glasgow every day at work,' Heather said politely, presuming that Janey wasn't as up to date on the nieces and nephews as other family members were who lived closer.

'I know you work in Glasgow,' Janey said, smiling over at

Sophie. 'I wasn't talkin' about your work, I was referring to you visiting the rich relations out in Giffnock – Claire and the husband.'

Fintan, Pat and Tommy Grace suddenly got up from their chairs and went into the kitchen, and Sophie wasn't sure whether it was a coincidence of timing or whether they didn't want to have any part in the conversation regarding their sister.

Heather looked over and saw her mother's anxious expression, and she knew that Sophie would want her to avoid any conflict with her aunts, especially with it being Lily's special night.

'No,' she said in as light-hearted a manner as she could muster, 'I haven't been back out to see Claire and Andy recently.'

'I'd say you'll be missin' the nuts and the fancy glasses of wine,' Janey said, leaning towards Mona, her tight little face smirking with amusement. 'Just the same way that Andy McPherson must often be missing a good dinner.'

Heather felt her blood run cold. Mona had obviously heard all the details of their visit out at Claire's and repeated it back to Janey with great delight.

Janey looked over at Mona now and shook her head. 'All their posh ways, and she can't even have a dinner on the table for her man comin' in from work!'

'Everyone has their own way of going on,' Heather said, unable to stop herself. 'And I think the way they live is actually very nice. They have a beautiful house and they made us all very welcome, and Claire really looked after me the day I took not well.'

'It's the least she could do,' Mona stated now. 'You're her brother's daughter. You surely don't think she was going to turn you away from the door when you were sick and didn't know anybody else in Glasgow?'

Heather bit down hard on her lip and took a deep breath. She knew perfectly well that nothing she said would make Mona or Janey agree with her, so there was absolutely no point in saying any more.

'I can knit again now,' Lily informed Kirsty, holding up a set of small plastic red needles and a ball of yellow wool that had been one of her rejected Christmas presents a few weeks ago. She had a little basket on the floor beside her filled with different coloured balls of wool.

'So, what are you going to knit?' Kirsty said, shifting Whiskey further along the couch. She lifted up a ball of black wool and placed it beside the yellow one.

'I don't know ...' Lily said, pondering the matter.

'You could always knit yourself a nice scarf,' Kirsty suggested, amusement flickering in her eyes. 'That black and yellow would go lovely together if you did it in stripes.' She started to laugh aloud now. 'You'd look like a lovely big bumble-bee!'

'You cheeky thing!' Lily said, wagging her finger like a teacher at her cousin.

'You're only supposed to say nice things to me tonight – I've decided that if people aren't nice to me all the time, I'll just go back and stay in the hospital.' She giggled away for a few moments, then her face suddenly became serious as she remembered. 'Did you not like Frankie the porter that was on my ward?'

'D'you mean the wee Teddy boy that was goin' out with the dental nurse?' Kirsty teased.

Lily tutted and folded her arms. 'He was really nice – and if you'd been nicer to him and not laughed at him, he might have finished with his girlfriend and started goin' out with you ... and then you could have brought him round here to visit me.' She smiled now. 'You could even have got married to him, and Heather could have been your bridesmaid and I could have been your flower girl.'

Kirsty shook her head and laughed, delighted that Lily was back to her old, devious ways of getting what she wanted. 'You should be a fairy-tale writer,' she told her young cousin, 'because you have the greatest imagination.' She prodded Lily gently on the arm. 'I wouldn't have taken that Frankie in a lucky-bag! And I'd love to have seen what the dental nurse was like – she must have been desperate to take him an' all.'

Lily rolled her eyes to the ceiling and sighed like a world-weary adult. 'I feel sorry for you, Kirsty Grace. You'll end up an oul' maid – for no one will have you the way you go on. You'll definitely never get a boyfriend.'

A male Irish voice suddenly boomed from the doorway that separated the kitchen and living-room. 'What are you talkin' about? Sure she already has a boyfriend!' It was her Uncle Tommy from Wishaw, and he looked as if he had already downed a few bottles of Pat's beer.

Kirsty looked at him, startled – as did her parents and Mona and Pat and Tommy's wife, Janey. She hadn't seen Tommy for ages – what on earth was he rambling on about?

'She not only has a boyfriend,' he said, smiling and nodding round the assembled group, 'she has a boyfriend wi' a big fancy car. Don't you, Kirsty?'

Kirsty shook her head, a sinking feeling suddenly coming to her stomach. 'No,' she said, trying to sound bright and breezy and wishing that everybody else hadn't stopped to listen. 'I'm not going out with anybody at the minute . . .'

'Who d'you think you're kidding?' he beamed, enjoying an audience for his banter. 'Sure, I saw you last Sunday afternoon getting off the bus at Carfin – I was driving the bus, so I couldn't miss you.' He shook his head now, laughing. 'She got off the bus as nice as you like, and there the fella was waitin' for her in his big fancy Wolseley car.' He looked at Fintan. 'Sure the price of that car would buy you a decent house!'

Fintan looked across at Kirsty, his face stiff and white. 'Who was this?' he asked.

Sophie was sitting beside him, looking from her husband to her daughter, not quite sure what was going on.

Kirsty felt her neck and chest burning up. She looked over at her mother. 'That was on Sunday when I was going over to that lassie's house in Carfin that I used to go to school with . . .' To her own ears now, the story sounded feeble.

'Now, don't be tryin' to kid us all!' Tommy went on, oblivious to the mayhem he was causing. 'I saw you with my own eyes, and that was no girl sitting in the car along with you. It was a fella – and no doubts about it! You and the fella were kissin' and cuddlin' in the front seat like a pair of lovebirds.' He shook his head. 'You can't tell me that he wasn't your boyfriend.'

398

Kirsty was so red-faced and stunned that she could do nothing except shake her head.

'And where did you say the car went?' Fintan asked Tommy in a low voice.

'Oh, it went tearin' off in the direction of Motherwell,' Tommy said, exaggerating wildly for effect. He held his hands up and slid one off against the other. 'It went tearin' off like a bullet out of a gun!'

Fintan slowly nodded his head. 'I see,' he said. But Kirsty knew from his tone of voice and the look on his face that it was going to be very hard to make Fintan Grace see anything about this situation at all.

Chapter 62

Kirsty had tried to explain the situation until she was blue in the face, but there was no shifting her father.

'And you can forget all about the singing!' he told her the minute they walked back into their own living-room. 'As far as I'm concerned that man has turned my daughter into a liar and a cheat – and it's to be hoped that that's as far as he's gone.'

'Fintan,' Sophie interrupted, her voice high and strained. 'At least give her a chance to explain—'

'Explain what?' he snapped. 'Do you not realise that your daughter was out all night with that man in a hotel? Do you not realise that she's been seeing him behind our backs for months?'

'Daddy,' Kirsty pleaded in a choked voice, 'I've already told you that nothing happened ... I told you the truth. We had separate rooms in the hotel, and all we did when we were together was talk.' Tears were running down her cheeks now. 'The only thing I didn't tell you was that I went to meet him on Sunday for a couple of hours.' She looked at her mother. 'I was going to see a friend and then I decided that I needed to see Larry ... I felt we needed to talk about everything.'

'And where did you go?' Fintan demanded. Sophie came

across the room to hold onto her husband's arm – half-comforting him and half-holding back his temper against their daughter.

There was a silence as Kirsty came to the conclusion that the only way out of this was to tell the truth. Or as much of the truth as she felt her father could take.

'We went for a run to Motherwell . . . and I asked him if I could see where he lived.'

Fintan gave a deep shuddering sigh. 'Are you that stupid, Kirsty?' he said, shaking his head in disbelief. 'The man's only after what he can get from a young, innocent girl.'

'He's not!' Kirsty almost screamed. 'He never laid a hand on me . . . and it was me that admitted I had feelings for him first.' She dug into her skirt pocket for her hanky to dab at her eyes. 'He thought it could never work between us. I've liked him for months.'

'It's true, Daddy,' Heather suddenly said from the doorway. She looked anxiously from her sister to her father. 'Kirsty told me all about liking him weeks ago . . . she came in one night all upset because he'd told her that he didn't want anything to do with her. He told her that she was too young and he didn't want her to be hanging around after an older man.'

Kirsty felt a little wave of relief at Heather standing up for her.

'Well, if that's true, what made him change his mind?' Fintan demanded.

'Well,' Kirsty said, swallowing back her tears, 'I tried to forget all about him, but when we got stranded up at the hotel last week . . . we got closer. We sat talking for hours.'

'And?' Fintan demanded.

'And we both realised that we really loved each other . . .'

'Loved?' Fintan repeated. 'Loved? You don't know the meaning of the word – you're only a girl, for God's sake. All he's interested in is getting you into bed, and you're so naive and stupid you can't see it.'

'For God's sake, Fintan!' Sophie said now. 'Will you give her a chance? She's told you what happened—'

'She hasn't told us *half* of what's happened . . .' he said in a broken voice. He went over to the armchair by the fire now and sank down into it, his head between his hands.

'Daddy,' Kirsty said, coming over to kneel by the side of his chair, 'I swear to God I haven't done anything wrong ... and apart from the age difference, there's no reason why me and Larry Delaney couldn't be together. He's Irish like yourself, and he was brought up as a Catholic ... he's got a lovely house and he's done very well for himself. A lot of fathers would be delighted for their daughter to meet a man like that.'

A silence fell on the room, where all three women looked across at each other and waited.

Eventually, Fintan Grace lifted his head. 'From tonight onwards,' he said, 'I want you to account for every move you make, and when you come in from work in the chemist's shop I don't want you to move outside this house.'

'But my singing ...' Kirsty whispered, thinking of the bookings she had this coming weekend and the weekends after. Thinking about Liz Mullen's wedding and the other people she would be letting down. Thinking of all the great plans that Larry had for her to become a top cabaret singer.

'You can forget the singing,' he told her, his face white and grim. 'And you can forget all about Larry Delaney.'

'I can't forget him,' Kirsty told him, her voice cracking.

'In that case,' Fintan said, looking her straight in the eye, 'you may walk out that door now and forget all about us.'

Chapter 63

After she had phoned Larry Delaney and told him that she could never see him again, Kirsty had just withdrawn into herself. She spent the evenings up in their room listening to her radio or she went across to Mona's to sit with Lily or watch television with her cousins. She had never spoken another word about what had happened and she had only had the most perfunctory conversations with anyone in the house.

Sophie was worried sick, and torn between Kirsty and Fintan. In all the years she'd known him, he had never taken such a stance over anything. And while Sophie knew that he had fairly strict views on religion and had insisted that the girls give it its proper place in their lives, he had still been a reasonable and open man.

And she was very worried about Kirsty. She was neither up nor down – her mood could only be described as completely flat. She was just going through the motions of living every day, but not really taking part. It was as though she had put her life on hold – as though she were waiting for something.

When Heather had had the awful upset over Gerry Stewart back in the New Year that had been bad enough. But at least her reaction had been fairly normal, and she was gradually getting back to her old self. But this with Kirsty was different, and Sophie instinctively knew that things weren't going to go back to the way they were. Something was going to have to give one way or another and Sophie had no idea what would make that happen.

She decided to leave them to it for the time being, and retreated upstairs to hide behind her mountain of sewing.

Heather felt equally awkward and decided she needed to talk over the situation with somebody – but there wasn't a single person she could think of that she could talk to about it. She had called up to Liz's house over the weekend, but Liz had only wanted to talk about Jim and how depressed he still was about what had happened to Gerry. The wedding had been put back until March, since there wasn't such a rush on it, and it would give them and their families more time to save up.

Although Heather would have loved to have talked the whole thing out about Kirsty and Larry, she knew that Liz might use the situation to hurt Kirsty in the future if it suited her. And Heather wasn't going to take that chance. She might not agree with what Kirsty was doing and she might not like Larry Delaney, but Kirsty was still her sister, and she didn't want anybody else hurting her.

One Wednesday, during her lunch break, Heather suddenly decided that she would phone her Auntie Claire and ask if she could come out at the weekend.

'That would be just perfect,' Claire told her, 'and it would be company for me because Andy's got some kind of conference on Friday and Saturday night in Edinburgh and he's staying over.' She'd halted. 'He doesn't like leaving me, with this fellow still on the loose.'

'It's the same out in Lanarkshire,' Heather had told her, 'all the shops are sold out of padlocks and chains, and all the women are too scared to go out at night on our own.'

'Well, Andy has plenty of locks on all our doors and windows,' Claire told her. 'So we needn't worry too much about it.' Then she'd asked, 'Would Kirsty like to come out as well? Has she got anything else on at the weekend?'

'No,' Heather said in a low voice. 'But I don't think she'll want to come . . . she's not feeling very sociable at the moment.'

Kirsty had only shrugged when Heather told her that she was going to stay in Glasgow the following weekend.

'Claire said you're welcome to come as well,' Heather ventured, when she went upstairs to find her sister lying on the bed staring up at the ceiling, the radio on low in the background.

Kirsty turned to look at her with dark-ringed eyes. 'I don't think so . . . and anyway, I'm sure my daddy wouldn't believe where I was. He'd probably turn up at Claire's house to check if I was really there.'

Heather paused. 'Are you all right, Kirsty?'

'What do you care?' Kirsty asked in a flat voice. She moved her gaze back to the ceiling. 'You're every bit as bad as my daddy . . . you never gave Larry a chance. You wouldn't even listen when I was trying to tell you all about him.'

'I'm sorry,' Heather said now. 'I wish I had listened properly . . . I wasn't feeling too good and I—'

'Don't bother,' Kirsty said, closing her eyes, shutting out her sister and shutting out the rest of the world. 'It's too late now.'

Chapter 64

Heather had been very grateful to get the train out to Giffnock on the Friday evening. She was glad of the chance to escape from home, and she also felt that Kirsty would be glad to have the bedroom all to herself.

It was a pity that this thing had happened with Kirsty, because everything else had started to look up a little bit. Lily was now home and improving every day and Liz was feeling and looking much better after her miscarriage. Heather felt that she, too, was finally getting back to her old self.

She had lain awake on numerous nights going over and over the situation about Gerry until she eventually realised that there were no answers to it all. However she thought about it and analysed it, there was nothing different she could have done about it. The bottom line was that she didn't love him and he just couldn't accept it. It was not her fault, and she now knew it.

In the same way, she had realised that she couldn't get involved with Danny in the office. Thankfully, he hadn't taken it at all badly, and had asked Marie to accompany him to the wedding instead. And things had improved with Sarah as well. When she heard the full story about Barbara, Heather had felt quite sorry for her workmate, and had made a point of joining her and Marie at the tea break the following day. Gradually, they had got back to their old way of working, and when Sarah insisted on apologising properly for the way the weekend out at her house had gone, Heather accepted it graciously.

Later in the week Sarah had brought her mum's knitting pattern for Heather to borrow, and had suggested that they might try another weekend together.

'Some time,' Heather had agreed. 'Maybe in the spring when the days are a bit longer – and after the murderer has been caught.' It had been weeks since it happened, but the story still dominated the newspapers and the radio news.

Although the other difficulties that Heather had experienced were now fading away, she felt very bad about Kirsty, and annoyed that it had all happened at the same time. Heather just hadn't been in the right frame of mind when Kirsty came home walking on air after spending the night with Larry Delaney. She regretted judging the situation so quickly and harshly and would do anything she could to repair it. But she knew, as Kirsty had said, that it was all too late. The situation had been taken out of her hands.

Claire was waiting for her at the station as arranged, waving profusely and excited in the way a young girl Heather's own age would be, with her perfectly bobbed hair bouncing up and down.

'Oh, you look so much better!' Claire said, examining her niece closely. 'Your eyes are much brighter and your cheeks have a lovely healthy glow.' She put her arm through Heather's then and said, 'We're going to have a great weekend, I've planned lots of nice things for us to do, starting with a meal out tonight at a lovely little local hotel.'

They walked along to Claire's Morris Minor and as they drove out towards the house, Heather thought how lovely it would be to live in a big city and just catch a train or a bus that would have you in the city centre in much less time than it took her to travel from Rowanhill.

Although she tried to avoid talking about it, later that night as they sat in the restaurant that Claire had booked for them, Heather found herself pouring out the whole story about Kirsty and her father.

'Oh, no!' Claire said, pressing the napkin to her mouth. 'I can't bear the thought of all this bitterness in the family. We've gone through enough bitterness in the Grace family – and it just shouldn't be happening all over again.'

Chapter 65

❧

Kirsty had forced down as much of her Sunday lunch as she could physically manage, and Sophie had said nothing as she scraped the leftover roast potatoes and chicken into the bin. It had been ten days since she last saw Larry and it felt like a lifetime away. There were times when she was even finding it difficult to remember what his face looked like or how his voice sounded.

She had spent a lot of the time up in her bedroom going over and over what had happened and wondering how she could have handled it better. She had only discovered Larry's feelings for her the night they were stranded and she couldn't possibly have told her father that the very next day. He had immediately been suspicious of the situation, and she had felt it best to give it all a bit of time to settle down before confessing that there was indeed a romance between her and Larry.

But of course she hadn't been patient enough ... she'd had to jump the gun and phone him and rush things on. Rush things on so quickly that she now couldn't see him at all. And if they waited to see how things worked out – as Larry was now suggesting – they might never see each other again. He would probably meet somebody else more suitable in the meantime, somebody nearer his own age.

Somebody like those glamorous McCluskey women.

There were always women around like that, desperate to get their clutches into someone like Larry Delaney. And somebody like Kirsty Grace would never be able to compete. As she lay back on her bed, she wondered for the hundredth time if there was any point in going down to speak to her father again. To try to make him understand things. So far she had followed her mother's advice and just let things lie for a while. But it looked as though it was going to lie for ever.

The doorbell sounded and when it went for the second time, Sophie called along the hallway from her sewing-room for Kirsty to answer it. Fintan had obviously gone out somewhere.

She moved from the bed and went downstairs, and as she walked along the hallway she could see, through the glass panel in the door, a figure in a red coat moving from side to side. For a moment she thought it was a child – as it was the kind of hopping, jittery movement that children made – then she realised it was too tall for a child.

When she opened the door she was both surprised and shocked to see Liz Mullen standing there with a letter in her hand and tears streaming unchecked down her face.

'Is Heather in?' she asked in a shaky voice, her face red and puffy from crying.

'No,' Kirsty said, opening the door wide. 'She's gone to Glasgow for the weekend ... she won't be back until tomorrow.'

If it was possible, Liz's face looked even more miserable at the news.

Kirsty stared at her now, not quite knowing what to say or do. 'As far as I know, she's staying at our auntie's, and then going straight into work tomorrow morning.' She wasn't quite sure as she hadn't paid any attention to Heather when she'd been telling their mother the arrangements. Kirsty stepped back now. 'Come on in, Liz,' she said kindly. 'You look as though you could do with a cup of tea or something ...'

Liz glanced back over her shoulder, checking there was no one else around. 'I'm nearly out of my mind ...' she whispered. 'Jim's gone – and he's not coming back.' She would have by far preferred to divulge all this to Heather, but since she wasn't there, she decided to take a chance on Kirsty. She couldn't face going back home straightaway, as she had felt she desperately needed to get out of the house.

'Gone where?' Kirsty said in a shocked voice, moving closer to her.

Liz held out the letter. 'I got it this morning. He must have pushed it through the door when we were all in bed last night.' She gave a little cough to clear her throat. 'You can read it for yourself. It says everything in it.'

'Come into the kitchen, it's freezing standing here,' Kirsty said, ushering her in and closing the door behind her.

Dear Liz, Kirsty read, sitting opposite Liz at the kitchen table.

By the time you read this I'll be a long way from Rowanhill. I was never sure about getting married, and I was only doing it because you were expecting. But now there's no baby, I think getting married would definitely be the wrong thing for me to do. Since Gerry died I've been thinking a lot, and I realise that we've only got one life to live and we don't know when that will end. It could be today or tomorrow – none of us knows. If Gerry had gone to Australia, I'd always planned on following him later, but now that will never happen. He's gone and he's never coming back.

If we'd got married and Gerry had stuck with Heather, things might have worked out here. The idea of getting married didn't seem as bad when there was the four of us. We could have all gone out together and got houses near each other and still all kept pals. But now Gerry's gone, it's all different.

I know getting married to you or any other girl at this time would be a big, big mistake. I've decided I'm going to go out to Australia on my own and start a brand-new life. Gerry's uncle has offered to give me the start he was going to give him.

I'm going to London for a bit until it's all organised then I'll go straight out. I won't be back home in between, as I think it's the best way.

I'm very sorry for hurting you like this, but better now than in a few years' time when we have a family.

I hope you find somebody else who is more suited to you,
Jim

Kirsty put the letter down on the table and shook her head. 'Oh, Liz,' she said, her own eyes filling up with tears, 'I'm so, so sorry . . .'

Liz nodded, grateful for Kirsty's sympathy. 'My mammy says she's delighted, she says it would never have worked . . . she said Jim wasn't dependable, and that I was the one that always did the running.'

'I don't know what to say to you,' Kirsty reached across the table and squeezed Liz's hand, 'because I know you really loved him. I'm not going to say the same things that your mother has said because I know it won't help you. You loved him and that's the only thing that matters to you.' And then, because she wanted to make this sad girl feel a bit better and because she needed to talk about it with somebody else, she suddenly blurted out, 'You're not going to believe it … but I'm in a similar position myself. I'm in love with a man, and I've lost him too.'

Liz looked up at Kirsty now, not sure if she was hearing right or whether Kirsty might even be joking. They had a very different sense of humour at times. 'Are you being serious?' she checked in a strained voce.

'Yes I am,' Kirsty told her. 'I'm being very serious.' Then she poured out the whole story about the romance between herself and Larry and all the trouble it had caused. Liz had sat open-mouthed, unable to believe that the skittish Kirsty, who was always teasing her about running after Jim, was sitting there telling her how she was madly in love with an older man.

Later, when they'd drunk two cups of strong tea and sympathised greatly with each other, Kirsty put her coat on and called upstairs to her mother that she was going to walk back up to Liz's house with her. She was glad that Sophie had stayed upstairs and that her father hadn't walked in on Liz breaking her heart over Jim. If they had been all understanding and sympathetic with Heather's friend, Kirsty would have had to walk out, because Fintan had certainly shown no sympathy where his own daughter was concerned. In fact, he had never appeared less understanding in the whole of his life.

The girls walked slowly, talking in low whispers all the way, and then they stood outside Liz's door, talking some more until they were both starting to get stiff from the chilled winter air.

'You better go,' Liz said. 'It's going to be dark soon, and you can't take a chance on being out on your own.'

'Aye, you're right,' Kirsty said. 'I wish they'd catch that blidey nuisance – you can't walk the streets at night now without bein' afraid of your life.'

'They're supposed to have brought somebody in for questioning,' Liz paused. 'You'll let Heather know,' she said, 'won't you? I'll need her more now that Jim's …' She stopped abruptly now, trying not to break down again.

Kirsty nodded. Even though she and Heather weren't great

friends now, she wouldn't leave Liz in the lurch. 'I might even give her a quick ring from the phone box on my way home. I think I have my auntie's number in my purse somewhere.' She had copied it down on a slip of paper the time she and her father went out to Claire's when Heather had fainted.

She looked at Liz now, and knew that however bad she was feeling herself, poor Liz's life was completely shattered. One minute she had a wedding and a baby to look forward to – and the next minute she didn't even have a boyfriend.

'Maybe when you're feeling a wee bit better we might have a night out ... Maybe just the pictures or something quiet like that?'

Liz gave a deep sigh. 'The way I'm feelin' I don't think I'll ever want to go out socially again. But thanks, Kirsty, you've been a big help.' She managed a terse little smile. 'I've known you for years – but I didn't know you could be so nice.'

The compliment almost took Kirsty's breath away, because the implication behind it was that she wasn't always nice to people. But today wasn't the day to start heaping more problems onto her already troubled mind.

Kirsty went into the phone box with the slip of paper with Claire's number written on it. She had her four pennies all ready, but when she dialled the number it was engaged. She waited and tried again but it was still engaged. She looked out of the grimy phone-box window at the darkening sky. She'd go home now and tell her mother what had happened and maybe in an hour or two they might both walk up and try phoning Claire's number again.

Then, just as she had her hand on the phone-box door to push it open, she suddenly halted. She turned back to the phone and before she could stop herself she had dialled Larry Delaney's number.

After only two rings he picked up the phone and at the sound of his voice Kirsty felt herself shaking so badly that she had difficulty pressing in the coins, fumbling and almost dropping them. Eventually the money went in, the pips stopped and the line became clear.

'It's Kirsty,' she said in a breathless voice. 'I was in the phone box and I—'

'Are you all right?' he cut across. 'I've been worried sick about you.'

'I'm OK,' she said, not sounding OK at all. 'I've missed you like mad.'

'And I've missed you, darling,' he told her. 'But I've been busy sorting things out – trying to make things easier for us to be together when it's all settled down.'

Her heart lifted at his faith in the fact that they would be together at some point. 'What do you mean?'

'About David,' he said. 'I've been out to see Helen and the fellow she's with, and they were going to see a lawyer this week to have something official signed to state that he is actually David's father.'

Kirsty caught her breath. 'How do you feel about it?'

'I've very mixed feelings,' he told her, his voice sounding weary now. 'But it couldn't go on the way it was … and although I love him, I think I always knew deep down that he wasn't mine. As I said before, it's better for him to be part of a real family with both his mother and father. That would never have happened with me and Helen.' There was a pause on the line. 'It means that there's one less thing for us to worry about with your family.'

'My father's been terrible,' Kirsty said now. 'We've hardly spoken all week. He's still convinced that you deliberately organised us to be in the hotel for the night together, and he won't believe that nothing happened in your flat when we were there together.'

Larry gave a big sigh. 'I wish you'd agree to me coming out to see him and explain the whole situation properly to him – man to man.'

'He won't listen, Larry. He wouldn't let you in the door.'

'But he needs to know that we were telling the truth about that night in the hotel. He needs to know that nothing *did* happen – and I would never have let it.'

'Well, it was me who wanted to go further,' Kirsty said.

'And you'll never know how much I wanted to make love to you,' Larry told her, his voice hoarse with emotion. 'But the fact is we *didn't*. But it was very unfortunate the way it all looked. I can actually see why your father is angry, and I would never have put us in that position if I'd known how it would turn out.' He halted. 'I was just trying to give us a bit of time on our own to make sure you really knew what you were getting into. I wanted you to know all about my background – I didn't want you to be under any illusions about me. I didn't want you to think I was somebody I wasn't.'

'After these few months together,' Kirsty told him, 'I know everything I need to know about you. I know enough to know I don't want anybody else.'

'Good,' he said in a low, gentle voice. 'That's all that matters.' The line was silent again for a few moments. 'Don't worry about anything, Kirsty,' he told her. 'It's all going to be sorted soon.'

'But how?' she asked. 'How can this be sorted?'

'I'll find a way ... I promise.'

Chapter 66

Heather had really enjoyed her weekend out at the McPhersons' house. Claire had planned everything down to the last minute, and it had taken her mind off all the things that had recently happened back in Rowanhill.

She loved everything about her aunt's house. She'd loved sleeping in the comfortable big double bed with the electric blanket, she loved all the vases with the fresh flowers and the fancy little ornaments and she loved all the unusual meals that Claire had cooked for her. She'd really enjoyed the meal they had out in the hotel on the Friday night, and then all the different but interesting things they'd done over the weekend.

On the Saturday morning after a breakfast of crispy rolls and bacon, they'd driven into Glasgow around eleven o'clock and spent the rest of the day shopping. They went into Lewis's department store where there were still loads of things left in the January sales. Claire had been very generous and bought

Heather a lovely grey tweed skirt with a matching grey sweater and made her pick a similar outfit in blue for Kirsty. Claire had brushed away Heather's offer of paying for them herself. 'They're less than half-price,' Claire had said, 'and anyway, I owe you and Kirsty a few presents for all those times I didn't see you.'

Later, when they were in the tea-room having a hot drink and a cake, Claire came back to the same subject. 'I feel I'll be trying to make it up to you and Kirsty for the next few years.' She stretched across the small table and rubbed Heather's arm affectionately. 'I'm really glad your father and Pat had the sense to forget all the differences we had, and I wish Mona would do the same thing.'

'She's always been awkward,' Heather said, lifting her teacup. 'She never seems happy unless she's something to snipe and moan about.' She gave a little giggle. 'My mammy says she's well named – *Moan-a*.'

Her aunt nodded but didn't smile. The wound between herself and Mona was too deep for that. 'I'll never forgive her if she stops me seeing Lily again,' she stated. 'Because that wee girl will grow up thinking I didn't care about her, when I think the world of her.' She sighed. 'And this is all because I married an older man who was a different religion. Surely people should realise that we can't choose who we fall in love with? And what does it matter what a grown adult chooses to do if it's not actually hurting anybody else?'

She looked straight at Heather now, her green eyes piercing and direct. 'Mona Grace is no angel, you know. She's not always followed the rules of the Catholic Church. In fact, she's the last one who should be throwing stones at anybody – but people are too afraid of her to speak out.'

'What do you mean?' Heather asked, intrigued now. Surely her sanctimonious Auntie Mona had nothing to hide?

'Look,' Claire said, putting her empty cup back into her saucer, 'if I were to start gossiping about Mona for the sake of it, it would make me just as bad as her. If people would just get on with their own lives and let others get on with theirs, we wouldn't have all this animosity.'

Heather felt a real pang of guilt when her aunt made the

statement, because she knew she had caused some of the animosity in her own family. She had been horrible to Kirsty about Larry Delaney, and she knew her sister was right. She hadn't got to know him. She hadn't even given him a chance.

When they came back from the shops Claire made a lovely meal with quiche and salad and chips and a glass of cold white wine, and then they had a homemade chocolate pudding to follow. They spent the rest of the evening watching television and reading fashion magazines and drinking coffee, and then Claire went into the kitchen to start preparing beef goulash for dinner the following day.

When she was on her own, Heather found her mind kept flitting back to Kirsty, and she wished they had a phone in the house, because she would have felt better if she could have phoned her and checked how she was.

Sunday was equally nice. They got up around nine o'clock and had a lovely cooked breakfast of bacon, sausages, black puddings and fried eggs, while still wearing their pyjamas and dressing-gowns. Heather wished that Mona could have seen them so easy and relaxed, sitting at the kitchen table, chatting and at times singing along with the radio. Heather felt every bit as relaxed as she would have done in her own house, and there was no way that anyone could have accused Claire of acting uppity or over-formal.

'Since you cooked all this, it's only fair that I should wash the dishes,' Heather offered as she gathered the plates and cups.

Claire checked her watch. 'We're not going to get time to get showered and dressed and do the dishes before we go out. Let's just stack them in the sink and leave them until we come back.'

'Where are we going?' Heather asked, collecting the knives and forks.

'Mass at the Cathedral – I thought you might like to go there for a change.'

'I didn't realise you went to Mass,' Heather said, suddenly feeling herself start to blush. She had already talked with her mother about the situation of Mass when she was at Claire's, and

Sophie had said not to mention it as it might make Claire feel awkward. She said quietly, and out of Fintan's earshot, that missing church for one week wouldn't be the end of the world.

'I go most Sundays,' Claire said smiling. 'And Andy often comes with me as well.' She lifted the butter dish to put back in the fridge. 'We've met a nice priest who's sympathetic to mixed marriages and we're hoping to have our marriage blessed some time.'

Heather's eyebrows shot up. 'I didn't realise ... I thought you'd completely left the Church.'

'I may have left the church in Rowanhill,' Claire said, 'but I never left the Church completely. It was just the way things happened when Andy and I wanted to get married. None of the Catholic churches around were prepared to do the service for us, so we went ahead and got married in a register office.'

'I don't think my daddy or anybody knows that,' Heather said, 'and I'm sure Mona doesn't think that.'

'Nobody asked,' Claire told her. 'The minute they heard that Andy wasn't a Catholic they just turned their back on me – they weren't interested in the details.'

'Will you tell them when you get the blessing?'

Claire shrugged and gave a wry little smile. 'I don't know ... if they couldn't accept me marrying him before, I don't know if I want them to accept him now just because the Church recognises our marriage and he attends Sunday Mass with me. Andy McPherson is the same man now as he was when they first met him.'

After Mass they drove out to a huge art gallery on the outskirts of Glasgow where they spent a few hours, and then they came back in time for Claire to finish preparing an evening meal for Andy's return.

The phone was ringing as they came in the door and Claire rushed to answer it. She chatted for a few moments then came back into the kitchen where Heather had started the washing-up.

'That was Andy,' she said, her face beaming. 'He's just leaving Edinburgh now and he said we have an extra two for dinner. He's bringing two men out who are staying the night in

Glasgow. Apparently the company have booked them into a hotel and it doesn't do an evening meal.'

Heather looked startled. 'Do you mind? Will you have time to get it all ready?'

'It's fine,' Claire said, 'and it's already half-made. I usually cook enough meat to last us two days, so the two men can have Monday's dinner. I don't like wasting time cooking when Andy's just arrived home so I do it in advance. I like to be able to sit down and have a drink and a chat with him when he gets in, so's we can catch up on what we've both been up to.' She went over to a large casserole dish on top of the cooker. 'The beef is cooked from last night, so I just have to make the sauce and do the vegetables.'

'Do you want me to help with anything?' Heather asked.

Claire thought for a minute. 'You could cut me up some fresh fruit if you don't mind, and then I'll get you to beat me up some egg whites to make up meringues. We'll put them all together with fresh cream and it'll make a nice dessert.' She pursed her lips together, thinking. 'Oh, I've got a fresh apple tart in the cupboard as well, so I think we've got plenty of everything.'

Two hours later the dining-table at the end of the long sitting-room was all set with the best cutlery and china, and Heather had put linen napkins at each place along with Claire's best crystal wine glasses. The casserole and vegetables were keeping hot in the oven, and there was a bottle of Italian red wine in the middle of the table and a chilled bottle of German white. Heather stood back to admire her handiwork, thinking with some satisfaction that she would now know how to set a table properly, and she would be able to make a beef casserole and a fancy meringue dessert if she ever had to host a meal. Not that she could imagine those skills being called for in the foreseeable future. Claire looked at her watch, checking how much time they had before Andy and the others arrived. 'I think we can treat ourselves to a glass of wine now, after all that hard work,' she said, taking the bottle of wine they had opened last night out of the fridge. 'And it might just help us to think of some scintillating conversation when we have Andy's two work colleagues.'

Heather laughed. 'I don't think you'd ever get stuck for conversation, Claire. I think you could talk to anybody. You're the most confident person I've ever met.'

'They always say the Irish have the gift of the gab,' Claire said, pouring wine into two of her more ordinary wine glasses. 'But the confidence is something I've learned over the years – and there are still plenty of occasions where I look more confident than I actually feel.' She handed Heather a glass, lifted her own and said 'cheers', and then took a sip of the delicious cold wine.

'How do you do it?' Heather asked in amazement. 'I'd love to always look confident at work and in all different kinds of situations . . . but I'm useless at pretending. How I feel is usually stamped all over my embarrassed face.' She sipped at her wine, finding she was getting used to the taste and was enjoying it more.

'The trick is to just keep calm and smile,' Claire told her, jokily demonstrating a sophisticated little smile. 'And to say absolutely nothing until you're sure of your ground.'

'When I get embarrassed,' Heather said, 'I just end up saying the first stupid thing that comes into my head . . .'

'Well, next time it happens,' Claire told her, 'just make sure you keep calm and smile!'

Then they both shouted out together 'and say nothing!' Then they both went into giggles of laughter.

'There's another little tip I should tell you,' Claire said, as they stood chatting. 'Always take the time to put on a little bit of mascara and some lipstick if you're going to be in a situation where people might be looking at you. It helps you to feel more confident, and it just gives you that little edge.' She shook her head. 'It would amaze you the number of women who don't make the effort to look their best, when a few minutes makes all the difference.'

Heather took a drink of her wine. 'Well, I'm going to take your advice right now,' she said, 'and put on a little bit of make-up, because I'm absolutely terrified at the thought of having dinner with Andy and the other two businessmen.'

'Oh, don't be silly!' Claire said. 'I was talking about when you were in a work situation or something like that – you look lovely as you are already. I wasn't suggesting that you needed to do anything to improve yourself now.'

'I know that,' Heather said, smiling back at her. 'But since we have a few minutes to spare I think I'll just go and tidy myself up a little bit.'

She went into the bedroom and on an impulse changed from her plain black skirt and cream blouse into the new skirt and soft grey sweater that Claire had bought her yesterday. She sat in front of the mirror and brushed out her glossy chestnut hair then put on a light coat of foundation, some brown mascara and a slick of lipstick. She studied herself for a few seconds, then she went back into her little make-up bag and took out an eye-shadow palette and brushed her eyelids over with a light bronze powder that she knew would really emphasise the hazel-brown of her eyes.

'You look great!' Claire told her when she went back into the kitchen. 'The colours make you look all warm and soft – very feminine.'

Just at that, the doorbell sounded and Andy's key could be heard turning in the lock, followed by the sound of men's laughter. As Claire rushed out from the kitchen and down the hallway to meet them, Heather finished the last couple of mouthfuls of her wine. Then, she took a deep breath and hoped that she would remember to smile and stay calm if she felt overwhelmed in the strange company of these mature business-men.

She could hear Claire chatting away to them in the hallway, and then she could hear her showing them into the sitting-room. Heather stood still in the kitchen now, wondering whether she should go and meet them or whether she should wait until somebody came for her. She decided to wait.

A few moments later she heard Claire's heels tapping towards the kitchen. 'Heather,' she called, 'you must come and meet everyone.'

Heather followed her aunt back into the sitting-room, where the two guests were politely on their feet waiting to be introduced. Feeling self-conscious amongst all the strangers –

because she hardly knew Andy that well – she kept her gaze lowered and was only aware of an immediate impression of typical businessmen: formal dark suits with white shirts and sober ties.

'Hello, Heather!' Andy said in a very hearty manner, a welcoming smile on his face. He motioned to the shorter of the two men, a pleasant-looking, sandy-haired man in his fifties who immediately came forward with his hand outstretched. 'This is Tony Ballantyne.'

'Delighted to meet you, Heather,' he said. 'You're Andy's niece, I believe?'

'Actually, she's Claire's niece,' Andy told him, then guided her over towards the younger man. 'And this is Tony's son – Paul Ballantyne.' Jokingly, he tapped his finger on the side of his nose. 'A great asset to his father's business.'

Ballantyne – Heather instinctively reacted to the name. They were obviously not Catholics with such a Scottish-sounding name. Too many years of hearing people like Mona analysing the Irish Catholics and Scots Protestants had obviously left their mark. She lifted her gaze and found herself looking at piercing blue eyes and probably the most handsome boy she had ever seen. His smiling, cheery face was topped by a thick but well-cut head of fair hair.

For just a second their eyes met and she suddenly felt all flustered and tongue-tied. She managed a vague smile, hoping that she looked calm and serene – the way that Claire had advised her. She glanced over to where Claire was standing, then realised her aunt had gone back into the kitchen.

'Hello, Heather,' Paul said, taking her hand and shaking it. His handshake felt warm and confidently firm for a young man. 'I'm pleased to meet you.'

'Hello,' she said, making herself look up at the deep blue eyes again. 'I'm pleased to meet you, too.'

Their gaze met fleetingly once again, but in that short time Heather felt a breathless, fluttery sensation in her chest and she had to quickly turn away.

'Well now!' Andy said, clapping his hands and rubbing them together. 'Let's get you all settled down and I'll bring everyone a drink. We deserve it after the work we've done over this weekend. Tony – whiskey and water?'

'Perfect!' Tony Ballantyne said, sitting down in one of the armchairs.

'Paul – beer or wine?' Andy asked.

'A glass of beer would be great,' Paul said, sitting down on the end of the sofa.

'Heather!' Andy suddenly said. 'My apologies, dear – I should have asked you. Ladies first and all that.'

'I'm OK, actually . . .' Heather said, moving out towards the hallway. 'I'll just go into the kitchen now and see if Claire needs a hand.' And as she turned away, she was acutely conscious of Paul Ballantyne's eyes on her.

'Go back in and chat to them,' Claire told her in the kitchen. 'Everything's under control here.'

'Oh, no,' Heather whispered. 'I couldn't . . . not with three businessmen. I wouldn't know what to say to them.'

Claire looked at her, her eyebrows raised in surprise. 'But the younger one – Paul – must be around the same age as yourself.'

Heather took a deep breath. 'I couldn't . . .' she repeated. 'I'd rather just stay here until we're taking the food through.'

'OK,' Claire said, nodding understandingly. 'You can take that dish of roast potatoes and put it on the mats in the centre of the table, because they'll probably need a few minutes to cool. And you'll find serving spoons in the top drawer of the sideboard. I think four will probably be enough.'

'Thanks, Claire, I feel better doing something.' Heather said, lifting the dish. For a split second she wished she was like Kirsty. Chatting to the three men wouldn't have bothered her in the slightest, and she probably would have been in there in the middle of them now, finding everything out about the good-looking Paul Ballantyne.

She walked back through to the sitting-room, trying to look relaxed and confident, which she certainly didn't feel, only to find it silent and empty. Then she heard voices coming from the front door, and she could hear Tony Ballantyne asking about a building away in the distance. The high-up aspect of the house gave a good view of the surrounding area.

Heather put the dish of potatoes on the table and then went over to the sideboard to get the spoons.

'It's a lovely house, isn't it?'

She turned around to find Paul Ballantyne standing casually at the sitting-room door, glass of beer in hand. The fluttery feeling started in her chest again. 'Aye,' she said, 'it's really lovely . . .'

'Where d'you live yourself?' he asked, coming across the room towards her.

'Out near Motherwell,' she said, 'in a wee village called Rowanhill.' She looked at him now, thinking that he really was a fine-looking fellow – and completely the opposite in looks to Gerry Stewart. Where Gerry had been of medium height and stocky, Paul Ballantyne was taller and slimmer, and of course fair-headed as opposed to dark.

He nodded, smiling straight at her. 'I've been through there a few times. It's near Wishaw and Cleland, isn't it?'

'That's right,' Heather said, thinking that he would know immediately that she didn't live in a big fancy house like this. He would know that the houses in Rowanhill were mainly very plain houses, two or four to a block. She turned back to the sideboard now, looking for the serving spoons, and sure she could feel his eyes still on her.

He put his glass on the table then pulled out the carver chair at the top of the table, and sat down. 'Do you come into Glasgow often?'

'I don't come out to this part that often,' she said, 'but I work in an office in the city centre, so I'm in every day.' She found the spoons and went back to the table to place them in the centre.

'Who do you work for?' he said, sounding very interested.

Heather explained all about Seafreight and the work she did in the office, then he asked where exactly the office was, as he only really knew the Central Station and Queen Street Station and the main shopping areas.

'What about at night?' he asked. 'Do you come in for the dancing or the picures or shows or anything?'

'Occasionally,' she hedged, wondering if the Christmas meal out with her office counted, because apart from that, she had only been in the once for the show with Sarah. 'I came in just after Christmas and stayed the night with a friend out in Govanhill.' She halted. 'You have to be careful travelling in and out on trains now with that fella still on the loose.'

Heather felt herself beginning to relax a little more now. Although he was handsome, he was actually quite easy to talk to, especially for someone who obviously had an important job. In fact, his manner was so down-to-earth she was sure that if she had met him in her office or somewhere ordinary like that, she wouldn't have felt at all intimidated by him.

Paul Ballantyne nodded. 'We live up in Edinburgh, and although there's been no evidence of the same man being around out there, Mother still worries about my two younger sisters. I suppose you never know ... and you can't blame parents for worrying.' He paused for a moment, his blond head tilted thoughtfully to the side. 'Do you like working in Glasgow?'

'Aye,' Heather said, wondering why he was so fascinated by the city. 'I love it. I enjoy the fact that it's lively and friendly, and I like being near the big shops and everything.'

'I think that's more a female priority than a male's,' he said, raising his eyebrows and laughing.

Heather caught her breath as she watched him. He really was *very* attractive – and he had something that she hadn't found in too many lads before. He was both very nice to look at and obviously intelligent and entertaining and interesting to talk to. So far he seemed to have all the things she would look for in a boyfriend. But she wondered what he would be like if she *really* got to know him. She wondered if after a while the flaws would start to show – the way they had with Gerry.

'The reason I'm so interested in Glasgow,' Paul said now, dropping his voice and glancing towards the doorway, 'is that I'm going to be moving there in the next couple of weeks, and I don't actually know that many people.' He rolled his eyes and laughed. 'Actually, I don't know anybody apart from Andy and his wife – and I certainly don't know anybody around my own age ...' He looked at her now. 'Andy has been good enough to offer me to stay here with them for a few weeks until I get a flat or something sorted.'

Heather's heart lifted at this news, as it meant she would

probably see him again if she was out visiting. 'That will give you a good start,' she ventured. 'Give you a chance to get to know Glasgow and decide where you want to live.'

'I was just thinking,' he went on, a slight hesitancy suddenly evident in his manner, 'maybe we could meet up for lunch or something like that when I do start? Would you mind?'

Would I mind going out for lunch with this gorgeous fellow? Heather thought. She couldn't imagine minding anything less. He was looking intently at her now, and she felt herself blushing.

'I wouldn't mind at all,' she told him. 'I would be happy to meet you for lunch. You can just let me know when and where.' She dropped her gaze back to the table, terrified that he might see just how delighted she was. Then, she suddenly thought that she should really be back in the kitchen helping Claire to carry out the other dishes. If she didn't move soon, the roast potatoes would start to get cold.

'Brilliant!' he said, his whole face lighting up. 'I'll get your address and everything before we go back to the hotel tonight.'

Claire came into the sitting-room now carrying the casserole dish. 'Paul, would you give Andy and your father a shout, please?' she asked. 'Tell them the meal's all ready.'

'Sure,' he said, getting up from the table.

'I'll help you to carry in the rest of the things now,' Heather said, following her back into the kitchen.

'You two seem to be hitting it off well,' Claire said, lifting her eyebrows and smiling. 'He seems a lovely young fellow and he's very good-looking as well, isn't he?'

Heather gave a little smile and nodded. 'He's really nice . . .'

So far, she thought, *so far*.

Heather was seated with Paul Ballantyne at one side of her and Andy at the other. Whether it was the second glass of wine or just the general cheery atmosphere, she felt more at ease and at times found she was actually enjoying herself.

Paul's father and Andy kept everybody entertained with stories about their respective offices and Claire joined in happily, telling the odd light-hearted story herself. On a couple of occasions when the older three ones were chatting, Paul Ballantyne leaned towards Heather to ask her questions about her office and Glasgow in general.

When the meal was finished, everyone congratulated Claire and then they moved to the more comfortable chairs and sofa to finish off with tea and coffee.

Andy turned to everyone. 'I have a nice brandy liqueur if anyone fancies a wee drop?' he offered.

Tony beamed. 'If you're having one, I'll happily join you.'

Then, before anyone else had replied, the phone rang out in the hallway.

'I'm on my feet, so I'll get it,' Andy said, striding out of the room. He came back a few moments later. 'It's for you, Heather. It's Kirsty.'

Heather felt a little pang of alarm as she rushed out to pick up the phone from the small, ornate marble table by the front door. She couldn't imagine what her sister would ring up for. Hopefully, there was nothing wrong, because it was heading on for six o'clock now and winter dark outside.

'Hi, it's me,' Kirsty said in a low voice. 'I'm sorry to ring you at Claire's house, but with you not coming home until tomorrow ...'

'What is it?' Heather whispered into the phone. 'Is there something wrong?'

'Aye,' Kirsty said. 'It's Liz again ... she's in a terrible state.'

'What's happened?' Heather's voice was fearful and her heart was thumping. 'Is she sick again?'

'No, no ...' Kirsty said quickly. 'It's Jim – he's disappeared.'

'What?' Heather said, her voice high now. 'Where to? Where's he disappeared to?'

'England,' Kirsty said, 'for a while, then if he's tellin' the truth he's going to Australia in a few months.'

'My God!' Heather said, trying to make sense of the information. 'And is Liz going with him?'

'No ... not at all,' Kirsty said. 'That's the whole reason I'm phoning you. He's done a runner ... that's why Liz is in such a state. He never told her. He just pushed a note to her through the letter box. He hadn't the guts to tell her to her face.'

Heather shook her head, speechless for a few moments. 'Is she taking it really bad?'

'Well,' Kirsty said, 'you can just imagine how she is, with a wedding booked and still being the talk of the place with the miscarriage.'

'Who knows?' Heather asked. *Poor Liz*, she thought, *Poor, poor Liz*. She didn't deserve this. She didn't deserve all that had happened to her.

'Just me so far,' Kirsty said, 'and I had to tell my mammy.' There was a pause. 'My mammy walked down to the phone box along with me since it was dark and everything. I tried to ring you a wee while ago but the phone was engaged,' she explained, 'so I got something to eat and then we came back out again.'

There was a long heavy pause. 'How are things with you?' Heather asked. 'Are you feeling any better?'

'Just the same,' came the crisp reply. 'Anyway,' Kirsty said, 'I just thought you would want to know ... Liz was very disappointed when you weren't here, but I think I managed to console her a wee bit.' Another little pause. 'Well, I tried my best anyway ...'

'I wish I could get home,' Heather said. 'If there was any way I could, I definitely would – but the trains on a Sunday night ...' Heather heard a little noise, and looked down the hallway to see Claire gesturing towards her, checking that everything was OK. Heather put her hand over the phone and said she'd be off in a minute and explain then.

'I know the trains are bad on a Sunday,' Kirsty agreed, 'and I told Liz that as well and she understood.'

'I feel terrible about it,' Heather said, 'but there's not a thing I can do.'

'I know, I know,' Kirsty reassured her. 'I wouldn't have phoned, but I didn't want to leave telling you until tomorrow night when you came in after work. I was afraid you might hear it on the train or maybe somebody might stop you when you were walkin' down from the train station.'

Heather was nodding her head and biting down on her thumbnail. 'Thanks,' she said, her voice cracking a little. 'It was really good of you to phone ...' She halted, then suddenly found herself rushing headlong into the proper apology that was long overdue. 'I'm really sorry for everything, Kirsty, and I want you to know I'm on your side.'

The phone line buzzing was the only thing which broke the ensuing silence.

'I'll see you tomorrow,' Kirsty finally said, her voice low and strained.

'OK then . . .' Heather said, reluctant to put down the phone.

The line went dead, signalling that the huge invisible barrier was still solidly between the two Grace sisters.

'I'll run you out to Rowanhill straightaway,' Claire said as soon as Heather told her the news. They had gone back into the privacy of the kitchen, leaving the men chatting over their drinks. 'You've got to go out and see your friend after all you've both been through.' She suddenly reached forward and gathered her niece into her arms. 'This is just terrible news . . . but things will eventually get better. They always do.'

Heather hugged her aunt, fighting back the overwhelming urge to break down into gigantic sobs. 'It's too far and it's dark,' she protested. 'I can wait until tomorrow night to see her.'

'No,' Claire insisted, patting Heather on the back before releasing her 'We're going *now*. It will only take around an hour, and it will give me the chance to see Lily.' She gave a little smile. 'Bringing you home gives me a brilliant excuse to sort a few things out.'

'Are you sure?' Heather checked. She desperately wanted to go and comfort her friend, and it might indeed be a good thing to have Claire back in their house. It would be another bridge mended – and it might just help to balance all the ones that had been broken.

'I'm positive,' Claire said. She turned towards the sitting-room. 'While you're getting your things together. I'll explain to Andy what's happening, then I'll pull on my trousers and a warm jumper for driving.'

It took only a few minutes to have the weekend case packed, and then Heather rummaged in her handbag for a piece of paper and a pen. She found a receipt from one of the shops the day before, so she quickly scribbled down her full name and home address on the back of it, then, after a moment's thought, she added the address of Seafreight as well.

It would be a bit embarrassing going into the sitting-room to give it to Paul Ballantyne, but it would be much worse if he thought she had deliberately snubbed him.

She pinned a brave little smile on her face and told herself to keep calm, and then she walked into the sitting-room.

Chapter 67

Larry Delaney's car pulled up outside the Graces' house. As soon as the engine was turned off, the door opened and he was out and striding through the gate and up to the front door. He pressed the bell and waited.

A few moments later, Fintan Grace opened the door. When he saw who the visitor was, his back and shoulders stiffened.

'I must apologise for calling unannounced,' Larry said, 'but I thought maybe it was time that we had a word together.'

Fintan's face was stony and his jaw clenched. 'I don't think I have anything to say to you.'

Larry looked him in the eye. 'Well, I have a few things to say to you ... and I'd first like to apologise for any worries I've caused you over Kirsty. It was unintentional and I want to assure you that nothing underhand happened between us when we were in the hotel overnight.'

Fintan was ramrod still and silent – and there was no indication that he was going to allow his visitor over the doorstep. But he was standing and he was listening.

'I also apologise for bringing her over to Motherwell to see where I lived.' Larry felt his throat dry now, and swallowed hard. 'She asked me if she could see the apartment, and ... looking back on it ... I can see now I should have said "no". But stupidly, I didn't see any harm in it at the time.' He halted. 'I can see how all this looks to you – but I can assure you that you have nothing to worry about where Kirsty is concerned.'

Fintan stared at him, his eyes flinty and hard. Then he sucked in his breath. 'You've only used the singing business to further your own ends. You're a hard-nosed Dublin businessman with your fancy cars and your fancy clothes – and that's not what I want for my daughter. I was far happier when she was out singing with the local band. We never had any problems like this.' His eyes narrowed. 'You're too old for her in every way – and I don't want her having anything more to do with you.'

Larry ran his hand through his hair, searching for the right words, the right approach to get through to this man. 'I've worked hard for every single thing I have,' he said in a low, even voice. 'And I'm honest and fair. That's why I've come out to see you this evening.'

'Well, you've wasted your time,' Fintan stated. He moved to close the door. 'I'll say goodnight to you.'

'I love Kirsty,' Larry said, 'and I want your permission to marry her.'

The door closed in his face.

Kirsty and Sophie came out of the phone box and started on the walk back down to the house, both drawing their scarves tighter around their necks against the chill.

'Do you want to call in on Liz for a few minutes?' Sophie asked as they came towards her house.

'No,' Kirsty said, her voice quiet and slightly hoarse. 'There's no point. What could we say?'

'Aye, I suppose you're right,' Sophie said, linking her daughter's arm as they walked along. 'There's nothing we can say that's going to make the poor girl feel better.' She gave an audible sigh. 'Och, it's terrible what that Jim Murray's done. He should be shot for the way he's treated her.'

'He's been an absolute rat,' Kirsty stated. 'And it was the greatest pity that Liz couldn't see it. She was completely blind to his faults.' She pursed her lips and shook her head. 'She was determined to have him one way or the other, and she thought that by getting pregnant everything would fall into place – that they'd get married, then have their family, and that they'd live happily ever after.'

'Nobody's life is happy ever after,' Sophie sighed. 'Every

couple have their ups and downs, even when you both go into the marriage with the very best of intentions. Look at this carry-on with your father. I would never have believed he'd take a stand like this. I don't know what's got into him ...' She squeezed Kirsty's arm. 'I'll do my best to keep working on him ...'

'I don't want to lose Larry, Mammy,' Kirsty said in a choked voice, her eyes glistening with tears, 'and I'm terrified that it's going to happen. I'm terrified that I'll spend the rest of my life regretting that I didn't stand up for us more.'

'Shush now,' Sophie said, squeezing her arm again. 'He'll wait ... it's only been a week or so.'

There was silence for a little while, the only sound being their heels as they stepped along, white clouds of breath coming out in the cold Scottish night air.

'What do you honestly think of Larry?' Kirsty suddenly asked.

Sophie hesitated for a moment, hating to be disloyal to her husband. 'I think he's a really nice fellow,' she admitted. 'From the first time I met him I thought that. He is a good bit older than you, but I don't think that's the worst thing in the world. At least he's sensible and he's past all the nonsense that young fellas can get up to.' They turned the corner to their street now. 'I'd rather you were with him than somebody like Jim Murray or Gerry Stewart.' She shook her head. 'God rest his soul, wherever it is – and his poor mother's heart is broken an' all.'

'I honestly don't feel the age difference is a problem,' Kirsty continued, heartened that her mother at least was on her side, and Heather was also coming round that way. 'I feel safe with him, I feel he looks after me every way he can. When I'm out singin', he's there at the side of the stage watching and encouraging me. And he's picked me up and brought me home every single night. He's terrified of anything happening to me with that nutter on the loose.'

'I know,' Sophie said in her vague manner. 'I know.'

'And I know my daddy won't believe me,' she said now, 'but there was nothing at all of a romantic nature between us until the night in the hotel ... and even then, although he is older than me, he never put a foot wrong.' A sudden picture of them lying on the bed came into her mind and, for a moment, Kirsty thought her heart would break. The thought of never feeling Larry's strong arms around her again or feeling his lips on hers made her feel almost sick.

'I don't think it's his foot your father is worried about,' Sophie said, attempting a light joke.

Kirsty drew her breath in sharply. 'Oh my God!'

'I was only kidding . . .' Sophie said, startled by her reaction.

'No, not that,' Kirsty said, pointing down towards their gate. 'I'm nearly certain that's Larry's car at our house . . .'

'Oh my God!' Sophie repeated, as they both moved into a fast trot.

They were just outside Mona's house when they heard their own front door closing and then saw Larry coming out of the gate. Kirsty called out to him and then rushed up to greet him, her heart thudding at the mere sight of him.

'My journey hasn't been totally wasted,' he said, putting his arms around her. Then he suddenly pulled away when he realised that Sophie was with her. 'Hello, Mrs Grace,' he said in a quiet voice.

'Did you not get anywhere with Fintan?' she asked anxiously.

'I'm afraid not,' he said. 'I did my best, but he didn't want to hear anything.'

Sophie gritted her teeth together. 'Och, he can be the most stubborn, pig-headed man when he has a mind to.' She shook her head. 'But I know him – I know this will be tearin' him apart. He's only torturing himself along with everybody else.'

'Will we try again?' Kirsty suggested, looking up at Larry.

Larry shook his head. 'Not tonight – it wouldn't be fair. The man's entitled to decide who he wants to have in his own house.'

Sophie stepped forward now, touching Larry on the arm. 'I want you to know that I have no argument with you . . . I think the two of you are well-matched with your interests in music and everything.'

Larry smiled warmly at her. 'Thanks for that, Mrs Grace . . . I appreciate it.'

'There's no need for Mrs . . . Sophie will do fine,' she told him.

He bent down now to kiss Kirsty lightly on the forehead. 'Let me know if anything changes,' he told her.

There was no sign of Fintan downstairs when they came into the house and when Sophie went upstairs, she found him lying on top of their bed in the darkened room. She sat down on the bottom of the bed.

'I met Larry Delaney outside the house, just as we were coming in . . .' she said.

Fintan made a sort of irritated grunting noise but he said nothing.

'We can't go on like this,' Sophie whispered. 'We're going to end up with another situation like Mona and Claire.'

'I'm only protecting her,' Fintan said, 'the way any decent father would protect his daughter. She's not yet nineteen, she's still only a young girl in many ways.'

'Well,' Sophie said, 'why don't you let Larry Delaney protect her too?'

'For God's sake, Sophie! Isn't *he* the very one I'm flamin' worried about!'

'Will you please listen to me?' she persisted, her voice rising. 'You know fine well that I very rarely have a strong opinion on anything. I usually sit back and let everybody else have their say . . . so please have the courtesy to listen to my opinion on this occasion.'

There was a strained silence but, tellingly, Fintan did not dispute his wife's statement.

'Aw . . . go on,' he grudgingly said.

'In a few years' time,' Sophie said, 'we'd both be delighted to see Kirsty with all the nice things that Larry Delaney has to offer her. We know he has a fine big car and a good job, and according to Kirsty he has a lovely flat in a good part of Motherwell.' She paused. 'And he's also a Catholic – an Irish Catholic.'

'And his age?' Fintan butted in.

'The thing is, Fintan,' Sophie went on, ignoring his point, 'I think he actually loves her and she definitely loves him. I can see it staring out of her eyes.'

Fintan made the grunting noise again. 'And if we stop her from seeing him, she might never meet anyone as good again. She might never meet anyone that would love her as much or look after her as well.' Her voice dropped now. 'And worse still – she might hold it against *you* for the rest of her life. Oh, it might not seem like it now – at this minute she's downstairs doing what you want. But it might rebound on you in years to come . . .'

Sophie got up from the bed and went to the bedroom door. She turned around, and looked at the forlorn figure on the bed. 'And don't forget, Fintan – I was only seventeen when I met you. There might not be the same age difference between us as there is between Kirsty and Larry, but you were no different from any other man. If you'd had your way, I might have been in the same boat poor Liz Mullen landed in.'

'That's blidey hittin' below the belt, Sophie!' he gasped.

There was a deadly silence as they both realised the inappropriate words he'd used to describe the situation. Normally they would have dissolved into laughter, enjoying the slightly risqué double meaning. But there was no laughing about it tonight.

'Imagine bringin' up something like that!' Fintan blustered on. 'And maybe that's exactly what I'm worried about – her landing in the same boat as Liz.'

'Well, don't worry about it,' Sophie told him. 'Kirsty has a lot more oil in her can than that. Apart from anything else, she has big ambitions about her singing – and there's no way she's going to spoil that.' She rested her hand on the doorknob. 'Larry Delaney's the best chance our Kirsty will ever get – he'll look after her in every way we could ever want. We'll never need to worry about her being out on her own at night, or going short of anything. I've just spoken to him outside, and I can tell just by the way he looks at her and talks to her that he loves her with all his heart. He'll always put her first.' She paused to catch her breath now. 'And I don't think any reasonable father could ask more for his daughter.'

Chapter 68

❦

K irsty and her mother were sitting opposite each other at the fire, one reading the *Sunday Post* and the other reading the *Sunday Mail*, when Mona came knocking on the front door. She had stopped going around and letting herself in the back door after dark since that poor family had been butchered – you never knew who could be creeping around. And Sophie had taken to locking the kitchen door when it got dark for the very same reason.

'I'll put the kettle on,' Sophie said, glad of something to do.

Mona stuck her head in the sitting-room as she followed Sophie down to the kitchen.

'Well, Miss,' she said, smiling at her favourite niece, 'any news?'

Kirsty shook her head, and forced herself to smile back. 'Not a ha'porth,' she said – a jokey retort they often used. She wondered if Mona knew about Jim Murray doing a bunk. She would soon hear if she did.

'Ah well,' Mona said, arms folded in the doorway, 'I suppose we've all had more than enough excitement, one way or another, since the New Year. We could do with things being quiet for a while.' She left Kirsty to her newspaper and went into the kitchen.

'Your Kirsty's awful quiet,' she remarked as she sat down at the table. 'Is she all right in herself?'

Sophie turned the tap on, letting the water drum into the empty, copper-bottomed kettle. She put the whistle in place and then put the kettle on one of the gas rings, all the while debating whether to trust Mona with the situation between Kirsty and Fintan. She decided against it.

'Och, she's fine,' Sophie said, striking a match and lighting the gas under the kettle. 'Just the usual Sunday night when they're not going out. The thought of getting up for work on these dark January mornings isn't very inspiring.'

'Oh, tell me about it,' Mona agreed. 'It's pitch black when I'm

433

up and trying to get fires lit and everything done for the boys getting up and out to work or school.' She paused. 'So you won't have Heather to get up for work in the morning?'

'That's right,' Sophie said, folding her arms. She had already been through this conversation with Mona on Friday when she told her that Heather was staying the weekend at Claire and Andy's house.

'It's to be hoped that she doesn't come back skin and bone with all they'll feed her out there,' she said, her mouth turning down at the corners. 'Oul' blidey nuts and glasses of wine.' She shook her head disapprovingly. 'And your Heather doesn't need that – she's lost enough weight recently and it doesn't suit her one bit. She needs feeding up now, and proper meals instead of all that nut and crisps nonsense that goes on out there.'

'I've told you already, Mona,' Sophie said with a definite edge to her voice, 'that that's their way. They just have a different routine. We can't all be the same – and anyway, plenty of people like that kind of thing, it's fashionable. They have their main meal later in the evening. Andy prefers to relax with a wee drink after a hard day at work, then have his dinner. Is there any harm in that? You had a priest a few years ago that had you over cooking dinners at seven o'clock in the evening and you didn't seem to mind.'

'That's different,' Mona stated, 'priests are from a very different class from the rest of us.' She raised her eyebrows. 'You know fine well that Claire Grace wasn't brought up to all those things – sure, she grew up in the same oul' farmhouse in Ballygrace as Jimmy, Fintan, Pat and Tommy. They don't carry on like that, do they? They're just ordinary working people, the same way we were brought up ourselves, who have their dinner the minute they walk in the door. And in my opinion, that's what any decent working man deserves.'

'Horses for courses, as far as I'm concerned,' Sophie stated. 'I couldn't care less whether they have champagne and frog's legs for their breakfast. It's their own business.' She ignored the tightness around Mona's mouth and the narrowing of her eyes. 'How's Lily doing?' she asked now, pointedly changing the subject. 'Has she adjusted to being back at home yet?'

'Adjusted?' Mona said, raising her eyes to heaven. 'She's ruling the blidey roost over there. She has the boys driven mad wi' getting them to switch the telly on and the radiogram off and vice versa, dependin' on her moods. She has them dancing to attention day and night. And if the telly money dares to run out when she's watchin' one of her programmes, there's hell to pay. She's screeching like a banshee for somebody to come and put the money in quick before she misses anythin'.' She shook her head. 'I'm waitin' on one of the lads turning on her one of these days. They're so meek and blidey mild and patient with her – big hulking fellas as they are.'

'She was always well able to twist them around her little finger.' Sophie laughed and shook her head. 'She's moving around a lot better though, isn't she? She'll soon be able to do all those things for herself.'

Mona smiled. 'Oh, thanks be to God an' his Blessed Mother, she has improved.' She put a finger to her lips now, thinking. 'I was wondering if you'd mind me droppin' her over here for a few hours during the week? You see, I'm supposed to be up at the priest's house at lunch times, and Pat's on the early bus shift and the boys are all out. It's the time that Lily would normally be in school.'

'No problem at all,' Sophie said. 'I'd be delighted to have her. She can sit up at the fire doing her reading or drawing or knitting, and I'll be up and down the stairs checking on her.'

'Oh, thanks,' Mona said. 'That would be a great help.' She made a little grimace of annoyance. 'It's that Cissy Dunne – you know, the one that's been covering for me when Lily was first in hospital then again since she came out of the hospital and couldn't be left?'

Sophie nodded that she knew the woman.

'Well,' Mona said, prodding her finger on the kitchen table for emphasis, 'she seems to think she has her feet well under the table in the Chapel House now, and I'm going to have to put in a few more hours to put her back in her place.'

'But surely Father Finlay wouldn't allow it?' Sophie said, surprised.

'You never know,' Mona stated. 'You can never take anythin' for granted when it comes to men – even if they are priests. They're very easily swayed with the forward, bossy types of women like that Cissy Dunne. Oh, if she got the chance to get my job full time she'd jump at it, and make no mistake.'

Sophie turned to the cupboard now for mugs, trying not to laugh in spite of all her own troubles. How on earth could her sister-in-law use words for someone else that exactly described herself and not notice?

'Where's Fintan?' Mona asked, noticing that Sophie had only put three mugs out on the table.

Sophie poured the boiling water into the teapot, then set it back on the edge of the gas ring to brew. 'Oh, he's upstairs at something,' she said vaguely. 'If he doesn't come down soon, I'll make him a fresh pot later.' She started rummaging in the cupboard to see what biscuits and cakes she had to offer her guest.

The sound of a key in the front door sounded and both women turned to look at each other. 'Who could that be?' Sophie said, looking alarmed. She moved across the kitchen floor towards the hall.

'Maybe Fintan went out and you didn't see him,' Mona suggested, sitting forward to get a good view of whoever it was.

'Hi, Mammy,' Heather said, letting herself in. 'Claire said she'd run me home tonight so that I could run up and see Liz.' She held back the front door to let her aunt in after her.

'I hope you don't mind us landing on you unexpectedly,' Claire said, 'but I thought Heather would be worrying all day tomorrow if she didn't see her friend . . .'

'Of course we don't mind, it was very good of you bringing her out all this way.' She moved down the hallway. 'I've just made tea . . . and I must give Fintan a shout. He was just upstairs fixing something.' *Oh God*, she thought to herself, *this above all nights for everyone to land in on the house, when Fintan was lying upstairs in the depths of despair over Kirsty and Larry Delaney. And lying down was a thing he never, ever did unless he was sick.*

'It's lovely and warm coming into the house,' Claire said. 'It's turned very cold outside – I wouldn't be surprised if we got a heavy frost later on tonight.'

As Heather followed her mother towards the kitchen, she glimpsed the heavy figure of Mona sitting at the kitchen table and her heart sank. This was all she needed. The plan was that Sophie was going to ask Fintan to go across to his brother's and check if Claire could come over for a few minutes to see Lily. She felt it was better than knocking at the door and having one of the boys answer it and then be put in an awkward spot. She had brought a box of Cadbury's Roses and a fancy little mirror for Lily to hang on her wall.

There was a silence as Heather and Claire walked into the kitchen. Mona immediately got to her feet, her roundish face stiff and grim. 'I'll leave youse all to it,' she said, bustling by on the opposite side of the table to where the two others were standing.

'Hello, Mona,' Claire said, stepping to the bottom of the table to bar her sister-in-law's way. 'I'm delighted to see you, because I had intended to drop over to see Lily while I was here.' She paused. 'I take it you won't mind?'

Mona came to a standstill in front of the taller, slimmer Claire – her gaze fixed somewhere around the chest area, refusing to meet her eye. 'She'll be getting ready for bed now, so it's not a good time.'

'I have a couple of little things in the car for her,' Claire said, standing solidly, 'and it won't take me a minute. It's a while since I saw her, and I told Pat I don't want things to start back the way they were. I don't want this barrier back down again that was there for the last two years.'

Mona's face turned an angry red. 'Well, that's just the way things are . . .'

'Well,' Claire said, in a firm, unwavering voice. 'It's not the way that the rest of us want it in the Grace family. From what Fintan and Pat and Sophie told me a few weeks ago, they want to have peace and harmony in the family as well. I also know that Heather and Kirsty and little Lily are delighted that most of us are back being friends again.' She paused. 'From where I'm standing, it seems that you're the only one, Mona, who is happy to keep this bitterness going on – and I want to know why.'

There was a creaking of floorboards in the hall as Kirsty came to stand at the door, having obviously heard the visitors arrive.

'This is neither the time nor the place,' Mona blustered. 'And I don't have to give you any reasons for anything.'

'Oh, but you do,' Claire told her, 'because this affects me directly. What you're doing is ostracising me from my whole family and I won't have it.'

Heather moved out from the table and went towards the door. She gave her sister a small comforting pat on the arm as she passed her by then she went straight upstairs. Her father should be here, she decided. He should know his sister was here for the first time in years and that there was a very serious row brewing. Her mother couldn't go for him as she was trapped at the sink, and in any case she wouldn't want to leave the situation in case it got very serious.

'Nobody *ostracised* you,' Mona said, deliberately mimicking Claire's use of the big word. 'You ostracised yourself when you took up with Andy McPherson. You knew perfectly well what that would mean in our family.'

'No,' Claire said in a low voice, 'I did not. It was my business and Andy's what happened when we got married – it has nothing to do with you or anybody else.'

'And what about the Catholic Church?' Mona said, her eyes moving up to meet Claire's for the first time. 'Did you not think you marrying somebody that wasn't a Catholic had anything to do with the Church?'

'That's my business,' Claire said, a steely, unflinching look in her eyes. 'And I don't think you're a fit person to be quoting the Church to me, Mona Grace.'

'What?' Mona said, astounded. 'What the hell are you sayin' now?'

'I'm saying that people in glass houses shouldn't be throwing stones,' Claire said. 'Or if you want me to quote the Bible, I'm saying "let he who is without sin, cast the first stone".' She bent her head down to Mona's level now, her dark bobbed hair swinging as she did. 'You cannot afford to throw stones, Mona – and if you don't stop this nastiness and bitterness, I'm going to land a very big stone down on you, and I don't care who hears it!'

Mona's face went chalk white. 'You're talkin' complete rubbish ...'

Claire turned to the doorway. 'Go into the sitting-room please, Kirsty. I don't want anyone other than your mother to hear this.' As soon as Kirsty had gone, she whirled back to Mona. 'Galway,' she stated, 'when you were a young girl helping out in the priest's house ...' She paused, waiting for the penny to drop.

'Rubbish ...' Mona said, her hand coming down on the table to steady herself. 'You're talking absolute rubbish. You know nothing about me when I was growing up in Galway ...'

Claire gave a big sigh. 'I hoped you wouldn't make me do this, Mona ...' She shook her head. 'Do you remember when me and you were over in Ballygrace with the children about five years ago? Do you remember the woman we met outside the church – the woman from your parish in Galway? The one you cut short and tried to ignore?'

Mona's face blanched, and her mouth opened and shut like a fish without a word coming out.

'Well,' Claire continued in an even voice, 'I met her again the following day up at the shop in Ballygrace, and she asked me if you were as friendly with the priests in Scotland as you were in Galway. And then she was delighted to tell me all about the newly ordained priest that had to be moved to another parish because—'

'We've heard enough,' Fintan's voice came from the door. 'I don't think we need it spelling out, Claire ...' He walked over to put an arm around his shocked wife's shoulders.

Mona lifted her apron skirt up to her face. 'You're cruel!' she said to Claire in a shocked, horrified tone. 'Pure cruel – there was no need for that!' Her voice took on a hysterical note. 'Bringin' all this up after what me and Pat have gone through wi' Lily!'

'I could have brought this up five years ago and I didn't,' Claire stated. 'I could have brought it up two and a half years ago when the family turned against me – and I didn't.' She paused. 'You forced me to bring this up, Mona. I asked you to be friends the nice way and you wouldn't have it. What I'm trying to tell you now is that I had the power to hurt you and cause mayhem in your family by telling Pat and I didn't. I chose to keep my mouth closed and my nose out of other people's business.'

Mona collapsed into a chair now, sobbing her heart out. 'I was only a young girl . . .'

'I'm aware of that,' Claire said in a softer voice, 'and I had no intentions of ever telling you or anybody else what that woman said.' She looked around the room. 'There's only me and Sophie and Fintan that heard this tonight, and I'm quite sure it's not going to go any further.'

'There won't be a word from me,' Fintan said.

'Nor me,' Sophie added in a whisper.

Mona's shoulders shook.

'I'm truly sorry for upsetting you,' Claire said, 'and I don't ever want to have to do it again. But,' she paused, taking a deep breath, 'you will never know the number of nights I lay in bed breaking my heart crying because I couldn't see my own brothers and their children. Just as recently as last month, I cried the whole night after I visited Lily. I cried that hard that I got sick and Andy nearly had to call the doctor.'

'We're all sorry for that now,' Fintan said, his voice thick and hoarse. 'God knows, I'm sorry for all the heartbreak that's been caused . . . and I certainly don't want to see anything else like this happening.'

Claire went to put a hand on Mona's shoulder but stopped herself. 'I'll go in and see the girls for a couple of minutes and then I'll head back to Glasgow.'

Both girls were sitting shocked and silent by the fire.

'Is everything OK?' Heather asked, her heart thumping in her chest. As she had passed by the kitchen door with her father, she could hear the raised and angry voices and she knew something monumental was happening.

'I hope so . . .' Claire said, sinking down into the sofa. 'I certainly hope so.' She gave a little smile. 'I'm absolutely drained . . .'

A short while later Fintan appeared with a tiny glassful of

brandy for his sister. 'Drink it up,' he told her, 'it'll do you good.' He turned to the doorway, where a white-faced Mona stood, clutching a good-sized glass of the medicinal alcohol. 'Come in, Mona,' he said quietly.

Without being asked, the two girls got to their feet and went out of the room, leaving the two women alone.

When Fintan came back to join his wife and two daughters, he closed the kitchen door firmly behind him. 'I think maybe we need to have a few words ourselves,' he said quietly.

All four sat down at the table, Heather glancing over anxiously at her mother and sister.

'I think we've seen and heard enough tonight to give us all a bit of a shake-up.' His throat felt dry again and he swallowed hard. 'I was thinking when I was upstairs that maybe I've let this business with you and the fellow get a wee bit out of hand, Kirsty.'

Kirsty's heart started racing. 'What do you mean?'

'I mean that maybe I jumped the gun a bit . . . that maybe I didn't give Larry Delaney a chance.' He glanced over at Sophie, as though checking with her that he was saying all the right things. The things she had told him upstairs – and the things he now knew were true. Sophie nodded so he continued. 'I think we should maybe start again . . . you going back to your singing . . . and maybe going out the odd night to the pictures or the dancing with him.'

'Are you sure?' Kirsty gasped, looking from her father to her mother. 'Can I really see him again – like a proper boyfriend?'

Fintan pursed his lips together and nodded. 'Just take it slow, mind.'

A huge, relieved smile spread across her face. 'And it's OK for him to come and pick me up for rehearsals and when I'm out singing like before?'

'Yes,' Fintan said. He was smiling back at her and nodding, but there was a hint of moisture at the corner of his eyes.

Twenty minutes later Mona and Claire came back out from the sitting-room together.

'I'm just going next door for a few minutes,' Claire said,

popping her head through the kitchen door, 'to give Lily her presents.' She moved back to let Mona look in.

'I'll see you in the morning,' Mona said to Sophie in a quiet, calm voice. 'I'd better get round or that wee devil, Lily, will be playin' them all up.'

When the front door closed behind them, a huge communal sigh reverberated around the kitchen table.

Chapter 69

About a quarter of an hour later, Claire came back into Fintan and Sophie's house. 'Just to let you know that everything is more or less sorted out between me and Mona,' she told all four Graces, as she leaned on the back of the couch in the sitting-room. She looked across at Kirsty. 'I'm sorry for asking you to leave the kitchen earlier . . . but I had to say something private to Mona, something I didn't want too many people to hear. I hope you didn't mind or feel offended.'

'Not a bit,' Kirsty said, beaming at her. She didn't mind anything at the moment. The whole world was suddenly a wonderful place and she was only counting the minutes until Claire left and she could rush up to the phone box to call Larry and tell him the great news.

'I didn't want to sit and listen to Mona ranting on anyway. I hear enough of it day in and day out.'

Claire looked over at her brother and his wife. 'I'm sure you didn't need all of this either . . .'

'You did the right thing,' Sophie told her. 'And I'm just delighted it's all worked out for you.'

'Well,' Claire said, giving a little weary sigh, 'I'm not going to get too elated about it, because I know Mona from old, and I know she's not the sort to change her colours. I'm not imagining that we're ever going to be the best of friends, but as long as she doesn't get in the way of me and Andy being friends with everybody else.'

'And I'm delighted that we all can get things on to a more normal footing,' Fintan said.

'We can have the odd visit out to each other at the weekends and that kind of thing.'

'Lovely,' Claire agreed. She looked over at Heather now. 'I'm hoping we'll see more of you out in Glasgow,' she said, smiling meaningfully. Heather had told her all about Paul Ballantyne asking to meet up with her some time soon in the city.

'Oh thanks, Claire ... I'll definitely be back out soon,' Heather said, feeling herself blush.

'And me and Larry will take a run out some evening or weekend,' Kirsty added, excited at the thought of all the things that lay ahead.

Claire looked at her watch. 'Right,' she said, 'I'd better get heading home now before the frost gets too thick.'

She gave them all a hug and a kiss. 'It was lovely seeing you all, and being back in your house again.'

Sophie and Fintan walked her out to the car.

'Keep an eye on Mona over the next few days,' Claire said to them as she got in the car. 'She's her own worst enemy, but I would hate to think I hurt her badly. I would never have done it if she hadn't forced me into a corner ...'

'She'll be fine,' Sophie reassured her. 'And it might not do her any harm to have a taste of her own medicine.'

Fintan leaned in through the car window. 'The door is open to you and Andy at any time,' he reminded his sister.

The engine revved up and Claire blew them both a kiss as the car pulled away.

'If you like,' Heather said, when the girls were on their own, 'I'll walk up to the phone box with you and then we can go on to Liz's.'

'OK,' Kirsty said, getting to her feet. 'It's a bit of a nuisance not being able to go anywhere on our own, but I suppose it's the sensible thing.'

'You know I'm really sorry about not sticking up for you over Larry, don't you?' Heather said.

Kirsty shrugged. 'It doesn't matter ...'

'But it *does* matter,' Heather insisted. She stood up now and went over and put her arms around her sister. 'It was just the timing ... all the trouble with Gerry and then Liz losing the baby.' She shook her head. 'I'm really sorry, I shouldn't have been so horrible and I'll never do it again. I think I was a wee bit depressed or something, especially when I think back to the day I fainted at work. I wasn't myself at all.'

'It's OK,' Kirsty said, patting Heather's arm. 'I know you didn't mean it. I know you weren't your normal self.'

'I promise I'll never be like that again ... and I'll really make a big effort to get to know Larry properly.' She moved back now to look Kirsty straight in the face, so that she would know that she was being sincere. 'Even though he is a wee bit older, he's very good-looking and he wears lovely clothes.'

A huge smile broke out on Kirsty's face. 'Even though I say it myself, he is very good-looking, isn't he?' She hugged herself with delight now. 'I just can't wait to get up to the phone box and tell him that everything's all right.' She suddenly stopped and put her hand to her mouth. 'I forgot – you missed all that earlier on!'

'What?' Heather asked, her face creasing into a worried frown. 'What did I miss?'

'Larry came out to the house about an hour before you arrived, and my daddy wouldn't let him over the doorstep.' Kirsty gave a little nervous giggle. 'It was certainly all happening in the Grace household tonight.'

'Let's just be glad it's all over and done with,' Heather said, suddenly feeling exhausted with the whole thing.

The front door opened again and the girls went out and had a few words with their parents then they threw on their coats and scarves and headed out into the cold night air.

'You're not going to believe it,' Heather said, linking her sister's arm, 'but I've met a really nice boy ...'

'When?' Kirsty asked. 'Where?'

'Just today, out at Claire's house. He's a young fellow who's going to be working with Andy.'

'So what's going to happen?' Kirsty said, all excited for her sister.

'Well, we were supposed to be meeting up,' Heather explained, 'but before I could make any real arrangements with him, I got your phone call and then I had to rush to get out here.' She looked at Kirsty and smiled. 'But at least I managed to give him my address, so I'll just have to wait and see what happens.'

Larry was delighted and relieved with Kirsty's news and after a brief chat they arranged to meet the following night. It was agreed that Larry would once again call out at the house to pick her up, and then they would go on to the pictures for their first real date.

The situation with Liz was much less cheery and there was little Heather could do or say that would make things any better.

'At least I still have my friends,' Liz said with a tear in her eye, 'and I suppose that's something to be grateful for.' She blew her nose. 'I'll never trust a man again after this.'

There was a little pause, then she looked up at Heather, her eyes hollow and sad. 'Although I can't help wondering what might have happened if Gerry Stewart hadn't got himself killed. Maybe you'd have got back together and the four of us would have all been happy together ...'

'No, Liz,' Heather said softly. 'We can't keep looking back and wondering what might have been. It's time for us all to start looking forward again.'

Chapter 70

Heather went into work the following morning, feeling that weeks had passed since Friday instead of days. She hung up her coat and outdoor things as usual and then stopped to have a few words with Muriel Ferguson, who was most interested to hear that Heather had spent the weekend at her aunt's.

'Lovely person,' Muriel had enthused again, 'and such a lovely house. We really must take a little trip out to visit her again when the weather is nice.'

'It was very frosty this morning, wasn't it?' Heather said, changing the subject. Hopefully, she thought to herself, Muriel's intended visit out to the McPhersons' house would be long forgotten by the time the nice weather came around.

Danny and Maurice came up to sit on Heather's desk later in the morning, full of stories from the weekend about the dancing and the pubs. And Danny took great delight in telling her all about a great new girl he had met in the Barrowland Dance Hall. 'I'm takin' her to the pictures on Wednesday night,' he told Heather, 'but I've already told her not to get any big ideas about us, as I'm not the kind to get tied down too easily.'

'I think I'd give her the chance to get to know *you* first,' Maurice had laughed, 'and then there will be no fear of her wantin' to get tied down too easily wi' you!'

Sarah and Marie had caught her at the break time and the three girls arranged to go to The Trees restaurant as usual for their lunch.

Just as they were all watching the time for the lunchtime buzzer, Muriel came rushing over to Heather's desk. 'There's a very well-dressed young man at the reception desk,' she whispered, 'and he's asked for you by name.'

Heather moved out from her desk, and looked down along the office to reception, to where the tall, fair-headed Paul Ballantyne was standing. Just looking at him started off the fluttery feeling again in her stomach and chest. She made herself take a long, deep breath. 'Thanks, Muriel,' she said to her curious colleague. 'It's a friend of mine who said he might be in the city today.'

Then, remembering Claire's advice, she walked straight towards him, smiling and calm.

'I hope you don't mind me calling up to the office,' he said apologetically, 'but I was afraid I might miss you if I left it too long.'

'I don't mind at all,' Heather told him. 'I wouldn't have given you the address if I did.'

The buzzer suddenly sounded and everyone started to make moves in the office.

'Are you free for lunch?' Paul asked. 'Or have you already made arrangements?'

446

Heather smiled at him. 'Nothing that important that I can't change. I'll just get my coat.'

She paused to tell the girls about her change of plan, then she grabbed her coat and scarf and bag and walked quickly back to Paul, ignoring all the curious stares.

They went in a different direction to where her workmates usually went and found a small, quiet café up in Sauchiehall Street, where they ordered coffee and sandwiches.

'I couldn't explain too much about my new job when we were in Andy's house yesterday,' Paul told Heather, 'because it was a wee bit awkward . . .'

Heather waited, not wanting to appear too keen or desperate to know everything about him – although that was exactly how she felt.

'You see, my dad's business hasn't been doing too well recently,' he explained, 'and Andy has been great. When we had the meeting over the weekend, he drew up a new business plan for the next two years for the factory. It involved cutting back on certain things, and staffing was one of them.' He gave a little shrug. 'I was one of the newest management staff there, and I felt it wasn't fair to keep me on when some of the older men were married with families.'

'So, what's happened?' Heather asked.

'Andy offered me a new job at his place,' he told her, 'which is just brilliant. There's far more scope for me there and if my father's business picks up, I can always go back with any new skills I've learned. It's just for a year initially, and we'll see what happens after that.' He paused. 'I start next Monday, so it'll give me time to tie things up back at the factory, and get myself all organised to move out to Glasgow next weekend.'

'It's a great opportunity,' Heather said. 'And going on my own experience, Glasgow's a great place.'

'I wondered,' he said now, 'if you fancy meeting me a couple of times a week for lunch, just until I get to know more people.'

'Sure,' Heather said, her chestnut wavy hair rippling down over her shoulders as she nodded.

'And maybe,' he said, 'we might meet up after work some

447

Friday and go out to the Barrowland Dance Hall. It's supposed to be great out there.'

Heather's heart soared. Going to the dancing together meant that it was a *proper* date. It meant that Paul Ballantyne must really like her.

'I have to confess that I was in two minds about moving to Glasgow,' he told her, looking straight into her dark brown eyes, 'but meeting you has made all the difference.' He gave a small laugh. 'I think somebody was smiling on me that day in Andy McPherson's house. The last thing I expected to happen was that I'd meet a really nice girl who just happened to be gorgeous-looking as well.'

Heather looked across the table at him and she suddenly found she was laughing too. She knew she should have just kept calm and given a little smile – but she just couldn't help herself.

While she was waiting for the train that evening, Heather decided to go to the row of public phone boxes and give Claire a ring to tell her what had happened with Paul Ballantyne.

'Oh, I'm so delighted for you!' her aunt exclaimed. 'And Andy will be delighted too.'

'He's really nice,' Heather said, pleased with the chance to talk it over with somebody who knew him. She would tell Kirsty all about it the minute she got home, but it was great to be able to talk to Claire about it now. 'We're going to meet up in Edinburgh on Saturday morning,' she continued, 'and then we're going to spend the whole day going around the castle and places like that.'

'Wonderful,' Claire breathed, her approval evident in her voice. Then there was a little silence on the line. 'Oh, Heather . . . there's just a little thing that you might like to know. Paul Ballantyne is actually a Catholic – the same as yourself. I just thought I'd mention it because Ballantyne is often taken for a Protestant name.'

'Is he?' Heather said in a surprised but pleased voice. It wouldn't have mattered, she would still have agreed to meet him – even if it meant starting the whole Mona thing all over again – but it just made things a whole lot easier.

'Andy told me last night,' Claire said. 'Apparently his

grandfather was originally a Protestant, but he changed when he married Paul's grandmother and the whole family are now Catholic.' She paused. 'I was actually relieved, because I wouldn't like anyone to think that I'd deliberately introduced you to him, given mine and Andy's situation. And it's one problem less after all the recent difficulties with Mona and poor Kirsty.'

'Well, it's all worked out well so far,' Heather said. 'So let's hope it continues. And I'm really glad I was at your house this weekend or I might never have met him.'

'Oh, I'm sure you would,' Clare said, laughing. 'I think Andy would have got you two together somehow. From the minute he first met Paul, he thought you and he would make a perfect couple.'

Heather found herself grinning into the phone box. 'Do you mean he deliberately tried to match us up?'

'Something like that,' Claire said. 'I'll tell you all about it the next time you're out at our house ... Oh, God!' she suddenly remembered. 'I meant to tell you about the experience I had driving home last night. You're not going to believe it!'

'What happened?' Heather asked.

'Well, I was just coming into Glasgow, at a dark bend just before Calderpark Zoo, when a man came out onto the road waving me down. He was smartly dressed in a dark overcoat and a shirt and tie and I thought it was somebody that had broken down, so I slowed down a bit ... I nearly stopped, and then I got a good look at him in the headlights.'

'What did he look like?' Heather asked in a low shocked voice.

'Quite good-looking,' Claire told her. 'He wasn't very tall but he was broad and fit-looking, with nice dark wavy hair. It was his smart looks that stupidly made me slow down, thinking he was genuine. I was crawling along when he came around to my side of the car and tried to open it – thank God I'd locked it when I got in.'

'What did you do then?' Heather's anxious voice echoed on the line. She was also feeling a little bit disturbed herself, as the description she'd just given was exactly how she would have described Gerry Stewart. She nearly said as much to Claire but then just as quickly she dismissed the idea. There were probably thousands of men in Scotland who fitted that description.

'It was his eyes that frightened me,' Claire told her niece. 'They were weird-looking – dark and piercing straight into me. So I just put my foot down and scooted off as quick as the car could go, and I never looked back until I hit the streetlights in Glasgow.' She paused. 'He was probably only a drunk or something like that, but I wasn't taking any chances – not with that lunatic still on the loose.'

'Well,' Heather said, 'I am really glad that you're OK ... and you did exactly the right thing.' She then went on to give Claire the good news about Kirsty and Larry, and how her father was now fine about the whole situation.

'Oh, I'm delighted,' Claire said. 'I feel much better hearing that.'

Heather glanced at the Departures board. 'That's my platform that's just been announced,' she told her aunt. 'I'll ring you next week.'

'And come out to the house again soon, especially now we're going to have Paul with us for a few weeks.'

'I will,' Heather promised. 'I will.'

Chapter 71

≋≋

JULY 1958

After a two-year engagement, Kirsty Grace married Larry Delaney in Rowanhill Church. Thankfully, Father Finlay was away on holiday, and they had a cheery, young, newly ordained priest to celebrate the wedding Mass. The summer's day was bright and sunny, and Kirsty looked more dazzling in her white fitted sequinned dress and her little diamond tiara and veil than she had ever looked on the stage.

Her career had really taken off in the last couple of years and she was now travelling as far as London to perform in bigger, more prestigious venues, with Larry – as always – by her side. There was even talk of a recording contract, but that would have to wait until after the honeymoon. They had booked two weeks off for their big event and had a trip to Italy planned for the day after the wedding. They would spend their first night as a married couple in Larry's newly decorated apartment.

Two of the bridesmaids, Heather and Liz Mullen, looked almost as stunning as the bride in their dusky-pink sequinned dresses – very similar in design to the bride's – and their delicate feathered pink head-dresses. They were watched closely by Paul Ballantyne – Heather's fiancé – and Liz's latest boyfriend, a nice quiet chap from Cleland.

The youngest bridesmaid, everyone agreed, stole the show.

Lily Grace – now a full head taller than when she was in hospital – wore the most beautiful dress that made her look like the fairy from the top of the Christmas tree, except that it was in the exact same pink as Heather and Liz's dresses.

Sophie had painstakingly made Lily's dress over the last few months, enduring endless anxious visits from Mona, and was overwhelmingly grateful when she sewed on the very last sequin.

As everyone watched Lily move gracefully up the aisle after the bridal party, numerous people discovered they had lumps in their throats, thinking back to the paralysed little girl she had been only two years before. Continuous physiotherapy and steely determination on the tenacious Lily's part had finally beaten the polio into submission.

Claire McPherson fought back tears of pride and emotion as she watched the three Grace girls standing at the altar, and she said a silent prayer of gratitude that all had worked out so well. She and Andy had had their marriage blessed the year before in a small private ceremony in a Catholic church in Glasgow, and they were now expecting their first baby.

Sophie Grace watched with pride as Fintan formally handed over his younger daughter to the care of Larry Delaney. And later, as they took their marriage vows, she watched the love shining out of Kirsty's eyes and she offered up a prayer of thanks that she'd had the courage to face Fintan on that cold winter's night.

The ceremony over, the group came out into the sunlight to

watch as wedding photographs were taken, with everybody cheering and laughing and enjoying the lovely summer's day.

As the guests milled around, they chatted about the usual wedding topics – how beautiful the bride and bridesmaids were, how very lucky they were with the weather and also about the man who had been convicted and hung earlier that week for the seven murders he had committed between January 1956 and January 1958 around the west of Scotland.

The people in Rowanhill commented again and again how uncanny the resemblance was between Gerry Stewart and the convicted man, Peter Manuel – leaving Kirsty and Lily to speculate about whether or not the prowler they had seen around the Graces' house was Gerry or Manuel. They plotted between them not to tell Heather anything about the incident at all, thinking that she should be left with the few good memories she still had of her former boyfriend.

When Claire McPherson saw the stark photographs of Peter Manuel in the newspapers, she was horrified to recognise the thick dark hair and the piercing dark eyes. She had no doubt that he was indeed the man who had flagged her down on the road just outside Calderpark Zoo in Glasgow. Claire joined the list of women who had had a narrow escape from the mass-murderer who, it transpired, had a string of convictions for rape and indecent assault prior to his murder conviction.

The summer of 1958 heralded a return to the earlier, carefree days that the Grace girls had enjoyed. The dark shadows of fear and suspicion slowly lifted and the long summery nights in Scotland replaced the two dark winters of endurance.

Heather and Kirsty and the fully recovered Lily Grace could now face the future confidently with all the hope and freedom their young hearts desired.